A Garland Series

Foundations of the Novel

Representative Early

Eighteenth-Century Fiction

A collection of 100 rare titles
reprinted in photo-facsimile in 71 volumes

Foundations of the Novel

compiled and edited by

Michael F. Shugrue

Secretary for English for the M.L.A.

with New Introductions for each volume by

Michael Shugrue, *City College of C.U.N.Y.*

Malcolm J. Bosse, *City College of C.U.N.Y.*

William Graves, *N.Y. Institute of Technology*

Memoirs
of a
Cavalier

by
Daniel Defoe

with a new introduction
for the Garland Edition by
Malcolm J. Bosse

Garland Publishing, Inc., New York & London

1972

The new introduction for the

Garland *Foundations of the Novel* Edition

is Copyright © 1972, by

Garland Publishing, Inc., New York & London

Bibliographical note:

*This facsimile has been made from a copy in the
Beinecke Library of Yale University
(IK D362 720f)*

Library of Congress Cataloging in Publication Data

Defoe, Daniel, 1661?-1731.
    Memoirs of a cavalier.

    (Foundations of the novel)
    Reprint of the 1720 ed.
    1. Thirty Years' War, 1618-1648--Fiction.
2. Great Britain--History--Civil War, 1642-1649--
Fiction. I. Title. II. Series.
PZ3.D362Mc8 [PR3404]   823'.5   74-170545
ISBN 0-8240-0546-5

Printed in the United States of America

Introduction

For Defoe perhaps the supreme virtue was courage. In Robinson Crusoe *he writes of the courage of a man pitted against nature; in* Moll Flanders *he describes the courage of a woman who survives the rebuffs of a pitiless social system; in* Captain Singleton *and similar adventure tales he examines the courage of men who uncomplainingly confront the appalling dangers of life at sea. Perhaps his most thoroughgoing treatment of courage, however, is found in* The Memoirs of a Cavalier, *an account of the religious and civil wars of the seventeenth century. It is a narrative so obsessively focused on the concept of courage that what ultimately emerges is a vivid portrait of a professional soldier whose chief object in life is to prove time and again his worthiness on the field of battle.*

Defoe had access to many published first-hand accounts of the Thirty Years' War in Germany, and it is likely that he personally interviewed survivors of the Civil War in England.[1] In his preface he argues for the authenticity of this military journal by using the fictional device of a manuscript found among a dead man's papers. Moreover, he emphasizes the intimacy of such a report, the special psychological value of an eyewitness account of warfare. Histories may be authoritative when they deal with facts, but "have they one half of the Circumstances and Incidents of the Actions themselves, that this man's Eyes were Witness to, and which his Memory has thus preserved?" Continuing his skillful and rather boastful advertisement, Defoe claims that the journal corrects historical errors and at all times demonstrates the most judicious objectivity: "The only Objection we find possible to make against this Work is, that it is not carried on farther."

The memoirs begins with the unnamed cavalier's birth in 1608. It is characteristic of Defoe to prefigure events through the medium of dreams, and, indeed, the cavalier's mother has a dream in which her son's career as a soldier is prophesied. Raised a gentleman and educated at Oxford, the restless young man decides to travel abroad. The cavalier's ensuing intense curiosity about the world suggests that Defoe was drawing for this portrait on his own insatiable desire to understand mankind, a desire that led him to become one of the greatest journalists of the age. The cavalier kills a man in a Paris duel, almost dies of the plague in Italy, and nearly gets killed during a skirmish between French and Italian armies. Curiosity drives him into Germany where the great war between the Protestant Union and the Catholic League has led the North Germans to ally themselves with the Swedish soldier-king Gustavus Adolphus. The cavalier becomes an eyewitness to the sack of Magdenburg, perhaps the bloodiest event in one of the most brutal wars of history. Defoe's account is typically detailed and dense, and it is a measure of his novelistic skill that he simulates convincingly the stunned consciousness of a young man newly exposed to the full horrors of war. Undeterred by what he has seen and still driven by his curiosity, the cavalier passes through the dangerous war-torn countryside and heads for the Swedish army's camp, anxious to judge at first hand the character of the famous Adolphus. He risks his own life in the company of the Swedes at the Battle of Breitenfeld, where they defeat the redoubtable Tilly despite the cowardice of their Saxon allies. He finally meets the Swedish king, who is portrayed as kind, generous, and always optimistic. The cavalier admires Adolphus so much that he volunteers to serve as a cavalry officer in the Swedish army; the cavalier has at last found his true profession.

Defoe describes the progress of the war sequentially and in telling detail: the Swedish march southward through Germany; the Battle of the Lech in which Tilly was mortally wounded; the winter quartering at Nuremberg; and the Protestant defeat at Alte Veste. Bluntly honest, the cavalier admits to fleeing once from a superior force: "Fear, which always encreases in a Flight, brought us to a plain Flight, the Enemy at our heels" (p. 125). This sort of detail attests to Defoe's ability to create characters rather than merely fictional types.

Captured, the cavalier is not with the army when the king dies at the Battle of Lutzen, but as a noncombatant he does attend the Battle of Nordlingen, and he witnesses the disastrous defeat of the Swedes at the hands of Gallas, the brilliant League general. Having spent more than three years fighting in Germany, the cavalier returns to England and soon enters the service of Charles I. Defoe maintains a high level of intensity for his story by refusing to vary it with domestic or romantic matters.

The cavalier embarks eagerly on a campaign during the Bishops' Wars (1639-41) in which the Scottish Covenanters take up arms against the English because of a hatred of enforced episcopacy. Defoe makes it clear through his protagonist that good soldiering is a profession and not a national characteristic; the Highland Scots are praised by the cavalier for their endurance and courage, whereas the English forces are scored by him for their amateurish behavior in the field. At the outset of the English Civil War the cavalier promptly joins the Royal Troop of Guards and sees the war from the viewpoint of a royalist. Defoe describes many important battles, often accounting for the deployment of specific regiments. The result is a sense of participation in the indecisive Battle of Edge Hill, Cromwell's surprise victory at Marston Moor, and the critical encounter at Naseby which paved the way for the New Model Army's complete triumph.

Although war is the subject, unrelieved by any other human activity, this historical novel includes more compassion than is usually found in Defoe's work. The cavalier, who had been a mercenary in Germany, now suffers the pangs of a soldier who fights against friend and neighbor:

INTRODUCTION

It grieved me to the Heart, even in the Rout of our Enemies, to see the Slaughter of them; and even in the Fight, to hear a Man cry for Quarter in English, moved me to a Compassion which I had never been used to; nay, sometimes it looked to me as if some of my own Men had been beaten; and when I heard a Soldier cry, O God, I am shot, I looked behind me to see which of my own Troop was fallen (p. 195).

The work is filled with the technicalities of seventeenth-century warfare, testament to Defoe's consuming interest in military affairs. The cavalier's judgment of friend and foe alike is always judicious and without rancor, befitting a man of honor whose profession has taught him to have sympathy for those of his fellowmen who must make difficult decisions in situations of mortal danger. He praises, for example, the parliamentary general Fairfax and acknowledges Cromwell's military genius. His disapproval of Prince Rupert's foolhardy charges is hardly more than implied, and his main criticism of Charles I is the king's reliance on bad advisors, who promoted the Bishops' War and who in the final stages of the Civil War encouraged the king to employ the hated Irish troops.

By the close of this study of war and the professionals who wage it, Defoe has not only illuminated a page of military history but he has also managed to create, largely by implication, a fictional character who is brave and modest, whose religion is honor, whose virtue is courage, and whose life of continuous soldiering has never brutalized him. This

9

INTRODUCTION

achievement seems to support the claim of John Robert Moore that "Memoirs of a Cavalier *was surely one of Defoe's own favorites."* [2] *Surely this work attests to the range, passion, and humanity of Defoe's imagination.*

Malcolm J. Bosse

NOTES

[1] *James Sutherland,* Defoe *(1950), p. 242.*

[2] Daniel Defoe: Citizen of the Modern World *(1958), p. 260.*

MEMOIRS

OF A

CAVALIER:

OR A

Military Journal

OF

The *WARS* in GERMANY,

AND

The *WARS* in ENGLAND;

From the Year 1632, to the Year 1648.

Written Threefcore Years ago by an *Englifh* Gentleman, who ferved firft in the Army of *Guftavus Adolphus*, the glorious King of *Sweden*, till his Death ; and after that, in the Royal Army of King *Charles* the Firft, from the Beginning of the Rebellion, to the End of that War.

LONDON:

Printed for *A. Bell* at the *Crofs Keys* in *Cornhill*, *J. Osborn* at the *Oxford Arms* in *Lombard-Street*, *W. Taylor* at the *Ship and Swan*, and *T. Warner* at the *Black Boy* in *Pater-Nofter-Row*.

THE
PREFACE.

S an Evidence that 'tis very probable
these Memorials were written many Years
ago, the Persons now concerned in the
Publication, assure the Reader, that they
have had them in their Possession finished,
as they now appear, above twenty Years : That they were
so long ago found by great Accident, among other valuable Papers in the Closet of an eminent publick Minister,
of no less Figure than one of King William's Secretaries
of State.

As it is not proper to trace them any farther, so neither is there any need to trace them at all, to give Reputation to the Story related, seeing the Actions here
mentioned have a sufficient Sanction from all the Histories of the Times to which they relate, with this Addition, that the admirable Manner of relating them, and
the wonderful Variety of Incidents, with which they are
beautified in the Course of a private Gentleman's Story,
add such Delight in the reading, and give such a Lustre,
as well to the Accounts themselves, as to the Person who

was

The *PREFACE.*

was the Actor; and no Story, we believe, extant in the World, ever came abroad with such Advantages.

It must naturally give some Concern in the reading, that the Name of a Person of so much Gallantry and Honour, and so many Ways valuable to the World, should be lost to the Readers : We assure them no small Labour has been thrown away upon the Enquiry, and all we have been able to arrive to of Discovery in this Affair is, that a Memorandum *was found with this Manuscript, in these Words, but not signed by any Name, only the two Letters of a Name, which gives us no Light into the Matter, which Memoir was as follows.*

Memorandum,

I found this Manuscript among my Father's Writings, and I understand that he got them as Plunder, at, or after, the Fight at *Worcester,* where he served as Major of ———'s Regiment of Horse on the Side of the Parliament.

I. K.

*As this has been of no Use but to terminate the Enquiry after the Person; so, however, it seems most naturally to give an Authority to the Original of the Work, (*viz.*) that it was born of a Soldier, and indeed it is thro' every Part, related with so Soldierly a Stile, and in the very Language of the Field, that it seems impossible any Thing, but the very Person who was present in every Action here related, could be the Relator of them.*

The Accounts of Battles, the Sieges, and the several Actions of which this Work is so full, are all recorded in the Histories of those Times; such as the great Battle of Leipsick, *the Sacking of* Magdeburgh, *the Siege of* Nurembergh, *the passing the River* Leck *in* Bavaria; *such also as the Battles of* Keynton, *or* Edge-Hill;
the

The PREFACE.

the Battles of Newberry, Marston-Moor, and Naseby, and the like: They are all, we say, recorded in
other Histories, and written by those who lived in
those Times, and perhaps had good Authority
for what they wrote. But do those Relations give
any of the beautiful Ideas of things formed in this
Account? Have they one half of the Circumstances and
Incidents of the Actions themselves, that this Man's
Eyes were Witness to, and which his Memory has thus
preserved? He that has read the best Accounts of those
Battles, will be surprized to see the Particulars of the
Story so preserved, so nicely, and so agreeably describ'd;
and will confess what we alledge, that the Story is in-
imitably told; and even the great Actions of the glorious King GUSTAVUS ADOLPHUS, receive a
Lustre from this Man's Relations, which the World
was never made sensible of before, and which the present Age has much wanted of late, in Order to give
their Affections a Turn in Favour of his late glorious
Successor.

In the Story of our own Country's unnatural Wars,
he carries on the same Spirit. How effectually does he
record the Virtues and glorious Actions of King
Charles the First, at the same Time that he frequently
enters upon the Mistakes of his Majesty's Conduct, and
of his Friends, which gave his Enemies all those fatal
Advantages against him, which ended in the Overthrow of his Armies, the Loss of his Crown and Life,
and the Ruin of the Constitution?

In all his Account he does Justice to his Enemies,
and honours the Merit of those whose Cause he fought
against; and many Accounts recorded in his Story,
are not to be found even in the best Histories of those
Times.

What Applause does he give to the Gallantry of Sir
Thomas Fairfax, to his Modesty, to his Conduct, under
which

The PREFACE.

which he himself was subdued, and to the Justice he did
the King's Troops when they laid down their Arms?

His Description of the Scots Troops in the beginning
of the War, and the Behaviour of the Party under the
Earl of Holland, who went over against them, are admirable; and his Censure of their Conduct, who push'd
the King upon the Quarrel, and then would not let him
fight, is no more than what many of the King's Friends,
tho' less knowing [as Soldiers, have often complained of.]

In a Word, this Work is a Confutation of many Errors in all the Writers upon the Subject of our Wars in
England, and even in that extraordinary History
written by the Earl of Clarendon; but the Editors
were so just, that when near twenty Years ago, a Person
who had written a whole Volume in Folio, by Way of
Answer to, and Confutation of Clarendon's History of
the Rebellion, would have borrowed the Clauses in this
Account, which clash with that History, and confront
it: We say the Editors were so just as to refuse
them.

There can be nothing objected against the general
Credit of this Work, seeing its Truth is established upon
universal History; and almost all the Facts, especially
those of Moment, are confirmed for their general Part by
all the Writers of those Times, if they are here embellished
with Particulars, which are no where else to be found,
that is the Beauty we boast of; and that it is that must
recommend this Work to all the Men of Sense and
Judgment that read it.

The only Objection we find possible to make against
this Work is, that it is not carried on farther; or, as we
may say finished, with the finishing the War of the Time;
and this we complain of also: But then we complain as
a Misfortune to the World, not as a Fault in the Author;
for how do we know but that this Author might carry it
on, and have another Part finished which might not
fall into the same Hands, or may still remain with
some

The PREFACE.

some of his Family, and which they cannot indeed publish, to make it seem any Thing perfect, for want of the other Part which we have, and which we have now made publick? Nor is it very improbable, but that if any such farther Part is in Being, the publishing these Two Parts may occasion the Proprietors of the Third to let the World see it; and that by such a Discovery, the Name of the Person may also come to be known, which would, no doubt, be a great Satisfaction to the Reader, as well as us.

This, however, must be said, that if the same Author should have written another Part of this Work, and carried it on to the End of those Times; yet as the Residue of those melancholly Days, to the Restoration, were filled with the Intrigues of Government, the Political Management of illegal Power, and the Dissentions and Factions of a People, who were then even in themselves but a FACTION, and that there was very little Action in the Field; it is more than probable that our Author, who was a Man of Arms, had little Share in those Things, and might not care to trouble himself with looking at them.

But besides all this, it might happen that he might go abroad again, at that Time, as most of the Gentlemen of Quality, and who had an Abhorrence for the Power that then govern'd, here did. Nor are we certain that he might live to the End of that Time, so we can give no Account whether he had any Post in the subsequent Actions of that Time.

'Tis enough that we have the Authorities above to recommend this Part to us that is now published; the Relation, we are perswaded, will recommend it self, and nothing more can be needful, because nothing more can invite than the Story it self, which when the Reader enters into, he will find it very hard to get out of, 'till he has gone thro' it.

MEMOIRS

MEMOIRS

OF A

CAVALIER.

PART I.

T may fuffice the Reader, without being very inquifitive after my Name, that I was born in the County of *SALOP*, in the Year 1608; under the Government of what Star I was never Aftrologer enough to examine; but the Confequences of my Life may allow me to fuppofe fome extraordinary Influence affected my Birth. If there be any thing in Dreams alfo, my Mother, who was mighty obfervant that Way, took Minutes, which I have fince feen in the firft Leaf of her Prayer Book, of feveral ftrange Dreams fhe had while fhe was with Child of her fecond Son, which was my

B   felf.

felf. Once fhe noted that fhe dreamed fhe was
carried away by a Regiment of Horfe, and delivered in the Fields of a Son, that as foon as
it was born had two Wings came out of its Back,
and in half an Hour's Time flew away from her :
And the very Evening before I was born, fhe dreamed fhe was brought to Bed of a Son, and that all
the while fhe was in Labour a Man ftood under her
Window beating on a Kettle-Drum, which very
much difcompofed her.

My Father was a Gentleman of a very plen-.
tiful Fortune, having an Eftate of above 5000
Pounds *per Annum*, of a Family nearly allied to
feveral of the principal Nobility, and lived about
fix Miles from the Town : And my Mother being at-----on fome particular Occafion, was furprized there at a Friend's Houfe, and brought
me very fafe into the World.

I was my Father's fecond Son, and therefore
was not altogether fo much flighted as younger
Sons of good Families generally are. But my
Father faw fomething in my Genius alfo which
particularly pleafed him, and fo made him take
extraordinary Care of my Education.

I was taught therefore, by the beft Mafters
that could be had, every Thing that was needful
to accompiifh a young Gentleman for the World ;
and at feventeen Years old my Tutor told my Father an Academick Education was very proper
for a Perfon of Quality, and he thought me very
fit for it : So my Father entered me of-----College
in *Oxford*, where I continued three Years.

A Collegiate Life did not fuit me at all, though
I loved Books well enough. It was never defigned that I fhould be either a Lawyer, Phy-
fician or Divine ; and I wrote to my Father,
that I thought I had ftaid there long enough
for

for a Gentleman, and with his Leave I defired to give him a Vifit.

During my Stay at *Oxford*, though I paffed through the proper Exercifes of the Houfe, yet my chief reading was upon Hiftory and Geography, as that which pleafed my Mind beft, and fupplied me with Ideas moft fuitable to my Genius : By one I underftood what great Actions had been done in the World ; and by the other I underftood where they had been done.

My Father readily complied with my Defire of coming home ; for befides that he thought, as I did, that three Years time at the Univerfity was enough, he alfo moft paffionately loved me, and began to think of my fettling near him.

At my Arrival I found my felf extraordinarily careffed by my Father, and he feemed to take a particular Delight in my Converfation. My Mother, who lived in a perfect Union with him, both in Defires and Affection, received me very paffionately : Apartments were provided for me by my felf, and Horfes and Servants allowed me in particular.

My Father never went a Hunting, an Exercife he was exceeding fond of, but he would have me with him ; and it pleafed him when he found me like the Sport. I lived thus, in all the Pleafures 'twas poffible for me to enjoy, for about a Year more ; when going out one Morning with my Father to hunt a Stag, and having had a very hard Chafe, and gotten a great Way off from home, we had Leifure enough to ride gently back : And as we returned, my Father took Occafion to enter into a ferious Difcourfe with me concerning the Manner of my fettling in the World.

He

He told me, with a great deal of Paſſion, that he loved me above all the reſt of his Children, and that therefore he intended to do very well for me ; that my eldeſt Brother being already married and ſettled, he had deſigned the ſame for me, and propoſed a very advantageous Match for me with a young Lady of very extraordinary Fortune and Merit, and offered to make a Settlement of 2000 *l. per Annum* on me, which he ſaid he would purchaſe for me without diminiſhing his paternal Eſtate.

There was too much Tenderneſs in this Diſcourſe not to affect me exceedingly. I told him, I would perfectly reſign my ſelf unto his Diſpoſal. But, as my Father had, together with his Love for me, a very nice Judgment in his Diſcourſe, he fixed his Eyes very attentively on me ; and though my Anſwer was without the leaſt Reſerve, yet he thought he ſaw ſome Uneaſineſs in me at the Propoſal, and from thence concluded that my Compliance was rather an Act of Diſcretion than Inclination ; and, that however I ſeemed ſo abſolutely given up to what he had propoſed, yet my Anſwer was really an Effect of my Obedience rather than my Choice : So he returned very quick upon me, *Look you, Son, though I give you my own Thoughts in the Matter, yet I would have you be very plain with me ; for if your own Choice does not agree with mine, I will be your Adviſer, but will never impoſe upon you ; and therefore let me know your Mind freely.* I don't reckon my ſelf capable, Sir, ſaid I, with a great deal of reſpect, *to make ſo good a Choice for my ſelf as you can for me ; and though my Opinion differed from yours, its being your Opinion would reform mine, and my Judgment would as readily comply as my Duty.* I gather at leaſt from thence, ſaid my Father, *that your Deſigns lay*
anoother

another Way before, however they may comply with mine : And therefore I would know what it was you would have asked of me if I had not offered this to you ; and you muſt not deny me your Obedience in this, if you expeĉt I ſhould believe your Readineſs in the other.

Sir, ſaid I, 'twas impoſſible I ſhould lay out for my ſelf juſt what you have propoſed ; but if my Inclinations were never ſo contrary, though at your Command you ſhall know them, yet I declare them to be wholly ſubjeĉted to your Order : I confeſs my Thoughts did not tend towards Marriage or a Settlement ; for though I had no Reaſon to queſtion your Care of me, yet I thought a Gentleman ought always to ſee ſomething of the World before he confined himſelf to any part of it : And if I had been to ask your Conſent to any Thing, it ſhould have been to give me leave to Travel for a ſhort Time, in order qualiſie my ſelf to appear at home like a Son to ſo good a Father.

In what Capacity would you Travel, replied my Father ? You muſt go abroad either as a private Gentleman, as a Scholar, or as a Soldier. If it were in the latter Capacity, Sir, ſaid I, returning pretty quick, I hope I ſhould not misbehave my ſelf ; but I am not ſo determined as not to be ruled by your Judgment. Truly, replied my Father, I ſee no War abroad at this Time worth while for a Man to appear in, whether we talk of the Cauſe or the Encouragement ; and indeed, Son, I am afraid you need not go far for Adventures of that Nature, for Times ſeem to look as if this Part of Europe would find us Work enough. My Father ſpake then relating to the Quarrel likely to happen between the King of England and the Spaniard, (*) for I believe he had no Notions of a Civil War in his Head.

(*) Upon the Breach of the Match between the King of England and the Infanta of Spain ; and particularly upon the old Quarrel of the King of Bohemia and the Palatinate.

In

In fhort, my Father perceiving my Inclinations very forward to go abroad, gave me Leave to Travel, upon Condition I would promife to return in two Years at fartheft, or fooner, if he fent for me.

While I was at *Oxford* I happened into the Society of a young Gentleman, of a good Family, but of a low Fortune, being a younger Brother, and who had indeed inftilled into me the firft Defires of going abroad, and who I knew paffionately longed to Travel, but had not fufficient Allowance to defray his Expences as a Gentleman. We had contracted a very clofe Friendfhip, and our Humours being very agreeable to one another, we daily enjoyed the Converfation of Letters. He was of a generous free Temper, without the leaft Affectation or Deceit, a handfome proper Perfon, a ftrong Body, very good Mien, and brave to the laft Degree: His Name was *Fielding*, and we called him *Captain*, though it be a very unufual Title in a College; but Fate had fome Hand in the Title, for he had certainly the Lines of a Soldier drawn in his Countenance. I imparted to him the Refolutions I had taken, and how I had my Father's Confent to go abroad; and would know his Mind, whether he would go with me:. He fent me Word, he would go with all his Heart.

My Father, when he faw him, for I fent for him immediately to come to me, mightily approved my Choice; fo we got our Equipage ready, and came away for *London*.

'Twas on the 22d of *April* 1630, when we embarked at *Dover*, landed in a few Hours at *Calais*, and immediately took Poft for *Paris*. I fhall not trouble the Reader with a Journal of my Travels, nor with the Defcription of Places; which
every

every Geographer can do better than I ; but thefe Memoirs being only a Relation of what happened either to our felves, or in our own Knowledge, I fhall confine my felf to that Part of it.

We had indeed fome diverting Paffages in our Journey to *Paris* ; as firft, the Horfe my Comrade was upon fell fo very lame with a Slip that he could not go, and hardly ftand : And the Fellow that rid with us Exprefs, pretended to ride away to a Town five Miles off to get a frefh Horfe, and fo left us on the Road with one Horfe between two of us : We followed as well as we could, but being Strangers, miffed the Way, and wandered a great Way out of the Road. Whether the Man performed in reafonable Time, or not, we could not be fure ; but if it had not been for an old Prieft, we had never found him. We met this Man, by a very good Accident, near a little Village whereof he was Curate : We fpoke *Latin* enough juft to make him underftand us, and he did not fpeak it much better himfelf ; but he carried us into the Village to his Houfe, gave us Wine and Bread, and entertained us with wonderful Courtefie : After this he fent into the Village, hired a Peafant, and a Horfe for my Captain, and fent him to guide us into the Road. At parting he made a great many Compliments to us in *French*, which we could juft underftand ; but the Sum was, to excufe him for a Queftion he had a mind to ask us. After leave to ask what he pleafed, it was, if we wanted any Money for our Journey, and pulled out two Piftoles, which he offered either to give or lend us.

I mention this exceeding Courtefie of the Curate, becaufe, though Civility is very much in Ufe in *France*, and efpecially to Strangers, yet

'tis

'tis a very unuſual thing to have them part with
their Money.

We let the Prieſt know, firſt, that we did not
want Money, and next that we were very
ſenſible of the Obligation he had put upon us;
and I told him in particular, if I lived to ſee
him again, I would acknowledge it.

This Accident of our Horſe, was, as we afterwards found, of ſome uſe to us: We had left
our two Servants behind us at *Calais* to bring our
Baggage after us, by reaſon of ſome Diſpute between the Captain of the Pacquet and the
Cuſtom-Houſe Officer which could not be
adjuſted; and we were willing to be at *Paris*:
The Fellows followed as faſt as they could, and
as near as we could learn, in the Time we loſt
our Way were robbed, and our Portmanteaus
opened. They took what they pleaſed; but
as there was no Money there, but Linen and Ne-
ceſſaries, the Loſs was not great.

Our Guide carried us to *Amiens*, where we
found the Expreſs and our two Servants, who
the Expreſs meeting on the Road with a ſpare
Horſe, had brought back with him thither.

We took this for a good Omen of our ſuc-
ceſsful Journey, having eſcaped a Danger which
might have been greater to us than it was to our
Servants; for the Highway-Men in *France* do
not always give a Traveller the Civility of
bidding him Stand and Deliver his Money, but
frequently Fire upon him firſt, and then take
his Money.

We ſtaid one Day at *Amiens*, to adjuſt this
little Diſorder, and walked about the Town,
and into the great Church, but ſaw nothing
very remarkable there; but going croſs a broad
Street near the great Church, we ſaw a Crowd of
People

People gazing at a Mountebank Doctor who made a long Harangue to them with a thousand antick Postures, and gave out Bills this Way, and Boxes of Physick that Way, and had a great Trade, when on a sudden the People raised a Cry, * *Larron, Larron,* on the other side the Street, and all the Auditors ran away from Mr. Doctor, to see what the matter was---- Among the rest, we went to see; and the case was plain and short enough. Two *English* Gentlemen, and a *Scotch-Man*, Travellers 'as we were, were standing gazing at this prating Doctor, and one of them catched a Fellow picking his Pocket: The Fellow had got some of his Money, for he dropt two or three Pieces just by him, and had got hold of his Watch; but being surprized, let it slip again: but the Reason of telling this Story, is for the Management of it. This Thief had his Seconds so ready, that as soon as the *English-Man* had seized him, they fell in, pretended to be mighty zealous for the Stranger, takes the Fellow by the Throat, and makes a great Bustle; the Gentleman not doubting but the Man was secured, let go his own Hold of him, and left him to them: The Hubbub was great, and 'twas these Fellows cried *Larron, Larron*; but with a Dexterity peculiar to themselves, had let the right Fellow go, and pretended to be all upon one of their own Gang. At last they bring the Man to the Gentleman, to ask him what the Fellow had done? who, when he saw the Person they seized on, presently told them that was not the Man: Then they seemed to be in more Consternation than before, and spread themselves all over the Street, crying

---

* In English, *Thief, Thief,*

Larron,

Larron, Larron, pretending to fearch for the Fellow; and fo one one Way, one another, they were all gone, the Noife went over, the Gentlemen ftood looking one at another, and the bawling Doctor began to have the Crowd about him again.

This was the firft *French* Trick I had the Opportunity of feeing; but I was told they have a great many more as dextrous as this.

We foon got Acquaintance with thefe Gentlemen, who were going to *Paris* as well as we; fo the next Day we made up our Company with them, and were a pretty Troop of five Gentlemen and four Servants.

As we had really no Defign to ftay long at *Paris,* fo indeed, excepting the City it felf, there was not much to be feen there. Cardinal *Richlieu,* who was not only a fupreme Minifter in the Church, but prime Minifter in the State, was now made alfo General of the King's Forces, with a Title never known in *France* before nor fince, *viz.* Lieutenant-General *au Place du Roy,* in the King's ftead, or as fome have fince tranflated it, reprefenting the Perfon of the King.

Under this Character he pretended to execute all the Royal Powers in the Army without Appeal to the King, or without waiting for Orders: and having parted from *Paris* the Winter before, had now actually begun the War againft the Duke of *Savoy;* in the procefs of which, he reftored the Duke of *Mantua,* and having taken *Pignerol* from the Duke, put it into fuch a ftate of Defence, as the Duke could never force it out of his hands, and reduced the Duke, rather by Manage and Conduct than by Force, to make Peace without it; fo as annexing it to the Crown of *France,* it has ever fince been a Thorn in his Foot, that has always made the

Peace

Peace of *Savoy* lame and precarious: and *France* has since made *Pignerol* one of the strongest Fortresses in the World.

As the Cardinal, with all the Military part of the Court, was in the Field; so the King, to be near him, was gone with the Queen and all the Court, just before I reached *Paris*, to reside at *Lyons*. All these considered, there was nothing to do at *Paris*: the Court looked like a Citizen's House when the Family was all gone into the Country: and I thought the whole City looked very melancholy, compared to all the fine things I had heard of it.

The Queen Mother and her Party were chagrin at the Cardinal, who, tho' he owed his Grandeur to her immediate Favour, was now grown too great any longer to be at the Command of Her Majesty, or indeed in her Interest; and therefore the Queen was under Dissatisfaction, and Her Party looked very much down.

The Protestants were every where disconsolate; for the Losses they had received at *Rochel*, *Nismes*, and *Montpelier*, had reduced them to an absolute Dependence on the King's Will, without all possible hopes of ever recovering themselves, or being so much as in a Condition to take Arms for their Religion; and therefore the wisest of them plainly foresaw their own entire Reduction, as it since came to pass: and I remember vere well, that a Protestant Gentleman told me once, as we were passing from *Orleans* to *Lyons*, That the *English* had ruined them; and therefore, says he, I think the next Occasion the King takes to use us ill, as I know 'twill not be long, before he does, we must all fly over to *England*, where you are bound to maintain us for having helped to turn us out

of

of our own Country. I asked him what he meant by saying the *Englifh* had done it? He returned fhort upon me; I do not mean, fays he, by not relieving *Rochel*, but by helping to ruin *Rochel*, when you and the *Dutch* lent Ships to beat our Fleet, which all the Ships in *France* could not have done without you.

I was too young in the World to be very fenfible of this before, and therefore was fomething ftartled at the Charge; but when I came to difcourfe with this Gentleman, I foon faw, the Truth of what he faid was undeniable, and have fince reflected on it with regret, that the Naval Power of the Proteftants, which was then fuperior to the Royal, would certainly have been the Recovery of all their Fortunes, had it not been unhappily broke by their Brethren of *England* and *Holland*, the former lending feven Men of War, and the latter twenty, for the Deftruction of the *Rocheller*'s Fleet; and by thofe very Ships the *Rocheller*'s Fleet were actually beaten and deftroyed, and they never afterward recovered their Force at Sea, and by confequence funk under the Siege, which the *Englifh* afterwards in vain attempted to prevent.

Thefe things made the Proteftants look very dull, and expected the Ruin of all their Party; which had certainly happened had the Cardinal lived a few Years longer.

We ftayed in *Paris* about three Weeks, as well to fee the Court, and what Rarities the Place afforded, as by an Occafion which had like to have put a fhort Period to our Ramble.

Walking one Morning before the Gate of the *Louvre*, with a Defign to fee the *Swifs* Drawn up, which they always did, and Exercifed juft before they Relieved the Guards; a Page came up
to

to me, and speaking *English* to me, Sir, says he the Captain must needs have your immediate Assistance. I that had not the knowledge of any Person in *Paris* but my own Companion, whom I called Captain, had no room to question, but it was he that sent for me; and crying out hastily to him, Where, followed the Fellow as fast as 'twas possible: he led me thro' several Passages which I knew not, and at last thro' a Tennis-Court, and into a large Room where three Men, like Gentlemen, were Engaged very briskly, two against one: the Room was very dark, so that I could not easily know them asunder; but being fully possessed with an Opinion before of my Captain's Danger, I ran into the Room with my Sword in my Hand: I had not particular-ly Engaged any of them, nor so much as made a Pass at any, when I received a very dangerous Thrust in my Thigh, rather occasioned by my hasty running in, than a real Design of the Person; but enraged at the Hurt, without examining who it was hurt me, I threw my self upon him, and run my Sword quite thro' his Body.

The Novelty of the Adventure, and the unexpected Fall of the Man by a Stranger come in no Body knew how, had becalmed the other two, that they really stood gazing at me. By this Time I had discovered that my Captain was not there, and that 'twas some strange Accident brought me thither. I could speak but little *French*, and supposed they could speak no *English*; so I stepped to the Door to see for the Page that brought me thither: but seeing no body there, and the Passage clear, I made off as fast as I could, without speaking a Word; nor did the other two Gentlemen offer to stop me.

But

But I was in a ſtrange Confuſion when coming into thoſe Entries and Paſſages which the Page led me thro', I could by no means find my way out; at laſt ſeeing a Door open that looked through a Houſe into the Street, I went in, and out at the other Door; but then I was at as great a Loſs to know where I was, and which was the way to my Lodging. The Wound in my Thigh bled apace, and I could feel the Blood in my Breeches. In this Interval came by a Chair, I called, and went into it, and bid them, as well as I could, go to the *Louvre*; for tho' I knew not the Name of the Street were I lodged, I knew I could find the way to it when I was at the *Baſtile*. The Chair-Men went on their own Way, and being ſtopp'd by a Company of the Guards as they went, ſet me down till the Soul-diers were marched by ; when looking out I found I was juſt at my own Lodging, and the Captain was ſtanding at the Door looking for me ; I beckon-ed him to me, and whiſpering told him I was very much hurt, but bid him pay the Chair-men, and ask no Queſtions but come to me.

I made the beſt of my Way up Stairs, but had loſt ſo much Blood that I had hardly Spirits enough to keep me from ſwooning till he came in : He was equally concerned with me to ſee me in ſuch a bloody Condition, and preſently called up our Landlord, and he as quickly called in his Neighbours, that I had a Room full of People about me in a quarter of an Hour. But this had like to have been of worſe Conſequence to me than the other ; for by this Time there was great enquiring after the Perſon who killed a Man at the Tennis-Court. My Landlord was then ſenſible of his Miſtake, and came to me, and told me the Danger I was in, and very honeſt-

ly

ly offered to convey me to a Friend's of his,
where I fhould be very fecure; I thanked him,
and fuffered my felf to be carried at Midnight
whether he pleafed; he vifited me very often
till I was well enough to walk about, which was
not in lefs than ten Days, and then we thought
fit to be gone, fo we took Poft for *Orleans*; but
when I came upon the Road I found my felf in
a new Error, for my Wound opened again with
riding, and I was in a worfe Condition than before, being forced to take up at a little Village
on the Road, called ·   about   Miles from
Orleans, where there was no Surgeon to be had,
but a forry Country Barber, who neverthelefs
dreffed me as well as he could, and in about a
Week more I was able to walk to *Orleans* at three
times.

Here I ftaid till I was quite well, and then
took Coach for *Lyons*, and fo through *Savoy* into
Italy.

I fpent near two Years Time after this bad beginning in travelling through *Italy*, and to the
feveral Courts of *Rome*, *Naples*, *Venice* and *Vienna*.

When I came to *Lyons* the King was gone from
thence to *Grenoble* to meet the Cardinal, but the
Queens were both at *Lyons*.

The *French* Affairs feemed at this Time to
have but an indifferent Afpect; there was no
Life in any Thing but where the Cardinal was,
he pufhed on every Thing with extraordinary
Conduct, and generally with Succefs; he had
taken *Suza* and *Pignerol* from the Duke of *Savoy*, and was preparing to pufh the Duke even out
of all his Dominions.

But in the mean Time every where elfe
Things looked ill ; the Troops were ill paid,
the Magazines empty, the People mutinous, and

a ge-

a general Diforder feized the Minds of the
Court; and the Cardinal, who was the Soul of
every Thing, defired this Interview at *Grenoble,*
in order to put Things into fome better Method.

This politick Minifter always ordered Matters fo, that if there was Succefs in any Thing
the Glory was his; but if Things mifcarried it
was all laid upon the King. This Conduct was
fo much the more Nice, as it is the direct contrary to the Cuftom in like Cafes, where Kings
affume the Glory of all the Succefs in an Action; and when a Thing mifcarries make themfelves eafie by facrificing their Minifters and Fa-
vourites to the Complaints and Refentments of
the People; but this accurate refined Statefman
got over this Point.

While we were at *Lyons,* and as I remember,
the third Day after our coming thither, we had
like to have been involved in a State Broil, without knowing where we were; it was of a *Sun-*
day in the Evening, the People of *Lyons,* who
had been forely oppreffed in Taxes, and the War
in *Italy* pinching their Trade, began to be very
tumultuous; we found the Day before the Mob
got together in great Crouds, and talked oddly;
the King was every where reviled, and fpoken
difrefpectfully of, and the Magiftrates of the City either winked at, or durft not attempt to
meddle, left they fhould provoke the People.

But on *Sunday* Night, about Midnight, we was
waked by a prodigious Noife in the Street; I
jumpt out of Bed, and running to the Window,
I faw the Street as full of Mob as it could hold,
fome armed with Mufquets and Halbards, marched in very good Order; others in diforderly
Crouds, all fhouting and crying out *du Paix le*
Roy, and the like: One that led a great Party
of

of this Rabble carried a Loaf of Bread upon the Top of a Pike, and other leſſer Loaves, ſignifying the Smallneſs of their Bread, occaſioned by Dearneſs.

By Morning this Croud was gathered to a great Heighth, they run roving over the whole City, ſhut up all the Shops, and forced all the People to join with them from thence; they went up to the Caſtle, and renewing the Clamour, a ſtrange Conſternation ſeized all the Princes.

They broke open the Doors of the Officers, Collectors of the new Taxes, and plundered their Houſes, and had not the Perſons themſelves fled in time they had been very ill treated.

The Queen Mother, as ſhe was very much diſpleaſed to ſee ſuch Conſequences of the Government, in whoſe Management ſhe had no Share, ſo I ſuppoſe ſhe had the leſs Concern upon her. However, ſhe came into the Court of the Caſtle and ſhewed her ſelf to the People, gave Money amongſt them, and ſpoke gently to them; and by a Way peculiar to her ſelf, and which obliged all ſhe talked with, ſhe pacified the Mob gradually, ſent them home with Promiſes of Redreſs and the like; and ſo appeaſed this Tumult in two Days, by her Prudence, which the Guards in the Caſtle had ſmall Mind to meddle with, and if they had, would, in all Probability, have made the better Side the worſe.

There had been ſeveral Seditions of the like Nature in ſundry other Parts of *France*, and the very Army began to murmur, though not to mutiny, for want of Proviſions.

This Sedition at *Lyons* was not quite over when we left the Place, for, finding the City all in a Broil, we conſidered we had no Buſineſs there, and

C　　　　what

what the Confequence of a popular Tumult might be, we did not fee, fo we prepared to be gone. We had not rid above three Miles out of the City but we were brought as Prifoners o° War, by a Party of Mutineers, who had been abroad upon the Scout, and were charged with being Meffengers fent to the Cardinal for Forces to reduce the Citizens: With thefe Pretences they brought us back in Triumph, and the Queen Mother being by this Time grown fomething familiar to them, they carried us before her.

When they enquired of us who we were, we called our felves *Scots*; for as the *Englifh* were very much out of Favour in *France* at this Time, the Peace having been made not many Months, and not fuppofed to be very durable, becau'e particularly difpleafing to the People of *England*; fo the *Scots* were on the other Extreme with the *French*. Nothing was fo much careffed as the *Scots*, and a Man had no more to do in *France*, if he would be well received there, than to fay he was a *Scotchman*.

When we came before the Queen Mother fhe feemed to receive us with fome Stiffnefs at firft, and caufed her Guards to take us into Cuftody; but as fhe was a Lady of moft exquifite Politicks, fhe did this to amufe the Mob, and we were immediately after difmiffed; and the Queen her felf made a handfome Excufe to us for the Rudenefs we had fuffered, alledging the Troubles of the Times; and the next Morning we had three Dragoons of the Guards to convoy us out of the Jurifdiction of *Lyons*.

I confefs this little Adventure gave me an Averfion to popular Tumults all my Life after, and if nothing elfe had been in the Caufe, would have byaffed me to efpoufe the King's Party in *England*,

England, when our popular Heats carried all before it at home.

But I muft fay, that when I called to mind fince the Addrefs, the Management, the Compliance in fhew, and in general the whole Conduct of the Queen Mother with the mutinous People of *Lyons*, and compared it with the Conduct of my unhappy Mafter the King of *England*, I could not but fee that the Queen underftood much better than King *Charles*, the Management of Politicks, and the Clamours of the People.

Had this Princefs been at the Helm in *England*, fhe would have prevented all the Calamities of the Civil War here, and yet not have parted with what that good Prince yielded in order to Peace neither; fhe would have yielded gradually, and then gained upon them gradually; fhe would have managed them to the Point fhe had defigned them, as fhe did all Parties in *France*; and none could effectually fubject her, but the very Man fhe had raifed to be her principal Support; I mean the Cardinal.

We went from hence to *Grenoble*, and arrived there the fame Day that the King and the Cardinal, with the whole Court, went out to view a Body of 6000 *Swifs* Foot, which the Cardinal had wheedled the Cantons to grant to the King to help ruin their Neighbour the Duke of *Savoy*.

The Troops were exceeding fine, well accoutred, brave, clean-limbed, ftout Fellows indeed. Here I faw the Cardinal; there was an Air of Church Gravity in his Habit, but all the Vigor of a General, and the Sprightlinefs of a vaft Genius in his Face; he affected a little Stiffnefs in his Behaviour, but managed all his Affairs with fuch Clearnefs, fuch Steddinefs, and fuch

C 2   Appli-

Application, that it was no Wonder he had such Succefs in every Undertaking.

Here I faw the King, whofe Figure was mean, his Countenance hollow, and always feemed dejected, and every Way difcovering that Weaknefs in his Countenance that appeared in his Actions.

If he was ever fprightly and vigorous it was when the Cardinal was with him; for he depended fo much on every Thing he did, that he was at the utmoft Dilemma when he was abfent, always timorous, jealous and irrefolute.

After the Review the Cardinal was abfent fome Days, having been to wait on the Queen Mother at *Lyons*, where, as it was difcourfed, they were at leaft feemingly reconciled.

I obferved while the Cardinal was gone there was no Court, the King was feldom to be feen, very fmall Attendance given, and no Buftle at the Caftle; but as foon as the Cardinal returned the great Councils were affembled, the Coaches of the Ambaffadors went every Day to the Caftle, and a Face of Bufinefs appeared upon the whole Court.

Here the Meafures of the Duke of *Savoy's* Ruine were concerted, and in Order to it the King and the Cardinal put themfelves at the Head of the Army, with which they immediately reduced all *Savoy*, took *Chamberry* and the whole Dutchy except *Montmelian*.

The Army that did this was not above 22000 Men, including the *Swifs*, and but indifferent Troops neither, efpecally the *French* Foot, who compared to the Infantry I have fince feen in the *German* and *Swedifh* Armies, were not fit to be called Soldiers. On the other hand, confidering the *Savoyards* and *Italian* Troops, they were

were good Troops; but the Cardinal's Conduct made amends for all thefe Deficiencies.

From hence I went to *Pignerol*, which was then little more than a fingle Fortification on the Hill near the Town called St. *Bride's*; but the Situation of that was very ftrong : I mention this becaufe of the prodigious Works fince added to it, by which it has fince obtained the Name of the Right Hand of *France*; they had begun a New Line below the Hill, and fome Works were marked out on the Side of the Town next the Fort; but the Cardinal afterwards drew the Plan of the Works with his own Hand, by which it was made one of the ftrongeft Fortreffes in *Europe*.

While I was at *Pignerol* the Governor of *Milan* for the *Spaniards* came with an Army and fat down before *Cafal*. The Grand Quarrel and for which the War in this Part of *Italy* was begun, was this; the *Spaniards* and *Germans* pretended to the Dutchy of *Mantua*; the Duke of *Nevers*, a French Man, had not only a Title to it, but had got Poffeffion of it, but being ill fupported by the *French*, was beaten out by the *Imperialifts*, and after a long Siege the *Germans* took *Mantua* it felf, and drove the poor Duke quite out of the Country.

The taking of *Mantua* elevated the Spirits of the Duke of *Savoy*, and the *Germans* and *Spaniards* being now at more Leifure, with a compleat Army came to his Affiftance, and formed the Siege of *Montferrat*.

For as the *Spaniards* pufhed the Duke of *Mantua*, fo the *French* by Way of Diverfion lay hard upon the Duke of *Savoy*; they had feized *Montferrat*, and held it for the Duke of *Mantua*, and had a ftrong *French* Garrifon under *Thoiras*, a brave and

expe-

experienced Commander ; and thus Affairs ftood when we came into the *French* Army.

I had no Bufinefs there, as a Soldier, but having paffed as a *Scotch* Gentleman with the Mob at *Lyons,* and after with her Majefty, the Queen Mother, when we obtained the Guard of her Dragoons; we had alfo her Majefty's Pafs, with which we came and went where we pleafed; and the Cardinal, who was then not on very good Terms with the Queen, but willing to keep fmooth Water there, when two or three times our Paffes came to be examined, fhewed a more than ordinary Refpeft to us on that very account, our Paffes being from the Queen.

Cafal being befieged, as I have obferved, began to be in Danger, for the Cardinal, who 'twas thought had formed a Defign to ruin *Savoy,* was more intent upon that than upon the Succour of the Duke of *Mantua* ; but Neceffity calling upon him to deliver fo great a Captain as *Thoiras,* and not to let fuch a Place as *Cafal* fall into the Hands of the Enemy, the King, or Cardinal rather, order'd the Duke of *Momorency* and the Marefchal D' *Effiat,* with 10000 Foot and 2000 Horfe, to march and joyn the Marefchals *De la Force* and *Schomberg,* who lay already with an Army on the Frontiers of *Genoa,* but too weak to attempt the raifing the Siege of *Cafal.*

As all Men thought there would be a Battle between the *French* and the *Spaniards,* I could not prevail with my felf to lofe the Opportunity, and therefore by the Help of the Paffes abovementioned, I came to the *French* Army under the Duke of *Momorency*; we marched through the Enemy's Country with great Boldnefs and no fmall Hazard, for the Duke of *Savoy* appeared frequently

quently with great Bodies of Horſe on the
Rear of the Army, and frequently skirmiſhed
with our Troops, in one of which I had the
Folly, *I can call it no better, for I had no Buſineſs
there*, to go out and ſee the Sport, as the *French*
Gentlemen called it; I was but a raw Soldier,
and did not like the Sport at all, for this Party
was ſurrounded by the Duke of *Savoy*, and almoſt
all killed, for as to Quarter, they neither asked
nor gave; I run away very fairly one of the
firſt, and my Companion with me, and by the
Goodneſs of our Horſes got out of the Fray, and
being not much known in the Army, we came into
the Camp an hour or two after, as if we had
been only riding abroad for the Air.

This little Rout made the General very cautious, for the *Savoyards* were ſtronger in Horſe by
3 or 4000, and the Army always marched in a
Body, and kept their Parties in or very near
Hand.

I 'ſcaped another Rub in this *French* Army
about five Days after, which had liked to have
made me pay dear for my Curioſity.

The Duke *de Momorency* and the Mareſchal
Schomberg joined their Army above four or five
Days after, and immediately, according to the
Cardinal's Inſtructions, put themſelves on the
March for the Relief of *Caſal*.

The Army had marched over a great Plain,
with ſome marſhy Grounds on the Right, and
the *Po* on the Left, and as the Country was
ſo well diſcovered that 'twas thought impoſſible
any Miſchief ſhould happen, the Generals obſerved
the leſs Caution. At the End of this Plain was
a long Wood, and a Lane or narrow Dehle thro'
the Middle of it.

Thro'

Thro' this Pass the Army was to march, and the Van began to file through it about four a Clock; by three Hours Time all the Army was got through, or into the Pass, and the Artillery was just entred when the Duke of *Savoy*, with 4000 Horse and 1500 Dragoons, with every Horse-man a Foot-man behind him; whether he had swam the *Po*, or passed it above at a Bridge, and made a long March after, was not examined, but he came boldly up the Plain and charged our Rear with a great deal of Fury.

Our Artillery was in the Lane, and as it was impossible to turn them about, and make way for the Army, so the Rear was. obliged to support themselves, and maintain the Fight for above an Hour and a half.

In this Time we lost abundance of Men, and if it had not been for two Accidents all that Line had been cut off; one was, that the Wood was so near that those Regiments which were disordered presently sheltred themselves in the Wood; the other was, that by this Time the Mareschal *Schomberg*, with the Horse of the Van, began to get back through the Lane, and to make good the Ground from whence the other had been beaten, till at last by this Means it came to almost a pitched Battle.

There were two Regiments of *French* Dragoons who did excellent Service in this Action, and maintained their Ground till they were almost all killed.

Had the Duke of *Savoy* contented himself with the Defeat of five Regiments on the Right, which he quite broke and drove into the Wood, and with the Slaughter and Havock which he had made among the rest, he had come off with Honour, and might have called it a Victory;

but

but endeavouring to break the whole Party, and carry off some Cannon, the obstinate Resistance of these few Dragoons lost him his Advantages, and held him in play till so many fresh Troops got through the Pass again, as made us too strong for him; and had not Night parted them he had been entirely defeated.

At last finding our Troops encrease and spread themselves on his Flank, he retired and gave over, we had no great Stomach to pursue him neither, tho' some Horse were ordered to follow a little Way.

The Duke lost above a thousand Men, and we almost twice as many, and but for those Dragoons, had lost the whole Rear-guard and half our Cannon. I was in a very sorry Case in this Action too, I was with the Rear in the Regiment of Horse of *Perigoort*, with a Captain of which Regiment I had contracted some Acquaintance; I would have rid off at first, as the Captain desired me, but there was no doing it, for the Cannon was in the Lane, and the Horse and Dragoons of the Van eagerly pressing back through the Lane, must have run me down, or carried me with them: As for the Wood, it was a good Shelter to save ones Life, but was so thick there was no passing it on Horseback.

Our Regiment was one of the first that was broke, and being all in Confusion, with the Duke of *Savoy*'s Men at our Heels, away we ran into the Wood; never was there so much Disorder among a Parcel of Runaways as when we came to this Wood, it was so exceeding bushy and thick at the Bottom there was no entring it, and a Volley of small Shot from a Regiment of *Savoy*'s Dragoons poured in upon us at our breaking into the Wood made terrible Work among our Horses.

For

For my Part I was got into the Wood, but was forced to quit my Horse, and by that means with a great deal of Difficulty got a little farther in, where there was a little open Place, and being quite spent with labouring among the Bushes, I sat down resolving to take my Fate there, let it be what it would, for I was not able to go any farther; I had twenty or thirty more in the same Condition came to me in less than half an Hour, and here we waited very securely the Success of the Battle, which was as before.

It was no small Relief to those with me to hear the *Savoyards* were beaten, for otherwise they had all been lost; as for me, I confess, I was glad as it was, because of the Danger, but otherwise I cared not much which had the better, for I designed no Service among them.

One Kindness it did me, that I began to consider what I had to do here, and as I could give but a very slender Account of my self for what it was I run all these Risques, so I resolved they should fight it out among themselves, for I would come among them no more.

The Captain with whom, as I noted above, I had contracted some Acquaintance in this Regiment, was killed in this Action, and the *French* had really a great Blow here, though they took Care to conceal it all they could; and I cannot, without smiling, read some of the Histories and Memoirs of this Action, which they are not ashamed to call a Victory.

We marched on to *Saluces*, and the next Day the Duke of *Savoy* presented himself in Batailla on the other Side of a small River giving us a fair Challenge to pass and engage him: We always said in our Camp that the Orders were to
fight

fight the Duke of *Savoy* where-ever we met him; but tho' he braved us in our View, we did not care to engage him, but we brought *Saluces* to furrender upon Articles, which the Duke could not relieve without attacking our Camp, which he did not care to do.

The next Morning we had News of the Surrender of *Mantua* to the *Imperial* Army; we heard of it firſt from the Duke of *Savoy*'s Cannon, which he fired by way of Rejoycing, and which ſeemed to make him Amends for the loſs of *Saluces*.

As this was a Mortification to the *French*, ſo it quite damped the Succeſs of the Campaign, for the Duke *de Momorency* imagining that the *Imperial* General would ſend immediate Aſſiſtance to the Marquis *Spinola*, who beſieged *Caſal*, they call'd frequent Councils of War what Courſe to take, and at laſt reſolved to halt in *Piedmont*.

A few Days after their Reſolutions were changed again, by the News of the Death of the Duke of *Savoy*, *Charles Emanuel*, who died, as ſome ſay, agitated with the Extreams of Joy and Grief.

This put our Generals upon conſidering again, whether they ſhould march to the Relief of *Caſal*, but the Chimera of the *Germans* put them by, and ſo they took up Quarters in *Piedmont*; they took ſeveral ſmall Places from the Duke of *Savoy*, making Advantage of the Conſternation the Duke's Subjects were in on the Death of their Prince, and ſpread themſelves from the Sea-ſide to the Banks of the *Po*.

But here an Enemy did that for them which the *Savoyards* could not, for the Plague got into their Quarters and deſtroyed abundance of People, both of the Army and of the Country.

I thought

I thought then it was Time for me to be gone, for I had no manner of Courage for that Rifque; and I think verily I was more afraid of being taken fick in a ftrange Country, than ever I was of being killed in Battle. Upon this Refolution I procured a Pafs to go for *Genoa*, and acordingly began my Journey, but was arrefted at *Villa Franca* by a flow lingring Fever, which held me about five Days, and then turned to a burning Malignancy, and at laft to the Plague: My Friend, the Captain, never left me Night nor Day; and though for four Days more I knew no Body, nor was capable of fo much as thinking of my felf, yet it pleafed God that the Diftemper gathered in my Neck, fwelled and broke; during the Swelling I was raging mad with the Violence of Pain, which being fo near my Head, fwelled that alfo in Proportion, that my Eyes were fwelled up, and for twenty four Hours my Tongue and Mouth; then, as my Servant told me, all the Phyficians gave me over, as paft all Remedy, but by the good Providence of God the Swelling broke.

The prodigious Collection of Matter which this Swelling difcharged, gave me immediate Relief, and I became fenfible in lefs than an Hour's Time; and in two Hours, or thereabouts, fell into a little Slumber which recovered my Spirits, and fenfibly revived me. Here I lay by it till the Middle of *September*, my Captain fell fick after me, but recovered quickly; his Man had the Plague, and died in two Days; my Man held it out well.

About the Middle of *September* we heard of a Truce concluded between all Parties, and being unwilling to winter at *Villa Franca*, I got Paffes, and

and though we were both but weak began to travel in Litters for *Milan*.

And here I experienced the Truth of an old *English* Proverb, *That Standers-by see more than the Gamesters.*

The *French*, *Savoyards* and *Spaniards* made this Peace or Truce all for separate and several Grounds, and every one were mistaken.

The *French* yielded to it because they had given over the Relief of *Casal*, and were very much afraid it would fall into the Hands of the Marquiss *Spinola*. The *Savoyards* yielded to it because they were afraid the *French* would winter in *Piedmont* ; the *Spaniards* yielded to it because the Duke of *Savoy* being dead, and the Count *de Colalto*, the *Imperial* General, giving no Assistance, and his Army weakened by Sickness and the Fatigues of the Siege, he foresaw he should never take the Town, and wanted but to come off with Honour.

The *French* were mistaken, because really *Spinola* was so weak, that had they marched on into *Montferrat* the *Spaniards* must have raised the Siege; the Duke of *Savoy* was mistaken, because the Plague had so weakened the *French* that they durst not have staid to winter in *Piedmont* ; and *Spinola* was mistaken, for tho' he was very flow, if he had staid before the Town one Fortnight longer *Thoiras* the Governour must have surrendred, being brought to the last Extremity.

Of all these Mistakes the *French* had the Advantage, for *Casal* was relieved, the Army had Time to be recruited, and the *French* had the best of it by an early Campaign.

I past through *Montferrat* in my Way to *Milan* just as the Truce was declared, and saw the miserable Remains of the *Spanish* Army, who

by

by Sicknefs, Fatigue, hard Duty, the Sallies of the Garrifon, and fuch like Confequences, were reduced to lefs than 2000 Men, and of them above 1000 lay wounded and fick in the Camp.

Here were feveral Reigments which I faw drawn out to their Arms that could not make up above 70 or 80 Men, Officers and all, and thofe half ftarved with Hunger, almoft naked, and in a lamentable Condition. From thence I went into the Town, and there Things were ftill in a worfe Condition, the Houfes beaten down, the Walls and Works ruined, the Garrifon, by continual Duty, reduced from 4500 Men to lefs than 800, without Clothes, Money, or Provifions. The brave Governour weak with continual Fatigue, and the whole Face of things in a miferable Cafe.

The *French* Generals had juft fent them Thirty Thoufand Crowns for prefent Supply, which heartened them a little, but had not the Truce been made as it was, they muft have furrendred upon what Terms the *Spaniards* had pleafed to make them.

Never were two Armies in fueh Fear of one another with fo little Caufe; the *Spaniards* afraid of the *French* whom the Plague had devoured, and the *French* afraid of the *Spaniards* whom the Siege had almoft ruined.

The Grief of this Miftake, together with the Senfe of his Mafter, the *Spaniards*, leaving him without Supplies to compleat the Siege of *Cafal*, fo affected the Marquefs *Spinola* that he died for Grief, and in him fell the laft of that rare breed of *Low Country* Soldiers who gave the World fo great and juft a Charafter of the *Spanifh* Infantry as the beft Soldiers of the World ;

World; a Character which we see them so very much degenerated from since, that they hardly deserve the Name of Soldiers.

I tarried at *Milan* the rest of the Winter, both for the Recovery of my Health, and also for Supplies from *England*.

Here it was I first heard the Name of *Gustavus Adolphus*, the King of *Sweden*, who now began his War with the Emperor ; and while the King of *France* was at *Lyons*, the League with *Sweden* was made, in which the *French* contributed 120000 Crowns in Money, and 600000 *per An.* to the Attempt of *Gustavus Adolphus:* About this Time he landed in *Pomerania*, took the Towns of *Stetin* and *Straelsund*, and from thence proceeded in that prodigious Manner, of which I shall have Occasion to be very particular in the Prosecution of these Memoirs.

I had indeed no Thoughts of seeing that King, or his Armies, I had been so roughly handled already that I had given over the Thoughts of appearing among the fighting People, and resolved in the Spring to pursue my Journey to *Venice*, and so for the rest of *Italy*.

Yet I cannot deny, that as every Gazette gave us some Accounts of the Conquests and Victories of this glorious Prince, it prepossessed my Thoughts with secret Wishes of seeing him, but these were so young and unsettled, that I drew no Resolutions from them for a long while after.

About the Middle of *January* I left *Milan* and came to *Genoa*, from thence by Sea to *Leghorn*, then to *Naples*, *Rome* and *Venice*, but saw nothing in *Italy* that gave me any Diversion.

As for what is modern, I saw nothing but Lewdness, private Murthers, stabbing Men at the Corner of a Street, or in the dark, hiring of
Bravoes,

Bravoes, and the like ; all the Diverfions here
ended in Whoring, Gaming and Sodomy, thefe
were to me the modern Excellencies of *Italy*;
and I had no Guft to Antiquities.

'Twas pleafant indeed when I was at *Rome* to
fay here ftood the Capitol, there the Coloffus of
Nero, here was the Amphitheatre of *Titus*, there
the Aqueduct of ——— here the Forum, there the
Catacombs, here the Temple of *Venus*, there of
Jupiter, here the Pantheon, and the like ; but I
never defigned to write a Book, as much as was
ufeful I kept in my Head ; and for the reft, I
left it to others.

I obferved the People degenerated from the an-
cient glorious Inhabitants, who were generous,
brave, and the moft valiant of all Nations, to a
vicious Bafenefs of Soul, barbarous, treacherous,
jealous and revengeful, lewd and cowardly, in-
tolerably proud and haughty, bigotted to blind,
incoherent Devotion, and the groffeft of Idolatry.

Indeed I think the Unfuitablenefs of the Peo-
ple made the Place unpleafant to me, for there
is fo little in a Country to recommend it when
the People difgrace it, that no Beauties of the
Creation can make up for the Want of thofe
Excellencies which fuitable Society procure the
Defect of ; this made *Italy* a very unpleafant
Country to me, the People were the Foil to the
Place, all manner of hateful Vices reigning in
their general Way of living.

I confefs I was not very religious my felf, and
being come abroad into the World young enough,
might eafily have been drawn into Evils that
had recommended themfelves with any tolerable
Agreeablenefs to Nature and common Manners ;
but when Wickednefs prefented it felf full grown
in its groffeft Freedoms and Liberties, it quite took
away

away all the Guft to Vice that the Devil had furnifhed me with, and in this I cannot but relate one Scene which paffed between no Body but the Devil and my felf.

At a certain Town in *Italy*, which fhall be namelefs, becaufe I won't celebrate the Proficiency of one Place more than another, when I believe the whole Country equally wicked, I was prevailed upon rather than tempted, *a la Courtezan:*

If I fhould defcribe the Woman I muft give a very mean Charaƈter of my own Virtue to fay I was allured by any but a Woman of an extraordinary Figure; her Face, Shape, Mein, and Drefs, I may, without Vanity, fay, the fineft that I ever faw: When I had Admittance into her Apartments, the Riches and Magnificence of them aftonifhed me, the Cupboard or Cabinet of Plate, the Jewels, the Tapeftry, and every Thing in Proportion, made me queftion whether I was not in the Chamber of fome Lady of the beft Quality; ----- but when after fome Converfation I found that it was really nothing but a Courtezan, in *Englifh*, a common Street Whore, a Punk of the Trade, I was amazed, and my Inclination to her Perfon began to cool; her Converfation exceeded, if poffible, the beft of Quality, and was, I muft own, exceeding agreeable; fhe fung to her Lute, and danced as fine as ever I faw, and thus diverted me two Hours before any Thing elfe was difcourfed of; ---- but when the vicious Part came on the Stage, I blufh to relate the Confufion I was in, and when fhe made a certain Motion by which I underftood fhe might be made ufe of, either as a Lady, or as ----- I was quite Thunder-ftruck, all the vicious Part of my Thoughts vanifhed, the Place filled me with Horror, and I was all over Diforder and Diftraƈtion.

D   I be-

I began however to recollect where I was, and that in this Country these were People not to be affronted; and though she easily saw the Disorder I was in, she turned it off with admirable Dexterity, began to talk again *a la Gallant*, received me as a Visitant, offered me Sweet-meats and some Wine.

Here I began to be in more Confusion than before, for I concluded she would neither offer me to eat or to drink now *without Poison*, and I was very shy of tasting her Treat, but she scattered this Fear immediately, by readily, and of her own accord, not only tasting but eating freely of every Thing she gave me; whether she perceived my Wariness, or the Reason of it, I know not, I could not help banishing my Suspicion, the obliging Carriage and strange Charm of her Conversation had so much Power of me, that I both eat and drank with her at all Hazards.

When I offered to go, and at parting presented her five Pistoles, I could not prevail with her to take them, when she spoke some *Italian* Proverb which I could not readily understand, but by my Guess it seemed to imply, *that she would not take the Pay, having not obliged me otherwise:* At last I laid the Pieces on her Toilet, and would not receive them again; upon which she obliged me to pass my Word to visit her again, else she would by no Means accept my Present.

I confess I had a strong Inclination to visit her again, and besides thought my self obliged to it in Honour to my Parole; but after some Strife in my Thoughts about it, I resolved to break my Word with her, when going at Vespers one Evening to see their Devotions, I happened to meet this very Lady very devoutly going to her Prayers.

At

At her coming out of the Church I fpoke to her, fhe paid me her Refpects with a *Seignior Inglefe*, and fome Words fhe faid in *Spanifh* fmiling, which I did not underftand ; I cannot fay here fo clearly as I would be glad I might, that I broke my Word with her ; but if I faw her any more I faw nothing of what gave me fo much Offence before.

The End of my relating this Story is anfwered in defcribing the Manner of their Addrefs, without bringing my felf to Confeffion ; if I did any Thing I have fome Reafon to be afhamed of, it may be a lefs Crime to conceal it than expofe it.

The Particulars related however, may lead the Reader of thefe Sheets to a View of what gave me a particular Difguft at this pleafant Part of the World, as they pretend to call it, and made me quit the Place fooner than Travellers ufe to do that come thither to fatisfy their Curiofity.

The prodigious ftupid Bigottry of the People alfo was irkfome to me ; I thought there was fomething in it very fordid, the entire Empire the Priefts have over both the Souls and Bodies of the People, gave me a Specimen of that Meannefs of Spirit which is no where elfe to be feen but in *Italy*, efpecially in the City of *Rome*.

At *Venice* I perceived it quite different, the Civil Authority having a vifible Superiority over the Ecclefiaftick ; and the Church being more fubject there to the State than in any other Part of *Italy*.

For thefe Reafons I took no Pleafure in filling my Memoirs of *Italy* with Remarks of Places or Things, all the Antiquities and valuable Remains of the *Roman* Nation are done better than

I can

I can pretend to by fuch People who made it more their Bufinefs; as for me, I went to fee, and not to write, and as little thought then of thefe Memoirs, as I ill furnifhed my felf to write them.

I left *Italy* in *April*, and taking the Tour of *Bavaria*, though very much out of the Way, I paffed through *Munick*, *Paffaw*, *Lints*, and at laft to *Vienna*.

I came to *Vienna* the 10th of *April* 1631, intending to have gone from thence down the *Danube* into *Hungary*, and by Means of a Pafs which I had obtained from the *Englifh* Ambaffador at *Conftantinople*, I defigned to have feen all thofe great Towns on the *Danube* which were then in the Hands of the *Turks*, and which I had read much of in the Hiftory of the War between the *Turks* and the *Germans*; but I was diverted from my Defign by the following Occafion.

There had been a long bloody War in the Empire of *Germany* for 12 Years, between the Emperor, the Duke of *Bavaria*, the King of *Spain*, and the Popifh Princes and Electors on the one Side, and the Proteftant Princes on the other; and both Sides having been exhaufted by the War, and even the Catholicks themfelves beginning to diflike the growing Power of the Houfe of *Auftria*, 'twas thought all Parties were willing to make Peace.

Nay, Things were brought to that Pafs that fome of the Popifh Princes and Electors began to talk of making Alliances with the King of *Sweden*.

Here it is neceffary to obferve, that the two Dukes of *Mecklenburgh* having been difpoffeffed of moft of their Dominions by the Tyranny of the Emperor *Ferdinand*, and being in danger of lofing the reft, earneftly follicited the King of
Sweden,

Sweden to come to their Affiftance; and that Prince, as he was related to the Houfe of *Mecklenburgh*, and efpecially as he was willing to lay hold of any Opportunity to break with the Emperor, againft whom he had laid up an implacable Prejudice, was very ready and forward to come to their Affiftance.

The Reafons of his Quarrel with the Emperor were grounded upon the *Imperialifts* concerning themfelves in the War of *Poland*, where the Emperor had fent 8000 Foot and 2000 Horfe to join the *Polifh* Army againft the King, and had thereby given fome Check to his Arms in that War.

In Purfuance therefore of his Refolution to quarrel with the Emperor, but more particularly at the Inftance of the Princes above-named, his *Swedifh* Majefty had landed the Year before at *Straelfund* with about 12000 Men, and having joined with fome Forces which he had left in *Polifh Pruffia*, all which did not make 30000 Men, he began a War with the Emperor, the greateft in Event, filled with the moft famous Battels, Sieges and extraordinary Actions, including its wonderful Succefs and happy Conclufion, of any War ever maintained in the World.

The King of *Sweden* had already taken *Stetin*, *Straelfund*, *Roftock*, *Wifmar*, and all the ftrong Places on the *Baltick*, and began to fpread himfelf in *Germany*; he had made a League with the *French*, as I obferved in my Story of *Saxony*, he had now made a Treaty with the Duke of *Brandenburg*, and, in fhort, began to be terrible to the Empire.

In this Conjuncture the Emperor called the General Diet of the Empire to be held at *Ratisbon*, where, as was pretended, all Sides were to treat of Peace and to join Forces to beat the

Swedes

Swedes out of the Empire. Here the Emperor, by a moft exquifite Management, brought the Affairs of the Diet to a Conclufion, exceedingly to his own Advantage and to the farther Oppreffion of the Proteftants ; and in particular, in that the War againft the King of *Sweden* was to be carried on in fuch Manner as that the whole Burthen and Charge would lie on the Proteftants themfelves, and they be made the Inftruments to oppofe their beft Friends. Other Matters alfo ended equally to their Difadvantage, as the Methods refolved on to recover the Church-Lands, and to prevent the Education of the Proteftant Clergy ; and what remained was referred to another General Diet to be held at *Frankfort au Main*, in *Auguft* 1631.

I won't pretend to fay the other Proteftant Princes of *Germany* had never made any Overtures to the King of *Sweden* to come to their Affiftance, but 'tis plain they had entred into no League with him ; that appears from the Difficulties which retarded the fixing the Treaties afterward, both with the Dukes of *Brandenburgh* and *Saxony* which unhappily occafioned the Ruine of *Magdenburgh*.

But 'tis Plain the *Swede* was refolved on a War with the Emperor ; his *Swedifh* Majefty might and indeed could not but forefee that if he once fhewed himfelf with a fufficient Force on the Frontiers of the Empire, all the Proteftant Princes would be obliged by their Intereft or by his Arms to fall in with him, and this the Confequence made appear to be a juft Conclufion ; for the Electors of *Brandenburgh* and *Saxony* were both forced to join with him.

Firft, They were willing to join with him, at leaft they could not find in their Hearts to join

join with the Emperor, of whofe Power they had fuch juft Apprehenfions; they wifhed the *Swedes* Succefs, and would have been very glad to have had the Work done at another Man's Charge; but like true *Germans* they were more willing to be faved than to fave themfelves, and therefore hung back and ftood upon Terms.

Secondly, They were at laft forced to it; the firft was forced to join by the King of *Sweden* himfelf, who being come fo far was not to be dallied with; and had not the Duke of *Brandenburgh* complied as he did, he had been ruined by the *Swede*; the *Saxon* was driven into the Arms of the *Swede* by Force, for Count *Tilly* Ravaging his Country made him comply with any Terms to be faved from Deftruction.

Thus Matters ftood at the End of the Diet at *Ratisbon*; the King of *Sweden* began to fee himfelf leagued againft at the Diet both by Proteftant and Papift; and, *as I have often heard his Maiefty fay fince*, he had refolved to try to force them off from the Emperor, and to treat them as Enemies equally with the Reft if they did not.

But the Proteftants convinced him foon after, that tho' they were tricked into the outward Appearance of a League againft him at *Ratisbon*, they had no fuch Intentions; and by their Ambaffadors to him let him know, that they only wanted his powerful Affiftance to defend their Councils, when they would foon convince him that they had a due Senfe of the Emperor's Defigns, and would do their utmoft for their Liberty; and thefe I take to be the firft Invitations the King of *Sweden* had to undertake the Proteftant Caufe as fuch, and which entitled him to fay he fought for the Liberty and Religion of the *German* Nation.

I have

I have had some particular Opportunities to hear these Things from the Mouths of some of the very Princes themselves, and therefore am the forwarder to relate them ; and I place them here, because previous to the part I acted on this bloody Scene, 'tis necessary to let the Reader into some Part of the Story, and to shew him in what Manner and on what Occasions this terrible War began.

The Protestants, alarmed at the Usage they had met with at the former Diet, had secretly proposed among themselves to form a general Union or Confederacy, for preventing that Ruin which they saw, unless some speedy Remedies were applied, would be inevitable. The Elector of *Saxony*, the Head of the Protestants, a vigorous and politick Prince, was the first that moved it ; and the Landgrave of *Hesse*, a zealous and gallant Prince, being consulted with, it rested a great while between those two; no Method being found practicable to bring it to pass ; the Emperor being so powerful in all Parts, that they foresaw the petty Princes would not dare to negotiate an Affair of such a Nature, being surrounded with the *Imperial* Forces, who by their two Generals, *Wallestein* and *Tilly*, kept them in continual Subjection and Terror.

This Dilemma had like to have stifled the Thoughts of the Union as a Thing impracticable, when one *Seigenfius*, a *Lutheran* Minister, a Person of great Abilities, and one whom the Elector of *Saxony* made great Use of in Matters of Policy as well as Religion, contrived for them this excellent Expedient.

I had the Honour to be acquainted with this Gentleman while I was at *Leipsick* ; it pleased him exceedingly to have been the Contriver

of

of fo fine a Structure as the *Conclufions of Leip-fick*, and he was glad to be entertained on that Subject ; I had the Relation from his own Mouth, when, but very modeftly, he told me he thought 'twas an Infpiration darted on a fudden into his Thoughts, when the Duke of *Saxony* calling him in-to his Clofet one Morning, with a Face full of Con-cern, fhaking his Head and looking very earneftly, *What will become of us, Doctor ?* faid the Duke, *we fhall all be undone at* Frankfort au Main. *Why fo; pleafe your Highnefs ?* fays the Doctor, *Why they will fight with the King of* Sweden *with our Armies and our Money*, fays the Duke, *and devour our Friends and our felves, by the help of our Friends and our felves : But what is become of the Confederacy then*, faid the Doctor, *which your Highnefs had fo happily framed in your Thoughts, and which the Landgrave of* Heffe *was fo pleafed with?* Become of it, fays the Duke, 'tis a good Thought enough, but 'tis impoffible to bring it to pafs among fo many Members of the Proteftant Princes as are to be confulted with, for we neither have Time to treat, nor will half of them dare to negotiate the Matter, the Imperialifts being quar-ter'd in their very Bowels. But may not fome Expedient be found out, fays the Doctor, to bring them all to-gether to treat of it in a General Meeting? 'Tis well propofed, fays the Duke, but in what Town or City fhall they affemble where the very Deputies fhall not be befieged by Tilly or Walleftein in 14 Days Time, and facrificed to the Cruelty and Fury of the Emperor Ferdi-nand? Will your Highnefs be the eafier in it, replies the Doctor, if a way may be found out to call fuch an Affembly upon other Caufes, at which the Emperor may have no Umbrage, and perhaps give his Affent? You know the Diet at Frankfort is at Hand ; 'tis neceffary the Proteftants fhould have an Affembly of their own, to prepare Matters for the General Diet, and it may be

na

no difficult Matter to obtain it. The Duke, furprized with Joy at the Motion, embraced the Doctor with an extraordinary Tranfport, *Thou haft
done it, Doctor,* faid he, and immediately caufed
him to draw a Form of a Letter to the Emperor, which he did with the utmoft Dexterity
of Style, in which he was a great Mafter, reprefenting to his *Imperial* Majefty, that in order to put an End to the Troubles of *Germany*,
his Majefty would be pleafed to permit the Proteftant Princes of the Empire to hold a Diet to
themfelves, to confider of fuch Matters as they
were to treat of at the General Diet, in order to
conform themfelves to the Will and Pleafure
of his *Imperial* Majefty, to drive out Foreigners,
and fettle a lafting Peace in the Empire; he alfo
infinuated fomething of their Refolutions unanimoufly to give their Suffrages in favour of the
King of *Hungary* at the Election of a King of
the *Romans*, a thing which he knew the Emperor
had in his Thought, and would pufh at with all
his Might at the Diet. This Letter was fent,
and the Bait fo neatly concealed, that the Electors
of *Bavaria* and *Mentz*, the King of *Hungary*, and
feveral of the Popifh Princes, not forefeeing that
the Ruin of them all lay in the bottom of it,
foolifhly advifed the Emperor to confent to it.

In confenting to this the Emperor figned his
own Deftruction, for here began the Conjunction
of the *German* Proteftants with the *Swede*, which
was the fataleft blow to *Ferdinand*, and which he
could never recover.

Accordingly the Diet was held at *Leipfick, Feb.*
8, 1630, where the Proteftants agreed on feveral
Heads for their mutual Defence, which were
the Grounds of the following War; thefe were
the Famous Conclufions of Leipfick, which fo alarmed
the

the Emperor and the whole Empire, that to crush it in the Beginning, the Emperor commanded Count *Tilly* immediately to fall upon the Landgrave of *Hesse*, and the Duke of *Saxony*, as the principal Heads of the Union; but it was too late.

The Conclusions were digested into ten Heads;

1. That since their Sins had brought God's Judgments upon the whole Protestant Church, they should command Publick Prayers to be made to Almighty God for the diverting the Calamities that attended them.

2. That a Treaty of Peace might be set on Foot, in order to come to a right Understanding with the Catholick Princes.

3. That a Time for such a Treaty being obtained, they should appoint an Assembly of Delegates to meet preparatory to the Treaty.

4. That all their Complaints should be humbly represented to his *Imperial* Majesty, and the Catholick Electors, in order to a peaceable Accommodation.

5. That they claim the Protection of the Emperor, according to the Laws of the Empire, and the present Emperor's solemn Oath and Promise.

6. That they would appoint Deputies who should meet at certain Times to consult of their common Interest, and who should be always empoured to conclude of what should be thought needful for their Safety.

7. That they will raise a competent Force to maintain and defend their Liberties, Rights and Religion.

8. That it is agreeable to the Constitution of the Empire, concluded in the Diet at *Ausburg* to do so.

9. That the arming for their neceffary Defence fhall by no Means hinder their Obedience to his *Imperial* Majefty, but that they will ftill continue their Loyalty to him.

10. They agree to Proportion their Forces, which in all amounted to 70000 Men.

The Emperor, exceedingly ftartled at the Conclufions, iffued out a fevere Proclamation or Ban againft them, which imported much the fame Thing as a Declaration of War, and commanded *Tilly* to begin, and immediately to fall on the Duke of *Saxony* with all the Fury imaginable, as I have already obferved.

Here began the Flame to break out; for upon the Emperor's Ban, the Proteftants fend away to the King of *Sweden* for Succour.

His *Swedifh* Majefty had already conquered *Mecklenburgh*, and Part of *Pomerania*, and was advancing with his victorious Troops, encreafed by the Addition of fome Regiments raifed in thofe Parts, in order to carry on the War againft the Emperor, having defigned to follow up the *Oder* into *Silefia*, and fo to pufh the War home to the Emperor's Hereditary Countries of *Auftria* and *Bohemia*, when the firft Meffengers came to him in this Cafe; but this changed his Meafures, and brought him to the Frontiers of *Brandenburgh*, refolved to anfwer the Defires of the Proteftants: But here the Duke of *Brandenburgh* began to halt, making fome Difficulties and demanding Terms which drove the King to ufe fome Extremities with him, and ftopt the *Swedes* for a while, who had otherwife been on the Banks of the *Elbe*, as foon as *Tilly* the *Imperial* General had entred *Saxony*, which if they had done, the miferable Deftruction of *Magdenburgh* had been prevented, as I obferved before.

The

The King had been invited into the Union, and when he firſt came back from the Banks of the *Oder* he had accepted it, and was preparing to back it with all his Power.

The Duke of *Saxony* had already a good Army, which he had with infinite Diligence recruited, and muſtered them under the Cannon of *Leipſick*. The King of *Sweden* having, by his Ambaſſador at *Leipſick*, entred into the Union of the Proteſtants, was advancing victoriouſly to their Aid, juſt as Count *Tilly* had enter'd the Duke of *Saxony*'s Dominions. The Fame of the *Swediſh* Conqueſts, and of the Hero who commanded them, ſhook my Reſolution of travelling into *Turkey*, being reſolved to ſee the Conjunction of the Proteſtants Armies, and before the Fire was broke out too far to take the Advantage of ſeeing both ſides.

While I remained at *Vienna*, uncertain which Way I ſhould proceed, I remember I obſerved they talked of the King of *Sweden* as a Prince of no Conſideration, one that they might let go on and tire himſelf in *Mecklenbergh*, and thereabout, till they could find Leiſure to deal with him, and then might be cruſhed as they pleaſed ; but as 'tis never ſafe to deſpiſe an Enemy, ſo this was not an Enemy to be *deſpiſed*, as they afterwards found.

As to the Concluſions of *Leipſick*, indeed at firſt they gave the *Imperial* Court ſome Uneaſineſs, but when they found the *Imperial* Armies began to fright the Members out of the Union, and that the ſeveral Branches had no conſiderable Forces on Foot, it was the general Diſcourſe at *Vienna*, that the Union at *Leipſick* only gave the Emperor an Opportunity to cruſh abſolutely the Dukes of *Saxony*, *Brandenburgh*, and the Landgrave

grave of *Heſſe*, and they looked upon it as a Thing certain.

I never ſaw any real Concern in their Faces at *Vienna*, 'till News came to Court that the King of *Sweden* had entered into the Union; but as this made them very uneaſie, they began to move the powerfulleſt Methods poſſible to divert this Storm; and upon this News *Tilly* was haſtened to fall into *Saxony* before this Union could proceed to a Conjunction of Forces. This was certainly a very good Reſolution, and no Meaſure could have been more exactly concerted had not the Diligence of the *Saxons* prevented it.

The gathering of this Storm, which from a Cloud began to ſpread over the Empire, and from the little Dutchy of *Mecklenburgh* began to threaten all *Germany*, abſolutely determined me, as I noted before, as to travelling; and laying aſide the Thoughts of *Hungary*, I reſolved, if poſſible, to ſee the King of *Sweden*'s Army.

I parted from *Vienna* the middle of *May*, and took poſt for *Great Glogau* in *Sileſia*, as if I had purpoſed to paſs into *Poland*, but deſigning indeed to go down the *Oder* to *Cuſtrin* in the Marquiſate of *Brandenburgh*, and ſo to *Berlin*; but when I came to the Frontiers of *Sileſia*, tho' I had Paſſes I could go no farther, the Guards on all the Frontiers were ſo ſtrict; ſo I was obliged to come back into *Bohemia*, and went to *Prague*.

From hence I found I could eaſily paſs through the *Imperial* Provinces to the *Lower Saxony*, and accordingly took Paſſes for *Hamburgh*, deſigning however to uſe them no farther than I found Occaſion.

By Virtue of theſe Paſſes I got into the *Imperial* Army, under Count *Tilly*, then at the Siege of *Magdenburgh*, *May* the 2d.

I con-

I confefs I did not forefee the Fate of this City, neither I believe did Count *Tilly* himfelf expect to glut his Fury with fo entire a Defolation, much lefs did the People expect it. I did believe they muft capitulate, and I perceived by Difcourfe in the Army, that *Tilly* would give them but very indifferent Conditions; but it fell out otherwife ; the Treaty of Surrender was as it were begun, nay fome fay concluded, when fome of the Out-guards of the *Imperialifts* finding the Citizens had abandoned the Guards of the Works, and looked to themfelves with lefs Diligence than ufual, they broke in, carried an Half-Moon Sword in Hand with little Refiftance ; and tho' it was a Surprize on both Sides, the Citizens neither fearing, nor the Army expecting the Occafion, the Garrifon, with as much Refolution as could be expected under fuch a Fright, flew to the Walls, twice beat the *Imperialifts* off, but frefh Men coming up, and the Adminiftrator of *Magdenburgh* himfelf being wounded and taken, the Enemy broke in, took the City by Storm, and entred with fuch terrible Fury, that without Refpect to Age or Condition, they put all the Garrifon and Inhabitants, Man, Woman and Child, to the Sword, plundered the City, and when they had done this, fet it on Fire.

This Calamity fure was the dreadfulleft Sight that ever I faw; the Rage of the *Imperial* Soldiers was moft intolerable, and not to be exprefied; of 25000, fome faid 30000 People, there was not a Soul to be feen alive, till the Flames drove thofe that were hid in Vaults and fecret Places to feek Death in the Streets, rather than perifh in the Fire : Of thefe miferable Creatures fome were killed too by the furious Soldiers, but at laft they faved the Lives of fuch as came out

of

of their Cellars and Holes, and so about 2000
poor desperate Creatures were left : The exact
Number of those that perished in this City could
never be known, because those the Soldiers had
first butcher'd, the Flames afterwards devour'd.

I was on the other Side the *Elbe* when this
dreadful Piece of Butchery was done ; the City
of *Magdenburgh* had a Sconce or Fort over against
it, called the Toll-House, which joined to the
City by a very fine Bridge of Boats.

This Fort was taken by the *Imperialists*
a few Days before, and having a Mind to see it,
and the rather because from thence I could have
a very good View of the City, I was gone over
Tilly's Bridge of Boats to view this Fort ; about
10 a Clock in the Morning I perceived they were
storming by the firing, and immediately all ran
to the Works, I little thought of the taking the
City, but imagined it might be some Out-work
attacked, for we all expected the City would
surrender that Day, or next, and they might
have capitulated upon very good Terms.

Being upon the Works of the Fort, on a sudden
I heard the dreadfullest Cry raised in the City
that can be imagined, 'tis not possible to express
the Manner of it, and I could see the Women and
Children running about the Streets in a most
lamentable Condition.

The City Wall did not run along the Side
where the River was with so great a Heighth
but we could plainly see the Market-Place and
the several Streets which run down to the River :
In about an Hour's Time after this first Cry all
was Confusion ; there was little shooting, the
Execution was all cutting of Throats and meer
House Murthers ; the resolute Garrison, with the
brave

brave Baron *Falconberg* fought it out to the laſt, and were cut in Pieces, and by this Time the *Imperial* Soldiers having broke open the Gates and entred on all Sides, the Slaughter was very dreadful, we could ſee the poor People in Crowds driven down the Streets, flying from the Fury of the Soldiers who followed butchering them as faſt as they could, and refuſed Mercy to any Body; 'till driving them to the River's Edge, the deſperate Wretches would throw themſelves into the River, where Thouſands of them periſhed, eſpecially Women and Children; ſeveral Men that could ſwim got over to our Side, where the Soldiers not heated with Fight gave them Quarter, and took them up, and I cannot but do this Juſtice to the *German* Officers in the Fort, they had five ſmall flat Boats, and they gave leave to the Soldiers to go off in them, and get what Booty they could, but charged them not to kill any Body, but take them all Priſoners.

Nor was their Humanity ill rewarded, for the Soldiers wiſely avoiding thoſe Places where their Fellows were employed in t he butchering the miſerable People, rowed to other Places, where Crouds of People ſtood crying out for help, and expeƈting to be every Minute either drowned or murdered; of theſe at ſundry Times they fetched over near Six hundred, but took Care to take in none but ſuch as offered them good Pay.

Never was Money or Jewels of greater Service than now, for thoſe that had any Thing of that ſort to offer were ſooneſt helped.

There was a Burgher of the Town, who ſeeing a Boat coming near him, but out of his Call, by the help of a ſpeaking Trumpet, told the Soldiers in it he would give them 20000 Dollers to fetch him off; they rowed cloſe to the Shore,

and

and got him with his Wife and fix Children into the Boat, but fuch Throngs of People got about the Boat that had like to have funk her, fo that the Soldiers were fain to drive a great many out again by main Force, and while they were doing this, fome of the Enemies coming down the Street defperately drove them all into the Water.

·The Boat however brought the Burgher and his Wife and Children fafe, and though they had not all that Wealth about them, yet in Jewels and Money. he gave them fo much as made all the Fellows very rich.

I cannot pretend to defcribe the Cruelty of this Day, the Town by five in the Afternoon was all on a Flame; the Wealth confumed was ineftimable, and a Lofs to the very Conqueror. I think there was little or nothing left but the great Church, and about 100 Houfes.

This was a fad Welcome into the Army for me, and gave me a Horror and Averfion to the Emperor's People, as well as to his Caufe. I quitted the Camp the third Day after this Execution, while the Fire was hardly out in the City; and from thence getting fafe Conduct to pafs into the *Palati-nate*, I turned out of the Road at a fmall Village on the *Elbe*, called *Emerfield*, and by Ways and Town I can give but fmall Account of, having a Boor for our Guide, who we could hardly underftand. I arrived at *Leipfick* on the 17th of *May*.

We found the Elector intenfe upon the ftrengthening of his Army, but the People, in the greateft Terror imaginable, every Day expecting *Tilly* with the *German* Army, who by his Cruelty at *Magdeburg* was become fo dreadful to the Proteftants, that they expected no Mercy where-ever he came.

The

The Emperor's Power was made so formidable to all the Protestants, particularly since the Diet at *Ratisbon* left them in a worse Case than it found them, that they had not only formed the Conclusions of *Leipsick*, which all Men looked on as the Effect of Desperation rather than any probable Means of their Deliverance, but had privately implored the Protection and Assistance of foreign Powers, and particularly the King of *Sweden*, from whom they had Promises of a speedy and powerful Assistance. And truly if the *Swede* had not with a very strong Hand rescued them, all their Conclusions at *Leipsick* had served but to hasten their Ruin. I remember very well when I was in the *Imperial* Army they discoursed with such Contempt of the Forces of the Protestants, that not only the *Imperialists* but the Protestants themselves gave them up as lost : the Emperor had not less than 200000 Men in several Armies on Foot, who most of them were on the back of the Protestants in every Corner. If *Tilly* did but write a threatning Letter to any City or Prince of the Union, they presently submittted, renounced the Conclusions of *Leipsick*, and received *Imperial* Garrisons, as the Cities of *Ulm* and *Memingen*, the Dutchy of *Wirtemberg*, and several others, and almost all *Suaben*.

Only the Duke of *Saxony* and the Landgrave of *Hesse* upheld the drooping Courage of the Protestants, and refused all Terms of Peace ; flighted all the Threatnings of the *Imperial* Generals, and the Duke of *Brandenburgh* was brought in afterward almost by Force.

The Duke of *Saxony* mustered his Forces under the Walls of *Leipsick*, and I having returned to *Leipsick* two Days before, saw them pass the Review. The Duke, gallantly mounted, rode

E 2   through

through the Ranks, attended by his Field Marshal *Arnheim*, and seemed mighty well pleased with them, and indeed the Troops made a very fine Appearance; but I that had seen *Tilly's* Army, and his old Weather-beaten Soldiers, whose Discipline and Exercises were so exact, and their Courage so often tried, could not look on the *Saxon* Army without some Concern for them, when I considered who they had to deal with; *Tilly's* Men were rugged surly Fellows, their Faces had an Air of hardy Courage, mangled with Wounds and Scars, their Armour shewed the Bruises of Musquet Bullets, and the Rust of the Winter Storms; I observed of them their Cloaths were always dirty, but their Arms were clean and bright; they were used to camp in the open Fields, and sleep in the Frosts and Rain; their Horses were strong and hardy like themselves, and well taught their Exercises; the Soldiers knew their Business so exactly that general Orders were enough; every private Man was fit to command, and their Wheelings, Marchings, Countermarchings and Exercises were done with such Order and Readiness that the distinct Words of Command were hardly of any use among them; they were flushed with Victory, and hardly knew what it was to fly.

There had passed some Messages between *Tilly* and the Duke, and he gave always such ambiguous Answers as he thought might serve to gain Time; but *Tilly* was not to be put off with Words, and drawing his Army towards *Saxony*, sends four Propositions to him to sign, and demands an immediate Reply, the Propositions were positive.

1. To cause his Troops to enter into the Emperor's Service, and to march in Person with them against the King of *Sweden*.

2. To give the *Imperial* Army Quarters in his Country, and supply them with necessary Provisions.

3. To relinquish the Union of *Leipsick*, and disown the 10 Conclusions.

4. To make Restitution of the Goods and Lands of the Church.

The Duke being pressed by *Tilly*'s Trumpeter for an immediate Answer, sat all Night, and part of the next Day in Council with his Privy Councillors, debating what Reply to give him, which at last was concluded, in short, that he would live and die in Defence of the Protestant Religion, and the Conclusions of *Leipsick*, and bad *Tilly* Defiance.

The Dye being thus cast, he immediately decamped with his whole Army for *Torgau*, fearing that *Tilly* should get there before him, and so prevent his Conjunction with the *Swede*. The Duke had not yet concluded any positive Treaty with the King of *Swedeland*, and the Duke of *Brandenburgh* having made some Difficulty of joining, they both stood on some Niceties till they had like to have ruined themselves all at once.

Brandenburgh had given up the Town of *Spandau* to the King by a former Treaty to secure a Retreat for his Army, and the King was advanced as far as *Francfort* upon the *Oder*, when on a sudden some small Difficulties arising *Brandenburgh* seems cold in the Matter, and with a sort of Indifference demands to have his Town of *Spandau* restored to him again. *Gustavus Adolphus*, who began presently to imagine the Duke had made his Peace with the

E 3 Emperor,

Emperor, and fo would either be his Enemy, or
pretend a Neutrality, generoufly delivered him
hisTown of *Spandau*; but immediately turns about,
and with his wholeArmy befieges him in his Capital City of *Berlin*. This brought the Duke to know
his Error, and by the Interpofition of the Ladies,
the Queen of *Sweden* being the Duke's Sifter, the
Matter was accommodated, and the Duke joined
his Forces with the King.

But the Duke of *Saxony* had like to have been
undone by this Delay, for the *Imperialifts*, under
Count *deFurftemburgh*,were entred his Country, and
had poffeffed themfelves of *Hall*, and *Tilly* was on
his March to join him, as he afterwards did, and
ravaging the whole Country laid Siege to *Leip-*
fick it felf; the Duke driven to this Extremity
rather flies to the *Swede* than treats with him, and
on the fecond of *September* the Duke's Army joined
with the King of *Sweden*.

I had not come to *Leipfick* but to fee the Duke
of *Saxony*'s Army, and that being marched as I
have faid for *Torgau*, I had no Bufinefs there;
but if I had, the approach of *Tilly* and the *Im-*
perial Army was enough to haften me away,
for I had no Occafion to be befieged there;
fo on the 27th of *Auguft* I left theTown, as feveral
of the principal Inhabitants had done before,
and more would have done had not the Governor
publifhed a Proclamation againft it; and befides
they knew not whether to fly, for all Places
were alike expofed, the poor People were under
dreadful Apprehenfions of a Siege, and of the
mercilefs Ufage of the *Imperial* Soldiers, the
Example of *Magdeburgh* being frefh before them,
the Duke and his Army gone from them, and
the Town, though well furnifhed, but indifferently fortified.

In

In this Condition I left them, buying up Stores of Provifions, working hard to fcour their Moats, fet up Palifadoes, repair their Fortifications, and preparing all Things for a Siege; and following the *Saxon* Army to *Torgau*, I continued in the Camp till a few Days before they joined the King of *Sweden*.

I had much ado to perfuade my Companion from entring into the Service of the Duke of *Saxony*, one of whofe Collonels, with whom we had contracted a particular Acquaintance, offering him a Commiffion to be Cornet in one of the old Regiments of Horfe; but the Difference I had obferved between this new Army and *Tilly*'s old Troops had made fuch an Impreffion on me, that I confefs I had yet no manner of Inclination for the Service; and therefore perfuaded him to wait a while till we had feen a little further into Affairs, and particularly till we had feen the *Swedifh* Army, which we had heard fo much of.

The Difficulties which the Elector Duke of *Saxony* made of joining with the King were made up by a Treaty concluded with the King on the 2d of *September* at *Cofwig*, a fmall Town on the *Elbe*, whither the King's Army was arrived the Night before; for General *Tilly* being now entered into the Duke's Country, had plundered and ruined all the lower part of it, and was now actually befieging the Capital City of *Leipfick*. Thefe Neceffities made almoft any Conditions eafy to him, the greateft Difficulty was that the King of *Sweden* demanded the abfolute Command of the Army, which the Duke fubmitted to with lefs good Will than he had Reafon to do, the King's Experience and Conduct confidered.

I had not Patience to attend the Conclufions of their particular Treaties, but as foon as ever the Paffage was clear I quitted the *Saxon* Camp,

and

and went to see the *Swedish* Army : I fell in with the Out-guards of the *Swedes* at a little Town called *Beltsig*, on the River *Werfa*, juft as they were relieving the Guards, and going to march, and having a Pafs from the *English* Ambaffador was very well received by the Officer who changed the Guards, and with him I went back into the Army ; by nine in the Morning the Army was in full March, the King himfelf at the Head of them on a gray Pad, and riding from one Brigade to another, ordered the March of every Line himfelf.

When I faw the *Swedish* Troops, their exact Difcipline, their Order, the Modefty and Familiarity of their Officers, and the regular living of the Soldiers, their Camp feemed a well ordered City ; the meaneft Country Woman with her *Market Ware* was as fafe from Violence as in the Streets of *Vienna* : There was no Regiments of Whores and Rags as followed the *Imperialifts* ; nor any Women in the Camp, but fuch as being known to the Provofts to be the Wives of the Soldiers, who were neceffary for wafhing Linen, taking Care of the Soldiers Cloaths, and dreffing their Victuals.

The Soldiers were well clad, not gay, furnifhed with excellent Arms, and exceeding careful of them ; and though they did not feem fo terrible as I thought *Tilly*'s Men did when I firft faw them, yet the Figure they made, together with what we had heard of them, made them feem to me invincible : The Difcipline and Order of their Marchings, Camping and Exercife was excellent and fingular, and which was to be feen in no Armies but the King's, his own Skill, Judgment and Vigilance having added much to the general Conduct of Armies then in ufe.

As

As I met the *Swedes* on their March I had no
Opportunity to acquaint my felf with any Body
'till after the Conjunction of the *Saxon* Army,
and then it being but four Days to the great
Battle of *Leipfick,* our Acquaintance was but
fmall, faving what fell out accidentally by Converfation.

I met with feveral Gentlemen in the King's
Army who fpoke *Englifh* very well, befides that
there were 3 Regiments of *Scots* in the Army,
the Collonels whereof I found were extraordinarily efteemed by the King, as the Lord *Rea,*
Collonel *Lumfdell,* and Sir *John Hepburn :* The
latter of thefe, after I had by an Accident become
acquainted with, I found had been for many
Years acquainted with my Father, and on that
Account I received a great deal of Civility from
him, which afterwards grew into a kind of
intimate Friendfhip; he was a compleat Soldier
indeed, and for that Reafon fo well beloved by
that galiant King, that he hardly knew how to go
about any great Action without him.

It was impoffible for me now to reftrain my
young Comrade from entring into the *Swedifh*
Service, and indeed every Thing was fo inviting that I could not blame him. A Captain in
Sir *John Hepburn*'s Regiment had picked Acquaintance with him, and he having as much Gallantry in his Face as real Courage in his Heart,
the Captain had perfuaded him to take Service,
and promifed to ufe his Intereft to get him a
Company in the *Scotch* Brigade. I had made him
promife me not to part from me in my Travels without my Confent, which was the only
Obftacle to his Defires of entring in the *Swedifh* Pay ; and being one Evening in the Captain's Tent with him, and difcourfing very freely

ly together, the Captain asked him very short but friendly, and looking earnestly at me, *Is this the Gentleman, Mr.* Fielding, *that has done so much Prejudice to the King of* Sweden's *Service?* I was doubly surprized at the Expression, and at the Collonel, Sir *John Hepburn,* coming at that very Moment into the Tent; the Collonel hearing something of the Question, but knowing nothing of the Reason of it, any more than as I seemed a little to concern my self at it; yet after the Ceremony due to his Character was over, would needs know what I had done to hinder his Majesty's Service. *So much truly,* says the Captain, *that if his Majesty knew it he would think himself very little beholding to him. I am sorry, Sir,* says I, *that I should offend in any Thing, who am but a Stranger; but if you would please to inform me, I would endeavour to alter any Thing in my Behaviour that is prejudicial to any one, much less to his Majesty's Service. I shall take you at your Word, Sir,* says the Captain; *the King of* Sweden, *Sir, has a particular Request to you. I should be glad to know two Things, Sir,* said I, *First, How that can be possible, since I am not known yet to any Man in the Army, much less to his Majesty? And, Secondly, What the Request can be? Why, Sir, his Majesty desires you would not hinder this Gentleman from entring into his Service, who it seems desires nothing more, if he may have your Consent to it. I have too much Honour for his Majesty,* return'd I, *to deny any Thing which he pleases to command me; but methinks 'tis some Hardship, you should make that the King's Order, which 'tis very probable he knows nothing of.* Sir *John Hepburn* took the Case up something gravely, and drinking a Glass of *Leipsick* Beer to the Captain, said, *Come, Captain, don't press these Gentlemen; the King desires no Man's Service but what is purely Voluntier.* So we entred into other Discourse, and the

the Collonel perceiving by my Talk that I had
feen *Tilly*'s Army, was mighty curious in his
Queftions, and feemed very well fatisfied with
the Account I gave him.

The next Day the Army having pafs'd the *Elbe*
at *Wittemberg*, and joyn'd the *Saxon* Army near
Torgau his Majefty caufed both Armies to draw
up in Battalia, giving every Brigade the fame Poft
in the Lines as he purpofed to fight in : I muft do
the Memory of that glorious General this Honour, that I never faw an Army drawn up with fo
much Variety, Order, and exact Regularity fince,
tho' I have feen many Armies drawn up by fome
of the greateft Captains of the Age ; the Order
by which his Men were directed to flank and relieve one another, the Methods of receiving one
Body of Men if difordered into another, and rallying one Squadron, without difordering another was fo admirable ; the Horfe every where
flank'd, lin'd and defended by the Foot, and the
Foot by the Horfe, and both by the Cannon, was
fuch, that if thofe Orders were but as punctually
obey'd, 'twere impoffible to put an Army fo
modell'd into any Confufion.

The View being over, and the Troops return'd
to their Camps, the Captain with whom we
drank the Day before meeting me, told me I muft
come and fup with him in his Tent, where he
would ask my Pardon for the Affront he gave me
before. I told him he needed not put himfelf to
the Trouble ; I was not affronted at all, that I
would do my felf the Honour to wait on him,
provided he wou'd give me his Word not to fpeak
any more of it as an Affront.

We had not been a quarter of an Hour in his
Tent but Sir *John Hepburn* came in again, and ad-
dreffing to me, told me he was glad to find me
there ; that he came to the Captain's Tent to enquire

quire how to fend to me ; and that I muft do him
the Honour to go with him to wait on the King,
who had a Mind to hear the Account I could give
him of the *Imperial* Army from my own Mouth.
I muft confefs I was at fome Lofs in my Mind how
to make my Addrefs to his Majefty ; but I had
heard fo much of the converfible Temper of the
King, and his particular Sweetnefs of Humour
with the meaneft Soldier, that I made no more
Difficulty, but having paid my Refpects to Collonel *Hepburn*, thank'd him for the Honour he had
done me, and offer'd to rife and wait upon him :
Nay, fays the Collonel, we will eat firft, for I find
Gourdon, which was the Captain's Name, has
got fomething for Supper, and the King's Order
is at feven a Clock : So we went to Supper, and
Sir *John* becoming very friendly, muft know my
Name ; which, when I had told him, and of what
Place and Family, he rofe from his Seat and em-
bracing me, told me he knew my Father very
well, and had been intimately acquainted with
him ; and told me feveral Paffages wherein my
Father had particularly obliged him. After this
we went to Supper, and the King's Health being
drank round, the Collonel moved the fooner becaufe he had a Mind to talk with me ; when we
were going to the King, he enquired of me where
I had been, and what Occafion brought me to the
Army. · I told him the fhort Hiftory of my Travels, and that I came hither from *Vienna* on purpofe to fee the King of *Sweden* and his Army ;
he ask'd me if there was any Service he could do
me, by which he meant, whether I defired an Employment ; I pretended not to take him fo, but
told him the Protection his Acquaintance would
afford me was more than I could have ask'd, fince
I might thereby have Opportunity to fatisfie my
Curi-

Curiofity, which was the chief End of my coming
abroad. He perceiving by this that I had no
Mind to be a Soldier, told me very kindly I
fhould command him in any thing; that his Tent
and Equipage, Horfes and Servants fhould always
have Orders to be at my Service : But that as a Piece
of Friendfhip, he would advife me to retire to
fome Place diftant from the Army, for that the
Army wou'd march to morrow, and the King was
refolved to fight General *Tily*, and he wou'd not
have me hazard my felf; that if I thought fit to
take his Advice, he wou'd have me take that Interval to fee the Court at *Berlin*, whither he
would fend one of his Servants to wait on me:
His Difcourfe was too kind not to extort the
tendereft Acknowledgment from me that I was
capable of; I told him his Care of me was fo o-
bliging, that I knew not what Return to make
him, but if he pleafed to leave me to my Choice
I defired no greater Favour than to trail a Pike
under his Command in the enfuing Battle. I
can never anfwer it to your Father, fays he, to
fuffer you to expofe your felf fo far. I told him
my Father would certainly acknowledge his
Friendfhip in the Propofal made me; but I be-
liev'd he knew him better than to think he wou'd
be well pleas'd with me if I fhould accept of it;
that I was fure my Father would have rod Poft 500
Miles to have been at fuch a Battle under fuch a
General, and it fhould never be told him that his
Son had rod 50 Miles to be out of it : He feem'd
to be fomething concern'd at the Refolution I had
taken, and replied very quickly upon me, that
he approved very well of my Courage; but, fays
he, no Man gets any Credit by running upon
needlefs Adventures, nor lofes any by fhunning
Hazards which he has no Order for. 'Tis enough,
fays

fays he, for a Gentleman to behave well when he
is commanded upon any Service; I have had fighting enough, fays he, upon thefe Points of Honour,
and I never got any thing but Reproof for it from
the King himfelf. Well, Sir, faid I, however if a
Man expects to rife by his Valour, he muft fhew
it fomewhere ; and if I were to have any Command in an Army, I wou'd firft try whether I
could deferve it ; I have never yet feen any Service, and muft have my Induction fome time or
other : I fhall never have a better Schoolmafter
than your felf, nor a better School than fuch an
Army. Well, fays Sir *John*, but you may have the
fame School and the fame teaching after this Battle is over ; for I muft tell you before-hand, this
will be a bloody Touch ; *Tilly* has a great Army
of old Lads that are ufed to boxing ; Fellows with
Iron Faces, and 'tis a little too much to engage fo
hotly the firft Entrance into the Wars : You may
fee our Difcipline this Winter, and make your
Campaign with us next Summer, when you need
not fear but we fhall have fighting enough, and you
will be better acquainted with Things : We do
never put our common Soldiers upon Pitcht Battles the firft Campaign, but place our new Men in
Garrifons and try them in Parties firft.   Sir, faid
I with a little more Freedom, I believe I fhall not
make a Trade of the War, and therefore need
not ferve an Apprenticefhip to it: 'Tis a hard Battle
where none efcapes : If I come off, I hope I fhall
not difgrace you, and if not, 'twill be fome Satisfaction to my Father to hear his Son died fighting, under the Command of Sir *John Hepburn* in the
Army of the King of *Sweden*, and I defire no better Epitaph upon my Tomb. Well, fays Sir
John, and by this time we were juft come to the
King's Quarters, and the Guards calling to us interrupted

terrupted his Reply; fo we went into the Court
Yard where the King was lodg'd, which
was in an indifferent Houfe of one of the Burghers of *Debien*, and Sir *John* ftepping up, met the
King coming down fome Steps into a large Room
which looked over the Town-Wall into a Field
where Part of the Artillery was drawn up. Sir
John Hepburn fent his Man prefently to me to come
up, which I did ; and Sir *John* without any Ceremony carries me directly up to the King, who
was leaning on his Elbow in the Window : The
King turning about, this is the *Englifh* Gentleman, fays Sir *John*, who I told your Majefty had
been in the *Imperial* Army. How then did he get
hither, fays the King, without being taken by the
Scouts? At which Queftion Sir *John* faying nothing;
By a Pafs, and pleafe your Majefty, from the *Englifh* Ambaffador's Secretary at *Vienna*, faid I,
making a profound Reverence. Have you then
been at *Vienna*, fays the King? Yes, and pleafe
your Majefty, faid I ; upon which the King fold-
ing up a Letter he had in his Hand, feemed much
more earneft to talk about *Vienna*, than about *Tilly* : And pray what News had you at *Vienna*? Nothing, Sir, faid I, but daily Accounts one in the
Neck of another of their own Misfortunes, and your
Majefty's Conquefts, which makes a very melancholy Court there. But pray, faid the King, what is
the common Opinion there about thefe Affairs?
The common People are terrified to the laft Degree,
faid I, and when your Majefty took *Frankfort* upon *Oder*, if your Army had march'd but 20
Miles into *Silefia*, half the People wou'd have run
out of *Vienna*, and I left them fortifying the City.
They need not, reply'd the King fmiling, I have
no Defign to trouble them, 'tis the Proteftant
Countries I muft be for : Upon this the Duke
of

of *Saxony* entred the Room, and finding the King
engag'd, offer'd to retire; but the King beckoning with his Hand call'd to him in *French*, Coufin,
fays the King, this Gentleman has been travelling and comes from *Vienna*, and fo made me repeat what I had faid before; at which the King
went on with me, and Sir *John Hepburn* informing his Majefty that I fpoke high *Dutch*, he
changed his Language, and ask'd me in *Dutch*
where it was that I faw General *Tilly's* Army; I
told his Majefty at the Siege of *Magdeburgh*. At
Magdeburgh! faid the King fhaking his Head,
Tilly muft anfwer to me one Day for that *City*,
and if not to me to a greater King than I : Can
you guefs what Army he had with him, faid the
King? He had two Armies with him, faid I, but
one I fuppofe will do your Majefty no harm : Two
Armies! faid the King. Yes Sir, he has one Army
of about 26000 Men, faid I, and another of above
15000 Whores and their Attendants; at which
the King laughed heartily; Ay, ay, fays the
King, thofe 15000 do us as much Harm as the
26000; for they eat up the Country, and devour the poor Proteftants more than the Men;
Well, fays the King, do they talk of fighting us?
They talk big enough, Sir, faid I, but your Majefty
has not been fo often fought with as beaten in
their Difcourfe. I know not for the Men, fays
the King, but the old Man is as likely to do it as
talk of it, and I hope to try them in a Day or
two : The King enquired after that, feveral Matters of me about the *Low Countries*, the Prince of
Orange, and of the Court and Affairs in *England*; and Sir *John Hepburn* informing his Majefty
that I was the Son of an *Englifh* Gentleman of his
Acquaintance, the King had the Goodnefs to ask
him what Care he had taken of me againft the

Day

Day of Battle. Upon which Sir *John* repeated to him the Difcourfe we had together by the Way ; the King feeming particularly pleafed with it, began to take me to Task himfelf : You *Engliſh* Gentlemen, fays he, are too forward in the Wars, which makes you leave them too foon again. Your Majefty, reply'd I, makes War in fo pleafant a Manner, as makes all the World fond of fighting under your Conduct. Not fo pleafant neither, fays the King, here's a Man can tell you that fometimes 'tis not very pleafant. I know not much of the Warrior, Sir, faid I, nor of the World, but if always to conquer be the Pleafure of the War, your Majefty's Soldiers have all that can be defired. Well, fays the King, but however confidering all Things, I think you would do well to take the Advice Sir *John Hepburn* has given you. Your Majefty may command me to any Thing, but where your Majefty and fo many gallant Gentleman hazard their Lives, mine is not worth mentioning ; and I fhould not dare to tell my Father at my return into *England* that I was in your Majefty's Army, and made fo mean a Figure that your Majefty would not permit me to fight under that Royal Standard. Nay, replied the King, I lay no Commands upon you, but you are young. I can never dye, Sir, faid I, with more Honour than in your Majefty's Service ; I fpake this with fo much Freedom, and his Majefty was fo pleafed with it, that he asked me how I would choofe to ferve, on Horfeback or on Foot ; I told his Majefty I fhould be glad to receive any of his Majefty's Commands, but if I had not that Honour I had purpos'd to trail a Pike under Sir *John Hepburn,* who had done me fo much Honour as to introduce me into his Majefty's Prefence. Do fo then, reply'd the King, and turning to Sir *John Hepburn,*

F   faid,

faid, and pray do you take Care of him; at which overcome with the Goodnefs of his Difcourfe I could not anfwer a Word, but made him a profound Reverence and retired.

The next Day but one, being the Seventh of *September*, before Day the Army march'd from *Dicben* to a large Field about a Mile from *Leipfick*, where we found *Tilly*'s Army in full Battalia in admirable Order, which made a fhew both glorious and terrible. *Tilly*, like a fair Gamfter, had taken up but one Side of the Plain, and left the other free, and all the Avenues open for the King's Army; nor did he ftir to the Charge 'till the King's Army was compleatly drawn up and advanced towards him: He had in his Army 44000 old Soldiers, every Way anfwerable to what I have faid of them before; and I fhall only add, a better Army I believe never was fo foundly beaten.

The King was not much inferior in Force, being joined with the *Saxons*, who were reckoned 22000 Men, and who drew up on the Left, making a main Battle and two Wings, as the King did on the Right.

The King placed himfelf at the right Wing of his own Horfe; *Guftavus Horn* had the main Battle of the *Swedes*, the Duke of *Saxony* had the main Battle of his own Troops, and General *Arnheim* the right Wing of his Horfe.

The fecond Line of the *Swedes* confifted of the two *Scotch* Brigades, and three *Swedifh*, with the *Finland* Horfe in the Wings.

In the beginning of the Fight, *Tilly*'s right Wing charg'd with fuch irrefiftible Fury upon the Left of the King's Army where the *Saxons* were pofted, that nothing could withftand them; the *Saxons* fled amain, and fome of them carried the News over

over the Country that all was loft, and the King's
Army overthrown; and indeed it paffed for an
Overfight with fome, that the King did not place
fome of his old Troops among the *Saxons* who were
new raifed Men; the *Saxons* loft here near 2000
Men, and hardly ever fhew'd their Faces again
all the Battle, except fome few o' their Horfe.

I was pofted with my Comrade, the Captain,
at the Head of three *Scottifh* Regiments of Foot,
commanded by Sir *John Hepburn*, with exprefs
Directions from the Collonel to keep by him : Our
Poft was in the fecond Line, as a Referve to the
King of *Sweden's* main Battle, and which was
ftrange, the main Battle, which confifted of four
great Brigades of Foot, were never charged during the whole Fight; and yet we, who had the
Referve, were obliged to endure the whole Weight
of the *Imperial* Army; the Occafion was, the
right Wing of the *Imperialifts* having defeated
the *Saxons*, and being eager in the Chace, *Tilly*,
who was an old Soldier, and ready to prevent all
Miftakes, forbids any Purfuit; let them go, fays
he, but let us beat the *Swedes*, or we do nothing.
Upon this the victorious Troops fall in upon the
Flank of the King's Army, which the *Saxons* being fled lay open to them; *Guftavus Horn* commanded the left Wing of the *Swedes*, and having
firft defeated fome Regiments which charged him,
falls in upon the Rear of the *Imperial* right Wing,
and feparates them from the Van, who were advanced a great Way forward in purfuit of the
Saxons; and having routed the faid Rear or Referve, falls on upon *Tilly's* main Battle, and defeated Part of them, the other Part was gone in
Chafe of the *Saxons*, and now alfo returned, fell
in upon the Rear of the left Wing of the *Swedes*,
charging them in the Flank; for they drew

up upon the very Ground which the *Saxons* had quitted. This changed the whole Front, and made the *Swedes* face about to the Left, and make a great Front on their Flank to make this good; our Brigades, who were placed as a Reserve for the main Battle, were by special Order from the King, wheeled about to the Left, and placed for the Right of this new Front to charge the *Imperialists*; they were about 12 Thousand of their best Foot, besides Horse; and flusht with the Execution of the *Saxons*, fell on like Furies: The King by this time had almost defeated the *Imperialist's* left Wing; their Horse with more Haste than good Speed, had charged faster than their Foot could follow, and having broke into the King's first Line, he let them go; where, while the second Line bears the Shock, and bravely resisted them; the King follows them on the Crupper with 13 Troops of Horse, and some Musqueteers, by which being hemm'd in, they were all cut down in a Moment as it were, and the Army never disordered with them. This fatal Blow to the left Wing, gave the King more Leisure to defeat the Foot which followed, and to send some Assistance to *Gustavus Horn* in his left Wing, who had his Hands full with the main Battle of the *Imperialists*.

But those Troops who, as I said, had routed the *Saxons*, being called off from the Pursuit, had charged our Flank, and were now grown very strong, renewed the Battle in a terrible Manner: Here it was I saw our Men go to Wrack; Collonel *Hall*, a brave Soldier, commanded the Rear of the *Swedes* left Wing; he fought like a Lion, but was slain, and most of his Regiment cut off, tho' not unrevenged; for they entirely ruined *Furstemberg's* Regiment of Foot: Collonel *Cullenbach* with his Regiment of Horse, was extreamly over-
laid

laid alſo, and the Collonel and many brave Officers killed, and in ſhort all that Wing was ſhattered, and in an ill Condition.

In this Juncture came the King, and having ſeen what Havock the Enemy made of *Cullembach*'s Troops, he comes riding along the Front of our three Brigades, and himſelf led us on to the Charge; the Collonel of his Guards, the Baron *Dyvel*, was ſhot dead juſt as the King had given him ſome Orders: When the *Scots* advanced, ſeconded by ſome Regiments of Horſe which the King alſo ſent to the Charge, the bloodieſt Fight began that ever Man beheld, for the *Scotiſh* Brigades giving Fire three Ranks at a Time over one anothers Heads, pour'd in their Shot ſo thick, that the Enemy were cut down like Graſs before a Scyth; and following into the thickeſt of their Foot with the Clubs of their Muſquets, made a moſt dreadful Slaughter, and yet was there no flying; *Tilly*'s Men might be killed and knocked down, but no Man turned his Back, nor would give an Inch of Ground, but as they were wheel'd, or marched, or retreated by their Officers.

There was a Regiment of Cuiraſſiers, which ſtood whole to the laſt, and fought like Lions, they went ranging over the Field when all their Army was broken, and no Body cared for charging them; they were commanded by Baron *Cronenburgh*, and at laſt went off from the Battle whole. Theſe were armed in black Armour from Head to Foot, and they carried off their General; about Six a Clock the Field was cleared of the Enemy, except at one Place on the King's Side, where ſome of them rallied, and though they knew all was loſt would take no Quarter, but fought it out to the laſt Man, being found

F 3   dead

dead the next Day in Rank and File as they were drawn up.

I had the good Fortune to receive no Hurt in this Battle, excepting a small Scratch on the side of my Neck by the push of a Pike; but my Friend received a very dangerous Wound when the Battle was as good as over ; he had engaged with a *German* Collonel whose Name we could never learn, and having killed his Man, and pressed very close upon him so that he had shot his Horse, the Horse in the fall kept the Collonel down, lying on one of his Legs, upon which he demanded Quarter, which Captain *Feilding* granting, helped him to quit his Horse, and having disarmed him, was bringing him into the Line, when the Regiment of Cuirassiers, which I mentioned, commanded by Baron *Crenenburgh*, came roving over the Field, and with a flying Charge saluted our Front with a Salvo of Carabin-shot, which wounded us a great many Men, and among the rest the Captain received a Shot in his Thigh, which laid him on the Ground, and being separated from the Line, his Prisoner got away with them.

This was the first Service I was in, and indeed I never saw any Fight since maintained with such Gallantry, such desperate Valour, together with such Dexterity of Management, both Sides being composed of Soldiers fully tried, bred to the Wars, expert in every Thing, exact in their Order, and uncapable of Fear, which made the Battle be much more bloody than usual. Sir *John Hepburn*, at my Request, took particular Care of my Comrade, and sent his own Surgeon to look after him; and afterwards when the City of *Leipsick* was retaken, provided him Lodgings there,

there, and came very often to fee him; and indeed I was in great Care for him too, the Surgeons being very doubtful of him a great while; for having lain in the Field all Night among the Dead, his Wound, for want of dreffing, and with the Extremity of Cold, was in a very ill Condition, and the Pain of it had thrown him into a Fever. 'Twas quite dusk before the Fight ended, efpecially where the laft rallied Troops fought fo long, and therefore we durft not break our Order to feek out our Friends, fo that 'twas near feven o' Clock the next Morning before we found the Captain, who though very weak by the lofs of Blood, had raifed himfelf up, and placed his Back againft the Buttock of a dead Horfe; I was the firft that knew him, and running to him, embraced him with a great deal of Joy: He was not able to fpeak, but made Signs to let me fee he knew me, fo we brought him into the Camp, and Sir *John Hepburn*, as I noted before, fent his own Surgeons to look after him.

The Darknefs of the Night prevented any Purfuit, and was the only Refuge the Enemy had left; for had there been three Hours more Day-light, ten Thoufand more Lives had been loft, for the *Swedes* (and *Saxons* efpecially) enraged by the Obftinacy of the Enemy, were fo throughly heated that they would have given Quarter but to few; the Retreat was not founded 'till feven o' Clock, when the King drew up the whole Army upon the Field of Battle, and gave ftrict Command that none fhould ftir from their Order; fo the Army lay under their Arms all Night, which was another reafon why the wounded Soldiers fuffered very much by the Cold; for the King, who had a bold Enemy to deal with, was not ignorant what a fmall Body of defpe-

rate

rate Men rallied together might have done in the Darknefs of the Night, and therefore he lay in his Coach all Night at the Head of the Line, though it froze very hard.

As foon as the Day began to peep the Trumpets founded to Horfe, and all the Dragoons and Light Horfe in the Army were commanded to the Purfuit; the Cuiraffiers and fome commanded Mufqueteers advanced fome Miles, if need were, to make good their Retreat, and all the Foot ftood to their Arms for a Referve; but in half an Hour Word was brought to the King, that the Enemy was quite difperfed, upon which Detachments were made out of every Regiment to fearch among the Dead for any of our Friends that were wounded; and the King himfelf gave a ftrict Order, that if any were found wounded and alive among the Enemy none fhould kill them, but take Care to bring them into the Camp: A Piece of Humanity which faved the Lives of near a Thoufand of the Enemies.

This Piece of Service being over, the Enemy's Camp was feized upon, and the Soldiers were permitted to plunder it; all the Cannon, Arms, and Ammunition was fecured for the King's Ufe, the reft was given up to the Soldiers, who found fo much Plunder that they had no Reafon to quarrel for Shares.

For my fhare, I was fo bufie with my wounded Captain that I got nothing but a Sword, which I found juft by him when I firft faw him; but my Man brought me a very good Horfe with a Furniture on him, and one Piftol of extraordinary Workmanfhip.

I bad him get upon his Back and make the beft of the Day for himfelf, which he did, and I faw
him

him no more till three Days after, when he found
me out at *Leipfick* fo richly dreffed that I hardly knew him; and after making his Excufe for
his long Abfence, gave me a very pleafant Account where he had been: He told me, that according to my Order being mounted on the Horfe
he had brought me, he firft rid into the Field
among the Dead, to get fome Clothes fuitable
to the Equipage of his Horfe, and having feized
on a laced Coat, a Helmet, a Sword, and an extraordinary good Cane, was refolved to fee
what was become of the Enemy, and following
the Track of the Dragoons, which he could eafily do, by the Bodies on the Road, he fell in
with a fmall Party of 25 Dragoons, under no
Command but a Corporal, making to a Village
where fome of the Enemies Horfe had been quartered; the Dragoons taking him for an Officer
by his Horfe, defired him to command them,
told him the Enemy was very rich, and they
doubted not a good Booty : He was a bold brisk
Fellow, and told them, with all his Heart; but
faid he had but one Piftol, the other being broke
with firing, fo they lent him a pair of Piftols,
and a fmall Piece they had taken, and he led
them on. There had been a Regiment of Horfe
and fome Troops of *Crabats* in the Village, but
they were fled on the firft Notice of the Purfuit, excepting three Troops, and thefe on Sight
of this fmall Party; fuppofing them to be only
the firft of a greater Number, fled in the greateft Confufion imaginable; they took the Village
and about 50 Horfes, with all the Plunder of
the Enemy, and with the Heat of the Service
he had fpoiled my Horfe, he faid, for which he
had brought me two more ; for he paffing for
the Commander of the Party, had all the Advantage

vantage the Cuſtom of War gives an Officer in like Caſes.

I was very well pleaſed with the Relation the Fellow gave me, and laughing at him, *Well, Captain*, ſaid I, *and what Plunder have ye got?* *Enough to make me a Captain, Sir*, ſays he, *if you pleaſe, and a Troop ready raiſed too*; *for the Party of Dragoons are poſted in the Village by my Command, till they have farther Orders.* In ſhort, he pulled out 60 or 70 Pieces of Gold, 5 or 6 Watches, 13 or 14 Rings, whereof 2 were diamond Rings, one of which was worth 50 Dollars; Silver as much as his Pockets would hold, beſides that he had brought three Horſes, two of which were laden with Baggage, and a Boor he had hired to ſtay with them at *Leipſick* till he had found me out. *But I am afraid Captain*, ſays I, *you have plundered the Village inſtead of plundering the Enemy.* *No indeed not we*, ſays he; *but the Crabats had done it for us, and we light of them juſt as they were carrying it off.* *Well*, ſaid I, *but what will you do with your Men*; *for when you come to give them Orders, they will know you well enough?* *No, no*, ſays he, *I took Care of that*; *for juſt now I gave a Soldier five Dollars to carry them News that the Army was marched to* Moersburgh, *and that they ſhould follow thither to the Regiment.*

Having ſecured his Money in my Lodgings, he asked me if I pleaſed to ſee his Horſes, and to have one for my ſelf? I told him I would go and ſee them in the Afternoon; but the Fellow being impatient goes and fetches them: There was three Horſes, one whereof was a very good one, and by the Furniture was an Officer's Horſe of the *Crabats*, and that my Man would have me accept, for the other he had ſpoiled, as he ſaid; I was but indifferently horſed before, ſo I accepted of the Horſe, and went down with him

to

to fee the reft of his Plunder there ; he had got
three or four pair of Piftols, two or three Bundles
of Officers Linen and Lace, a Field-Bed and a
Tent, and feveral other Things of Value ; but
at laft coming to a fmall Fardel, and this, fays
he, I took whole from a *Crabat* running away
with it under his Arm, fo he brought it up into my Chamber ; he had not looked into it, he
faid, but he underftood 'twas fome Plunder the
Soldiers had made, and finding it heavy took it
by Confent ; we opened it and found 'twas a
Bundle of fome Linen, 13 or 14 Pieces of
Plate, and in a fmall Cup three Rings, a fine
Necklace of Pearl, and the Value of 100 Rix-
dollars in Money. The Fellow was amazed at
his own good Fortune, and hardly knew what
to do with himfelf: I bid him go take Care of
his other Things, and of his Horfes, and come
again ; fo he went and difcharged the Boor that
waited, and packed up all his Plunder, and came
up to me in his old Clothes again. *How now,*
Captain, fays I, *what have you altered your Equipage*
already ? I am no more afhamed, Sir, of your Livery,
anfwered he, *than of your Service, and neverthelefs*
your Servant for what I have got by it. Well, fays
I to him, *but what will you do now with all your Mo-*
ney ? I wifh my poor Father had fome of it, fays he,
and for the reft I got it for you, Sir, and defire you
would take it. He fpoke it with fo much Honefty
and Freedom that I could not but take it very
kindly ; but however, I told him I would not
take a Farthing from him, as his Mafter ; but I
would have him play the good Husband with
it now he had fuch good Fortune to get it: He told
me he would take my Directions in every Thing.
Why then, fays I, *I'll tell you what I would advife you*
to do, turn it all into ready Money, and convey it by
Return

Return home into England, *and follow your self the first Opportunity, and with good Management you may put your self in a good Posture of living with it.* The Fellow, with a sort of Dejection in his Looks, asked me, if he had disobliged me in any Thing? *Why,* says I: That I was willing to turn him out of his Service. *No,* George, (that was his Name) says I, *but you may live on this Money without being a Servant.* I'd throw it all into the Elbe, says he, *over* Torgaw *Bridge, rather than leave your Service; and besides,* says he, *can't I save my Money without going from you? I got it in your Service, and I'll never spend it out of your Service, unless you put me away. I hope my Money won't make me the worse Servant, if I thought it would, I'd soon have little enough.* Nay, George, says I, *I shall not oblige you to it, for I am not willing to lose you neither: come then,* says I, *let us put it all together, and see what it 'twill come to.* So he laid it all together on the Table, and by our Computation he had gotten as much Plunder as was worth about 1400 Rix-dollars, besides 3 Horses with their Furniture, a Tent, a Bed, and some wearing Linen. Then he takes the Necklace of Pearl, a very good Watch, a Diamond Ring, and 100 Pieces of Gold, and lays them by themselves, and having according to our best Calculation valued the Things, he put up all the rest, and as I was going to ask him what they were left out for, he takes them up in his Hand, and coming round the Table, told me, that if I did not think him unworthy of my Service and Favour, he begged I would give him leave to make that Present to me; that it was my first thought, his going out; that he had got it all in my Service, and he should think I had no Kindness for him if I should refuse it. I was resolved in my Mind not to take it from him, and yet I could find no

Means

Means to refift his Importunity; at laft I told him, I would accept of Part of his Prefent, and that I efteemed his Refpect in that as much as the whole; and that I would not have him importune me farther, fo I took the Ring and Watch with the Horfe and Furniture as before, and made him turn all the reft into Money at *Leipfick*, and not fuffering him to wear his Livery, made him put himfelf into a tolerable Equipage, and taking a young *Leipficker* into my Service, he attended me as a Gentleman from that Time forward.

The King's Army never entred *Leipfick* but proceeded to *Moersburg*, and from thence to *Hall* and fo marched on into *Franconia*, while the Duke of *Saxony* employed his Forces in recovering *Leipfick* and the driving the *Imperialifts* out of his Country. I continued at *Leipfick* 12 Days, being not willing to leave my Comrade 'till he was recovered; but Sir *John Hepburn* fo often importuned me to come into the Army, and fent me Word that the King had very often enquired for me, that at laft I confented to go without him; fo having made our Appointment where to meet and how to correfpond by Letters, I went to wait on Sir *John Hepburn*, who then lay with the King's Army at the City of *Erfurt* in *Saxony*. As I was riding between *Leipfick* and *Hall* I obferved my Horfe went very aukwardly and uneafy, and fweat very much, though the Weather was cold, and we had rid but very foftly; I fancied therefore that the Saddle might hurt the Horfe, and calls my new Captain up; *George* fay I, I believe this Saddle hurts the Horfe; fo we alighted and looking under the Saddle found the Back of the Horfe extreamly galled; fo I bid him take off the Saddle, which he did and giving the Horfe to my

young

young *Leipficker* to lead, we fat down to fee if we could mend it, for there was no Town near us; Says *George*, pointing with his Finger, if you pleafe to cut open the Pannel there, I'll get fomething to ftuff into it which will bear it from the Horfe's Back; fo while he look'd for fomething to thruft in, I cut a Hole in the Pannel of the Saddle, and following it with my Finger I felt fomething hard, which feemed to move up and down; again as I thruft it with my Finger, here's fomething that fhould not be here, fays I, not yet imagining what afterwards fell out, and calling, run back, bad him put up his Finger; whatever 'tis, fays he, 'tis this hurts the Horfe, for it bears juft on his Back when the Saddle is fet on; fo we ftrove to take hold on it, but could not reach it; at laft we took the upper Part of the Saddle quite from the Pannel, and there lay a fmall Silk Purfe wrapt in a Piece of Leather, and full of Gold Ducats; thou art born to be rich, *George*, fays I to him, here's more Money, we opened the Purfe and found in it 438 fmall Pieces of Gold, there I had a new Skirmifh with him whofe the Money fhould be; I told him 'twas his, he told me no, I had accepted of the Horfe and Furniture and all that was about him was mine, and folemnly vow'd he wou'd not have a Penny of it: I faw no Remedy but put up the Money for the Prefent, mended our Saddle, and went on; we lay that Night at *Hall*, and having had fuch a Booty in the Saddle, I made him fearch the Saddles of the other two Horfes; in one of which, we found Three *French* Crowns, but nothing in the other.

We arrived at *Erfurt* the 28th of *September*, but the Army was removed, and entred into *Franconia*, and at the Siege of *Koningfhoven* we came up with them. The firft thing I did, was to pay my

Civilities

Civilities to Sir *John Hepburn*, who received me very kindly, but told me withal, that I had not done well to be so long from him; that the King had particularly enquired for me, had commanded him to bring me to him at my return: I told him the Reason of my Stay at *Leipsick*, and how I had left that Place and my Comrade, before he was cured of his Wounds, to wait on him according to his Letters. He told me the King had spoken some Things very obliging about me, and he believed would offer me some Command in the Army, if I thought well to accept of it; I told him I had promised my Father not to take Service in an Army without his Leave; and yet if his Majesty should offer it, I neither knew how to resist it, nor had I an Inclination to any thing more than the Service, and such a Leader; tho' I had much rather have serv'd as a Volunteer at my own Charge, (which as he knew was the Custom of our *English* Gentlemen) than in any Command. He replied, do as you think fit; but some Gentlemen would give 20000 Crowns to stand so fair for Advancement as you do.

The Town of *Koningshoven* capitulated that Day, and Sir *John* was ordered to treat with the Citizens, so I had no farther Discourse with him then; and the Town being taken, the Army immediately advanced down the River *Main*, for the King had his Eye upon *Frankford* and *Mentz*, two great Cities, both which he soon became Master of, chiefly by the prodigious Expedition of his March; For within a Month after the Battle, he was in the lower Parts of the Empire, and had passed from the *Elb* to the *Rhine*, an incredible Conquest; had taken all the Strong Cities, the Bishopricks of *Bambergh*, of *Wirtsburgh*, and almost all the Circle of *Franconia*, with Part of *Schawber-*
land;

land; a Conqueſt large enough to be ſeven Year a making by the common Courſe of Arms.

Buſineſs going on thus, the King had not Leiſure to think of ſmall Matters, and I being not thoroughly reſolved in my Mind, did not preſs Sir *John* to introduce me ; I had wrote to my Father with an Account of my Reception in the Army, the Civilities of Sir *John Hepburn*, the Particulars of the Battle, and had indeed preſs'd him to give me Leave to ſerve the King of *Sweden :* To which Particular I waited for an Anſwer, but the following Occaſion determined me before an Anſwer cou'd poſſibly reach me.

The King was before the Strong Caſtle of *Marienburgh*, which commands the City of *Wurtsburgh*; he had taken the *City*, but the Garriſon and richer Part of the Burghers were retir'd into the Caſtle, and truſting to the Strength of the Place, which was thought impregnable, they bad the *Swedes* do their worſt ; 'twas well provided with all Things, and a ſtrong Garriſon in it ; ſo that the Army indeed expected 'twould be a long Piece of Work. The Caſtle ſtood on a high Rock, and on the Steep of the Rock was a Baſtion, which defended the only Paſſage up the Hill into the Caſtle ; the *Scots* were choſe out to make this attack, and the King was an Eye Witneſs of their Gallantry : In the Action Sir *John* was not commanded out, but Sir *James Ramſey* led them on, but I obſerved that moſt of the *Scotch* Officers in the other Regiments prepared to ſerve as Volunteers for the Honour of their Countrymen, and Sir *John Hepburn* led them on : I was reſolved to ſee this Piece of Service, and therefore joined my ſelf to the Volunteers ; we were armed with Partizans, and each Man two Piſtols at our Belt ; it was a Piece of Service that ſeemed perfectly deſperate,

the

the Advantage of the Hill, the Precipice we were
to mount, the height of the Baftion, the refolute
Courage and Number of the Garrifon, who from
a compleat Covert made a terrible Fire upon us,
all joined to make the Action hopelefs; but the
Fury of the *Scots* Mufqueteers was not to be a-
bated by any Difficulties; they mounted the
Hill, fcaled the Works like Madmen, running
upon the Enemies Pikes, and after two Hour's defperate Fight in the midft of Fire and Smoke, took
it by Storm, and put all the Garrifon to the Sword.
The Voluntiers did their part, and had their Share
of the Lofs too, for 13 or 14 were killed out of
37, befides the wounded, among whom I received
a Hurt more troublefome than dangerous, by a
Thruft of a Halberd into my Arm, which proved
a very painful Wound, and I was a great while
before it was thoroughly recovered.

The King received us as we drew off at the
Foot of the Hill, calling the Soldiers *his brave
Scots*, and commending the Officers by Name.
The next Morning the Caftle was alfo taken by
Storm, and the greateft Booty that ever was
found in any one Conqueft in the whole War;
the Soldiers got here fo much Money that they
knew not what to do with it and the Plunder they
got here and at the Battle of *Leipfick* made them fo
unruly, that had not the King been the beft
Mafter of Difcipline in the World they had never
been kept-in any reafonable Bounds.

The King had taken Notice of our fmall Party
of Voluntiers, and though I thought he had not
feen me, yet he fent the next Morning for Sir
John Hepburn, and asked him if I were not come
to the Army? *Yes*, fays Sir *John*, *he has been here two
or three Days:* And as he was forming an Excufe

G   for

for not having brought me to wait on his Majesty, says the King interrupting him, *I wonder you would let him thruft himfelf into fuch a hot Piece of Service as ftorming the* Port Graft: *Pray let him know I faw him, and have a very good Account of his Behaviour.* Sir *John* returned with this Account to me, and preffed me to pay my Duty to his Majefty the next Morning; and accordingly, though I had but an ill Night with the Pain of my Wound, I was with him at the Levee in the Caftle.

I cannot but give fome fhort Account of the Glory of that Morning; the Caftle had been cleared of the dead Bodies of the Enemies, and what was not pillaged by the Soldiers, was placed under a Guard. There was firft a Magazine of very good Arms for about 18 or 20000 Foot, and 4000 Horfe, a very good Train of Artillery of about 18 Pieces of Battery, 32 brafs Field-pieces and four Mortars. The Bifhop's Treafure, and other publick Monies not plundered by the Soldiers, was telling out by the Officers, and amounted to 400000 Florins in Money; and the Burghers of the Town in folemn Proceffion, bareheaded, brought the King three Tun of Gold as a Compofition to exempt the City from Plunder. Here was alfo a Stable of gallant Horfes which the King had the Curiofity to go and fee.

When the Ceremony of the Burghers was over the King came down into the Caftle Court, walked on the Parade (where the great Train of Artillery was placed on their Carriages) and round the Walls, and gave Order for repairing the Baftion that was ftormed by the *Scots*; and as at the Entrance of the Parade Sir *John Hepburn* and I made our Reverence to the King, *Ho, Cavalier,* faid said the King to me, *I am glad to see you,* and so passed forward ; I made my bow very low, but his Majesty said no more at that Time.

When the View was over the King went up into the Lodgings, and Sir *John* and I walked in an Anti-Chamber for about a Quarter of an Hour, when one of the Gentlemen of the Bed-Chamber came out to Sir *John,* and told him the King ask'd for him ; he staid but a little with the King and came out to me, and told me the King had ordered him to bring me to him.

His Majesty, with a Countenance full of Honour and Goodness interrupted my Compliment, and asked me how I did ; at which answering only with a bow, says the King, *I am sorry to see you are hurt, I would have laid my Commands on you not to have shewn your self in so sharp a Piece of Service, if I had known you had been in the Camp. Your Majesty does me too much Honour,* said I, *in your Care of a Life that has yet done nothing to deserve your Favour.* His Majesty was pleased to say something very kind to me relating to my Behaviour in the Battle of *Leipsick,* which I have not Vanity enough to write ; at the Conclusion whereof, when I replyed very humbly, that I was not sensible that any Service I had done or could do could possibly merit so much Goodness ; he told me he had ordered me a small Testimony of his Esteem, and withal gave me his Hand to kiss : I was now conquered, and with a sort of Surprize, told his Majesty, I found my self so much engaged by his Goodness, as well as my own Inclination, that if his Majesty would please to accept of my Devoir I was resolved to serve in his Army, or whereever he pleased to command me. *Serve me,* says the King, *why so you do, but I must not have you be a Musketter ; a poor Soldier at a Dollar a Week will do*

G 2   *that.*

that. Pray, *Sir* John, says the King, give him what Commiffion he defires. No Commiffion, Sir, fays I, *would pleafe me better than Leave to fight near your Majefty's Perfon, and to ferve you at my own Charge till I am qualified by more Experience to receive your Commands. Why then it fhall be fo,* faid the King, *and I charge you,* Hepburn, fays he, *when any Thing offers that is either fit for him, or he defires, that you tell me of it,* and giving me his Hand again to kifs I withdrew.

I was followed before I had paffed the Caftle-Court by one of the King's Pages, who brought me a Warrant directed to Sir *John Hepburn* to go to the Mafter of the Horfe for an immediate delivery of Things ordered by the King himfelf for my Account, where being come, the Querry produced me a very good Coach with four Horfes, Harnefs and Equipage, and two very fine Saddle-Horfes out of the Stable of the Bifhop's Horfes, afore-mentioned; with thefe there was a Lift for three Servants, and a Warrant to the Steward of the King's Baggage to defray me, my Horfes and Servants at the King's Charge till farther Order. I was very much at a Lofs how to manage my felf in this fo ftrange freedom of fo great a Prince, and confulting with Sir *John Hepburn,* I was propofing to him whether it was not proper to go immediately back to pay my Duty to his Majefty and acknowledge his Bounty in the beft Terms I could; but while we were refolving to do fo, the Guards ftood to their Arms, and we faw the King go out at the Gate in his Coach to pafs into the City, fo we were diverted from it for that Time. I acknowledge the Bounty of the King was very furprifing, but I muft fay it was not fo very ftrange to me when I afterward faw the Courfe of his Management;

Bounty

Bounty in him was his natural Talent, but he never diftributed his Favours but where he thought himfelf both loved and faithfully ferved, and when he was fo, even the fingle Actions of his private Soldiers he would take particular Notice of himfelf, and publickly own, acknowledge and reward them, of which I am obliged to give fome Inftances.

A private Mufqueteer at the ftorming the Caftle of *Wurtzberg*, when all the Detachment was beaten off ftood in the Face of the Enemy, and fired his Piece, and though he had 1000 fhot made at him, ftood uuconcerned, and charged his Piece again, and let fly at the Enemy, continuing to do fo three Times, at the fame Time beckoning with his Hand to his Fellows to come on again, which they did, animated by his Example, and carried the place for the King.

When the Town was taken the King ordered the Regiment to be drawn out, and calling for that Soldier, thanked him before them all for taking the Town for him, gave him 1000 Dollars in Money, and a Commiffion with his own Hand for a Foot Company, or Leave to go home, which he would; the Soldier took the Commiffion on his Knees, kiffed it, and put it into his Bofom, and told the King, he would never leave his Service as long as he lived.

This Bounty of the King's, timed and fuited by his Judgment, was the Reafon that he was very well ferved, intirely beloved, and moft punctually obeyed by his Soldiers, who were fure to be cherifhed and encouraged, if they did well, having the King generally an Eye-witnefs of their Behaviour.

My Indifcretion rather than Valour had engaged me fo far at the Battle of *Leipfick*, that be-

ing

ing in the Van of Sir *John* *Hepburn*'s Brigade, almoft three whole Companies of us were fepa-rated from our Line, and furrounded by the Enemies Pikes; I cannot but fay alfo that we were difengaged rather by a defperate Charge Sir *John* made with the whole Regiment to fetch us out, than by our own Valour, though we were not wanting to our felves neither, but this Part of the Action being talked of very much to the Advantage of the young *Englifh* Voluntier, and poffibly more than I deferved, was the Occafion of all the Diftinction the King ufed me with ever after.

I had by this Time Letters from my Father, in which, though with fome Reluctance, he left me at Liberty to enter into Arms if I thought fit, always obliging me to be directed, and, as he faid, commanded by Sir *John Hepburn*; at the fame Time he wrote to Sir *John Hepburn*, com-mending his Son's Fortunes, as he called it, to his Care; which Letters Sir *John* fhewed the King, unknown to me.

I took Care always to acquaint my Father of every Circumftance, and forgot not to men-tion his Majefty's extraordinary Favour, which fo affected my Father that he obtained a very honourable mention of it in a Letter from King *Charles* to the King of *Sweden*, written by his own Hand.

I had waited on his Majefty with Sir *John Hepburn*, to give him Thanks for his magnificent Prefent, and was received with his ufual Good-nefs, and after that I was every Day among the Gentlemen of his ordinary Attendance; and if his Majefty went out on a Party, as he would often do, or to view the Country, I always at-tended him among the Voluntiers of whom a great many

many always followed him ; and he would often call me out, talk with me, send me upon Meſſages to Towns, to Princes, free Cities, and the like, upon extraordinary Occaſions.

The firſt Piece of Service he put me upon had like to have embroiled me with one of his favourite Collonels ; the King was marching through the *Bergſtract*, a low Country on the edge of the *Rhine*, and, as all Men thought, was going to beſiege *Heidelberg*, but on a ſudden orders a Party of his Guards, with five Companies of *Scots*, to be drawn.out ; while they were drawing out this Detachment the King calls me to him, *Ho, Cavalier*, ſays he, *that was his uſual Word*, you ſhall command this Party ; and thereupon gives me Orders to march back all Night, and in the Morning, by break of Day, to take Poſt under the Walls of the Fort of *Oppenheim*, and immediately to entrench my ſelf as well as I could : *Grave Neels*, the Collonel of his Guards, thought himſelf injured by this Command, but the King took the Matter upon himſelf, and *Grave Neels* told me very familiarly afterwards, We have ſuch a Maſter, ſays he, that no Man can be affronted by : I thought my ſelf wronged, ſays he, when you commanded my Men over my Head; and for my Life, ſays he, I knew not which way to be angry.

I executed my Commiſſion ſo punƐtually that by break of Day I was ſet down within Muſquet-ſhot of the Fort, under covert of a little Mount, on which ſtood a Wind-mill, and had indifferently fortified my ſelf, and at the ſame Time had poſted ſome of my Men on two other Paſſes, but at farther Diſtance from the Fort, ſo that the Fort was effeƐtually block'd up on the Land-ſide ; in the Afternoon the Enemy ſal-

lied

lied on my firſt Entrenchment, but being covered from their Cannon, and defended by a Ditch which I had drawn croſs the Road, they were ſo well received by my Muſqueteers that they retired with the loſs of 6 or 7 Men.

The next Day Sir *John Hepburn* was ſent with two Brigades of Foot to carry on the Work, and ſo my Commiſſion ended; the King expreſſed himſelf very well pleaſed with what I had done; and when he was ſo was never ſparing of telling of it, for he uſed to ſay that publick Commendations were a great Encouragement to Valour.

While Sir *John Hepburn* lay before the Fort, and was preparing to ſtorm it, the King's Deſign was to get over the *Rhine*, but the *Spaniards* which where in *Oppenheim* had ſunk all the Boats they could find; at laſt the King being informed where ſome lay that were ſunk cauſed them to be weighed with all the Expedition poſſible, and in the Night of the 7th of *December* in three Boats paſſed over his Regiment of Guards, about three Miles above the Town, and as the King thought ſecure from Danger; but they were no ſooner landed and not drawn into Order but they were charged by a Body of *Spaniſh* Horſe, and had not the Darkneſs given them Opportunity to draw up in the Encloſures in ſeveral little Parties, they had been in great Danger of being diſordered, but by this Means they lined the Hedges and Lanes ſo with Muſqueteers, that the remainder had Time to draw up in Battalia, and ſaluted the Horſe with their Muſquets ſo that they drew farther off.

The King was very impatient, hearing his Men engaged, having no Boats nor poſſible Means to get over to help them; at laſt, about Eleven a Clock at Night the Boats came back, and the

King

King thruft another Regiment into them, and though his Officers diffuaded him, would go over himfelf with them on Foot, and did fo. This was three Months that very Day when the Battle of *Leipfick* was fought, and winter Time too, that the Progrefs of his Arms had fpread from the *Elbe*, where it parts *Saxony* and *Brandenburgh*, to the *Lower Palatinate* and the *Rhine*.

I went over in the Boat with the King, I never faw him in fo much Concern in my Life, for he was in Pain for his Men; but before we got on fhore the *Spaniards* retired, however the King landed, ordered his Men, and prepared to entrench, but he had not Time; for by that Time the Boats were put off again, the *Spaniards*, not knowing more Troops were landed, and being reinforced from *Oppenheim*, came on again, and charged with great Fury; but all Things were now in Order; and they were readily received and beaten back again: They came on again the third Time, and with repeated Charges attacked us; but at laft finding us too ftrong for them they gave it over. By this Time another Regiment of Foot was come over, and as foon as Day appeared the King with the three Regiments marched to the Town, which furrendred at the firft Summons, and the next Day the Fort yielded to Sir *John Hepburn*.

. The Caftle at *Oppenheim* held out ftill with a Garrifon of 800 *Spaniards*, and the King leaving 200 *Scots* of Sir *James Ramfey*'s Men in the Town, drew out to attack the Caftle; Sir *James Ramfey* being left wounded at *Wartsburgh* the King gave me the Command of thofe 200 Men, which were a Regiment, that is to fay, all that were left of a Gallant Regiment of 2000 *Scots* which the King brought out of *Sweden* with him, under that Brave Collonel; there

there was about 30 Officers, who having no Soldiers were yet in Pay, and ferved as Reformadoes
with the Regiment, and were over and above the
200 Men.

The King defigned to ftorm the Caftle on the
lower fide by the Way that leads to *Mentz*, and
Sir *John Hepburn* landed from the other Side and
marched up to ftorm on the *Rhine* Port.

My Reformado *Scots* having obferved that the
Town Port of the Caftle was not fo well guarded
as the reft, all the Eyes of the Garrifon being
bent towards the King and Sir *John Hepburn*; came
running to me, and told me, they believed they
could enter the Caftle Sword in Hand if
I would give them Leave; I told them I durft
not give them Orders, my Commiffion being
only to keep and defend the Town; but they
being very importunate, I told them they were
Voluntiers, and might do what they pleafed,
that I would lend them 50 Men and draw up
the reft to fecond them, or bring them off, as I
faw Occafion, fo as I might not hazard the
Town; this was as much as they defired, they
fallied immediately, and in a trice the Voluntiers
fcaled the Port, cut in Pieces the Guard and
burft open the Gate, at which the 50 entered:
finding the Gate won I advanced immediately
with 100 Mufqueteers more, having locked up
all the Gates of the Town but the Caftle-Port,
and leaving 50 ftill for a Referve juft at that
Gate; the Townfmen too feeing the Caftle as it
were taken, run to Arms, and followed me with
above 200 Men; the *Spaniards* were knocked down
by the *Scots* before they knew what the Matter
was, and the King and Sir *John Hepburn* advancing
to ftorm, were furprized, when inftead of Refift-
ence, they faw the *Spaniards* throwing themfelves
over

over the Walls to avoid the Fury of the *Scots*;
few of the Garrison got away, but were either
killed or taken; and having cleared the Castle,
I set open the Port on the King's Side, and sent
his Majesty Word the Castle was his own. The
King came on, and entered on Foot, I received him
at the Head of the *Scots* Reformadoes, who all
saluted him with their Pikes. The King gave
them his Hat, and turning about, *Brave* Scots, *Brave*
Scots, says he smiling, *you were too quick for me*;
then beckoning to me, made me tell him· how and
in what Manner we had managed the Storm,
which he was exceeding well pleased with, but
especially at the Caution I had used to bring them
off if they had miscarried, and secure the Town.

From hence the Army marched to *Mentz*,
which in 4 Days Time capitulated, with the Fort
and Citadel, and the City paid his Majesty
300000 Dollars to be exempted from the Fury
of the Soldiers ; here the King himself drew the
Plan of those invincible Fortifications which
to this Day makes it one of the strongest Cities
in *Germany*.

Friburg, *Koningstien*, *Niustat*, *Keiser-Lautern*, and
almost all the *Lower Palatinate*, surrendered at
the very Terror of the King of *Sweden*'s Approach,
and never suffered the Danger of a Siege.

The King held a most Magnificent Court at
Mentz, attended by the Landgrave of *Hesse*,
with an incredible Number of Princes and
Lords of the Empire, with Ambassadors and
Residents of Foreign Princes; and here his
Majesty staid till *March* when the Queen,
with a great Retinue of *Swedish* Nobility came
from *Erfurt* to see him. The King attended by
a gallant Train of *German* Nobility went to
Frankfort,

Frankfort, and from thence on to *Hoeft*, to meet the Queen, where her Majefty arrived *Feb.* 8th.

During the King's ftay in thefe Parts, his Armies were not idle, his Troops on one fide under the *Rhinegrave*, a brave and ever-fortunate Commander, and under the Landgrave of *Heffe*, on the other, ranged the Country from *Lorrain* to *Luxemburgh*, and paft the *Mofelle* on the Weft, and the *Wefer* on the North. Nothing could ftand before them, the *Spanifh* Army which came to the Relief of the Catholick Electors was every where defeated and beaten quite out of the Country, and the *Lorrain* Army quite ruined; 'twas a moft pleafant Court fure as ever was feen, where every Day Expreffes arrived of Armies defeated, Towns furrendered, Contributions a-greed upon, Parties routed, Prifoners taken, and Princes fending Ambaffadours to fue for Truces and Neutralities, to make Submiffions and Com-pofitions, and to pay Arrears and Contri-butions.

Here arrived, *Febr.* 10th, the King of *Bohe-mia* from *England*, and with him my Lord *Craven*, with a Body of *Dutch Horfe*, and a very fine Train of *Englifh* Voluntiers, who immediately, without any ftay, marched on to *Hoeft* to wait upon his Majefty of *Sweden*, who received him with a great deal of Civility, and was treated at a Noble Collation, by the King and Queen, at *Frankfort*. Never had the Unfortunate King fo fair a Profpect of being reftored to his Inhe-ritance of the *Palatinate* as at that Time, and had King *James*, his Father-in-Law, had a Soul an-fwerable to the Occafion, it had been effected be-fore, but it was a ftrange Thing to fee him equip-ped from the *Englifh* Court with one Lord and about 40 or 50 *Englifh Gentlemen* in his Attend-ance,

ance, whereas had the King of *England* now, as 'tis well known he might have done, furnished him with 10 or 12000 *English* Foot, nothing could have hindered him taking a full Poffeffion of his Country ; and yet even without that Help did the King of *Sweden* clear almoft his whole Country of *Imperialifts*, and after his Death reinftal his Son in the Electorate, but no Thanks to us.

The Lord *Craven* did me the Honour to enquire for me by Name, and his Majefty of *Sweden* did me yet more by prefenting me to the King of *Bohemia*, and my Lord *Craven* gave me a Letter from my Father, and fpeaking fomething of my Father having ferved under the Prince of *Orange* in the Famous Battle of *Neuport*, the King fmiling returned, *And pray tell him from me his Son has ferved as well in the warm Battle of* Leipfick.

My Father being very much pleafed with the Honour I had received from fo great a King, had ordered me to acquaint his Majefty, that if he pleafed to accept of their Service he would raife him a Regiment of *English* Horfe at his own Charge to be under my Command, and to be fent over into *Holland* ; and my Lord *Craven* had Orders from the King of *England* to fignify his Confent to the faid Levy. I acquainted my old Friend Sir *John Hepburn* with the Contents of the Letter, in order to have his Advice, who being pleafed with the Propofal, would have me go to the King immediately with the Letter, but prefent Service put it off for fome Days.

The taking of *Creutznach* was the next Service of any Moment; the King drew out in Perfon to the Siege of this Town ; the Town foon came to a Parly, but the Caftle feemed a Work of Difficulty; for its Situation was fo ftrong and fo furrounded

with

with Works behind and above one another, that
moſt People thought the King would receive a
Check from it; but it was not eaſy to reſiſt the
Reſolution of the King of *Sweden*.

He never battered it but with two ſmall Pieces,
but having viewed the Works himſelf, ordered
a Mine under the firſt Ravelin, which being ſprung
with Succeſs, he commands a ſtorm; I think there
was not more commanded Men than Voluntiers,
both *Engliſh, Scots, French* and *Germans:* My old
Comrade was by this Time recovered of his
Wound at *Leipſick,* and made one. The firſt Body
of Voluntiers of about 40, were led on by my Lord
Craven, and I led the ſecond, among whom were
moſt of the Reformade *Scots* Officers who
took the Caſtle of *Oppenheim*; the firſt Party was
not able to make any Thing of it, the Garriſon
fought with ſo much Fury that many of the
Voluntier Gentlemen being wounded, and ſome
killed, the reſt were beaten off with Loſs. The
King was in ſome Paſſion at his Men, and rated
them for running away, as he called it, though
they really retreated in good Order, and commanded the Aſſault to be renewed. 'Twas our
Turn to fall on next; our *Scots* Officers not being
uſed to be beaten, advanced immediately, and my
Lord *Craven,* with his Voluntiers, pierced in with
us, fighting gallantly in the Breach with a Pike
in his Hand, and to give him the Honour due to
his Bravery, he was with the firſt on the Top of
the Rampart, and gave his Hand to my Comrade,
and lifted him up after him; we helped one
another up, till at laſt almoſt all the Voluntiers
had gained the Height of the Ravelin, and maintained it with a great Deal of Reſolution, expecting when the commanded Men had gained the
ſame Height to advance upon the Enemy, when
one

one of the Enemies Captains called to my Lord *Craven*, and told him if they might have honourable Terms they would capitulate, which my Lord telling him he would engage for, the Garrison fired no more, and the Captain leaping down from the next Rampart came with my Lord *Craven* into the Camp, where the Conditions were agreed on, and the Castle surrendered.

After the taking of this Town, the King hearing of *Tilly's* Approach, and how he had beaten *Gustavus Horn*, the King's Field Marshal out of *Bamberg*, began to draw his Forces together, and leaving the Care of his Conquests in these Parts to his Chancellor *Oxenstern*, prepares to advance towards *Bavaria*.

I had taken an Opportunity to wait upon his Majesty with Sir *John Hepburn*, and being about to introduce the Discourse of my Father's Letter, the King told me he had received a Compliment on my account in a Letter from King *Charles*: I told him his Majesty had by his exceeding Generosity bound me and all my Friends to pay their Acknowledgments to him, and that I supposed my Father had obtained such a mention of it from the King of *England* as Gratitude moved him to; that his Majesty's Favour had been shewn in me to a Family both willing and ready to serve him, that I had received some Commands from my Father, which if his Majesty pleased to do me the Honour to accept of, might put me in a Condition to acknowledge his Majesty's Goodness in a Manner more proportioned to the Sense I had of his Favour; and with that I produced my Father's Letter, and read that Clause in it which related to the Regiment of Horse, which was as follows.

I read

I Read with a great deal of Satisfaction the Account you give of the great and extraordinary Conquests of the King of Sweden, and with more his Majesty's Singular Favour to you, I hope you will be careful to value and deserve so much Honour; I am glad you rather chose to serve as a Voluntier at your own Charge, than to take any Command, which for want of Experience you might misbehave in.

I have obtained of the King that he will particularly Thank his Majesty of Sweden for the Honour he has done you, and if his Majesty gives you so much Freedom, I could be glad you should in the humblest Manner thank his Majesty in the Name of an old broken Soldier.

If you think your self Officer enough to command them, and his Majesty pleased to accept them, I would have you offer to raise his Majesty a Regiment of Horse, which I think I may near compleat in our Neighbourhood with some of your old Acquaintance who are very willing to see the World. If his Majesty gives you the Word, they shall receive his Commands in the Maes, the King having promised me to give them Arms, and transport them for that Service into Holland; and I hope they may do his Majesty such Service as may be for your Honour and the Advantage of his Majesty's Interest and Glory,

Your loving Father.

'Tis an Offer like a Gentleman and like a Soldier, says the King, and I'll accept of it on two Conditions; first, says the King, that I will pay your Father the Advance Money for the raising the Regiment; and next, that they shall be landed in the Weser or the Elbe, for which if the King of England will not, I will pay the Passage, for if they land in Holland, it may prove very difficult to get them to us when the Army shall be marched out of this Part of the Country.

I rea-

I returned this Anfwer to my Fat'ier, and fent my Man *George* into *England* to Order that Regiment, and made him Quarter-Mafter ; I fent blank Commiffions for the Officers, figned by the King, to be filled up as my Father fhould think fit ; and when I had the King's Order for the Commiffions, the Secretary told me I muft go back to the King with them. Accordingly I went back to the King, who opening the Packet, laid all the Commiffions but one upon a Table before him, and bad me take them, and keeping that one ftill in his Hand, *Now,* fays he, *you are one of my Soldiers,* and therewith gave me his Commiffion, as Collonel of Horfe in prefent Pay. I took the Commiffion kneeling, and humbly thanked his Majefty ; *But,* fays the King, *there is one Article of War I expect of you more than of others. Your Majefty can expect nothing of me which I fhall not willingly comply with,* faid I, *as foon as I have the Hcnour to underftand what it is. Why it is,* fays the King, *that you fhall never fight but when you have Orders; for I fhall not be willing to lofe my Collonel before I have the Regiment. I fhall be ready at all Times, Sir,* returned I, *to obey your Majefty's Orders.*

I fent my Man Exprefs with the King's Anfwer, and the Commiffion to my Father, who had the Regiment compleated in lefs than 2 Months time, and 6 of the Officers with a Lift of the reft came away to me, who I prefented to his Majefty when he lay before *Neurenburg,* where they kiffed his Hand.

One of the Captains offered to bring the whole Regiment travelling as private Men into the Army in fix Weeks Time, and either to tranfport their Equipage, or buy it in *Germany;* but 'twas thought impracticable ; however, I had fo many came in that Manner that I had a compleat

H   Troop

Troop always about me, and obtained the King's Order to mufter them as a Troop.

On the 8th of *March* the King decampt, and marching up the River *Mayn*, bent his Courfe directly for *Bavaria*, taking feveral fmall Places by the Way, and expecting to engage with *Tilly*, who he thought would difpute his Entrance into *Bavaria*, kept his Army together; but *Tilly* finding himfelf too weak to encounter him, turned away, and leaving *Bavaria* open to the King, marched into the *Upper Palatinate*. The King finding the Country clear of the *Imperialifts*, comes to *Norimberg*, made his Entrance into that City the 21ft of *March*, and being nobly treated by the Citizens, he continued his March into *Bavaria*; and on the 26th fat down before *Donawert* : The Town was taken the next Day by Storm, fo fwift were the Conquefts of this invincible Captain. Sir *John Hepburn*, with the *Scots* and the *Englifh* Voluntiers at the Head of them, entred the Town firft, and cut all the Garrifon to Pieces, except fuch as efcaped over the Bridge.

I had no Share in the Bufinefs of *Donawert*, being now among the Horfe, but I was pofted on the Roads with five Troops of Horfe, where we picked up a great many Stragglers of the Garrifon, who we made Prifoners of War.

'Tis obfervable, that this Town of *Donawert* is a very ftrong Place and well fortified, and yet fuch Expedition did the King make, and fuch Refolution did he ufe in his firft Attacks, that he carried the Town without putting himfelf to the Trouble of formal Approaches; 'twas generally his way when he came before any Town with a Defign to befiege it; he never would encamp at a Diftance and begin his Trenches a great Way off, but bring his Men immediately

within

within half Mufquet-fhot of the Place, there getting under the beft Cover he could, he would immediately begin his Batteries and Trenches before their Faces; and if there was any Place poffible to be attacked, he would fall to ftorming immediately: By this refolute way of coming on he carried many a Town in the firft heat of his Men, which would have held out many Days againft a more Regular Siege.

This March of the King broke all *Tilly*'s Meafures, for now was he obliged to face about, and leaving the *Vpper Palatinate*, to come to the Affiftance of the Duke of *Bavaria*; for the King being 20000 ftrong, befides 10000 Foot and 4000 Horfe and Dragoons which joined him from the *Duringer Wald*, was refolved to ruin the Duke, who lay now open to him, and was the moft powerful and inveterate Enemy of the Proteftants in the Empire.

Tilly was now joined with the Duke of *Bavaria*, and might together make about 22000 Men, and in Order to keep the *Swedes* out of the Country of *Bavaria*, had planted themfelves along the Banks of the River *Lech*, which runs on the Edge of the Duke's Territories; and having fortified the other Side of the River, and planted his Cannon for feveral Miles at all the convenient Places on the River, refolved to difpute the King's Paffage.

I fhall be the longer in relating this Account of the *Lech*, being efteemed in thofe Days as great an Action as any Battle or Siege of that Age, and particularly famous for the Difafter of the gallant old General *Tilly*; and for that I can be more particular in it than other Accounts, having been an Eye-witnefs to every part of it.

The

The King being truly informed of the Difposition of the *Bavarian* Army, was once of the Mind to have left the Banks of the *Lech*, have repaffed the *Danube*, and fo fetting down before *Ingolftat*, the Duke's Capital City, by the taking that ftrong Town to have made his Entrance into *Bavaria*, and the Conqueft of fuch a Fortrefs, one entire Action; but the Strength of the Place, and the Difficulty of maintaining his Leaguer in an Enemy's Country, while *Tilly* was fo ftrong in the Field, diverted him from that Defign; he therefore concluded that *Tilly* was firft to be beaten out of the Country, and then the Siege of *Ingolftat* would be the eafier.

Whereupon the King refolved to go and view the Situation of the Enemy; his Majefty went out the 2d of *April* with a ftrong Party of Horfe, which I had the Honour to command; we marched as near as we could to the Banks of the River, not to be too much expofed to the Enemy's Cannon, and having gained a little Height, where the whole Courfe of the River might be feen, the King halted, and Commanded to draw up. The King alighted, and calling me to him, Examined every Reach and Turning of the River by his Glafs, but finding the River run a long and almoft a ftraight Courfe, he could find no Place which he liked, but at laft turning himfelf North, and looking down the ftream, he found the River fetching a long Reach, doubles fhort upon it felf, making a round and very narrow Point, *There's a Point will do our bufinefs*, fays the King, *and if the Ground be good I'll pafs there, let* Tilly *do his worft.*

He immediately ordered a fmall Party of Horfe to view the Ground, and to bring him
Word

Word particularly how high the Bank was on
each Side and at the Point; and he shall have
50 Dollars, says the King, that will bring me
Word how deep the Water is. I asked his Majesty
Leave to let me go, which he would by no
Means allow of; but as the Party was drawing
out, a Serjeant of Dragoons told the King, if he
pleafed to let him go difguifed as a Boor, he
would bring him an Account of every Thing he
defired. The King liked the Motion well e-
nough, and the Fellow being very well acquainted with the Country, puts on a Ploughman's
Habit, and went away immediately with a long
Pole upon his Shoulder; the Horfe lay all this
while in the Woods, and the King ftood undif-
cerned by the Enemy on the little Hill aforefaid. The Dragoon with his long Pole comes
down boldly to the Bank of the River, and calling to the Centinels which *Tilly* had placed on
the other Bank, talked with them, asked them,
if they could not help him over the River; and
pretended he wanted to come to them; at laft
being come to the Point, where, as I faid, the
River makes a fhort Turn, he ftands parlying
with them a great while, and fometimes pretending to wade over, he puts his long Pole into the
Water, then finding it pretty Shallow he pulls
off his Hofe and goes in, ftill thrufting his Pole in
before him, till being gotten up to his middle,
he could reach beyond him, where it was too
deep, and fo fhaking his Head, comes back again.
The Soldiers on the other Side laughing at him,
asked him if he could fwim? He faid, No. Why
you Fool you, says one of the Centinels, the
Channel of the River is 20 Foot deep. How
do you know that? says the Dragoon. Why our

Engi-

Engineer, fays he, meafured it Yefterday. This
was what he wanted, but not yet fully fatisfied;
Av but, fays he, may be it may not be very
broad, and if one of you would wade in to meet
me till I could reach you with my Pole, I'd give
him half a Ducat to pull me over. The innocent
way of his Difcourfe fo deluded the Soldiers,
that one of them immediately ftrips and goes in
up to the Shoulders, and our Dragoon goes in on
this Side to meet him ; but the Stream took the
t'other Soldier away, and he being a good Swim-
mer, came fwimming over to this Side. The
Dragoon was then in a great deal of Pain for fear
of being difcovered, and was once going to kill
the Fellow, and make off; but at laft refolved
to carry on the Humour, and having entertained the Fellow with a Tale of a Tub, about
the *Swedes* ftealing his Oats, the Fellow being a
cold wanted to be gone, and he as willing to be
rid of him, pretended to be very forry he could
not get over the River, and fo makes off.

By this however he learned both the Depth and
Breadth of the Channel, the Bottom and Nature of
both Shores, and every Thing the King wanted to
know ; we could fee him from the Hill by our
Glaffes very plain, and could fee the Soldier naked with him : Says the King, he will certainly
be difcovered and knocked on the Head from
the other Side : He is a Fool, fays the King, he
does not kill the Fellow and run off; but when
the Dragoon told his Tale, the King was extremely well fatisfied with him, gave him 100
Dollars, and made him a Quarter-mafter to a
Troop of Cuiraffiers.

The King having farther examined the Dragoon, he gave him a very diftinct Account of
the

the Shore and the Ground on this Side, which he found to be higher than the Enemy's by 10 or 12 Foot, and a hard Gravel.

Hereupon the King refolves to pafs there, and in order to it gives, himfelf, particular Directions for fuch a Bridge as I believe never Army paffed a River on before nor fince.

His Bridge was only loofe Plank laid upon large Treffels in the fame homely Manner as I have feen Bricklayers raife a low Scaffold to build a Brick Wall; the Treffels were made higher than one another to anfwer to the River as it become deeper or fhallower, and was all framed and fitted before any Appearance was made of attempting to pafs.

When all was ready the King brings his Army down to the Bank of the River, and plants his Cannon as the Enemy had done, fome here and fome there, to amufe them.

At Night *April* 4th, the King commanded about 2000 Men to march to the Point, and to throw up a Trench on either Side, and quite round it with a Battery of fix Pieces of Cannon, at each End befides three fmall Mounts, one at the Point and one of each Side, which had each of them two Pieces upon them. This Work was begun fo briskly, and fo well carried on, the King firing all the Night from the other Parts of the River, that by Day-light all the Batteries at the new Work were mounted, the Trench lined with 2000 Mufqueteers, and all the Utenfils of the Bridge lay ready to be put together.

Now the *Imperialifts* difcovered the Defign, but it was too late to hinder it, the Mufqueteers in the great Trench, and the five new Batteries, made fuch continual Fire that the other Bank, which, as before, lay 12 Foot below them, was too

H 4   hot

hot for the *Imperialifts*; whereupon *Tilly*, to be
provided for the King at his coming over, falls
to work in a Wood right againft the Point, and
raifes a great Battery for 20 Pieces of Cannon,
with a Breaft-Work, or Line, as near the River
as he could, to cover his Men, thinking that
when the King had built his Bridge he might
eafily beat it down with his Cannon.

But the King had doubly prevented him, firft
by laying his Bridge fo low that none of *Tilly's*
Shot could hurt it ; for the Bridge lay not above
half a Foot above the Water's edge, by which
Means the King, who in that fhewed himfelf an
excellent Engineer, had fecured it from any
Batteries to be made within the Land, and the
Angle of the Bank fecured it from the remoter Batteries, on the other Side, and the continual Fire
of the Cannon and fmall Shot beat the *Imperialifts*
from their ftation juft againft it, they having no
Works to cover them.

And in the fecond Place, to fecure his Paffage
he fent over about 200 Men, and after that 200
more, who had Orders to caft up a large Ravelin
on the other Bank, juft where he defigned to
land his Bridge; this was done with fuch Expedition too, that it was finifhed before Night,
and in a Condition to receive all the Shot of
Tilly's great Battery, and effectually covered his
Bridge. While this was doing the King on his
Side lays over his Bridge. Both Sides wrought
hard all Day and all Night, as if the Spade,
not the Sword, had been to decide the Contro-
verfy, and that he had got the Victory whofe
Trenches and Batteries were firft ready; in the
mean while the Cannon and Mufquet Bullets
flew like Hail, and made the Service fo hot,
that both Sides had enough to do to make their
Men

Men stand to their Work; the King in the
hottest of it, animated his Men by his Presence,
and *Tilly*, to give him his Due, did the same;
for the Execution was so great, and so many Officers killed, General *Attringer* wounded, and two
Sergeant Majors killed, that at last *Tilly* himself
was obliged to expose himself, and to come up
to the very Face of our Line to encourage his
Men, and give his necessary Orders.

And here about one a Clock, much about the
Time that the King's Bridge and Works were
finished, and just as they said he had ordered to
fall on upon our Ravelin with 3000 Foot, was
the Brave old *Tilly* slain with a Musquet Bullet
in the Thigh; he was carried off to *Ingolstat*,
and lived some Days after, but died of that
Wound the same Day as the King had his Horse
shot under him at the Siege of that Town.

We made no question of passing the River here,
having brought every Thing so forward, and
with such extraordinary Success, but we should
have found it a very hot Piece of Work if *Tilly*
had lived one Day more; and if I may give my
Opinion of it, having seen *Tilly's* Battery and
Breast-work, in the Face of which we must have
passed the River, I must say, that whenever we
had marched, if *Tilly* had fallen in with his Horse
and Foot, placed in that Trench, the whole
Army would have passed as much Danger *as in
the Face of a strong Town in the storming a Counterscarp.*
The King himself, when he saw with what
Judgment *Tilly* had prepared his Works, and
what Danger he must have run, would often say,
that Day's Success was every way. equal to the
Victory of *Leipsick*.

Tilly being hurt and carried off, as if the Soul
of the Army had been lost, they begun to draw
off;

off; the Duke of *Bavaria* took Horse and rid away as if he had fled out of Battle for his Life.

The other Generals, with a little more Caution, as well as Courage, drew off by Degrees, sending their Cannon and Baggage away first, and leaving some to continue firing on the Bank of the River to conceal their Retreat; the River preventing any Intelligence, we knew nothing of the Disaster befallen them; and the King, who looked for Blows, having finished his Bridge and Ravelin, ordered to run a Line with Palisadoes to take in more Ground on the Bank of the River, to cover the first Troops he should send over: This being finished the same Night, the King sends over a Party of his Guards to relieve the Men who were in the Ravelin, and commanded 600 Musqueteers to Man the new line out of the *Scots* Brigade.

Early in the Morning a small Party of *Scots*, commanded by one Captain *Forbes*, of my Lord *Reas* Regiment, were sent out to learn something of the Enemy, the King observing they had not fired all Night; and while this Party were abroad, the Army stood in Battalia; and my old Friend Sir *John Hepburn*, whom of all Men the King most depended upon for any desperate Service, was ordered to pass the Bridge with his Brigade, and to draw up without the Line, with Command to advance as he found the Horse who were to second him came over

Sir *John* being passed without the Trench, meets Captain *Forbes* with some Prisoners, and the good News of the Enemy's Retreat; he sends him directly to the King, who was by this Time at the Head of his Army, in full Battalia ready to follow his Vanguard, expecting a hot Day's
Work

Work of it. Sir *John* fends Meffenger after Meffenger to the King, intreating him to give him
Orders to advance; but the King would not fuffer him; for he was ever upon his Guard, and
would not venture a Surprize; fo the Army
continued on this Side the *Lech* all Day, and the
next Night. In the Morning the King fent for
me, and ordered me to draw out 300 Horfe, and
a Collonel with 600 Horfe, and a Collonel with
800 Dragoons, and ordered us to enter the Wood
by 3 Ways, but fo as to be able to relieve one
another; and then ordered Sir *John Hepburn* with
his Brigade to advance to the edge of the Wood
to fecure our Retreat; and at the fame Time commanded another Brigade of Foot to pafs the
Bridge, if need were, to fecond Sir *John Hepburn*,
fo warily did this prudent General proceed.

We advanced with our Horfe into the *Bavarian*
Camp, which we found forfaken; the plunder
of it was inconfiderable, for the exceeding Caution the King had ufed gave them Time to carry
off all their Baggage; we followed them three or
four Miles and returned to our Camp.

I confefs I was moft diverted that Day with
viewing the Works which *Tilly* had caft up, and
muft own again, that had he not been taken
off, we had met with as defperate a Piece of
Work as ever was attempted. The next Day the
reft of the Cavalry came up to us, commanded
by *Guftavus Horn*, and the King and the whole
Army followed; we advanced through the Heart
of *Bavaria*, took *Rain* at the firft Summons, and
feveral other fmall Towns, and fat down before
Ausburg.

Ausburg, though a Proteftant City, had a popifh *Bavarian* Garrifon in it of above 5000 Men,
commanded by a *Fugger* a great Family in *Bavaria*.

varia. The Governour had posted several little Parties as out Scouts at the Distance of two Miles and half, or three Miles from the Town. The King, at his coming up to this Town, sends me with my little Troop, and 3 Companies of Dragoons to beat in these out Scouts; the first Party I light on was not above 16 Men, who had made a small Barricado cross the Road, and stood resolutely upon their Guard; I commanded the Dragoons to alight, and open the Barricado, which while they resolutely performed, the 16 Men gave them 2 Volleys of their Musquets, and through the Enclosures made their Retreat to a Turn-pike about a quarter of a Mile farther. We past their first Traverse, and coming up to the Turn-pike, I found it defended by 200 Musqueteers: I prepared to attack them, sending word to the King how strong the Enemy was, and desired some Foot to be sent me. My Dragoons fell on, and tho' the Enemy made a very hot Fire, had beat them from this Post before 200 Foot, which the King had sent me, had come up; being joined with the Foot, I followed the Enemy, who retreated fighting, till they came under the Cannon of a strong Redoubt, where they drew up, and I could see another Body of Foot of about 300 join them out of the Works; upon which I halted, and considering I was in View of the Town, and a great way from the Army, I faced about and began to march off; as we marched I found the Enemy followed, but kept at a Distance, as if they only designed to observe me; I had not marched far, but I heard a Volly of small Shot, answered by 2 or 3 more, which I presently apprehended to be at the Turn-pike, where I had left a small Guard of 26 Men, with a Lieutenant. Immediately I detached 100 Dragoons

to

to relieve my Men, and secure my Retreat, following my self as fast as the Foot could march. The Lieutenant sent me back word the Post was taken by the Enemy, and my Men cut off; upon this I doubled my Pace, and when I came up I found it as the Lieutenant said; for the Post was taken and manned with 300 Musqueteers, and three Troops of Horse; by this Time also I found the Party in my Rear made up towards me, so that I was like to be charged in a narrow Place, both in Front and Rear.

I saw there was no Remedy but with all my Force to fall upon that Party before me, and so to break through before those from the Town could come up with me; wherefore commanding my Dragoons to alight, I ordered them to fall on upon the Foot; their Horse were drawn up in an enclosed Field on one Side of the Road, a great Ditch securing the other Side, so that they thought if I charged the Foot in Front they would fall upon my Flank, while those behind would charge my Rear; and indeed had the other come in Time, they had cut me off; my Dragoons made three fair Charges on their Foot, but were received with so much Resolution, and so brisk a Fire that they were beaten off, and sixteen Men killed: Seeing them so rudely handled, and the Horse ready to fall in, I relieved them with 100 Musqueteers and they renewed the Attack, at the same Time with my Troop of Horse, flanked on both Wings with 50 Musqueteers, I faced their Horse, but did not offer to charge them; the Case grew now desperate, and the Enemy behind were just at my Heels with near 600 Men; the Captain who commanded the Musqueteers who flanked my Horse came up to me, says he, if we do not force

this

this Pafs all will be loft; if you will draw out your Troop and 20 of my Foot, and fall in, I'll engage to keep off the Horfe with the reft. With all my Heart, fays I.

Immediately I wheel'd off my Troop, and a fmall Party of the Mufqueteers followed me, and fell in with the Dragoons and Foot, who feeing the Danger too, as well as I, fought like Mad Men; the Foot at the Turn-pike were not able to hinder our Breaking through, fo we made our way out, killing about 150 of them, and put the reft into Confufion.

But now was I in as great a Difficulty as before how to fetch off my brave Captain of Foot, for they charged home upon him; he defended himfelf with extraordinary Gallantry, having the Benefit of a Piece of a Hedge to cover him; but he loft half his Men, and was juft upon the Point of being defeated, when the King, informed by a Soldier that efcaped from the Turn-pike, one of 26, had fent a Party of 600 Dragoons to bring me off; thefe came upon the Spur, and joined with me juft as I had broke through the Turn-pike; the Enemy's Foot rallied behind their Horfe, and by this Time their other Party was come in, but feeing our Relief they drew off together.

I loft above 100 Men in thefe Skirmifhes, and kill'd them about 180; we fecured the Turn-pike, and placed a Company of Foot there with 100 Dragoons, and came back well beaten to the Army. The King, to prevent fuch uncertain Skirmifhes, advanced the next Day in View of the Town, and according to his Cuftom, fits down with his whole Army within Cannon-fhot of their Walls.

The

The King won this great City by Force of Words, for by two or three Meffages and Letters to and from the Citizens, the Town was gained, the Garrifon not daring to defend them againft their Wills. His Majefty made his publick Entrance into the City on the 14th of *April,* and receiving the Compliments of the Citizens, advanced immediately to *Ingolftat,* which is accounted, and really is the ftrongeft Town in all thefe Parts.

The Town had a very ftrong Garrifon in it, and the Duke of *Bavaria* lay entrenched with his Army under the Walls of it, on the other Side of the River. The King, who never loved long Sieges, having viewed the Town, and brought his Army within Mufquet-fhot of it, called a Council of War, where it was the King's Opinion, in fhort, that the Town would lofe him more than 'twas worth, and therefore he refolved to raife his Siege.

Here the King going to view the Town had his Horfe fhot with a Cannon-bullet from the Works, which tumbled the King and his Horfe over one another, that every Body thought he had been killed, but he received no Hurt at all; that very Minute, as near as could be learnt, General *Tilly* died in the Town of the Shot he received on the Bank of the *Lech* as aforefaid.

I was not in the Camp when the King was hurt, for the King had fent almoft all the Horfe and Dragoons, under *Guftavus Horn,* to face the Duke of *Bavaria's* Camp, and after that to plunder the Country, which truly was a Work the Soldiers were very glad of, for it was very feldom they had that Liberty given them, and they made very good ufe of it when it was; for the Country of *Bavaria* was rich and plentiful, having

having feen no Enemy before during the whole
War.

The Army having left the Siege of *Ingolftat,*
proceeds to take in the reft of *Bavaria*; Sir *John
Hepburn* with 3 Brigades of Foot, and *Guftavus
Horn* with 3000 Horfe and Dragoons, went to
the *Landfhut,* and took it the fame Day ; the
Garrifon was all Horfe, and gave us feveral Ca-
mifadoes at our Approach, in one of which I loft
two of my Troops, but when we had beat them
into clofe Quarters, they prefently capitulated.
The General got a great Sum of Money of the
Town befides a great many Prefents to the Officers : And from thence the King went on to
Munick, the Duke of *Bavaria*'s Court ; fome of
the General Officers would fain have had the
plundering of the Duke's Palace; but the King
was too generous, the City paid him 400000
Dollars; and the Duke's Magazine was there
feized, in which was 140 Pieces of Cannon, and
fmall Arms for above 20000 Men. The great
Chamber of the Duke's Rarities was preferved
by the Kings fpecial Order with a great deal of
Care. I expected to have ftaid here fome Time,
and to have taken a very exact Account of this
curious Labaratory ;.but being commanded away,
I had no Time, and the Fate of the War never
gave me Opportunity to fee it again.

The *Imperialifts* under the Command of Comif-
fary *Ofta* had befieged *Bibrach,* an Imperial
City not very well fortified, and the Inhabitants
being under the *Swede*'s Protection, defended
themfelves as well as they could, but were in
great Danger, and fent feveral Expreffes to the
King for Help.

The King immediately detaches a ftrong Body
of Horfe and Foot, to relieve *Bibrach,* and would
be

be the Commander himself; I marched among the Horfe, but the *Imperialifts* faved us the Labour; for the News of the King's coming frighted away *Ofta*, that he left *Bibrach*, and hardly looked behind him 'till he got up to the *Bodenfee*, on the Confines of *Swifferland*.

At our Return from this Expedition, the King had the firft News of *Wallestein*'s Approach, who on the Death of Count *Tilly*, being declared Generaliffimo of the Emperor's Forces, had plaid the Tyrant in *Bohemia*, and was now advancing with 60000 Men, as they reported, to relieve the Duke of *Bavaria*.

The King therefore, in order to be in a Pofture to receive this great General, refolves to quit *Bavaria*, and to expect him on the Frontiers of *Franconia*; and becaufe he knew the *Norembergers*, for their Kindnefs to him, would be the firft Sacrifice, he refolved to defend that City againft him whatever it coft.

Neverthelefs he did not leave *Bavaria* without a Defence; but on the one Hand he left Sir *John Bannier* with 10000 Men about *Ausburgh*, and the Duke of *Saxe-Weymar* with another like Army about *Ulme* and *Meningen*,with Orders fo to direct their March, as that they might join him upon any Occafion in a few Days.

We encamped about *Noremberg* the Middle of *June*. The Army, after fo many Detachments,was not above 19000 Men. The Imperial Army joined with the *Bavarian*, were not fo numerous as was reported, but were really 60000 Men. The King, not ftrong enough to fight yet, as he ufed to fay, was ftrong enough not to be forced to to fight, formed his Camp fo under the Cannon of *Noremberg*, that there was no befieging the

Town,

Town, but they muft befiege him too; and he fortified his Camp in fo formidable a Manner, that *Walleftein* never durft attack him. On the 30th of *June*, *Walleftein*'s Troops appeared, and on the 5th of *July*, encamped clofe by the King, and pofted themfelves not on the *Bavarian* Side, but between the King and his own Friends of *Schwaben*, and *Frankenland* in order to intercept his Provifions, and, as they thought, to ftarve him out of his Camp.

Here they lay to fee, as it were, who could fubfift longeft; the King was ftrong in Horfe, for we had full 8000 Horfe and Dragoons in the Army, and this gave us great Advantage in the feveral Skirmifhes we had with the Enemy. The Enemy had Poffeffion of the whole Country, and had taken effectual Care to furnifh their Army with Provifions; they placed their Guards in fuch excellent Order, to fecure their Convoys, that their Waggons went from Stage to Stage as quiet as in a time of Peace, and were relieved every five Miles by Parties conftantly pofted on the Road. And thus the Imperial General fat down by us, not doubting but he fhould force the King either to fight his Way through, on very difadvantageous Terms, or to rife for want of Provifions, and leave the City of *Noremberg* a Prey to his Army; for he had vowed the Deftruction of the City, and to make it a fecond *Magdeburg*.

But the King, who was not to be eafily deceived, had countermined all *Walleftein*'s Defigns; he had paffed his Honour to the *Norembergers*, that he would not leave them, and they had undertaken to Victual his Army, and fecure him from Want, which they did fo effectually, that

he

he had no Occasion to expose his Troops to any Hazard or Fatigues for Convoys or Forage on any Account whatever.

The City of *Noremberg* is a very rich and populous City; and the King being very sensible of their Danger, had given his Word for their Defence : And when they, being terrified at the Threats of the *Imperialists*, sent their Deputies to beseech the King to take care of them, he sent them Word, he would, and be besieged with them. They on the other Hand laid in such Stores of all Sorts of Provision, both for Men and Horse, that had *Wallestein* lain before it six Months longer, there would have been no Scarcity. Every private House was a Magazine, the Camp was plentifully supplied with all Manner of Provisions, and the Market always full, and as cheap as in Times of Peace. The Magistrates were so careful, and preserved so excellent an Order in the Disposal of all sorts of Provision, that no engrossing of Corn could be practised; for the Prices were every Day directed at the Town-house: And if any Man offered to demand more Money for Corn, than the stated Price, he could not sell, because at the Town Store-house you might buy cheaper. Here are two Instances of good and bad Conduct; the City of *Magdeburgh* had been intreated by the King to settle Funds, and raise Money for their Provision and Security, and to have a sufficient Garrison to defend them, but they made Difficulties, either to raise Men for themselves, or to admit the King's Troops to assist them, for fear of the Charge of maintaining them; and this was the Cause of the City's Ruin.

The City of *Noremberg* open'd their Arms to receive the Assistance proferred by the *Swedes*, and

their

their Purfes to defend their Town, and Common Caufe, and this was the faving them abfolutely from Deftruction. The rich Burghers and Magiftrates kept open Houfes, where the Officers of the Army were always welcome; and the Council of the City took fuch Care of the Poor, that there was no Complaining nor Diforders in the whole City. There is no doubt but it coft the City a great deal of Money; but I never faw a publick Charge borne with fo much Chearfulnefs, nor managed with fo much Prudence and Conduct in my Life. The City fed above 50000 Mouths every Day, including their own Poor, befides themfelves; and yet when the King had lain thus 3 Months, and finding his Armies longer in coming up than he expected, asked the Burgrave how their Magazines held out? He anfwered, they defired his Majefty not to haften things for them, for they could maintain themfelves and him 12 Months longer, if there was Occafion. This Plenty kept both the Army and City in good Health, as well as in good Heart; whereas nothing was to be had of us but Blows; for we fetched nothing from without our Works, nor had no Bufinefs without the Line, but to interrupt the Enemy.

The Manner of the King's Encampment deferves a particular Chapter. He was a compleat Surveyor, and a Mafter in Fortification, not to be outdone by any Body. He had pofted his Army in the Suburbs of the Town, and drawn Lines round the whole Circumference, fo that he begirt the whole City with his Army; his Works were large, the Ditch deep, flanked with innumerable Baftions, Ravelins, Horn-works, Forts, Redoubts, Batteries and Pallifadoes, the inceffant Work of 8000 Men for about 14 Days; befides
that

that the King was adding some thing or other to it every Day; and the very Posture of his Camp was enough to tell a bigger Army than *Wallestein's*, that he was not to be assaulted in his Trenches.

The King's Design appeared chiefly to be the Preservation of the City; but that was not all: He had three Armies acting abroad in three several Places; *Gustavus Horn* was on the *Mosel*, the Chancellor *Oxenstern* about *Mentz*, *Colcgn*, and the *Rhine*, Duke *William* and Duke *Bernard*, together with General *Bannier* in *Bavaria*.: And though he designed they should all join him, and had wrote to them all to that purpose, yet he did not hasten them, knowing that while he kept the main Army at Bay about *Noremberg*, they would without Opposition reduce those several Countries they were acting in to his Power. This occasioned his lying longer in the Camp at *Noremberg* than he would have done, and this occasioned his giving the *Imperialists* so many Alarms by his strong Parties of Horse, of which he was well provided, that they might not be able to make any considerable Detachments for the Relief of their Friends: And here he shewed his Mastership in the War; for by this means his Conquests went on as effectually as if he had been abroad himself.

In the mean Time, it was not to be expected two such Armies should lye long so near without some Action; the Imperial Army being Masters of the Field, laid the Country for 20 Miles round *Noremberg* in a manner desolate; what the Inhabitants could carry away had been before secured in such strong Towns as had Garrisons to protect them, and what was left, the hungry *Crabats* devoured, or set on Fire; but sometimes they were

I 3   met

met with by our Men, who often paid them home
for it. There had passed several small Rencoun-
ters between our Parties and theirs; and as it
falls out in such Cases, sometimes one Side, sometimes the other, got the better; but I have
observed there never was any Party sent out by
the King's special Appointment, but always came
home with Victory.

The first considerable Attempt, as I remember,
was made on a Convoy of Ammunition: The Party
sent out was commanded by a *Saxon* Collonel, and
consisted of a 1000 Horse, and 500 Dragoons,
who burnt above 600 Waggons, loaden with
Ammunition and Stores for the Army, besides ta-
ing about 2000 Musquets which they brought
back to the Army.

The latter end of *July* the King received Advice, that the *Imperialists* had formed a Magazine
for Provision at a Town called *Freynstat*, 20 Miles
from *Noremberg*. Hither all the Booty and Contributions raised in the *Upper Palatinate*, and
Parts adjacent, was brought and laid up as in a
Place of Security; a Garrison of 600 Men being
placed to defend it; and when a Quantity of Provisions was got together, Convoys were appointed
to fetch it off.

The King was resolved, if possible, to take or de-
stroy this Magazine; and sending for Collonel
Dubalt, a *Swede,* and a Man of extraordinary Conduct, he tells him his Design, and withal, that
he must be the Man to put it in Execution, and
ordered him to take what Forces he thought convenient. The Collonel, who knew the Town
very well, and the Country about it, told his
Majesty, he would attempt it with all his Heart;
but he was affraid 'twould require some Foot to
make the Attack; but we can't stay for that, says
the

the King, you muſt then take ſome Dragoons with you, and immediately the King called for me. I was juſt coming up the Stairs, as the King's Page was come out to enquire for me; ſo I went immediately in to the King. Here is a Piece of hot Work for you, ſays the King, *Dubalt* will tell it you; go together and contrive it.

We immediately withdrew, and the Collonel told me the Deſign, and what the King and he had diſcourſed; that in his Opinion Foot would be wanted: But the King had declared there was no Time for the Foot to march, and had propoſed Dragoons. I told him, I thought Dragoons might do as well; ſo we agreed to take 1600 Horſe and 400 Dragoons. The King, impatient in his Deſign, came into the Room to us to know what we had reſolved on, approved our Meaſures, gave us Orders immediately; and turning to me, you ſhall command the Dragoons, ſays the King, but *Dubalt* muſt be General in this Caſe, for he knows the Country. Your Majeſty, ſaid I, ſhall be always ſerved by me in any Figure you pleaſe. The King wiſhed us good Speed, and hurried us away the ſame Afternoon, in order to come to the Place in Time. We marched ſlowly on becauſe of the Carriages we had with us, and came to *Freynſtat* about One a Clock in the Night perfectly undiſcover'd; the Guards were ſo negligent, that we came to the very Port before they had Notice of us, and a Serjeant with 12 Dragoons thruſt in upon the Out-Centinels, and killed them without Noiſe.

Immediately Ladders were placed to the Half-Moon which defended the Gate, which the Dragoons mounted and carried in a trice, about 28 Men being cut in Pieces within. As ſoon as the

I 4   Ravelin

Ravelin was taken, they burſt open the Gate, at which I entered at the Head of 200 Dragoons, and ſeized the Drawbridge. By this Time the Town was in Alarm, and the Drums beat to Arms, but it was too late; for by the help of a Petard we broke open the Gate, and entered the Town. The Garriſon made an obſtinate Fight for about half an Hour, but our Men being all in, and 3 Troops of Horſe diſmounted coming to our Aſſiſtance with their Carabines, the Town was entirely maſtered by Three of the Clock, and Guards ſet to prevent any Body running to give Notice to the Enemy. There were about 200 of the Garriſon killed, and the reſt taken Priſoners. The Town being thus ſecured, the Gates were opened, and Collonel *Dubalt* came in with the Horſe.

The Guards being ſet, we entered the Magazine where we found an incredible Quantity of all ſorts of Proviſion. There was 150 Tun of Bread, 8000 Sacks of Meal, 4000 Sacks of Oats, and of other Proviſions in Proportion. We cauſed as much of it as could be loaded to be brought away in ſuch Waggons and Carriages as we found, and ſet the reſt on Fire, Town and all; we ſtaid by it till we ſaw it paſt a Poſſibility of being ſaved, and then drew off with 800 Waggons, which we found in the Place, moſt of which we loaded with Bread, Meal and Oats. While we were doing this we ſent a Party of Dragoons into the Fields, who met us again as we came out, with above a 1000 Head of Black Cattle, beſides Sheep.

Our next Care was to bring this Booty home without meeting with the Enemy; to ſecure which, the Collonel immediately diſpatch'd an Expreſs to the

the King, to let him know of our Succefs, and to defire a Detachment might be made to fecure our Retreat, being charged with fo much Plunder.

And it was no more than Need; for tho' we had ufed all the Diligence poffible to prevent any Notice, yet fome body more forward than ordinary, had fcap'd away and carried News of it to the *Imperial* Army. The General upon this bad News detaches Major General *Sparr*, with a Body of 6000 Men to cut off our Retreat. The King, who had Notice of this Detachment, marches out in Perfon with 3000 Men to wait upon General *Sparr* : All this was the Account of one Day; the King met General *Sparr* at the Moment when his Troops were divided, fell upon them, routed one Part of them, and the reft in a few Hours after; killed them a 1000 Men, and took the General Prifoner.

In the Interval of this Action, we came fafe to the Camp with our Booty, which was very confiderable, and would have fupplied our whole Army for a Month. Thus we feafted at the Enemy's Coft, and beat them into the Bargain.

The King gave all the live Cattle to the *Norembergers*, who, tho' they had really no want of Provifions, yet frefh Meat was not fo plentiful as fuch Provifions which were ftored up in Veffels and laid by.

After this Skirmifh, we had the Country more at Command than before, and daily fetch'd in frefh Provifions and Forage in the Fields.

The two Armies had now lain a long Time in fight of one another, and daily Skirmifhes had confiderably weakened them; and the King beginning to be impatient, haftened the Advancement of his Friends to join him, in which alfo they were not backward; but having drawn together

gether their Forces from feveral Parts, and all joined the Chancellor *Oxenftern,* News came the 15th of *Auguft,* that they were in full March to join us; and being come to a fmall Town called *Brock,* the King went out of the Camp with about 1000 Horfe to view them. I went along with the Horfe, and the 21ft of *Auguft* faw the Review of all the Armies together, which were 30000 Men in extraordinary Equipage, old Soldiers, and commanded by Officers of the greateft Conduct and Experience in the World. There was the rich Chancellor of *Sweden* who commanded as General, *Guftavus Horn* and *John Bannier,* both *Swedes* and old Generals; Duke *William* and Duke *Bernard* of *Weymar,* the Landgrave of *Heffe Caffel,* the Palatine of *Birkenfelt,* and Abundance of Princes and Lords of the Empire.

The Armies being joined, the King who was now a Match for *Walleftein,* quits his Camp and draws up in Battalia before the *Imperial* Trenches; but the Scene was changed; *Walleftein* was no more able to fight now than the King was before; but keeping within his Trenches, ftood upon his Guard. The King coming up clofe to his Works, plants Batteries, and cannonaded him in his very Camp.

The *Imperialifts* finding the King prefs upon them, retreat into a woody Country about three Leagues, and taking Poffeffion of an old ruin'd Caftle, pofted their Army behind it.

This old Caftle they fortified, and placed a very ftrong Guard there. The King having viewed the Place, tho' it was a very ftrong Poft, refolved to attack it with the whole right Wing. The Attack was made with a great deal of Order and Refolution, the King leading the firft Party on with Sword in Hand, and the Fight was maintained

on

on both Sides with the utmost Gallantry and Obstinacy all the Day and the next Night too; for the Cannon and Musquet never gave over 'till the Morning; but the *Imperialists* having the Advantage of the Hill, of their Works and Batteries, and being continually relieved, and the *Swedes* naked, without Cannon or Works, the Post was maintained; and the King finding it would cost him too much Blood, drew off in the Morning.

This was the famous Fight at *Attembergh*, where the *Imperialists* boasted to have shewn the World the King of *Sweden* was not invincible. They call it the Victory at *Attembergh*; 'tis true, the King failed in his Attempt of carrying their Works, but there was so little of a Victory in it, that the *Imperial* General thought fit not to venture a second Brush, but to draw off their Army as soon as they could to a safer Quarter.

I had no Share in this Attack, very few of the Horse being in the Action; but my Comerade, who was always among the *Scots* Voluntiers was wounded and taken Prisoner by the Enemy. They used him very civilly, and the King and *Wallestein* straining Courtesies with one another, the King released Major General *Sparr* without Ransom, and the *Imperial* General sent home Collonel *Tortenson* a *Swede*, and 16 Voluntier Gentlemen who were taken in the Heat of the Action, among whom my Captain was one.

The King lay 14 Days facing the *Imperial* Army, and using all the Stratagems possible to bring them to a Battle, but to no purpose; during which Time, we had Parties continually out, and very often Skirmishes with the Enemy.

I had a Command of one of these Parties in an Adventure, wherein I got no Booty, nor much Honour. The King had received Advice of a Con-

voy

voy of Provifions which was to come to the Enemy's Camp from the *Upper Palatinate*, and having a great Mind to furprize them, he commanded us to way-lay them with 1200 Horfe, and 800
Dragoons. I had exact Directions given me of the
Way they were to come, and pofting my Horfe
in a Village a little out of the Road, I lay with my
Dragoons in a Wood, by which they were to pafs
by break of Day. The Enemy appeared with
their Convoy, and being very wary, their Out-
Scouts difcovered us in the Wood, and fired upon
the Centinel I had pofted in a Tree at the Entrance of the Wood. Finding my felf difcovered,
I would have retreated to the Village where my
Horfe were pofted, but in a Moment the Wood
was skirted with the Enemy's Horfe, and a Thoufand commanded Mufqueteers advanced to beat
me out. In this Pickle I fent away three Meffengers one after another for the Horfe, who were
within two Miles of me, to advance to my Relief;
but all my Meffengers fell into the Enemy's Hands.
400 of my Dragoons on foot, whom I had plac'd at a
little Diftance before me, ftood to their Work, and
beat off two Charges of the Enemy's Foot with fome
Lofs on both Sides : Mean Time 200 of my Men
fac'd about, and rufhing out of the Wood, broke
through a Party of the Enemy's Horfe who ftood
to watch our coming out. I confefs I was exceedingly furprized at it, thinking thofe Fellows
had done it to make their Efcape, or elfe were
gone over to the Enemy; and my Men were fo
difcouraged at it, that they began to look about
which way to run to fave themfelves, and were
juft upon the Point of disbanding to fhift for
themfelves, when one of the Captains called to
me aloud to beat a Parle and Treat. I made no Anfwer, but, as if I had not heard him, immediately
gave

gave the Word for all the Captains to come together. The Confultation was but fhort, for the
Mufqueteers were advancing to a third Charge,
with Numbers which we were not likely to deal
with. In fhort, we refolved to beat a Parle, and
demand Quarter, for that was all we could expect; when on a fudden the Body of Horfe I had
pofted in the Village being directed by the Noife,
had advanced to relieve me, if they faw Occafion,
and had met the 200 Dragoons who guided them
directly to the Spot where they had broke thro',
and all together fell upon the Horfe of the Enemy who were pofted on that Side, and maftering
them before they could be relieved, cut them all
to Pieces and brought me off. Under the Shelter
of this Party, we made good our Retreat to the
Village, but we loft above 300 Men, and were
glad to make off from the Village too, for the
Enemy were very much too ftrong for us.

Returning thence towards the Camp, we fell
foul with 200 *Crabats* who had been upon the
plundering Account : We made our felves fome
Amends upon them for our former Lofs, for we
fhew'd them no Mercy ; but our Misfortunes were
not ended, for we had but juft difpatch'd thofe
Crabats when we fell in with 3000 *Imperial* Horfe,
who, on the Expectation of the aforefaid Convoy,
were fent out to fecure them.

All I could do, could not perfuade my Men
to ftand their Ground againft this Party ; fo that
finding they would run away in Confufion, I a-
greed to make off, and facing to the Right, we
went over a large Common a full Trot, 'till at laft
Fear, which always encreafes in a Flight, brought
us to a plain Flight, the Enemy at our Heels;
I muft confefs I was never fo mortified in my
Life ; 'twas to no Purpofe to turn Head, no Man
would

would ftand by us, we run for Life, and a great many we left by the Way who were either wounded by the Enemy's Shot, or elfe could not keep Race with us.

At laft having got over the Common, which was near two Miles, we came to a Lane; one of our Captains, a *Saxon* by Country, and a Gentleman of a good Fortune alighted at the Entrance of the Lane, and with a bold Heart faced about, fhot his own Horfe, and called his Men to ftand by him and defend the Lane. Some of his Men halted, and we rallied about 600 Men which we pofted as well as we could, to defend the Pafs; but the Enemy charged us with great Fury. The *Saxon* Gentleman, after defending himfelf with exceeding Gallantry and refufing Quarter, was killed upon the Spot: A *German* Dragoon as I thought him, gave me a rude Blow with the Stock of his Piece on the Side of my Head, and was juft going to repeat it, when one of my Men fhot him dead. I was fo ftunn'd with the Blow, that I knew nothing; but recovering, I found my felf in the Hands of two of the Enemy's Officers, who offered me Quarter, which I accepted; and indeed, to give them their due, they ufed me very civilly. Thus this whole Party was defeated, and not above 500 Men got fafe to the Army, nor had half the Number efcaped, had not the *Saxon* Captain made fo bold a Stand at the Head of the Lane.

Several other Parties of the King's Army revenged our Quarrel, and paid them home for it; but I had a particular Lofs in this Defeat, that I never faw the King after; for tho' his Majefty fent a Trumpet to reclaim us as Prifoners the very next Day, yet I was not delivered, fome Scruple happening about exchanging, 'till after the

Battle

Battle of *Lutzen*, where that Gallant Prince loft his Life.

The Imperial Army rife from their Camp about eight or ten Days after the King had removed, and I was carried Prifoner in the Army 'till they fat down to the Siege of *Coburgh Caftle*, and then was left with other Prifoners of War, in the Cuftody of Collonel *Spezuter*, in a fmall Caftle near the Camp called *Newftad*. Here we continued indifferent well treated, but could learn nothing of what Action the Armies were upon, 'till the Duke of *Friedland* having been beaten off from the Caftle of *Coburgh*, marched into *Saxony*, and the Prifoners were fent for into the Camp, as was faid, in order to be exchanged.

I came into the Imperial Leager at the Siege of *Leipfick*, and within three Days after my coming, the City was furrendred, and I got Liberty to lodge at my old Quarters in the Town upon my Parole.

The King of *Sweden* was at the Heels of the *Imperialifts*; for finding *Walleftein* refolved to ruin the Elector of *Saxony*, the King had recollected as much of his divided Army as he could, and came upon him juft as he was going to befiege *Torgau*.

As it it is not my Defign to write a Hiftory of any more of thefe Wars than I was actually concerned in, fo I fhall only note, that upon the King's Approach, *Walleftein* halted, and likewife called all his Troops together; for he apprehended the King would fall on him; and we that were Prifoners, fancied the *Imperial* Soldiers went unwillingly out; for the very Name of the King of *Sweden* was become terrible to them. In fhort, they drew all the Soldiers of the Garrifon they could fpare, out of *Leipfick*, fent for *Papenheim* again, who was gone but three Days before,

fore with 6000 Men on a private Expedition. On the 16th of *November*, the Armies met on the Plains of *Lutzen*; a long and bloody Battle was fought; the *Imperialists* were entirely routed and beaten, 12000 slain upon the Spot, their Cannon, Baggage and 2000 Prisoners taken, but the King of *Sweden* lost his Life, being killed at the Head of his Troops in the Begining of the Fight.

It is impossible to describe the Consternation the Death of this conquering King struck into all the Princes of *Germany*; the Grief for him exceeded all Manner of human Sorrow: All People looked upon themselves as ruined and swallowed up; the Inhabitants of two Thirds of all *Germany* put themselves into Mourning for him; when the Ministers mentioned him in their Sermons or Prayers, whole Congregations would burst out into Tears: The Elector of *Saxony* was utterly inconsolable, and would for several Days walk about his Palace like a distracted Man, crying the Saviour of *Germany* was lost, the Refuge of abused Princes was gone; the Soul of the War was dead, and from that Hour was so hopeless of out-living the War, that he sought to make Peace with the Emperor.

Three Days after this mournful Victory, the *Saxons* recovered the Town of *Leipsick* by Stratagem. The Duke of *Saxony*'s Forces lay at *Torgau*, and perceiving the Confusion the *Imperialists* were in at the News of the Overthrow of their Army, they resolved to attempt the Recovery of the Town. They sent about 20 scattering Troopers who pretending themselves to be *Imperialists* fled from the Battle, were let in one by one, and still as they came in, they staid at the Court of Guard in the Port, entertaining the Souldiers with Discourse about the Fight, and how they escaped, and

the

the like; 'till the whole Number being got in at
a Watch Word, they fell on the Guard, and cut
them all in Pieces; and immediately opening the
Gate to three Troops of *Saxon* Horse, the Town
was taken in a Moment.

It was a welcome Surprise to me, for I was
at Liberty of Course; and the War being now
on another Foot, as I thought, and the King dead,
I resolved to quit the Service.

I had sent my Man, as I have already noted into *England*, in Order to bring over the Troops
my Father had raised for the King of *Sweden*.
He executed his Commission so well, that he
landed with five Troops at *Embden*, in very good
Condition; and Orders were sent them by the
King, to join the Duke of *Lunenberg's* Army;
which they did at the Siege of *Boxtude*, in the
Lower *Saxony*. Here by long and very sharp Service they were most of them cut off, and though
they were several Times recruited, yet I under-
stood there were not three full Troops left.

The Duke of *Saxe-Weymar*, a Gentleman of
great Courage, had the Command of the Army
after the King's Death, and managed it with so
much Prudence, that all things were in as much
Order as could be expected, after so great a Loss;
for the *Imperialists* where every where beaten, and
Wallestein never made any Advantage of the King's
Death.

I waited on him at *Hailbron*, whither he was
gone to meet the great Chancellor of *Sweden*,
where I paid him my Respects, and desired he
would bestow the Remainder of my Regiment
on my Comerade the Captain, which he did with
all the Civility and Readiness imaginable: So I took
my Leave of him, and prepared to come for
England.

K   I shall

I shall only note this, that at this Dyet, the Protestant Princes of the Empire renewed their League with one another, and with the Crown of *Sweden,* and came to several Regulations and Conclusions for the carrying on the War, which they afterwards prosecuted under the Direction of the said Chancellor of *Sweden.* 'But it was not the Work of a small Difficulty, nor of a short Time; and having been perswaded to continue almost two Years afterwards at *Frankfort, Hailbron,* and thereabout, by the particular Friendship of that noble wise Man, and extraordinary Statesman *Axell Oxenstern,* Chancellor of *Sweden,* I had Opportunity to be concerned in, and present at several Treaties of extraordinary Consequence, sufficient for a History, if that were my Design.

Particularly I had the Happiness to be present at, and have some Concern in the Treaty for the restoring the Posterity of the truly noble *Palsgrave* King of *Bohemia.* King *James* of *England* had indeed too much neglected the whole Family; and I may say with Authority enough, from my own Knowledge of Affairs, had nothing been done for them but what was from *England,* that Family had remained desolate and forsaken to this Day.

But that glorious King, whom I can never mention without some Remark of his extraordinary Merit, had left particular Instructions with his Chancellor to rescue the *Palatinate* to its rightful Lord, as a Proof of his Design to restore the the Liberty of *Germany,* and reinstate the oppressed Princes who were subjected to the Tyranny of the House of *Austria.*

Pursuant to this Resolution, the Chancellor proceeded very much like a Man of Honour; and tho' the King of *Bohemia* was dead a little
before,

before, yet he carefully managed the Treaty, anſwered the Objections of ſeveral Princes, who, in the general Ruin of the Family, had reaped private Advantages, ſettled the Capitulations for the Quota of Contributions, very much for their Advantage, and fully reinſtalled the Prince *Charles* in the Poſſeſſion of all his Dominions in the *Lower Palatinate*, which afterwards was confirmed to him and his Poſterity by the Peace of *Weſt-Phalia*, where all theſe bloody Wars were finiſhed in a Peace, which has ſince been the Foundation of the *Proteſtants* Liberty, and the beſt Security of the whole Empire.

I ſpent two Years rather in wandring up and down, than travelling; for tho' I had no Mind to ſerve, yet I could not find in my Heart to leave *Germany*; and I had obtained ſome ſo very cloſe Intimacies with the General Officers, that I was often in the Army, and ſometimes they did me the Honour to bring me into their Councils of War.

Particularly, at that eminent Council before the Battle of *Nordlingen*, I was invited to the Council of War, both by Duke *Bernard* of *Weymar*, and by *Guſtavus Horne*. They were Generals of equal Worth, and their Courage and Experience had been ſo well, and ſo often tried, that more than ordinary Regard was always given to what they ſaid. Duke *Bernard* was indeed the younger Man, and *Guſtvaus* had ſerved longer under our Great Schoolmaſter the King; but 'twas hard to judge which was the better General, ſince both had Experience enough, and ſhewn undeniable Proofs both of their Bravery and Conduct.

I am obliged, in the Courſe of my Relation, ſo often to mention the great Reſpect I often received

ceived from thefe great Men, that it makes me fometimes jealous, leaft the Reader may think I affect it as a Vanity. The Truth is, and I am ready to confefs the Honours I received, upon all Occafions, from Perfons of fuch Worth, and who had fuch an eminent Share in the greateft Action of that Age, very much pleafed me; and particularly, as they gave me Occafions to fee every thing that was doing on the whole Stage of the War: For being under no Command, but at Liberty to rove about, I could come to no *Swedifh* Garrifon or Party, but fending my Name to the commanding Officer I could have *the Word* fent me; and if I came into the Army, I was often treated as I was now at this famous Battle of *Nordlingen.*

But I cannot but fay, that I always looked upon this particular Refpect to be the Effect of more than ordinary Regard the great King of *Sweden* always fhewed me, rather than any Merit of my own; and the Veneration they all had for his Memory, made them continue to fhew me all the Marks of a fuitable Efteem.

But to return to the Council of War, the great, and indeed the only Queftion before us was, fhall we give Battle to the *Imperialifts,* or not? *Guftavus Horn* was againft it, and gave, as I thought, the moft invincible Arguments againft a Battle that Reafon could imagine.

Firft, They were weaker than the Enemy by above 5000 Men.

Secondly, The Cardinal Infant of *Spain,* who was in the *Imperial* Army with 8000 Men, was but there *en Paffant,* being going from *Italy* to *Flanders,* to take upon him the Government of the *Low Countries*; and if he faw no Profpect of immediate Action, would be gone in a few Days.

Thirdly,

Thirdly, They had two Reinforcements, one of 5000 Men, under the Command of Collonel *Cratz*, and one of 7000 Men under the Rhinegrave, who were juft at Hand, the laft within three Days March of them: And

Laftly, They had already faved their Honour, in that they had put 600 Foot into the Town of *Nordlingen*, in the Face of the Enemy's Army, and confequently the Town might hold out fome Days the longer.

Fate rather than Reafon certainly blinded the reft of the Generals againft fuch Arguments as thefe. Duke *Barnard* and almoft all the Generals were for Fighting, alledging, the Affront it would be to the *Swedifh* Reputation, to fee their Friends in the Town loft before their Faces.

Guftavus Horn ftood ftiff to his cautious Advice, and was againft it; and I thought the Baron *D'Offkirk* treated him a little indecently; for being very warm in the Matter, he told them; *That if* Guftavus Adolphus *had been governed by fuch cowardly Council, he had never been Conqueror of half* Germany *in two Years.* No, replied old General *Horn*, very fmartly, *But he had been now alive to have teftified for me, that I was never taken by him for a Coward; and yet* fays he, *the King was never for a Victory with a Hazard, when he could have it without.*

I was asked my Opinion, which I would have declined, being in no Commiffion; but they preffed me to fpeak. I told them, I was for ftaying at leaft till the Rhinegrave came up; who at leaft might, if Expreffes were fent to haften him, be up with us in 24 Hours. But *Offkirk* could not hold his Paffion, and had not he been over-rul'd, he would have almoft quarrelled with Marfhal *Horn*. Upon which the old General, not

to

to foment him, with a great deal of Mildnefs ftood up, and fpoke thus.

Come, Offkirk, fays he, *I'll fubmit my Opinion to you and the Majority of our Fellow-Soldiers: We will fight, but upon my Word we fhall have our Hands full.*

The Refolution thus taken, they attacked the *Imperial* Army. I muft confefs the Councils of this Day feemed as confufed as the Refolutions of the Night.

Duke *Bernard* was to lead the Van of the Left Wing, and to poft himfelf upon a Hill which was on the Enemy's Right without their Entrenchments; fo that having fecured that Poft, they might level their Cannon upon the Foot who ftood behind the Lines, and relieved the Town at Pleafure. He marched accordingly by Break of Day, and falling with great Fury upon 8 Regiments of Foot which were pofted at the Foot of the Hill, he prefently routed them and made himfelf Mafter of the Poft. Flufhed with this Succefs, he never regards his own concerted Meafures of ftopping there, and poffeffing what he had got, but pufhes on and falls in with the Main Body of the Enemy's Army.

While this was doing, *Guftavus Horn* attacks another Poft on a Hill, were the *Spaniards* had pofted and lodged themfelves behind fome Works they had caft up on the fide of the Hill; here they defended themfelves with extreme Obftinacy for five Hours, and at laft obliged the *Swedes* to give it over with Lofs. This extraordinary Gallantry of the *Spaniards* was the faving of the *Imperial* Army; for Duke *Barnard* having all this while refifted the frequent Charges of the *Imperialifts,* and borne the Weight of two

Thirds

Thirds of their Army, was not able to ſtand any
longer, but ſending one Meſſenger in the Neck
of another to *Guſtavus Horn* for more Foot, he
finding he could not carry his Point, had givẽn
it over, and was in full March to ſecond the
Duke. But now 'twas too late; for the King of
Hungary ſeeing the Duke's Men as it were wave-
ring, and having Notice of *Horn*'s wheeling about
to ſecond him, falls in with all his Force upon
his Flank, and with his *Hungarian* Huſſars, made
ſuch a furious Charge, that the *Swedes* could
ſtand no longer.

The Rout of the Left Wing was ſo much the
more unhappy, as it happened juſt upon *Guſtavus
Horn*'s coming up; for being puſhed on with the
Enemies at their Heels, they were driven upon
their own Friends, who having no Ground, to
open, and give them way, were trodden down
by their own run-away Brethren. This brought
all into the utmoſt Confuſion. The *Imperialiſts*
cried *Victoria*, and fell into the Middle of the Infantry with a terrible Slaughter.

I have always obſerved, 'tis fatal to upbraid
an old experienced Officer with want of Courage. If *Guſtavus Horn* had not been whetted with
the Reproaches of the Baron *D'Offkirk*, and ſome
of the other General Officers, I believe it had
ſaved the Lives of a 1000 Men; for when all was
thus loſt, ſeveral Officers adviſed him to make
a Retreat with ſuch Regiments as he had yet unbroken; but nothing could perſwade him to
ſtir a Foot: But turning his Flank into a Front,
he ſaluted the Enemy as they paſs'd by him in
Purſuit of the reſt, with ſuch terrible Volleys of
ſmall Shot, as coſt them the Lives of Abundance of
their Men.

The

The *Imperialifts*, eager in the Purfuit, left him
unbroken, till the *Spanifh* Brigade came up and
charged him: Thefe he bravely repulfed with
a great Slaughter, and after them a Body of
Dragoons; till being laid at on every Side, and
moft of his Men killed, the brave old General,
with all the reft who were left, were made Prifoners.

The *Swedes* had a terrible Lofs here; for almoft
all their Infantry were killed or taken Prifoners.
Guftavus Horn refufed Quarter feveral times; and
ftill thofe that attacked him were cut down by
his Men, who fought like Furies, and by the
Example of their General, behaved themfelves
like Lions. But at laft, thefe poor Remains
of a Body of the braveft Men in the World were
forced to fubmit. I have heard him fay, he had
much rather have died than been taken, but
that he yeilded in Compaffion to fo many brave
Men as were about him; for none of them would
take Quarter till he gave his Confent.

I had the worft Share in this Battle that ever
I had in any Action of my Life; and that was
to be pofted among as brave a Body of Horfe as
any in *Germany*, and yet not be able to fuccour
our own Men; but our Foot were cut in Pieces
(as it were) before our Faces; and the Situation
of the Ground was fuch as we could not fall in.
All that we were able to do, was to carry off about
2000 of the Foot, who running away in the Rout
of the Left Wing, rallied among our Squadrons,
and got away with us. Thus we ftood till we faw
all was loft, and then made the beft Retreat we
could to fave our felves, feveral Regiments having never charged, nor fired a Shot; for the
Foot had fo embaraffed themfelves among the
Lines and Works of the Enemy, and in the Vine-
yards

yards and Mountains, that the Horfe were rendered abfolutely unferviceable.

The Rhinegrave had made fuch Expedition to join us, that he reached within three Miles of the Place of Action that Night, and he was a great Safeguard for us in rallying our difperfed Men, who elfe had fallen into the Enemy's Hands, and in checking the Purfuit of the Enemy.

And indeed, had but any confiderable Body of the Foot made an orderly Retreat, it had been very probable they had given the Enemy a Brufh that would have turned the Scale of Victory; for our Horfe being whole, and in a manner untouched, the Enemy found fuch a Check in the Purfuit, that 1600 of their forwardeft Men following too eagerly, fell in with the Rhinegrave's advanced Troops the next Day, and were cut in Pieces without Mercy.

This gave us fome Satisfaction for the Lofs, but it was but fmall compared to the Ruin of that Day. We loft near 8000 Men upon the Spot, and above 3000 Prifoners, all our Cannon and Baggage, and 120 Colours. I thought I never made fo indifferent a Figure in my Life, and fo we thought all; to come away, lofe our Infantry, our General, and our Honour, and never fight for it. Duke *Barnard* was utterly difconfolate for old *Guftavus Horn*; for he concluded him killed; he tore the Hair from his Head like a mad Man, and telling the Rhinegrave the Story of the Council of War, would reproach himfelf with not taking his Advice, often repeating it in his Paffion, *'Tis I,* faid he, *have been the Death of the braveft General* in Germany; would call himfelf Fool and Boy, and fuch Names, for not liftening to the Reafons of an old experienced Soldier. But

when

when he heard he was alive in the Enemy's Hands, he was the easier, and applied himself to the recruting his Troops, and the like Business of the War ; and it was not long before he paid the *Imperialists* with Interest.

I returned to *Frankfort au Main* after this Action, which happened the 17th of *August* 1634; but the Progress of the *Imperialists* was so great, that there was no staying at *Frankfort*. The Chancellor *Oxenstern* removed to *Magdeburg*, Duke *Barnard* and the Landgrave marched into *Alsatia*, and the *Imperialists* carried all before them, for all the rest of the Campaign: They took *Philipsburgh* by Surprize; they took *Ausburgh* by Famine, *Spire* and *Treves* by Sieges, taking the Elector Prisoner. But this Success did one Piece of Service to the *Swedes*, that it brought the *French* into the War on their Side ; for the Elector of *Treves* was their Confederate. The *French* gave the Conduct of the War to Duke *Barnard*. This, though the Duke of *Saxony* fell off, and fought against them, turned the Scale so much in their Favour, that they recovered their Losses, and proved a Terror to all *Germany*. The farther Accounts of the War I refer to the Histories of those Times, which I have since read with a great deal of Delight.

I confess, when I saw the Progress of the *Imperial* Army after the Battle of ·*Nordlingen*, and the Duke of *Saxony* turning his Arms against them, I thought their Affairs declining; and giving them over for lost, I left *Frankfort*, and came down the Rhine to *Cologn*, and from thence into *Holland*.

I came to the *Hague* the 8th of *March* 1635, having spent three Years and a half in *Germany* and the greatest Part of it in the *Swedish* Army.

I spent

I spent some Time in *Holland* viewing the wonderful Power of Art which I observed in the Fortifications of their Towns, where the very Bastions stand on bottomless Morasses, and yet are as firm as any in the World. There I had the Opportunity to see the *Dutch* Army, and their famous General Prince *Maurice*. 'Tis true, the Men behaved themselves well enough in Action, when they were put to it, but the Prince's way of beating his Enemies without Fighting, was so unlike the Gallantry of my Royal Instructer, that it had no manner of Relish with me. Our way in *Germany* was always to seek out the Enemy and fight him; and, give the *Imperialists* their due, they were seldom hard to be found, but were as free of their Flesh as we were.

Whereas Prince *Maurice* would lye in a Camp till he starved half his Men, if by lying there he could but starve two Thirds of his Enemies; so that indeed the War in *Holland* had more of Fatigues and Hardships in it, and ours had more of Fighting and Blows: Hasty Marches, long and unwholesome Encampments, Winter Parties, Counter-marching, Dodging, and Entrenching, were the Excercises of his Men, and often times killed him more Men with Hunger, Cold, and Diseases, than he could do with Fighting: Not that it required less Courage, but rather more; for a Soldier had at any time rather die in the Field *a la Coup de Mousquet*, than be starved with Hunger, or frozen to Death in the Trenches.

Nor do I think I lessen the Reputation of that Great General; for tis most certain he ruined the *Spaniard* more by spinning the War thus out in Length, than he could possibly have done by

a swift

a fwift Conqueft: For had he, *Guftavus* like, with a Torrent of Victory diflodged the *Spaniard* of all the 12 Provinces in 5 Years, whereas he was 40 Years, a beating them out of 7, he had left them rich and ftrong at Home, and able to keep them in conftant Apprehenfions of a Return of his Power: Whereas, by the long Continuance of the War, he fo broke the very Heart of the *Spanifh* Monarchy, fo abfolutely and irrecoverably impoverifhed them, that they have ever fince languifhed of the Difeafe, till they are fallen from the moft powerful, to be the moft defpicable Nation in the World.

The prodigious Charge the King of *Spain* was at in lofing the Seven Provinces, broke the very Spirit of the Nation; and that fo much, that all the Wealth of their *Peruvian* Mountains have not been able to retrieve it; King *Philip* having often declared, that War, befides his Armada for invading *England,* had coft him 370 Millions of Ducats, and 4000000 of the beft Soldiers in *Europe*; whereof, by an unreafonable *Spanifh* Obftinacy, above Sixty Thoufand loft their Lives before *Oftend,* a Town not worth a fixth Part, either of the Blood or Money it coft in a Siege of three Years; and which at laft he had never taken, but that Prince *Maurice* thought it not worth the Charge of defending it any longer.

However, I fay, their Way of fighting in *Holland* did not relifh with me at all. The Prince lay a long time before a little Fort called *Shenkfcans,* which the *Spaniard* took by Surprize, and I thought he might have taken it much fooner. Perhaps it might be my Miftake; but I fancied my Heroe, the King of *Sweden,* would have carried it Sword in Hand, in Half the Time.

How-

However it was, I did not like it; so in the latter End of the Year I came to the *Hague*, and took Shipping for *England*, where I arrived, to the great Satisfaction of my Father and all my Friends.

My Father was then in *London*, and carried me to kiss the King's Hand. His Majesty was pleased to received me very well, and to say a great many very obliging things to my Father upon my Account.

I spent my Time very retired from Court, for I was almost wholly in the Country; and it being so much different from my Genius, which hankered after a warmer Sport than Hunting among our *Welch* Mountains, I could not but be peeping in all the foreign Accounts from *Germany*, to see who and who was together. There I could never hear of a Battle, and the *Germans* being beaten, but I began to wish my self there. But when an Account came of the Progress of *John Bannier*, the *Swedish* General in *Saxony*, and of the constant Victories he had there over the *Saxons*, I could no longer contain my self, but told my Father this Life was very disagreeable to me; that I lost my Time here, and might to much more Advantage go into *Germany*, where I was sure I might make my Fortune upon my own Terms: That, as young as I was, I might have been a General Officer by this Time, if I had not laid down my Commission: That General *Bannier*, or the Marshal *Horn*, had either of them so much Respect for me, that I was sure I might have any thing of them: And that if he pleased to give me Leave, I would go for *Germany* again. My Father was very unwilling to let me go, but seeing me uneasy, told me, that if I was resolv'd,

he

he would oblige me to ſtay no longer in *Eng-land* than the next Spring, and I ſhould have his Conſent.

The Winter following began to look very un-pleaſant upon us in *England*, and my Father uſed often to ſigh at it ; and would tell me ſometimes, he was afraid we ſhould have no need to ſend *Engliſhmen* to fight in *Germany*.

The Cloud that ſeemed to threaten moſt was from *Scotland*. My Father, who had made him-ſelf Maſter of the Arguments on both Sides, uſed to be often ſaying, he feared there was ſome about the King who exaſperated him too much againſt the *Scots*, and drove things too high. For my part, I confeſs I did not much trouble my Head with the Cauſe ; but all my Fear was, they would not fall out, and we ſhould have no Fighting. I have often reflected ſince, that I ought to have known better, that had ſeen how the moſt flouriſhing Provinces of *Germany* were reduced to the moſt miſerable Condition that ever any Country in the World was, by the Ravagings of Soldiers, and the Calamities of War.

How much ſoever I was to blame, yet ſo it was, I had a ſecret Joy at the News of the King's raiſing an Army, and nothing could have with-held me from appearing in it ; but my Eagerneſs was anticipated by an Expreſs the King ſent to my Father, to know if his Son was in *England* ; and my Father having ordered me to carry the Anſwer my ſelf, I waited upon his Majeſty with the Meſſenger. The King received me with his uſual Kindneſs, and asked me if I was willing to ſerve him againſt the *Scots* ?

I anſwered, I was ready to ſerve him againſt any that his Majeſty thought fit to account his

Enemies,

Enemies, and fhould count it an Honour to receive his Commands. Hereupon his Majefty offered me a Commiffion. I told him, I fuppofed there would not be much Time for raifing of Men ; that if his Majefty pleafed I would be at the Rendezvous with as many Gentlemen as I could get together, to ferve his Majefty as Voluntiers.

The Truth is, I found all the Regiments of Horfe the King defigned to raife, were but two, as Regiments ; the reft of the Horfe were fuch as the Nobility raifed in their feveral Counties, and commanded them themfelves ; and, as I had commanded a Regiment of Horfe abroad, it looked a little odd to ferve with a 'fingle Troop at home ; and the King took the thing prefently. *Indeed 'twill be a Voluntier War*, faid the King, *for the Northern Gentry have fent me an Account of above* 4000 *Horfe they have already.* I bowed, and told his Majefty I was glad to hear his Subjects were fo forward to ferve him ; fo taking his Majefty's Orders to be at *York* by the End of *March*, I returned to my Father.

My Father was very glad I had not taken a Commiffion, for I know not from what kind of Emulation between the Weftern and Northern Gentry. The Gentlemen of our Side were not very forward in the Service ; their Loyalty to the King in the fucceeding. Times made it appear it was not from any Difaffection to his Majefty's Intereft or Perfon, or to the Caufe ; but this however made it difficult for me when I came home, to get any Gentleman of Quality to ferve with me, fo that I prefented my felf to his Majefty only as a Voluntier, with eight Gentlemen, and about 36 Countrymen well mounted and armed.

And

And as it proved, thefe were enough, for this
Expedition ended in an Accomodation with the
Scots; and they not advancing fo much as to
their own Borders, we never came to any Action; but the Armies lay in the Counties of
Northumberland and Durham, eat up the Country,
and fpent the King a vaft Sum of Money, and
fo this War ended, a Pacification was made, and
both Sides returned.

The Truth is, I never faw fuch a defpicable
Appearance of Men in Arms to begin a War, in
my Life; whether it was that I had feen fo
many braver Armies abroad that prejudiced me
againft them, or that it really was fo; for to
me they feemed little better than a Rabble met
together to devour, rather than fight for their
King and Country. There was indeed a great
Appearance of Gentlemen, and thofe of extraordinary Quality; but their Garb, their Equipages,
and their Mein, did not look like War; their
Troops were filled with Footmen and Servants,
and wretchedly armed, God wot. I believe I
might fay, without Vanity, one Regiment of Finland Horfe would have made Sport at beating them
all. There were fuch Crouds of Parfons, (for this
was a Church War in particular) that the Camp
and Court was full of them; and the King was
fo eternally befieged with Clergymen of one fort
or another, that it gave Offence to the chief of
the Nobility.

As was the Appearance, fo was the Service;
the Army marched to the Borders, and the Head
Quarter was at Berwick upon Tweed; but the Scots
never appeared, no, not fo much as their Scouts;
whereupon the King called a Council of War,
and there it was refolved to fend the Earl of
Holland with a Party of Horfe into Scotland, to
learn

learn fome News of the Enemy; and truly the
firft News he brought us was, that finding their
Army encamped about *Coldingham*, 15 Miles from
Berwick, as foon as he appeared, the *Scots* drew
out a Party to chaige him, upon which moft of
his Men halted, I don't fay run away, but 'twas
next Door to it; for they could not be perfwaded to fire their Piftols, and wheel off like Soldiers, but retreated in fuch a diforderly and
fhameful Manner, that had the Enemy but had
either the Courage or Conduct to have followed
them, it muft have certainly ended in the Ruin
of the whole Party.

THE

THE
SECOND PART.

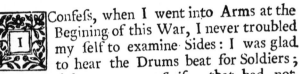

Confefs, when I went into Arms at the Begining of this War, I never troubled my felf to examine Sides : I was glad to hear the Drums beat for Soldiers ; as if I had been a meer *Swifs*, that had not car'd which Side went up or down, fo I had my Pav. I went as eagerly and blindly about my Bufinefs, as the meaneft Wretch that lifted in the Army ; nor had I the leaft compaffionate Thought for the Miferies of my native Country, 'till after the Fight at *Edgehill*. I had known as much, and perhaps more than moft in the Army, what it was to have an Enemy ranging in the Bowels of a Kingdom ; I had feen the moft flourifhing Provinces of *Germany* reduced to perfect Defarts, and the voracious *Crabats*, with inhuman Barbarity, quenching the Fires of the plundered Villages with the Blood of the Inhabitants. Whether this had hardened me againft the natural Tendernefs which I afterwards found return upon me, or not, I cannot tell; but I reflected upon my felf afterwards with a great deal of Trouble, for the Unconcernednefs of my Temper at the approaching Ruin of my native Country.

I was

I was in the firſt Army at *York*, as I have already noted, and I muſt confeſs, had the leaſt
Diverſion there that ever I found in an Army in
my Life; for when I was in *Germany* with the
King of *Sweden*, we uſed to ſee the King with the
General Officers every Morning on Horſeback,
viewing his Men, his Artillery, his Horſes, and
always ſomething going forward: Here we ſaw
nothing but Courtiers and Clergymen, Biſhops and
Parſons, as buſy as if the Direction of the War had
been in them; the King was ſeldom ſeen among us,
and never without ſome of them always about him.

Thoſe few of us that had ſeen the Wars, and
would have made a ſhort End of this for him,
began to be very uneaſy; and particularly a certain Nobleman took the Freedom to tell the
King, that the Clergy would certainly ruin the Expedition; *the Caſe was this* he would ha' had the King
have immediately marched into *Scotland*, and put
the Matter to the Trial of a Battle; and he urged it
every Day; and the King finding his Reaſons
very good, would often be of his Opinion; but
next Morning he would be of another Mind.

This Gentleman was a Man of Conduct enough,
and of unqueſtioned Courage, and afterwards loſt
his Life for the King. He ſaw we had an Army
of young ſtout Fellows, numerous enough; and
tho' they had not yet ſeen much Service, he was
for bringing them to Action, that the *Scots* might
not have time to ſtrengthen themſelves; nor they
have time by Idleneſs and Sotting, *the Bane of
Soldiers*, to make themſelves unfit for any thing.

I was one Morning in Company with this Gentleman; and as he was a warm Man, and eager
in his Diſcourſe, a Pox of theſe Prieſts, ſays he,
'tis for them the King has raiſed this Army, and

put

put his Friends to a vaſt Charge ; and now we are come, they won't let us fight.

But I was afterwards convinced, the Clergy ſaw farther into the Matter than we did ; they ſaw the Scots had a better Army than we had ; bold and ready, commanded by brave Officers ; and they foreſaw, that if we fought, we ſhould be beaten, and if beaten, they were undone. And 'twas very true, we had all been ruined, if we had engaged.

It is true, when we came to the Pacification which followed, I confeſs I was of the ſame Mind the Gentleman had been of; for we had better have fought, and been beaten, than have made ſo diſhonourable a Treaty, without ſtriking a Stroke. This Pacification ſeems to me to have laid the Scheme of all the Blood and Confuſion which followed in the Civil War ; for whatever the King and his Friends might pretend to do by talking big, the Scots ſaw he was to be bullied into any thing, and that when it came to the Puſh, the Courtiers never cared to bring it to Blows.

I have little or nothing, to ſay as to Action, in this Mock-Expedition. The King was perſwaded at laſt to march to Berwick ; and as I have ſaid already, a Party of Horſe went out to learn News of the Scots, and as ſoon as they ſaw them, run away from them, bravely.

This made the Scots ſo inſolent, that whereas before they lay encamped behind a River, and never ſhewed themſelves, in a ſort of modeſt Deference to their King, which was the Pretence of not being Aggreſſors or Invaders, only arming in their own Defence ; now, having been invaded by the Engliſh Troops entring Scotland, they had what they wanted : And to ſhew it was not Fear that reſtrained them before, but Policy, now

they

they came up in Parties to our very Gates, braving, and facing us every Day.

I had, with more Curiofity than Difcretion, put my felf as a Voluntier at the Head of one of our Parties of Horfe, under my Lord *Holland*, when they went out to difcover the Enemy; they went, they faid, to fee what the *Scots* were a-doing.

We had not marched far, but our Scouts brought Word, they had difcovered fome Horfe, but could not come up to them, becaufe a River parted them. At the Heels of thefe came another Party of our Men upon the Spur to us, and faid the Enemy was behind, which might be true, for ought we knew; but it was fo far behind, that no Body could fee them; and yet the Country was plain and open for above a Mile before us: Hereupon we made a Halt, and indeed I was afraid 'twould have been an odd Sort of a Halt; for our Men began to look one upon another, as they do in like Cafes, when they are going to break; and when the Scouts came galloping in, the Men were in fuch Diforder, that had but one Man broke way, I am fatisfied they had all run for it.

I found my Lord *Holland* did not perceive it; but after the firft Surprize was a little over, I told my Lord what I had obferved; and that unlefs fome Courfe was immediately taken, they would all run at the firft Sight of the Enemy. I found he was much concerned at it, and began to confult what Courfe to take, to prevent it. I confefs 'tis a hard Queftion, how to make Men ftand and face an Enemy, when Fear has poffeffed their Minds with an Inclination to run away: But I'll give that Honour to the Memory of that noble Gentleman, who tho' his Experience in Matters of War was fmall, having never been in much Ser-

vice;

vice ; yet his Courage made amends for it ; for I dare fay he would not have turned his Horfe from an Army of Enemies, nor have faved his Life at the Price of running away for it.

My Lord foon faw, as well as I, the Fright the Men were in, after I had given him a Hint of it ; and to encourage them, rode thro' their Ranks, and fpoke chearfully to them, and ufed what Arguments he thought proper to fettle their Minds I remembred a Saying which I had heard old Marfhal *Guftavus Horn* fpeak in *Germany*, If you find your Men faulter, or in Doubt, never fuffer them to halt, but keep them advancing ; for while they are going forward, it keeps up their Courage.

As foon as I could get Opportunity to fpeak to him, I gave him this as my Opinion. That's very well, fays my Lord, but I am ftudying, fays he, to poft them fo as that they can't run if they would ; and if they ftand but once to face the Enemy, I do'nt fear them afterwards.

While we were difcourfing thus, Word was brought, that feveral Parties of the Enemies were feen on the farther Side of the River, upon which my Lord gave the Word to march, and as we were marching on, my Lord calls out a Lieutenant who had been an old Soldier, with only five Troopers whom he had moft Confidence in ; and having given him his Leffon, he fends him away ; in a Quarter of an Hour, one of the five Troopers comes back galloping and hallowing, and tells us his Lieutenant had with his fmall Party beaten a Party of 20 of the Enemy's Horfe over the River, and had fecured the Pafs, and defired my Lord would march up to him immediately.

'Tis a ftrange thing that Mens Spirits fhould be fubjeffed to fuch fudden Changes, and capable of fo much Alteration from Shadows of things.

They

They were for running before they faw the Enemy; now they are in hafte to be led on, and but that in raw Men we are obliged to bear with any thing, the Diforder in both was intolerable.

The Story was a premeditated Sham, and not a Word of Truth in it, invented to raife their Spirits, and cheat them out of their cowardly flegmatick Apprehenfions, and my Lord had his End in it; for they were all on Fire to fall on: And I am perfwaded, had they been led immediately into a Battle begun to their Hands, they would have laid about them like Furies; for there is nothing like Victory to flufh a young Soldier. Thus while the Humour was high, and the Fermentation lafted, away we marched; and paffing one of their great Commons which they call *Moors*, we came to the River, as he called it, where our Lieutenant was pofted with his four Men; 'twas a little Brook fordable with Eafe, and leaving a Guard at the Pafs, we advanced to the Top of a fmall Afcent, from whence we had a fair View of the *Scots* Army, as they lay behind another River larger than the former.

Our Men were pofted well enough, behind a fmall Enclofure, with a narrow Lane in their Front: And my Lord had caufed his Dragoons to be placed in the Front to line the Hedges; and in this Pofture he ftood viewing the Enemy at a Diftance. The *Scots* who had fome Intelligence of our coming, drew out three fmall Parties, and fent them by different Ways to obferve our Number; and forming a fourth Party, which I gueffed to be about 600 Horfe, advanced to the Top of the Plain, and drew up to face us, but never offered to attack us.

One of the fmall Parties making about 100 Men, one third Foot paffes upon our Flank in View,

L 4   but

but out of reach; and as they marched, shouted
at us, which our Men better pleafed with that
Work than with Fighting, readily enough anfwered, and would fain have fired at them for the
Pleafure of making a Noife; for they were too
far off to hit them.

I obferved that thefe Parties had always fome
Foot with them; and yet if the Horfe galloped,
or pufhed on ever fo forward, the Foot were as
forward as they, which was an extraordinary
Advantage.

Guftavus Adolphus that King of Soldiers, was the
firft that I have ever obferved found the Advantage of mixing fmall Bodies of Mufqueteers a-
mong his Horfe; and had he had fuch nimble
ftrong Fellows as thefe, he would have prized
them above all the reft of his Men. Thefe were
thofe they call *Highlanders*; they would run on
Foot with their Arms, and all their Acoutre-
ments, and keep very good Order too, and yet
keep Pace with the Horfe, let them go at what
Rate they would. When I faw the Foot thus in-
terlined among the Horfe, together with the Way
of ordering their flving Parties, it prefently oc-
curred to my Mind, that here was fome of our
old *Scots*, come home out of *Germany*, that had the
ordering of Matters; and if fo, I knew we were
not a Match for them.

Thus we ftood facing the Enemy 'till our Scouts
brought us Word the whole *Scots* Army was in
Motion, and in full march to attack us; and
though it was not true, and the Fear of our Men
doubled every Object, yet 'twas thought convenient to make our Retreat. The whole Matter
was, that the Scouts having informed them what
they could, of our Strength; the 600 were ordered

to

to march towards us, and three Regiments of Foot were drawn out to support the Horse.

I know not whether they would have ventured to attack us, at least before their Foot had come up; but whether they would have put it to the Hazard or no, we were resolved not to hazard the Trial, so we drew down to the Pass; and, as retreating looks something like running away, especially when an Enemy is at hand, our Men had much a-do to make there Retreat pass for a March, and not a Flight; and, by their often looking behind them, any Body might know what they would have done if they had been pressed.

I confess, I was heartily ashamed when the *Scots* coming up to the Place where we had been posted, stood and shouted at us. I would have perswaded my Lord to have charged them, and he would have done it with all his Heart, but he saw it was not practicable; so we stood at gaze with them above 2 Hours, by which time their Foot were come up to them, and yet they did not offer to attack us. I never was so ashamed of my self in my Life; we were all dispirited, the *Scots* Gentlemen would come out single, within Shot of our Post, which in a time of War is always accounted a Challenge to any single Gentleman, to come out and exchange a Pistol with them, and no Body would stir; at last our old Lieutenant rides out to meet a *Scotchman* that came pickeering on his Quarter. This Lieutenant was a brave and a strong Fellow, had been a Soldier in the *Low Countries*; and though he was not of any Quality, only a meer Soldier, had his Preferment for his Conduct. He gallops bravely up to his Adversary, and exchanging their Pistols, the Lieutenant's Horse happened

to

to be killed. The *Scotchman* very generously dismounts, and engages him with his Sword, and fairly masters him, and carries him away Prisoner; and I think this Horse was all the Blood was shed in that War.

The Lieutenant's Name thus conquered was *English*, and as he was a very stout old Soldier, the Disgrace of it broke his Heart. The *Scotchman* indeed used him very generously; for he treated him in the Camp very courteously, gave him another Horse, and set him at Liberty, *gratis*. But the Man laid it so to Heart, that he never would appear in the Army, but went home to his own Country and died.

I had enough of Party-making, and was quite sick with Indignation at the Cowardise of the Men; and my Lord was in as great a Fret as I, but there was no Remedy; we durst not go about to retreat, for we should have been in such Confusion, that the Enemy must have discovered it: So my Lord resolved to keep the Post, if possible, and send to the King for some Foot. Then were our Men ready to fight with one another who should be the Messenger; and at last when a Lieutenant with 20 Dragoons was dispatched, he told us afterwards he found himself an Hundred strong before he was gotten a Mile from the Place.

In short, as soon as ever the Day declined, and the Dusk of the Evening began to shelter the Designs of the Men, they dropt away from us one by one; and at last in such Numbers, that if we had stayed till the Morning, we had not had 50 Men left, out of 1200 Horse and Dragoons.

When I saw how 'twas, consulting with some of the Officers, we all went to my Lord *Holland*, and

and preffed him to retreat, before the Enemy fhould difcern the Flight of our Men; fo he drew us off, and we came to the Camp the next Morning, in the fhamefulleft Condition that ever poor Men could do. And this was the End of the worft Expedition ever I made in my Life.

To fight and be beaten, is a Cafualty common to a Soldier, and I have fince had enough of it; but to run away at the Sight of an Enemy, and neither ftrike or be ftricken, this is the very Shame of the Profeffion, and no Man that has done it, ought to fhew his Face again in the Field, unlefs Difadvantages of Place or Number make it tolerable, neither of which was our Cafe.

My Lord *Holland* made another March a few Days after, in hopes to retrieve this Mifcarriage; but I had enough of it, fo I kept in my Quarters: And though his Men did not defert him as before, yet upon the Appearance of the Enemy, they did not think fit to fight, and came off with but little more Honour than they did before.

There was no need to go out to feek the Enemy after this; for they came, as I have noted, and pitched in Sight of us, and their Parties came up every Day to the very Out-works of *Berwick*; but no Body cared to meddle with them: And in this Pofture things ftood when the Pacification was agreed on by both Parties; which, like a fhort Truce, only gave both Sides Breath to prepare for a new War more ridiculoufly managed than the former. When the Treaty was fo near a Conclufion, as that Converfation was admitted on both Sides, I went over to the *Scotch* Camp to fatisfy my Curiofity, as many of our *Englifh* Officers did alfo.

I con-

I confess, the Soldiers made a very uncouth
Figure, especially the *Highlanders*: The Oddness
and Barbarity of their Garb and Arms seemed
to have something in it remarkable.

They were generaly tall swinging Fellows; their
Swords were extravagantly, and I think insignifi-
cantly broad, and they carried great wooden Targets large enough to cover the upper part of their
Bodies. Their Dress was as antique as the rest; a
at Cap on their Heads, called by them a Bonnet,
long hanging Sleeves behind, and their Doublet,
Breeches and Stockings, of a Stuff they called
Plaid, striped a-cross red and yellow, with short
Cloaks of the same. These Fellows looked, when
drawn out, like a Regiment of *Merry Andrews*
ready for *Bartholomew* Fair. They are in Companies
all of a Name, and therefore call one another
only by their Christian Names, as *Jemy, Jockey,*
that is *John*; and *Sawny*, that is, *Alexander*, and the
like. And they scorn to be commanded but by
one of their own Clan or Family. They are
all Gentlemen, and proud enough to be Kings.
The meanest Fellow among them is as tenacious
of his Honour, as the best Nobleman in the Country, and they will fight, and cut one another's
Throats for every trifling Affront.

But to their own Clans or Lairds, they are the
willingest and most obedient Fellows in Nature.
Give them their due, were their Skill in Excercises and Discipline proportioned to their Courage, they would make the bravest Soldiers in
the World. They are large Bodies, and pro-
digiously strong; and two Qualities they have
above other Nations, *viz*. hardy to endure Hunger,
Cold, and Hardships, and wonderfully swift of
Foot. The latter is such an Advantage in the
Field, that I know none like it; for if they conquer

quer, no Enemy can efcape them; and if they run, even the Horfe can hardly overtake them. Thefe were fome of them, who, as I obferved before, went out in Parties with their Horfe.

There were three or four Thoufand of thefe in the *Scots* Army, armed only with Swords and Targets; and in their Belts fome of them had a Piftol, but no Mufquets at that time among them.

But there were alfo a great many Regiments of difciplined Men, who by their carrying their Arms, looked as if they underftood their Bufinefs, and by their Faces, that they durft fee an Enemy.

I had not been Half an Hour in their Camp, after the Ceremony of giving our Names, and paffing their Out-Guards and Main Guard was over, but I was faluted by feveral of my Acquaintance; and in particular, by one who led the *Scotch* Voluntiers at the Taking the Caftle of *Openheim*, of which I have given an Account. They ufed me with all the Refpect they thought due to me, on Account of old Affairs, gave me the Word, and a Sergeant waited upon me whenever I pleafed to go abroad.

I continued 12 or 14 Days among them, till the Pacification was concluded; and they were ordered to march home. They fpoke very refpectfully of the King, but I found were exafperated to the laft Degree at Arch-bifhop *Laud* and the *Englifh* Bifhops, for endeavouring to impofe the *Common-Prayer-Book* upon them; and they always talked with the utmoft Contempt of our Soldiers and Army. I always waved the Difcourfe about the Clergy, and the Occafion of the War; but I could not but be too fenfible what they faid of our Men was true; and by this I perceived they had an univerfal Intelligence
from

from among us, both of what we were doing,
and what fort of People we were that were doing it; and they were mighty defirous of coming to Blows with us. I had an Invitation from
their General, but I declined it, left I fhould give
Offence. I found they accepted the Pacification
as a thing not likely to hold, or that they
did not defign fhould hold; and that they were
refolved to keep their Forces on Foot, notwithftanding the Agreement. Their whole Army
was full of brave Officers, Men of as much Experience and Conduct as any in the World; and all
Men who know any thing of the War, know
good Officers prefently make a good Army.

Things being thus huddled up, the *Englifh* came
back to *York*, were the Army feparated, and the
Scots went home to encreafe theirs; for I eafily
forefaw, that Peace was the fartheft thing from
their Thoughts.

The next Year the Flame broke out again,
the King draws his Forces down into the North,
as before, and Expreffes were fent to all the Gentlemen that had Commands, to be at the Place
by the 15th of *July.* As I had accepted of no
Command in the Army, fo I had no Inclination
at all to go; for I forefaw there would be nothing but Difgrace attend it. My Father obferving fuch an Alteration in my ufual Forward-
nefs, asked me one Day, what was the Matter,
that I, who ufed to be fo forward to go into the
Army, and fo eager to run abroad to fight, now
fhewed no Inclination to appear when the Service of the King and Country called me to it? I
told him, I had as much Zeal as ever for the
King's Service, and for the Country too: But
he knew a Soldier could not abide to be beaten;
and being from thence a little more inquifitive,
I told

I told him the Obfervations I had made in the
Scots Army, and the People I had converfed with
there; and, Sir, fays I, affure your felf, if the
King offers to fight them, he will be beaten; and
I don't love to engage, when my Judgement tells
me before-hand, I fhall be worfted: And as I
had forefeen, it came to pafs; for the *Scots* refolving to proceed, never ftood upon the Ceremony of Aggreffion, as before, but on the 20th
of *Auguft* they entered *England* with their
Army.

However, as my Father defired, I went to the
King's Army, which was then at *York*, but not
gotten all together: The King himfelf was at
London; but upon this News takes Poft for the
Army, and advancing a Part of his Forces, he
pofted the Lord *Conway* and Sir *Jacob Aftley*,
with a Brigade of Foot and fome Horfe at *Newborn*, upon the River *Tine*, to keep the *Scots* from
paffing that River.

The *Scots* could have paffed the *Tine* without
Fighting; but to let us fee that they were able
to force their Paffage, they fall upon this Body
of Men; and notwithftanding all the Advantages of the Place, they beat them from the Poft,
took their Baggage and two Pieces of Cannon,
with fome Prifoners. Sir *Jacob Aftley* made what
Refiftance he could; but the *Scots* charged with
fo much Fury, and being alfo over-powered, he
was foon put into Confufion. Immediately the
Scots made themfelves Mafters of *Newcaftle*, and
the next Day of *Durham*, and laid thofe two
Counties under intolerable Contributions.

Now was the King abfolutely ruined; for
among his own People the Difcontents before
were fo plain, that had the Clergy had any
Forecaft, they would never have embroiled him

I   with

with the *Scots*, till he had fully brought Matters
to an Underſtanding at Home : But the Caſe was
thus : The King, by the good Husbandry of
Biſhop *Juxon*, his Treaſurer, had a Million of ready
Money in his Treaſury, and upon that Account
having no need of a Parliament, had not called
one in 12 Years; and perhaps had never called
another, if he had not by this unhappy Circum-
ſtance been reduced to a Neceſſity of it ; for now
this ready Money was ſpent in two fooliſh Ex-
peditions, and his Army appeared in a Condition not fit to engage the *Scots* ; the Detatch-
ment under Sir *Jacob Aſtley*, which were of the
Flower of his Men, had been routed at *Newborn*,
and the Enemy had Poſſeſſion of two intire
Counties.

All Men blamed *Laud* for prompting the King
to provoke the *Scots*, a headſtrong Nation, and
zealous for their own Way of Worſhip ; and
Laud himſelf found too late the Conſequences of
it, both to the whole Cauſe and to himſelf ;
for the *Scots*, whoſe native Temper is not eaſily to
forgive an Injury, purſued him by their Party
in *England*, and never gave it over, till they
laid his Head on the Block.

The ruined Country now clamoured in his
Majeſty's Ears with daily Petitions, and the
Gentry of other Neighbour Counties cry
out for Peace and a Parliament. The King, em-
baraſſed with theſe Difficulties, and quite empty of Money, calls a Great Council of the Nobility at *York*, and demands their Advice, which
any one could have told him before, would be
to call a Parliament.

I cannot, without Regret, look back upon the
Misfortune of the King, who, as he was one of
the beſt Princes in his perſonal Conduct that
ever

ever reigned in *England*, had yet fome of the
greateft Unhappineffes in his Conduct as a King,
that ever Prince had, and the whole Courfe of
his Life demonftrated it.

1. An impolitick Honefty. His Enemies called it Obftinacy : But as I was perfectly acquainted with his Temper, I cannot but think
it was his Judgment, when he thought he was
in the right to adhere to it as a Duty tho' againft
his Intereft.

2. Too much Compliance when he was complying.

No Man but himfelf would have denied what
at fometimes he denied, and have granted what
at other times he granted ; and this Uncer-
t   c Counfel proceeded from two things.

the Heat of the Clergy, to whom he was
exceedingly devoted, and for whom indeed he
ruined himfelf.

2. The Wifdom of his Nobility.

Thus when the Counfel of his Priefts prevailed, all was Fire and Fury; the *Scots* were Rebels, and muft be fubdued; and the Parliament's Demands were to be rejected as exorbitant; but whenever the King's Judgment was
led by the grave and fteady Advice of his Nobility and Counfellors, he was always enclined
by them to temperate his Meafures between
the two Extremes : And had he gone on in
fuch a Temper, he had never met with the
Misfortunes which afterward attended him, or
had fo many Thoufands of his Friends loft their
Lives and Fortunes in his Service.

I am fure, we that knew what it was to fight
for him, and that loved him better than any of
the Clergy could pretend to, have had many a
Confultation how to bring over our Mafter from

M   fo

fo efpoufing their Intereft, as to ruin himfelf for
it ; but 'twas in vain.

I took this interval, when I fat ftill and only
looked on, to make thefe Remarks, becaufe I remember the beft Friends the King had were at
this time of that Opinion. That 'twas an unaccountable Piece of Indifcretion, to commence a
Quarrel with the *Scots*, a poor and obftinate People, for a Ceremony and Book of Church Difcipline, at a time when the King ftood but upon
indifferent Terms with his People at Home.

The Confequence was, it put Arms into the
Hands of his Subjects to rebel againft him ; it
embroiled him with his Parliament in *England*,
to whom he was fain to ftoop in a fatal and unufual Manner to get Money, all his own being
fpent, and fo to buy off the *Scots* whom he cou'd
not beat off.

I cannot but give one Inftance of the unaccountable Politicks of his Minifters. If they over-
ruled this unhappy King to it, with Defign to ex-
hauft and impoverifh him, they were the worft
of Traytors ; if not, the groffeft of Fools. They
prompted the King to equip a Fleet againft the
Scots, and to put on board it 5000 Land Men.
Had this been all, the Defign had been good, that
while the King had faced the Army upon the
Borders, thefe 5000 landing in the Frith of *Edinburgh* might have put that whole Nation into Diforder. But in Order to this, they advife the
King to lay out his Money in fitting out the biggeft Ships he had, and the Royal Sovereign, the
biggeft Ship the World had ever feen, which
coft him no lefs than 100000 Pounds was now
built, and fitted out for this Voyage.

This was the moft incongruous and ridiculous
Advice that could be given, and made us all believe

lieve we were betrayed, tho' we knew not by whom.

To fit out Ships of 100 Guns to invade *Scotland*, which had not one Man of War in the World, nor any open Confederacy with any Prince or State that had any Fleet! 'twas a moft ridiculous thing. An Hundred Sail of *Newcaftle* Colliers, to carry the Men with their Stores and Provifions, and ten Frigates of 40 Guns each, had been as good a Fleet as Reafon, and the Nature of the thing could ha' made tolerable.

Thus things were carried on, 'till the King, beggar'd by the Mifmanagement of his Counfels, and beaten by the *Scots*, was driven to the Neceffity of calling a Parliament in *England*.

It is not my Defign to enter into the Feuds and Brangles of this Parliament. I have noted, by Obfervations of their Miftakes, who brought the King to this unhappy Neceffity of calling them.

His Majefty had tried Parliaments upon feveral Occafions before, but never found himfelf fo much embroiled with them but he could fend them Home, and there was an End of it; but as he could not avoid Calling thefe, fo they took Care to put him out of a Condition to difmifs them.

The *Scots* Army was now quartered upon the *Englifh*. The Counties, the Gentry, and the Affembly of Lords at *York*, petitioned for a Parliament.

The *Scots* prefented their Demands to the King, in which it was obferved, that Matters were concerted between them and a Party in *England*; and I confefs, when I faw that, I began to think the King in an ill Cafe; for as the *Scots* pretended Grievances, we thought, the King redreffing thofe Grievances, they could ask no more; and there-

M 2   fore

fore all Men advifed the King to grant their full
Demands. And whereas the King had not Money to fupply the *Scots* in their March home, I know
there were feveral Meetings of Gentlemen with a
Defign to advance confiderable Sums of Money
to the King to fet him free, and in order to rein-
ftate his Majefty, as before. Not that we ever advifed the King to rule without a Parliament, but
we were very defirous of putting him out of the
Neceffity of calling them, at leaft, juft then.

But the Eighth Article of the *Scots* Demands ex-
prefly required, That an *Englifh* Parliament might
be called to remove all Obftructions of Commerce,
and to fettle Peace, Religion and Liberty; and
in another Article they tell the King, the 24th
of *September* being the Time his Majefty appointed
for the Meeting of the Peers, will make it too
long e'er the Parliament meet.

And in another, That a Parliament was the only
Way of fettling Peace, and bringing them to his
Majefty's Obedience.

When we faw this in the Army, 'twas time to
look about. Every body perceived that the *Scots*
Army would call an *Englifh* Parliament; and whatever Averfion the King had to it, we all faw he
would be obliged to comply with it; and now
they all began to fee their Error, who advifed
the King to this *Scotch* War.

While thefe things were tranfacting, the Affembly of the Peers meet at *York*; and by their Advice a Treaty was begun with the *Scots.* I had
the Honour to be fent with the firft Meffage which
was in Writing.

I brought it, attended with a Trumpet, and a
Guard of 500 Horfe, to the *Scots* Quarters. I was
ftoped at *Darlington,* and my Errand being
known, General *Lefly* fent a *Scots* Major and 50
Horfe,

Horfe, to receive me, but would let neither my
Trumpet or Guard fet Foot within their Quarters. In this Manner, I was conducted to Audi-
ence in the Chapter-Houfe at *Durham*, where a
Committee of *Scots* Lords who attended the Army, received me very courteoufly, and gave me
their Anfwer in Writing alfo.

'Twas in this Anfwer that they fhewed at leaft
to me their Defign of embroiling the King with
his *Englifh* Subjects; they difcourfed very freely
with me, and did not order me to withdraw when
they debated their private Opinions : They drew
up feveral Anfwers but did not like them ; at laft,
they gave me one which I did not receive ; I
thought it was too infolent to be born with, as
near as I can remember, it was thus.

The Commiffioners of Scotland *attending the Service
in the Army, do refufe any Treaty in the City of* York.

One of the Commiffioners who treated me with
more Diftinction than the reft, and difcourfed
freely with me, gave me an Opportunity to
fpeak more freely of this than I expected.

I told them, if they would return to his Majefty an Anfwer fit for me to carry, or if they
would fay they would not treat at all, I would
deliver fuch a Meffage : But I entreated them to
confider the Anfwer was to their Sovereign, and
to whom they made a great Profeffion of Duty
and Refpect ; and at leaft they ought to give their
Reafons, why they declined a Treaty at *York* ;
and to name fome other Place, or humbly to defire his Majefty to name fome other Place : But to
fend Word they would not treat at *York*, I could
deliver no fuch Meffage, for when put into *Englifh* it would fignify, they would not treat at all.

I ufed a great many Reafons and Arguments
with them on this Head: And at laft, with fome Difficulty,

ficulty, obtained of them to give the Reaſon, which
was the Earl of *Strafford's* having the chief Command at *York*, whom they declared their mortal E-
nemy, he having declared them Rebels in *Ireland*.
With this Anſwer I returned. I could make
no Obſervation in the ſhort time I was with them;
for as I ſtaid but one Night, ſo I was guarded as
a cloſe Priſoner all the while. I ſaw ſeveral of
their Officers whom I knew, but they durſt not
ſpeak to me; and if they would ha' ventured,
my Guard would not ha' permitted them.

In this Manner I was conducted out of their
Quarters to my own Party again, and having
delivered my Meſſage to the King, and told his
Majeſty the Circumſtances, I ſaw the King receive the Account of the haughty Behaviour of the
Scots with ſome Regret; however it was his Majeſty's time now to bear, and therefore the *Scots*
were comply'd with, and the Treaty appointed
at *Rippon*; where, after much Debate, ſeveral
preliminary Articles were agreed on, as a Ceſſa-
tion of Arms, *Quarters and Bounds to the Armies,
Subſiſtence to the* Scots *Army*, and the Reſidue of the
Demands was referred to a Treaty at *London, &c.*

We were all amazed at the Treaty, and I cannot
but remember we uſed to wiſh much rather we had
been ſuffered to fight; for tho' we had been worſted at firſt, the Power and Strength of the King's
Intereſt which was not yet tried, muſt, in fine,
ha' been too ſtrong for the *Scots*: Whereas now we
ſaw the King was for complying with any thing,
and all his Friends would be ruined.

I confeſs, I had nothing to fear, and ſo was not
much concerned; but our Predictions ſoon came
to paſs: For no ſooner was this Parliament called,
but Abundance of thoſe who had embroiled their
King with his People of both Kingdoms, like the
Diſci-

Difciples, when their Mafter was betrayed to the *Jews, forfook him and fled*; and now Parliament Tyranny began to fucceed Church Tyranny, and we Soldiers were glad fee it at firft : The Bifhops trembled, the Judges went to Goal ; the Officers of the Cuftoms were laid hold on ; and the Parliament began to lay their Fingers on the great ones, particularly Arch-Bifhop *Laud*, and the Earl of *Strafford*. We had no great Concern for the firft, but the laft was a Man of fo much Conduct and Gallantry, and fo beloved by the Soldiers and principal Gentry of *England*, that every Body was touched with his Misfortune.

The Parliament now grew mad in their Turn, and as the Profperity of any Party is the time to fhew their Difcretion, the Parliament fhewed they knew as little where to ftop as other People. The King was not in a Condition to deny any thing, and nothing could be demanded but they pufh'd it. They attainted the Earl of *Strafford*, and thereby made the King cut off his right Hand, to fave his left, and yet not fave it neither : They obtain another Bill, to empower them to fit during their own Pleafure, and after them, Triennial Parliaments to meet, whether the King call them or no ; and Granting this compleated his Majefty's Ruin.

Had the Houfe only regulated the Abufes of the Court, punifhed evil Counfellours, and reftor'd Parliaments to their original and juft Powers, all had been well ; and the King, tho' he had been more than mortified, had yet reaped the Benefit of future Peace ; for now the *Scots* were fent Home, after having eaten up two Counties, and received a prodigious Sum of Money to boot : And the King, tho' too late, goes in Perfon to *Edinburgh*, and grants them all they could defire, and more

M 4   than

than they asked; but in *England*, the Defires of ours were unbounded, and drove at all Extremes.

They threw out the Bifhops from fitting in the Houfe, make a Proteftation equivalent to the *Scotch* Covenant; and this done, print their Remonftrance. This fo provoked the King, that he refolves upon feizing fome of the Members, and in an ill Hour enters the Houfe in Perfon to take them. Thus one imprudent thing on one Hand produced another of the other Hand, 'till the King was obliged to leave them to themfelves, for fear of being mobbed into fomething or other unworthy of himfelf.

Thefe Proceedings began to alarm the Gentry and Nobility of *England*; for however willing we were to have evil Counfellours removed, and the Government return to a fettled and legal Courfe, according to the happy Conftitution of this Nation, and might ha' been forward enough to have owned the King had been mifled, and impofed upon to do things which he had rather had not been done; yet it did not follow, that all the Powers and Prerogatives of the Crown fhould devolve upon the Parliament, and the King in a Manner be depofed, or elfe facrificed to the Fury of the Rabble.

The Heats of the Houfe running them thus to all Extremes, and at laft to take from the King the Power of the Militia, which indeed was all that was left to make him any thing of a King, put the King upon oppofing Force with Force; and thus the Flame of Civil War began.

However backward I was in engaging in the fecond Year's Expedition againft the *Scots*, I was as forward now; for I waited on the King at *York*, where a gallant Company of Gentlemen as ever were feen in *England*, engaged themfelves to enter

ter

ter into his Service; and here some of us formed our selves into Troops for the Guard of his Person.

The King having been waited upon by the Gentry of *Yorkshire*, and having told them his Resolution of erecting his Royal Standard, and received from them hearty Assurances of Support; dismisses them, and marches to *Hull*, where lay the Train of Artillery, and all the Arms and Amunition belonging to the *Northern* Army which had been disbanded. But here the Parliament had been before-hand with his Majesty, so that when he came to *Hull*, he found the Gates shut, and Sir *John Hotham* the Governour upon the Walls, tho' with a great deal of seeming Humility and Protestations of Loyalty to his Person, yet with a positive Denial to admit any of the King's Attendants into the Town. If his Majesty pleased to enter the Town in Person with any reasonable Number of his Houshould, he would submit, but would not be prevailed on to receive the King, as he would be received, with his Forces, tho' those Forces were then but very few.

The King was exceedingly provoked at this Repulse, and indeed it was a great Surprize to us all; for certainly never Prince began a War against the whole Strength of his Kingdom, under the Circumstances that he was in. He had not a Garrison, or a Company of Soldiers in his Pay, not a Stand of Arms, or a Barrel of Powder, a Musquet, Cannon or ·Mortar, not a Ship of all the Fleet, or Money in his Treasury to procure them; whereas the Parliament had all his Navy, and Ordinance, Stores, Magazines, Arms, Ammunition, and Revenue, in their Keeping. And this I take to be another Defect of the King's Counsel, and a sad Instance of the Distraction of this Affairs; that when he saw how

all

all things were going to wreck, as it was impoffible but he fhould fee it, and 'tis plain he
did fee it, that he fhould not long enough before
it came to Extremities, fecure the Navy, Magazines, and Stores of War, in the Hands of his
trufty Servants that would have been fure to
have preferved them for his Ufe, at a Time
when he wanted them.

It cannot be fuppofed, but the Gentry of
England, who generally preferved their Loyalty
for their Royal Mafter, and at laft heartily
fhewed it, were exceedingly difcouraged at
firft, when they faw the Parliament had all the
Means of making War in their own Hands, and
the King was naked and deftitute either of Arms,
or Ammunition, or Money to procure them.

Not but that the King, by extraordinary Application, recovered the Diforder the Want of
thefe things had thrown him into, and fupplied
himfelf with all things needful.

But my Obfervation was this, had his Majefty had the Magazines, Navy, and Forts in his
own Hand, the Gentry, who wanted but the
Profpect of fomething to encourage them, had
come in at firft, and the Parliament being un-
provided, would have been prefently reduced
to Reafon.

But this was it that baulked the Gentry of
Yorkfhire, who went home again, giving the King
good Promifes, but never appeard for him, till
by raifing a good Army in *Shropfhire* and *Wales*,
he marched towards *London*, and they faw there
was a Profpect of their being fupported.

In this Condition the King erected his Standard at *Nottingham*, *Auguft* the 22d 1642, and,
I confefs, I had very melancholy Apprehenfions
of the King's Affairs; for the Appearance to
the

the Royal Standard was but small. The Affront the King had met with at *Hull*, had baulked and difpirited the Northern Gentry, and the King's Affairs looked with a very difmal Afpect. We had Expreffes from *London* of the prodigious Succefs of the Parliament's Levies, how their Men came in fafter than they could entertain them, and that Arms were delivered out to whole Companies lifted together, and the like: And all this while the King had not got together a Thoufand Foot, and had no Arms for them neither. When the King faw this, he immediately difpatches five feveral Meffengers, whereof one went to the Marquefs of *Worcefter* into *Wales*; one went to the Queen, then at *Windfor*; one to the Duke of *Newcaftle*, then Marquefs of *Newcaftle*, into the *North*; one into *Scotland*, and one into *France*, where the Queen foon after arrived to raife Money, and buy Arms, and to get what Affiftance fhe could among her own Friends: Nor was her Majefty idle, for fhe fent over feveral Ships laden with Arms and Ammunition, with a fine Train of Artillery, and a great many very good Officers; and though one of the firft fell into the Hands of the Parliament, with 300 Barrels of Powder and fome Arms, and 150 Gentlemen, yet moft of the Gentlemen found Means, one Way or other, to get to us, and moft of the Ships the Queen freighted arrived; and at laft her Majefty came her felf, and brought an extraordinary Supply, both of Men, Money, Arms, &c. with which fhe joined the King's Forces under the Earl of *Newcaftle* in the *North*. Finding his Majefty thus beftirring himfelf to mufter his Friends together, I ask'd him, if he thought it might not be for his Majefty's Service to let me go among my Friends, and his loyal Subjects,

about

about *Shrewsbury*? Yes, fays the King, fmiling, I intend you fhall, and I defign to go with you my felf. I did not underftand what the King meant then, and did not think it good Manners to enquire; but the next Day I found all things difpofed for a March, and the King on Horfeback by Eight of the Clock; when calling me to him, he told me I fhould go before, and let my Father and all my Friends know, he would be at *Shrewsbury* the *Saturday* following. I left my Equipages, and taking Poft with only one Servant, was at my Father's the next Morning by Break of Day. My Father was not furprized at the News of the King's coming at all; for, it feems, he, together with the loyal Gentry of thofe Parts, had fent particularly to give the King an Invitation to move that Way, which I was not made privy to; with an Account what Encouragement they had there in the Endeavours made for his Intereft. In fhort, the whole Country was entirely for the King, and fuch was the univerfal Joy the People fhewed when the News of his Majefty's coming down was pofitively known, that all Manner of Bufinefs was laid afide, and the whole Body of the People feemed to be refolved upon the War.

As this gave a new Face to the King's Affairs, fo I muft own it filled me with Joy; for I was aftonifhed before, when I confidered what the King and his Friends were like to be expofed to. The News of the Proceedings of the Parliament, and their powerful Preparations were now no more terrible; the King came at the Time appointed, and having lain at my Father's Houfe one Night, entered *Shrewsbury* in the Morning. The Acclamations of the People, the Concourfe of the Nobility and Gentry about his Perfon, son, and the Crouds which now came every Day in to his Standard, were incredible.

The Loyalty of the *English* Gentry was not only worth Notice, but the Power of the Gentry is extraordinary visible in this Matter: The King, in about six Weeks time, which was the most of his Stay at *Shrewsbury*, was supplied with Money, Arms, Ammunition, and a Train of Artillery, and lifted a Body of an Army upwards of 20000 Men.

His Majesty seeing the general Alacrity of his People, immediately issued out Commissions, and form'd Regiments of Horse and Foot; and having some experienced Officers about him, together with about 16 who came from *France*, with a Ship loaded with Arms and some Field-pieces which came very seasonably into the *Severn*; the Men were excercised, regularly disciplined, and quartered, and now we began to look like Soldiers. My Father had raised a Regiment of Horse at his own Charge, and compleated them, and the King gave out Arms to them from the Supplies which I mentioned came from Abroad. Another Party of Horse, all brave stout Fellows, and well mounted, came in from *Lancashire*, and the Earl of *Derby* at the Head of them. The *Welchmen* came in by Droves; and so great was the Concourse of People, that the King began to think of Marching, and gave the Command, as well as the Trust of Regulating the Army, to the brave Earl of *Lindsey*, as General of the Foot. The Parliament General being the Earl of *Essex*, two braver men, or two better Officers, were not in the Kingdom; they had both been old Soldiers, and had served together as Voluntiers, in the *Low Country* Wars, under Prince *Maurice*. They had been Comrades and Companions Abroad,

I   and

and now came to face one another as Enemies
in the Field.

Such was the Expedition ufed by the King
and his Friends, in the Levies of this firft Army,
that notwithftanding the wonderful Expedition
the Parliament made, the King was in the Field
before them; and now the Gentry in other Parts
of the Nation beftirred themfelves, and fiezed
upon, and Garrifoned feveral confiderable Places
for the King. In the North, the Earl of *Newcaftle*
not only Garrifoned the moft confiderable Places,
but even the general Poffeffion of the North
was for the King, excepting *Hull*, and fome few
Places, which the old Lord *Fairfax* had taken
up for the Parliament. On the other Hand,
entire *Cornwall*, and moft of the Weftern Counties
were the King's. The Parliament had their
chief Intereft in the South and Eaftern Part of
England, as *Kent*, *Surry*, and *Suffex*, *Effex*, *Suffolk*,
Norfolk, *Cambridge*, *Bedford*, *Huntington*, *Hertford*,
Buckinghamfhire, and the other midland Counties.
Thefe were called, or fome of them at leaft, the
Affociated Counties, and felt little of the War,
other than the Charges; but the main Support of
the Parliament was the City of *London*. The King
made the Seat of his Court at *Oxford*, which he
caufed to be regularly fortified. The Lord *Say* had
been here, and had Poffeffion of the City for the Enemy, and was debating about fortifying it, but came
to no Refolution, which was a very great Overfight in them; the Situation of the Place, and
the Importance of it, on many Accounts, to the
City of *London*, confidered; and they would have
retrieved this Error afterwards, but then 'twas
too late; for the King made it the Head Quarter, and received great Supplies and Affiftance
from the Wealth of the Colleges, and the Plenty
of

of the neighbouring Country. *Abingdon, Walling-ford, Bafing* and *Reading,* were all Garrifoned and fortified as Outworks to defend this as the Center. And thus all *England* became the Theater of Blood, and War was fpread into every Corner of the Country, though as yet there was no Stroke ftruck. I had no Command in this Army; my Father led his own Regiment, and old as he was, would not leave his royal Mafter, and my elder Brother ftaid at home to fupport the Family. As for me, I rode a Voluntier in the royal Troop of Guards, which may very well deferve the Title of a royal Troop; for it was compófed of young Gentlemen Sons of the Nobility and fome of the prime Gentry of the Nation, and I think not a Perfon of fo mean a Birth or Fortune as my felf. We reckoned in this Troop Two and Thirty Lords, or who came afterwards to be fuch, and Eight and Thirty of younger Sons of the Nobility, five *French* Noblemen, and all the reft Gentlemen of very good Families and Eftates.

And that I may give the due to their perfonal Valour, many of this Troop lived afterwards to have Regiments and Troops under their Command, in the Service of the King; many of them loft their Lives for him, and moft of them their Eftates: Nor did they behave unworthy of themfelves in their firft fhewing their Faces to the Enemy, as fhall be mentioned in its Place.

While the King remained at *Shrewsbury,* his loyal Friends beftirred themfelves in feveral Parts of the Kingdom. *Goring* had fecured *Portf-mouth*; but being young in Matters of War, and not in Time relieved, though the Marquefs of *Hertford* was marching to relieve him, yet he

was

was obliged to quit the Place, and shipped himself for *Holland*, from whence he returned with Relief for the King, and afterwards did very good Service upon all Occasions, and so effectually cleared himself of the Scandal the hasty Surrender of *Portsmouth* had brought upon his Courage.

The chief Power of the King's Forces lay in three Places, in *Cornwall*, in *Yorkshire*, and at *Shrewsbury*: In *Cornwall*, Sir *Ralph Hopton*, afterwards Lord *Hopton*; Sir *Bevil Granvil* and Sir *Nicholas Slamming*, secured all the Country, and afterwards spread themselves over *Devonshire* and *Somersetshire*, took *Exeter* from the Parliament, fortified *Bridgwater*, and *Barnstable*, and beat Sir *William Waller* at the Battle of *Roundway Down*, as I shall touch at more particularly when I come to recite the Part of my own Travels that Way.

In the *North*, the Marquess of *Newcastle* secured all the Country, Garrisoned *York*, *Scarborough*, *Carlisle*, *Newcastle Pomfret*, *Leeds*, and all the considerable Places, and took the Field with a very good Army, though afterwards he proved more unsuccessful than the rest, having the whole Power of a Kingdom at his Back, the *Scots* coming in with an Army to the Assistance of the Parliament; which indeed was the general Turn of the Scale of the War; for had it not been for this *Scots* Army, the King had most certainly reduced the Parliament, at least to good Terms of Peace, in two Years time.

The King was the third Article: His Force at *Shrewsbury* I have noted already ; the Alacrity of the Gentry filled him with Hopes, and all his Army with Vigour, and the 8th of *October* 1642, his Majesty gave Orders to march. The Earl of *Essex* had spent above a Month after his leaving

ving

ing *London* (for he went thence the 9th of *September*) in modelling and drawing together his Forces; his Rendezvous was at St. *Albans*, from whence he marched to *Northampton, Coventry*, and *Warwick*, and leaving Garrisons in them, he comes on to *Worcester*. Being thus advanced, he possesses *Oxford*, as I noted before, *Banbury, Bristol, Gloucester*, and *Worcester*, out of all which Places, except *Gloucester*, we drove him back to *London* in a very little while.

Sir *John Biron* had raised a very good Party of 500 Horse, most Gentlemen, for the King, and had possessed *Oxford*; but on the Approach of the Lord *Say* quitted it, being now but an open Town, and retreated to *Worcester:* From whence, on the Approach of *Essex*'s Army, he retreated to the King. And now all things grew ripe for Action, both Parties having secured their Posts, and settled their Schemes of the War, taken their Posts and Places as their Measures and Opportunities directed, the Field was next in their Eye, and the Soldiers began to enquire when they should fight; for as yet there had been little or no Blood drawn, and 'twas not long before they had enough of it; for I believe I may challenge all the Historians in *Europe* to tell me of any War in the World where, in the Space of four Years, there were so many pitched Battles, Sieges, Fights, and Skirmishes, as in this War; we never encamped or entrenched, never fortified the Avenues to our Posts, or lay fenced with Rivers and Defiles; here was no Leaguers in the Field, as at the Story of *Noremberg*, neither had our Soldiers any Tents, or what they call heavy Baggage. 'Twas the general Maxim of this War, Where is the Enemy? Let us go and fight them: Or, on the other Hand, if the

N   Enemy

Enemy was coming, what was to be done? Why, what fhould be done? Draw out into the Fields, and fight them. I cannot fay 'twas the Prudence of the Parties, and had the King fought lefs he had gained more: And I fhall remark feveral times, when the Eagernefs of Fighting was the worft Counfel, and proved our Lofs. This Benefit however happened in general to the Country, that it made a quick, though a bloody End, of the War, which otherwife had lafted till it might have ruined the whole Nation.

On the 10th of *October* the King's Army was in full March, his Majefty Generaliffimo, the Earl of *Lindfey* General of the Foot, Prince *Rupert* General of the Horfe; and the firft Action in the Field was by Prince *Rupert* and Sir *John Biron.* Sir *John* had brought his Body of 500 Horfe, as I noted already, from *Oxford* to *Worcefter*; the Lord *Say*, with a ftrong Party, being in the Neighbourhood of *Oxford*, and expected in the Town, Collonel *Sandys*, a hot Man, and who had more Courage than Judgment, advances with about 1500 Horfe and Dragoons, with Defign to beat Sir *John Biron* out of *Worcefter*, and take Poft there for the Parliament.

The King had notice that the Earl of *Effex* defigned for *Worcefter*, and Prince *Rupert* was ordered to advance with a Body of Horfe and Dragoons, to face the Enemy, and bring off Sir *John Biron*. This his Majefty did to amufe the Earl of *Effex*, that he might expect him that Way; whereas the King's Defign was to get between the Earl of *Effex's* Army and the City of *London*; and his Majefty's End was doubly anfwered; for he not only drew *Effex* on to *Worcefter*, where he fpent more Time than he needed, but he beat the Party into the Bargain.

I went

I went Voluntier in this Party, and rid in my Father's Regiment; for though we really expected not to fee the Enemy, yet I was tired with lying ftill. We came to *Worcefter* juft as Notice was brought to Sir *John Biron*, that a Party of the Enemy was on their March for *Worcefter*, upon which the Prince immediately confulting what was to be done, refolves to march the next Morning, and fight them.

The Enemy, who lay at *Perfhore*, about eight Miles from *Worcefter*, and, as I believe, had no Notice of our March, came on very confidently in the Morning, and found us fairly drawn up to receive them: I muft confefs this was the blunteft downright Way of making War that ever was feen. The Enemy, who, in all the little Knowledge I had of War ought to have difcovered our Numbers, and guefled by our Pofture what our Defign was, might eafily have informed themfelves, that we intended to attack them, and fo might have fecured the Advantage of a Bridge in their Front; but without any Regard to thefe Methods of Policy, they came on at all Hazards. Upon this Notice, my Father propofed to the Prince, to halt for them, and fuffer ourfelves to be attacked, fince we found them willing to give us the Advantage: The Prince approved of the Advice, fo we halted within View of a Bridge, leaving Space enough on our Front for about half the Number of their Forces to pafs and draw up; and at the Bridge was pofted about 50 Dragoons, with Orders to retire as foon as the Enemy advanced, as if they had been afraid. On the Right of the Road was a Ditch, and a very high Bank behind, where we had placed 300 Dragoons, with Orders to lye flat on their Faces till the Enemy had

paffed

paſſed the Bridge, and to let fly among them
as ſoon as our Trumpets ſounded a Charge. No
Body but Collonel *Sandys* would have been caught
in ſuch a Snare; for he might eaſily have ſeen,
that when he was over the Bridge, there was not
Room enough for him to fight in: But the Lord
of Hoſts was ſo much in their Mouths, *for that was
the Word for that Day,* that they took little heed
how to conduct the Hoſt of the Lord to their
own Advantage.

As we expected, they appeared, beat our Dragoons from the Bridge, and paſſed it : We ſtood
firm in one Line with a Reſerve, and expected a
Charge; but Collonel *Sandys* ſhewing a great deal
more Judgment than we thought he was Maſter of,
extends himſelf to the Left, finding the Ground
too ſtreight, and began to form his Men with
a great deal of Readineſs and Skill; for by this
time he ſaw our Number was greater than he expected : The Prince perceiving it, and foreſeeing
that the Stratagem of the Dragoons would be
fruſtrated by this, immediately charges with
the Horſe, and the Dragoons at the ſame time
ſtanding upon their Feet, poured in their Shot
upon thoſe that were paſſing the Bridge : This
Surprize put them into ſuch Diſorder, that we
had but little Work with them ; for though Collonel *Sandys* with the Troops next him ſuſtained
the Shock very well, and behaved themſelves gallantly enough, yet the Confuſion beginning in
their Reer, thoſe that had not yet paſſed the
Bridge were kept back by the Fire of the Dragoons, and the reſt were eaſily cut in Pieces. Collonel *Sandys* was mortally wounded and taken Priſoner, and the Crowd was ſo great, to get back,
that many puſhed into the Water; and were rather ſmothered than drowned. Some of them who
never

never came into the Fight, were fo frighted, that they never looked behind them, 'till they came to *Perfhore* ; and as we were afterwards informed, the Life-Guards of the General who had quartered in the Town, left it in Diforder enough, expecting us at the Heels of their Men.

If our Bufinefs had been to keep the Parliament Army from coming to *Worcefter*, we had a very good Opportunity to have fecured the Bridge at *Perfhore* ; but our Defign lay another Way, as I have faid, and the King was for drawing *Effex* on to the *Severn*, in hopes to get behind him, which fell out accordingly.

Effex, fpurred by this Affront in the Infancy of their Affairs, advances the next Day, and came to *Parfhore* time enough to be at the Funeral of fome of his Men ; and from thence he advances to *Worcefter*.

We marched back to *Worcefter* extremely pleafed with the good Succefs of our firft Attack ; and our Men were fo flufhed with this little Victory, that it put Vigour into the whole Army. The Enemy loft about 3000 Men, and we carried away near 150 Prifoners, with 500 Horfes, fome Standards and Arms, and among the Prifoners their Collonel, but he died a little after of his Wounds.

Upon the Approach of the Enemy, *Worcefter* was quitted, and the Forces marched back to join the King's Army which lay then at *Bridgnorth*, *Ludlow*, and thereabout. As the King expected, it fell out ; *Effex* found fo much Work at *Worcefter* to fettle Parliament Quarters, and fecure *Briftol*, *Gloucefter*, and *Hereford*, that it gave the King a full Day's March of him ; fo the King having the Start of him, moves towards *London* ; and *Effex*, nettled to be both beaten in Fight, and outdone in Conduct, decamps, and follows the King.

N 3   The

The Parliament, and the *Londoners* too, were in a ftrange Confternation at this Miftake of their General ; and had the King, whofe great Misfortune was always to follow precipitant Advices: Had the King, I fay, pufhed on his firft Defign, which he had formed with very good Reafon, and for which he had been dodging with *Effex* eight or ten Days, *viz.* Of marching directly to *London*, where he had a very great Intereft, and where his Friends were not yet oppreffed and impoverifhed, as they were afterwards, he had turned the Scale of his Affairs: And every Man expected it; for the Members began to fhift for themfelves, Expreffes were fent on the Heels of one another to the Earl of *Effex*, to haften after the King, and if poffible to bring him to a Battle. Some of thefe Letters fell into our Hands, and we might eafily difcover, that the Parliament were in the laft Confufion at the Thoughts of our coming to *London*: Befides this, the City was in a worfe Fright than the Houfe, and the great moving Men began to go out of Town. In fhort, they expected us, and we expected to come, but Providence for our Ruine had otherwife determined it.

Effex, upon News of the King's March, and upon Receipt of the Parliament's Letters, makes long Marches after us, and on the 23d of *October* reaches the Village of *Keynton* in *Warwickfhire*. The King was almoft as far as *Banbury*, and there calls a Council of War. Some of the old Officers that forefaw the Advantage the King had, the Concern the City was in, and the vaft Addition both to the Reputation of his Forces, and the Encreafe of his Intereft, it would be, if the King could gain that Point, urged the King to march on to *London*. Prince *Rupert*, and the frefh Collonells

nells preffed for Fighting, told the King, it diſpirited their Men to march with the Enemy at their Heels; that the Parliament Army was inferiour to him by 6000 Men, and fatigued with haſty Marching; that their Orders were to fight, he had nothing to do, but to poſt himſelf to Advantage, and receive them to their Deſtruction; that the Action near *Worceſter* had let him know how eaſy it was to deal with a raſh Enemy; and that 'twas a Diſhonour for him, whoſe Forces were ſo much ſuperior, to be purſued by his Subjects in Rebellion. Theſe and the like Arguments prevailed with the King to alter his wiſer Meaſures, and reſolve to fight. Nor was this all, when a Reſolution of fighting was taken, that Part of the Advice which they who were for fighting gave, as a Reaſon for their Opinion, was forgot, and inſtead of halting, and poſting our ſelves to Advantage till the Enemy came up, we were ordered to march back, and meet them.

Nay, ſo eager was the Prince for fighting, that when from the Top of *Edgehill*, the Enemy's Army was deſcried in the Bottom between them and the Village of *Keynton*, and that the Enemy had bid us Defiance, by diſcharging three Cannons, we accepted the Challenge, and anſwering with two Shot from our Army, we muſt needs forſake the Advantages of the Hills, which they muſt have mounted under the Command of our Cannon, and march down to them into the Plain. I confeſs, I thought here was a great deal more Gallantry than Diſcretion; for it was plainly taking an Advantage out of our own Hands, and puting it into the Hands of the Enemy. An Enemy that *muſt fight*, may always be fought with to Advantage. My old Heroe, the Glorious *Guſtavus Adolphus*, was

as

as forward to fight as any Man of true Valour mixt with any Policy need to be, or ought to be ; but he ufed to fay, *An Enemy reduced to a Neceffity of Fighting, is half Beaten.*

'Tis true, we were all but young in the War ; the Souldiers hot and forward, and eagerly defired to come to Hands with the Enemy. But I take the more Notice of it here, becaufe the King in this acted againft his own Meafures: For it was the King himfelf had laid the Defign of getting the Start of *Effex,* and marching to *London.* His Friends had invited him thither, and expected, him and fuffered deeply for the Omiffion ; and yet he gave way to thefe hafty Counfels, and fuffered his Judgment to be over-ruled by Majority of Voices; an Error, I fay, the King of *Sweden* was never guilty of: For if all the Officers at a Council of War were of a different Opinion, yet unlefs their Reafons maftered his Judgment, their Votes never altered his Meafures: But this was the Error of our good, but unfortunate Mafter, three times in this War, and particularly in two of the greateft Battles of the time, *viz.* this of *Edgehill,* and that of *Nafeby.*

The Refolution for Fighting being publifhed in the Army, gave an univerfal Joy to the Soldiers, who expreffed an extraordinary Ardour. for Fighting. I remember, my Father talking with me about it, asked me what I Thought of the approaching Battle : I told him, I Thought the King had done very well; for at that time I did not confult the Extent of the Defign, and had a mighty Mind, like other rafh People, to fee it brought to a Day, which made me anfwer my Father as I did: But faid I, Sir, *I Doubt there will be but indifferent Doings on both Sides, between two Armies both made up of frefh Men, that have never feen any Service.*

My

My Father minded little what I fpoke of that; but when I feemed pleafed that the King had refolved to fight, he looked angrily at me, and told me he was forry I could fee no farther into things. I tell you, fays he haftily, *If the King fhould kill, and take Prifoners, this whole Army, Gene- ral and all, the Parliament will have the Victory; for we have loft more by flipping this Opportunity of getting into* London, *than we fhall ever get by ten Battles.* I faw enough of this afterwards to convince me of the Weight of what my Father faid, and fo did the King too; but it was then too late, Advantages flipt in War are never recovered.

We were now in a full March to fight the Earl of *Effex.* It was on *Sunday* Morning the 24th of *October,* 1642, fair Weather over Head, but the Ground very heavy and dirty. As foon as we came to the Top of *Edgehill,* we difcovered their whole Army. They were not drawn up, having had two Miles to march that Morning; but they were very bufy forming their Lines, and po- fting the Regiments as they came up. Some of their Horfe were exceedingly fatigued, having marched 48 Hours together; and had they been fuffered to follow us three or four Days March farther, feveral of their Regiments of Horfe would have been quite ruined, and their Foot would have been rendered unferviceable for the prefent. But we had no Patience.

As foon as our whole Army was come to the Top of the Hill, we were drawn up in Order of Battle: The King's Army made a very fine Ap- pearance; and indeed they were a Body of gal- lant Men as ever appeared in the Field, and as well furnifhed at all Points: The Horfe exceeding well accoutred, being moft of them Gentlemen and Voluntiers; fome whole Regiments ferving
without

without Pay. Their Horfes very good and fit for Service as could be defired. The whole Army were not above 18000 Men, and the Enemy not a 1000 over or under, though we had been told they were not above 12000; but they had been reinforced with 4000 Men from *Northampton*.

The King was with the General, the Earl of *Lindfey*, in the Main Battle; Prince *Rupert* commanded the Right Wing, and the Marquefs of *Hertford*, the Lord *Willoughby*, and feveral other very good Officers, the Left.

The Signal of Battle being given with two Cannot Shot, we marched in Order of Battalia down the Hill, being drawn up in two Lines with Bodies of Referve; the Enemy advanced to meet us much in the fame Form, with this Difference only, that they had placed their Cannon on their Right, and the King had placed ours in the Center, before, or rather between two great Brigades of Foot. Their Cannon began with us firft, and did fome Mifchief among the Dragoons of our left Wing; but our Officers perceiving the Shot took the Men, and miffed the Horfes, ordered all to alight, and every Man leading his Horfe, to advance in the fame Order; and this faved our Men, for moft of the Enemy's Shot flew over their Heads. Our Cannon made a terrible Execution upon their Foot for a Quarter of an Hour, and put them into great Confufion, till the General obliged them to halt, and changed the Pofture of his Front, marching round a fmall rifing Ground by which he avoided the Fury of our Artillery.

By this time the Wings were engaged, the King having given the Signal of Battle, and ordered the Right Wing to fall on. Prince *Rupert* who as is faid, commanded that Wing, fell on with fuch

Fury,

Fury, and pushed the Left Wing of the Parliament Army so effectually, that in a Moment he filled all with Terror and Confusion: Comissary General *Ramsey*, a Scochman, a Low Country Soldier, and an experienced Officer, commanded their Left Wing; and though he did all that an expert Soldier, and a brave Commander could do, yet 'twas to no Purpose; his lines were immediately broken, and all overwhelmed in a trice: Two Regiments of Foot, whether as Part of the Left Wing, or on the Left of the Main Body, I know not, were disordered by their own Horse, and rather trampled to Death by the Horses, than beaten by our Men; but they were so entirely broken and disordered, that I do not remember that ever they made one Volley upon our Men; for their own Horse running away, and falling foul on these Foot, were so vigorously followed by our Men, that the Foot never had a Moment to rally, or look behind them. The Point of the left Wing of Horse were not so soon broken as the rest, and three Regiments of them stood firm for some Time: The dexterous Officers of the other Regiments taking the Opportunity, rallied a great many of their scattered Men behind them, and pieced in some Troops with those Regiments; but after two or three Charges, which a Brigade of our second Line following the Prince, made upon them, they also were broken with the rest.

I remember, that at the great Battle of *Leipsick*, the Right Wing of the *Imperialists* having fallen in upon the *Saxons* with like Fury to this, bore down all before them, and beat the *Saxons* quite out of the Field; upon which the Soldiers cried, *Victoria, Let us follow*. *No, no*, said the old General *Tilly*, *let them go, but let us beat the*

Swedes

Swedes *too, and then all's our own.* Had Prince
Rupert taken this Method, and inftead of following the Fugitives, who were difperfed fo
effectually, that two Regiments would have
fecured them from rallying; I fay, had he fallen in upon the Foot, or wheeled to the Left,
and fallen in upon the Rear of the Enemy's Right
Wing of Horfe, or returned to the Affiftance of the
Left Wing of our Horfe, we had gained the moft
abfolute and compleat Victory that could be; nor
had 1000 Men of the Enemy's Army got off: But
this Prince, who was full of Fire, and pleafed
to fee the Rout of the Enemy, purfued them
quite to the Town of *Keynton,* where indeed he
killed Abundance of their Men, *and fome Time alfo was loft in plundering the Baggage:* But in the
mean Time, the Glory and Advantage of the Day
was loft to the King; for the right Wing of the
Parliament Horfe could not be fo broken. Sir
William Balfour made a defperate Charge upon
the Point of the King's Left; and had it not been
for two Regiments of Dragoons who were planted in the Referve, had routed the whole Wing;
for he broke through the firft Line, and ftaggered the fecond, who advanced to their Affiftance, but was fo warmly received by thofe
Dragoons, who came feafonably in, and gave their
firft Fire on Horfeback, that his Fury was checked, and having loft a great many Men, was forced
to wheel about to his own Men; and had the
King had but three Regiments of Horfe at hand,
to have charged him, he had been routed. The reft
of this Wing kept their Ground, and received
the firft Fury of the Enemy with great Firm-
nefs; after which, advancing in their Turn, they
were once Mafters of the Earl of *Effex's* Cannon.
And here we loft another Advantage; for if any

Foot had been at hand to fupport thefe Horfe, they had carried off the Cannon, or turned it upon the main Battle of the Enemy's Foot ; but the Foot were otherwife engaged. The Horfe on this Side fought with great Obftinacy, and Variety of Succefs a great while. Sir *Philip Stapylton*, who commanded the Guards of the Earl of *Effex*, being engaged with a Party of our *Shrewsbury* Cavaliers, as we called them, was once in a fair way to have been cut off by a Brigade of our Foot, who being advanced to fall on upon the Parliament's main Body, flanked Sir *Philip's* Horfe in their way, and facing to the Left, fo furioufly charged him with their Pikes, that he was obliged to retire in great Diforder, and with the Lofs of a great many Men and Horfes.

All this while the Foot on both Sides were defperately engaged, and coming clofe up to the Teeth of one another with the clubbed Mufquet and Pufh of Pike, fought with great Refolution, and a terrible Slaughter on both Sides, giving no Quarter for a great while ; and they continued to do thus, till, as if they were tired, and out of Wind, either Party feemed willing enough to leave off, and take Breath. Thofe which fuffered moft were that Brigade which had charged Sir *William Stapylton's* Horfe, who being bravely engaged in the Front which the Enemy's Foot, were, on the fudden, charged again in Front and Flank, by Sir *William Balfour's* Horfe, and difordered, after a very defperate Defence. Here the King's Standard was taken, the Standard-bearer, Sir *Edward Varney*, being killed ; but it was refcued again by Captain *Smith*, and brought to the King the fame Night, for which the King Knighted the Captain.

This

This Brigade of Foot had fought all the Day, and had not been broken at laft, if any Horfe had been at Hand to fupport them: The Field began to be now clear, both Armies ftood, as it were, gazing at one another, only the King, having rallied his Foot, feemed inclined to renew the Charge, and began to cannonade them, which they could not return, moft of their Cannon being nailed while they were in our Poffeffi- on, and all the Cannoniers killed or fled, and our Gunners did Execution upon Sir *William Bal- four*'s Troops for a good while.

My Father's Regiment being in the Right with the Prince, I faw little of the Fight, but the Rout of the Enemy's Left, and we had as full a Victory there as we could defire, but fpent too much Time in it; we killed about 2000 Men in that Part of the Action, and having totally difperfed them, and plundred their Baggage, be- gan to think of our Fellows when 'twas too late to help them. We returned however victorious to the King, juft as the Battle was over; the King asked the Prince what News? He told him he could give his Majefty a good Account of the Enemy's Horfe; *ay by G---d, fays a Gentleman that ftood by me, and of their Carts too.* That word was fpoken with fuch a Senfe of the Misfortune, and made fuch an Impreffion in the whole Army, that it occa- fioned fome ill Blood afterwards among us; and but that the King took up the Bufinefs, it had been of ill Confequence; for fome Perfon who had heard the Gentleman fpeak it, informed the Prince who it was, and the Prince refenting it, fpoke fomething about it in the hearing of the Party when the King was prefent: The Gentle- man not at all furprized, told his Highnefs open- ly, he had faid the Words; and though he owned

I   he

he had no Difrefpect for his Highnefs, yet he
could not but fay, if it had not been fo, the
Enemy's Army had been better beaten. The
Prince replied fomething very difobliging; upon
which the Gentleman came up to the King, and
kneeling, humbly befought his Maiefty to accept
of his Commiffion, and to give him leave to tell
the Prince, that whenever his Highnefs pleafed,
he was ready to give him Satisfaction. The Prince
was exceedingly provoked, and as he was very
paffionate, began to talk very odly, and without
all Government of himfelf: The Gentleman, as
bold as he, but much calmer, preferved his Temper, but maintained his Quarrel; and the King
was fo concerned, that he was very much out of
Humour with the Prince about it. However,
his Majefty upon Confideration, foon ended the
Difpute, by laying his Commands on them both
to fpeak no more of it for that Day; and refufing the Comiffion from the Collonel, for he was
no lefs, fent for them both next Morning in private, and made them Friends again.

But to return to our Story, we came back to
the King timely enough to put the Earl of *Effex's*
Men out of all Humour of renewing the Fight;
and as I obferved before, both Parties ftood gazing at one another, and our Cannon playing upon
them, obliged Sir *William Balfour's* Horfe to
wheel off in fome Diforder, but they returned us
none again; which, as we afterwards underftood,
was, as I faid before, for want of both Powder
and Gunners; for the Cannoniers and Firemen
were killed, or had quitted their Train in the
Fight, when our Horfe had Poffeffion of their
Artillery; and as they had fpiked up fome of the
Cannon, fo they had carryed away 15 Carriages
of Powder.

Night

Night coming on, ended all Difcourfe of more fighting; and the King drew off and marched towards the Hills. . I know no other Token of Victory which the Enemy had, than their lying in the Field of Battle all Night, which *they did* for no other Reafon, than that having loft their Baggage and Provifions, they had no where to go; and which we *did not*, becaufe we had good Quarters at Hand.

The Number of Prifoners, and of the flain, were not very unequal; the Enemy loft more Men, we moft of Quality. Six Thoufand Men on both Sides were killed on the Spot, whereof, when our Rolls were examined, we miffed 2500. We loft our brave General the old Earl of *Lindfey*, who was wounded and taken Prifoner, and died of his Wounds; Sir *Edward Stradling*, Collonel *Lundf-ford*, Prifoners; and Sir *Edward Varney*, and a great many Gentlemen of Quality flain. On the other Hand, we carried off Collonel *Effex*, Collonel *Ramfey*, and the Lord St. *John*, who alfo died of his Wounds; we took five Ammunition Waggons, full of Powder, and brought off about 500 Horfe in the Defeat of the Left Wing, with 18 Standards and Colours, and loft 17.

The Slaughter of the Left Wing was fo great, and the Flight fo effectual, that feveral of the Officers rid clear away, coafting round, and got to *London*, where they reported, that the Parliament Army was entirely defeated, all loft, killed, or taken, as if none but them were left alive to carry the News. This filled them with Confternation for a while; but when other Meffengers followed, all was reftored to Quiet again, and the Parliament cried up their Victory, and fufficiently mocked God and their General, with their publick Thanks for it. Truly, as the Fight

was

was a Deliverance to them, they were in the right to give Thanks for it; but as to its being a Victory, neither Side had much to boaft of, and they lefs a great deal than we had.

I got no Hurt in this Fight; and indeed we of the Right Wing had but little fighting; I think I difcharged my Piftols but once, and my Carabin twice, for we had more Fatigue than Fight; the Enemy fled, and we had little to do but to follow and kill thofe we could overtake. I fpoiled a good Horfe, and got a better from the Enemy in his Room, and came home weary enough. My Father loft his Horfe, and in the Fall was bruifed in his Thigh by another Horfe, treading on him, which difabled him for fome Time, and, at his Requeft, by his Majefty's Confent; I commanded the Regiment in his Abfence.

The Enemy received a Recruit of 4000 Men the next Morning; if they had not, I believe they had gone back towards *Worcefter*; but, encouraged by that Reinforcement, they called a Council of War, and had a long Debate whether they could attack us again? but notwithftanding their great Victory, they durft not attempt it, though this Addition of Strength made them fuperiour to us by 3000 Men.

The King indeed expected, that when thefe Troops joined them they would advance, and we were preparing to receive them at a Village called *Aino*, where the Head Quarter continued three or four Days; and had they really efteemed the firft Day's Work a Victory, as they called it, they would have done it, but they thought not good to venture, but march away to *Warwick*, and from thence to *Coventry*. The King, to urge them to venture upon him, and come to a fecond Battle, fits down before *Banbury*, and takes

O   both

both Town and Caftle, and two entire Regiments of Foot, and one Troop of Horfe, quit the Parliament Service, and take up their Arms for the King. This was done almoſt before their Faces, which was a better Proof of a Victory on our Side, than any they could pretend to. From *Banbury* we marched to *Oxford*; and now all Men faw the Parliament had made a great Miſtake, *for they were not always in the right any more than we,* to leave *Oxford* without a Garrifon. The King caufed new regular Works to be drawn round it, and feven royal Baſtions with Ravelins and and Out-works, a double Ditch, Counterfcarp and Covered Way ; all which added to the Advantage of its Situation, made it a formidable Place, and from this Time it became our Place of Arms, and the Center of Affairs on the King's Side.

If the Parliament had the Honour of the Field, the King reaped the Fruits of the Victory ; for all this Part of the Country fubmitted to him : *Effex's* Army made the beſt of their Way to *London,* and were but in an ill Condition when they came there, efpecially their Horfe.

The Parliament, fenfible of this, and receiving daily Accounts of the Progrefs we made, began to cool a little in their Temper, abated of their firſt Rage, and voted an Addrefs for Peace; and fent to the King, to let him know they were defirous to prevent the Effufion of more Blood, and to bring things to an Accommodation, or, as they called it, a *Right Underſtanding.*

I was now, by the King's particular Favour, fummoned to the Councils of War, my Father continuing abfent and ill; and now I began to think of the real Grounds, and which was more, of the fatal Iffue of this War. I fay, I now began

gan it; for I cannot fay that I ever rightly ſta-
ted Matters in my own Mind before, though I
had been enough uſed to Blood, and to ſee the Deſtruction of People, ſacking of Towns, and plundering the Country; yet 'twas in *Germany*, and
among Strangers; but I found a ſtrange ſecret
and unaccountable Sadneſs upon my Spirits to ſee
this acting in my own native Country. It grieved me to the Heart, even in the Rout of our
Enemies, to ſee the Slaughter of them; and even
in the Fight, to hear a Man cry for Quarter in
Engliſh, moved me to a Compaſſion which I had
never been uſed to; nay, ſometimes it looked to
me as if ſome of my own Men had been beaten; and
when I heard a Soldier cry, *O God, I am ſhot*, I
looked behind me to ſee which of my own Troop
was fallen. Here I ſaw my ſelf at the cutting
of the Throats of my Friends; and indeed ſome
of my near Relations. My old Comerades and
Fellow-ſoldiers in *Germany* were ſome *with us*, ſome
againſt us, as their Opinions happened to differ
in Religion. For my part, I confeſs I had not
much Religion in me, at that time; but I
thought Religion rightly practiſed on both Sides
would have made us all better Friends; and therefore ſometimes I began to think, that both the
Biſhops of our Side, and the Preachers on theirs,
made Religion rather *the Pretence* than *the Cauſe*
of the War; and from thoſe Thoughts I vigorouſly argued it at the Council of War againſt
marching to *Brentford*, while the Addreſs for a
Treaty of Peace from the Parliament was in Hand;
for I was for taking the Parliament by the Handle
which they had given us, and entring into a
Negotiation with the Advantage of its being
at their own Requeſt.

I thought the King had now in his Hands an Opportunity to make an honourable Peace; for this Battle at *Edgehill*, as much as they boafted of the Victory to hearten up their Friends, had forely weakened their Army, and difcouraged their Party too, which in Effect was worfe as to their Army. The Horfe were particularly in an ill Cafe, and the Foot greatly diminifhed; and the Remainder very fickly : But befides this, the Parliament, were greatly alarmed at the Progrefs we made afterward ; and ftill fearing the King's furprizing them, had fent for the Earl of *Effex* to *London*, to defend them; by which the Country was as it were, deferted and abandoned, and left to be plundered ; our Parties over-run all Places at Pleafure. All this while I confidered, that whatever the Soldiers of Fortune meant by the War, our Defires were to fupprefs the exorbitant Power of a Party, to eftablifh our King in his juft and legal Rights; but not with a Defign to deftroy the Conftitution of Government, and the Being of Parliament; and therefore I thought now was the Time for Peace, and their were a great many worthy Gentlemen in the Army of my Mind ; and, had our Mafter had Ears to hear us, the War might have had an End here.

This Addrefs for Peace was received by the King at *Maidenhead*, whither this Army was now advanced, and his Majefty returned Anfwer by Sir *Peter Killegrew*, that he defired nothing more, and would not be wanting on his Part. Upon this the Parliament name Commiffioners, and his Majefty excepting againft Sir *John Evelyn*, they left him out, and fent others ; and defired the King to appoint his Refidence near *London*, where the Commiffioners might wait upon

upon him. Accordingly the King appointed
Windfor for the Place of Treaty, and defired the
Treaty might be haftened. And thus all things
looked with a favourable Afpect, when one un-
lucky Action knocked it all on the Head, and
filled both Parties with more implacable Ani-
mofities than they had before, and all Hopes of
Peace vanifhed.

During this Progrefs of the King's Armies, we
were always abroad with the Horfe ravaging the
Country, and plundering the Roundheads. Prince
Rupert, a moft active vigilant Party-man, and I
muft own, fitter for fuch than for a General, was
never lying ftill, and I feldom ftayed behind; for
our Regiment being very well mounted, he
would always fend for us, if he had any extraordinary Defign in Hand.

One time in particular he had a Defign upon
Alisbury, the Capital of *Buckinghamfhire*; indeed
our View at firft was rather to beat the Enemy
out of Town and demolifh their Works, and perhaps raife fome Contributions on the rich Country round it, than to Garrifon the Place, and keep
it; for we wanted no more Garrifons, being
Mafters of the Field.

The Prince had 2500 Horfe with him in
this Expedition, but no Foot; the Town had
fome Foot raifed in the Country by Mr. *Hambden*, and two Regiments of the Country Militia,
whom we made light of, but we found they ftood
to their Tackle better than *well enough*. We
came very early to the Town, and thought they
had no Notice of us; but fome falfe Brother had
given them the Alarm and we found them all in
Arms, the Hedges without the Town lined with
Mufqueteers, on that Side in particular where
they expected us, and the two Regiments of Foot

drawn

drawn up in View to fupport them, with fome
Horfe in the Rear of all.

The Prince willing however to do fome thing,
caufed fome of his Horfe to alight, and ferve as
Dragoons; and having broken a Way into the
Enclofures, the Horfe beat the Foot from behind
the Hedges, while the reft who were alighted
charged them in the Lane which leads to the
Town. Here they had caft up fome Works, and
fired from their Lines very regularly, confidering
them as Militia only, the Governour encouraging
them by his Example; fo that finding without
fome Foot there would be no good to be done, we
gave it over, and drew off; and fo *Alisbury* fcaped a
fcouring for that Time.

I cannot deny but thefe flying Parties of Horfe
committed great Spoil among the Country People; and fometimes the Prince gave a Liberty to
fome Cruelties which were not at all for the
King's Intereft; becaufe it being ftill upon our
own Country, and the King's own Subjects,
whom, in all his Declarations, he protefted to be
careful of. It feemed to contradict all thofe pro-
teftations and Declarations, and ferved to aggra-
vate and exafperate the Common People; and
the King's Enemies made all the Advantages of
it that was poffible, by crying out of twice as
many Extravagancies as were committed.

'Tis true, the King, who naturally abhorred
fuch things, could not reftrain his Men, no nor
his Generals, fo abfolutely as he would have
done. The War, on his Side, was very much
a la Voluntier; many Gentlemen ferved him at
their own Charge, and fome paid whole Regiments themfelves: Sometimes alfo the King's
Affairs were ftrait er than ordinary, and his
Men were not very well paid, and this obliged
him

him to wink at their Excurfions upon the Country, though he did not approve of them; and
yet I muft own, that in thofe Parts of *England*
were the War was hotteft, there never was feen
that Ruin and Depopulation, Murthers, Ravifh-
ments, and Barbarities, which I have feen even
among Proteftant Armies abroad in *Germany*, and
other foreign Parts of the World. And if the
Parliament People had feen thofe things abroad,
as I had, they would not have complained.

The moft I have feen was plundering the
Towns for Provifions, drinking up their Beer,
and turning our Horfes into their Fields, or
Stacks of Corn; and fometimes the Soldiers would
be a little rude with the Wenches; but alas!
what was this to Count *Tilly*'s Ravages in *Saxony?*
Or what was our taking of *Leicefter* by Storm,
where they cried out of our Barbarities, to the
facking of *New Brandenburgh*, or the taking of
Magdeburgh? In *Leicefter*, of 7 or 8000 People in
the Town, 300 were killed; in *Magdeburgh*, of
25000 fcarce 2700 were left, and the whole
Town burnt to Afhes. I my felf, have feen 17
or 18 Villages on Fire in a Day, and the People
driven away from their Dwellings, like Herds of
Cattle; the Men murthered, the Women ftript;
and, 7 or 800 of them together, after they had
fuffered all the Indignities and Abufes of the
Soldiers, driven ftark naked in the Winter through
the great Towns, to feek Shelter and Relief
from the Charity of their Enemies. I do not
inftance thefe greater Barbarities to juftify leffer
Actions, which are neverthelefs irregular; but,
I do fay, that Circumftances confidered, this War
was managed with as much Humanity on both
Sides as could be expected, efpecially alfo confidering the Animofity of Parties.

O 4   Bu

But to Return to the Prince, he had not always the fame Succefs in thefe Enterprizes, for fometimes we came fhort home. And I cannot omit one pleafant Adventure which happened to a Party of ours in one of thefe Excurfions into *Buckinghamfhire*. The Major of our Regiment was foundly beaten by a Party which, as I may fay was led by a Woman; and, if I had not refcued him, I know not but he had been taken Prifoner by a Woman. It feems our Men had befieged fome fortified Houfe about *Oxfordfhire*, towards *Tame*, and the Houfe being defended by the Lady in her Husband's Abfence, fhe had yielded the Houfe upon a Capitulation; one of the Articles of which was, to march out with all her Servants, Soldiers, and Goods, and to be convey'd to *Tame*: Whether fhe thought to have gone no farther, or that fhe reckoned her felf fafe there, I know not; but my Major, with two Troops of Horfe meets with this Lady and her Party, about five Miles from *Tame*, as we were coming back from our defeated Attack of *Alisbury*. We reckoned our felves in an Enemy's Country, and had lived a little at large, or at Difcretion, *as 'tis called abroad*; and thefe two Troops with the Major, were returning to our Detachment from a little Village, where, at a Farmer's Houfe, they had met with fome Liquor, and truly fome of his Men were fo drunk they could but juft fit upon their Horfes. The Major himfelf was not much better, and the whole Body were but in a forry Condition to fight. Upon the Road they meet this Party; the Lady having no Defign of Fighting, and being as fhe thought under the Protection of the Articles, founds a Parley, and defired to fpeak with the Officer. The Major *as drunk as he was*, could tell her, that by the Articles fhe

was

was to be affured no farther than *Tame*, and being now five Miles beyond it, fhe was a fair
Enemy, and therefore demanded to render themfelves Prifoners. The Lady feemed furprized,
but being fenfible fhe was in the wrong, offered
to compound for her Goods, and would have
given him 300 l. and, I think, feven or eight
Horfes: The Major would certainly have taken
it, if he had not been drunk; but he refufed it,
and gave threatning Words to her, bluftering in
Language which he thought proper to fright a
Woman, *viz.* that he would cut them all to
Pieces, and give no Quarter, *and the like.* The
Lady, who had been more ufed to the Smell of
Powder than he imagined, called fome of her
Servants to her, and confulting with them what
to do, they all unanimoufly encouraged her to
let them fight; told her, it was plain that the
Commander was drunk, and all that were with
him were rather worfe than he, and hardly
able to fit their Horfes; and that therefore one
bold Charge would put them all into Confufion.
In a Word, fhe confented, and, as fhe was a Woman, they defired her to fecure her felf among
the Waggons; but fhe refufed, and told them
bravely, fhe would take her Fate with them.
In fhort, fhe boldly bad my Major Defiance, and
that he might do his worft, fince fhe had offered him fair, and he had refufed it; her
Mind was altered now, and fhe would give him
nothing, and bad his Officer that parlied longer
with her, be gone; fo the Parly ended. After
this, fhe gave him fair Leave to go back to his Men;
but before he could tell his Tale to them, fhe was
at his Heels, with all her Men, and gave him
fuch a home Charge as put his Men into Diforder; and, being too drunk to rally, they were
knocked

knocked down before they knew what to do
with themfelves; and, in a few Minutes more,
they took to a plain Flight. But what was
ftill worfe, the Men, being fome of them very
drunk, when they came to run for their Lives,
fell over one another, and tumbled over their
Horfes, and made fuch Work, that a Troop of
Women might have beaten them all. In this
Pickle, with the Enemy at his Heels, I came
in with him, hearing the Noife; when I appeared, the Purfuers retreated, and, feeing what
a Condition my People were in, and not knowing the Strength of the Enemy, I contented my
felf with bringing them off without purfuing
the other; nor could I ever hear pofitively
who this Female Captain was. We loft 17 or
18 of our Men, and about 30 Horfes; but when
the Particulars of the Story were told us, our
Major was fo laughed at by the whole Army,
and laughed at every where, that he was a-
fhamed to fhew himfelf for a Week or a Fortnight after.

But, to return to the King; his Majéfty, as
I obferved, was at *Maidenhead* addreffed by the
Parliament for Peace, and *Windfor* being appointed for the Place of Treaty, the Van of his Army lay at *Colebrook*. In the mean time, whether
it were true, or only a Pretence, but it was reported the Parliament General had fent a Body
of his Troops, with a Train of Artillery, to *Ham-
merfmith*, in order to fall upon fome part of our
Army, or to take fome advanced Poft, which was
to the Prejudice of our Men; whereupon the
King ordered the Army to march, and, by the
Favour of a thick Mift, came within half a Mile
of *Brentford* before he was difcovered. There
were two Regiments of Foot, and about 600
Horfe

Horfe in the Town, of the Enemy's beft Troops;
thefe taking the Alarm, pofted themfelves on
the Bridge at the Weft End of the Town. The
King attacked them with a felect Detachment
of his beft Infantry, and they defended themfelves with incredible Obftinacy. I muft own,
I never faw *raw Men*, for they could not have
been in Arms above four Months, act like them
in my Life. *In fhort*, there was no forcing thefe
Men; for, though two whole Brigades of our
Foot, backed by our Horfe, made five feveral
Attacks upon them, they could not break them,
and we loft a great many brave Men in that
Action. At laft, feeing the Obftinacy of thefe
Men, a Party of Horfe was ordered to go round
from *Ofterly*; and, entering the Town on the
North Side, where, though the Horfe made
fome Refiftance, it was not confiderable, the
Town was prefently taken. I led my Regiment
through an Enclofure, and came into the Town
nearer to the Bridge than the reft, by which
Means I got firft into the Town; but I had
this Lofs by my Expedition, that the Foot
charged me before the Body was come up, and
pouring in their Shot very furioufly, my Men
were but in an ill Cafe, and would not have
ftood much longer, if the reft of the Horfe coming up the Lane had not found them other
Employment. When the Horfe were thus entered, they immediately difperfed the Enemy's
Horfe, who fled away towards *London;* and falling in Sword in Hand upon the Rear of the
Foot, who were engaged at the Bridge, they
were all cut in Pieces, except about 200, who
fcorning to ask Quarter, defperately threw themfelves into the River of *Thames*, where they were
moft of them drowned.

The

The Parliament, and their Party, made a great
Outcry at this Attempt; that it was bafe and
treacherous while in a Treaty of Peace; and
that the King, having amufed them with hearken-
ing to a Treaty, defigned to have feized upon
their Train of Artillery firft, and, after that, to
have furprized both the City of *London* and the
Parliament. And I have obferved fince, that
our Hiftorians note this Action as contrary to
the Laws of Honour and Treaties; though as
there was no Ceffation of Arms agreed on, nothing is more contrary to the Laws of War
than to fuggeft it.

That it was a very unhappy thing to the
King and whole Nation, as it broke off the
Hopes of Peace, and was the Occafion of bringing the *Scots* Army in upon us, I readily acknowledge; but that there was any thing difhonourable in it, I cannot allow : For though the Parliament had addreffed to the King for Peace,
and fuch Steps were taken in it, as before; yet,
as I have faid, there was no Propofals made on
either Side for a Ceffation of Arms; and all the
World muft allow, that in fuch Cafes the War
goes on in the Field, while the Peace goes on
in the Cabinet. And if the War goes on, admit the King had defigned to furprize the City
or Parliament, or all of them, it had been no
more than the Cuftom of War allows, and what
they would have done by him, if they could.
The Treaty of *Weftphalia*, or Peace of *Munfter*,
which ended the bloody Wars of *Germany*, was
a Precedent for this. That Treaty was actually
negotiating feven Years, and yet the War went
on with all the Vigour and Rancour imaginable,
even to the laft: Nay, the very Time after the
Conclufion of it, but before the News could be
brought

brought to the Army, did he that was afterwards King of *Sweden, Carolus Guſtavus,* take the City of *Prague,* by Surprize, and therein an ineſtimáble Booty. Beſides, all the Wars of *Europe* are full of Examples of this Kind; and therefore I cannot ſee any Reaſon to blame the King for this Aſtion as to the Fairneſs of it. Indeed as to the Policy of it, I can ſay little; but the Caſe was this, the King had a gallant Army, fluſhed with Succeſs, and things hitherto had gone on very proſpe-rouſly, both with his own Army and elſewhere; he had above 35000 Men in his own Army, including his Garriſons left at *Banbury, Shrewsbury, Worceſter, Oxford, Wallingford, Abbingdon, Reading,* and Places adjacent. On the other Hand, the Parliament Army came back to *London* in but a very * ſorry Condition; for what with their Loſs *in their Viſtory, as they called it,* at Edgehill, their Sickneſs, and a haſty March to *London,* they were very much diminiſhed; though at *London* they ſoon recruited them again. And this Pro-ſperity of the King's Affairs might encourage him to ſtrike this Blow, thinking to bring the Parliament to the better Terms, by the Appre-henſions of the ſuperior Strength of the King's Forces.

But *however it was,* the Succeſs did not equal-ly anſwer the King's Expeſtation; the vigorous Defence the Troops poſted at *Brentford* made as above, gave the Earl of *Eſſex* Opportunity, with extraordinary Application, to draw his Forces out to *Turnham-Green;* and the exceeding Alacri-

---

* Note, General *Ludlow,* in his Memoirs, p. 52. ſays, their Men returned from *Warwick* to *London,* not like Men who had obtained a Viſtory, but like Men that had been beaten.

ty of the Enemy was fuch, that their whole
Army appeared with them, making together an
Army of 24000 Men, drawn up in View of our
Forces, by 8 o' Clock the next Morning. The
City Regiments were placed between the regular
Troops, and all together offered us Battle, but
we were not in a Condition to accept it. The
King indeed was fometimes of the Mind to charge
them, and once or twice ordered Parties to ad-
vance to begin to skirmifh; but upon better
Advice, altered his Mind; and indeed it was the
wifeft Counfel to defer the fighting at that Time.
The Parliament Generals were as unfixed in their
Refolutions on the other Side, as the King: Sometimes they fent out Parties, and then called them
back again. One ftrong Party, of near 3000
Men marched off towards *Acton*, with Orders
to amufe us on that Side, but were counter-
manded. Indeed I was of the Opinion, we might
have ventured the Battle; for though the Parliament's Army were more numerous, yet the City
Trained-Bands, which made up 4000 of their
Foot, were not much efteemed, and the King was
a great deal ftronger in Horfe than they; but
the main Reafon that hindred the Engagement,
was want of Ammunition, which the King having duly weighed, he caufed the Carriages and
Cannon to draw off firft, and then the Foot, the
Horfe continuing to face the Enemy till all was
clear gone, and then we drew off too, and marched to *Kingfton*, and the next Day to *Reading*.
Now the King faw his Miftake, in not continuing his March for *London*, inftead of Facing
about to fight the Enemy at *Edgehill*. And all
the Honour we had gained in fo many fuccefsful
Enterprizes lay buried in this fhameful Retreat
from an Army of Citizens Wives: For, truly
that

that Appearance at *Turnham-Green* was gay, but not great. There was as many Lookers on as Actors; the Crouds of Ladies, 'Prentices and Mob was so great, that when the Parties of our Army advanced, and, as they thought, to Charge, the Coaches, Horsemen, and Croud, that cluttered away, to be out of Harm's way, looked little better than a Rout: And I was perswaded a good home Charge from our Horse would have sent their whole Army after them; but so it was, that this Croud of an Army was to triumph over us, and they did it; for all the Kingdom was carefully informed how their dreadful Looks had frightened us away.

Upon our Retreat, the Parliament resent this Attack, which they called treacherous, and vote no Accommodation; but they considered of it afterwards, and sent six Commissioners to the King with Propositions; but the Change of the Scene of Action changed the Terms of Peace; and now they made Terms like Conquerors, petition him to desert his Army, and return to the Parliament, and the like. Had his Majesty, at the Head of his Army, with the full Reputation they had before, and in the Ebb of their Affairs, rested at *Windsor*, and commenced a Treaty, they had certainly made more reasonable Proposals; but now the Scabbard seemed to be thrown away on both Sides.

The rest of the Winter was spent in strengthening Parties, and Places also in fruitless Treaties of Peace, Messages, Remonstrances, and Paper War on both Sides, and no Action remarkable happened any where that I remember: Yet the King gained Ground every where, and his Forces in the *North* encreased under the Earl of *Newcastle*; also my Lord *Goring*, then only called

I Collonel

Collonel *Goring*, arrived from *Holland*, bringing
three Ships loaden with Arms and Ammunition;
and Notice, that the Queen was following with
more. *Goring* brought 4000 Barrels of Gunpowder, and 20000 ſmall Arms ; all which came
very ſeaſonably, for the King was in great want
of them, eſpecally the Powder. Upon this Recruit the Earl of *Newcaſtle* draws down to *York*,
and being above 16000 ſtrong, made Sir *Thomas
Fairfax* give Ground, and retreat to *Hull*.

Whoever lay ſtill, Prince *Rupert* was always
abroad, and I choſe to go out with his High-
neſs as often as I had Opportunity ; for hitherto
he was always ſuccesful. About this Time the
Prince, being at *Oxford*, I gave him Intelligence
of a Party of the Enemy who lived a little at
large, too much for good Soldiers, about *Cirenceſter :* The Prince glad of the News, reſolved to
attack them, and though it was a wet Seaſon,
and the Ways exceeding bad, being in *February*,
yet we marched all Night in the Dark, which
occaſioned the Loſs of ſome Horſes and Men too,
in Sloughs and Holes, which the Darkneſs of the
Night had ſuffered them to fall into. We were
a very ſtrong Party, being about 3000 Horſe and
Dragoons, and coming to *Cirenceſter* very early
in the Morning, to our great Satisfaction the Enemy were perfectly ſurprized, not having the leaſt
Notice of our March, which anſwered our End
more Ways than one. However, the Earl of
Stamford's Regiment made ſome Reſiſtance; but
the Town having no Works to defend it, ſaving
a ſlight Breaſt-Work at the Entrance of the
Road, with a Turn-pike, our Dragoons alighted,
and forcing their Way over the Bellies of *Stamford's* Foot, they beat them from their Defence,
and followed them at their Heels into the Town.

Stamford's

Stamford's Regiment was entirely cut in Pieces, and several others, to the Number of about 800 Men, and the Town entered without any other Refiftance. We took 1200 Prifoners, 3000 Arms, and the County Magazin, which at that was confiderable; for there was about 120 Barrels of Powder, and all things in Proportion.

I received the firft Hurt I got in this War, at this Aftion; for having followed the Dragoons, and brought my Regiment within the Barricado which they had gained, a Mufquet Bullet ftruck my Horfe juft in the Head; and that fo effectually, that he fell down as dead as a Stone, all at once. The Fall plunged me into a Puddle of Water, and daubed me; and my Man having brought me another Horfe, and cleaned me a little, I was juft getting up, when another Bullet ftrook me on my left Hand, which I had juft clapt on the Horfe's Mane, to lift my felf into the Saddle. The Blow broke one of my Fingers, and bruifed my Hand very much, and it proved a very painful Hurt to me. For the prefent I did not much concern my felf about it, but made my Man tye it up clofe in my Handkerchief, and led up my Men to the Market Place, where we had a very fmart Brufh with fome Mufqueteers who were pofted in the Church-yard; but our Dragoons foon beat them out there, and the whole Town was then our own. We made no Stay here, but marched back with all our Booty to *Oxford*, for we knew the Enemy were very ftrong at *Gloucefter*, and that way.

Much about the fame Time, the Earl of *Northampton*, with a ftrong Party, fet upon *Litchfield*, and took the Town, but could not take the Clofe; but they beat a Body of 4000 Men coming to

P   the

the Relief of the Town, under Sir *John Gell* of *Darbyshire* and Sir *William Brereton* of *Chefhire*, and killing 600 of them, difperfed the reft.

Our fecond Compaign now began to open; the King marched from *Oxford* to relieve *Reading*, which was befieged by the Parliament Forces; but Collonel *Felding*, Lieutenant Governour, Sir *Arthur Afhton* being wounded, furrendred to *Effex* before the King could come up; for which he was tried by Martial Law, and condemned to die; but the King forbore to execute the Sentence. This was the firft Town we had loft in the War; for ftill the ·Succefs of the King's Affairs was very encouraging. This bad News however was over-balanced by an Account brought the King at the fame time, by an Exprefs from *York*, that the Queen had landed in the *North*, and had brought over a great Magazin of Arms and Ammunition, befides fome Men. Some time after this, her Majefty marching Southward to meet the King, joined the Army near *Edgehill*, where the firft Battle was fought. She brought the King 3000 Foot, 1500 Horfe and Dragoons, fix Pieces of Cannon, 1500 Barrels of Powder, 12000 fmall Arms.

During this Profperity of the King's Affairs, his Armies encreafed mightily in the Weftern Counties alfo. Sir *William Waller* indeed commanded for the Parliament in thofe Parts too, and particularly in *Dorfetfhire*, *Hampfhire*, and *Berkfhire*, where he carried on their Caufe but too faft; but farther Weft, Sir *Nicholas Flamming*, Sir *Ralph Hopton*, and Sir *Bevil Greenvil*, had extended the King's Quarters from *Cornwall* through *Devonfhire*, and into *Somerfetfhire*, where they took *Exeter*, *Barnftable*, and *Biddiford*; and the firft of thefe they fortified very well, making it a Place of

of Arms for the West, and afterwards it was
the Residence of the Queen.

At last, the Famous Sir *William Waller*, and
the King's Forces met, and came to a pitched
Battle, where Sir *William* lost all his Honour
again. This was at *Roundway-down* in *Wiltshire.*
Waller had engaged our *Cornish* Army at *Lansf-
down*, and in a very obstinate Fight had the
better of them, and made them retreat to
the *Devizes.* Sir *William Hopton* however having a good Body of Foot untouched, sent Ex-
presses and Messengers one in the Neck of
another to the King for some Horse, and the
King being in great Concern for that Army,
who were composed of the Flower of the *Cornish*
Men, commanded me to march with all possible
Secresy, as well as Expedition, with 1200 Horse
and Dragoons from *Oxford*, to join them. We set
out in the Depth of the Night, to avoid, if possible, any Intelligence being given of our Rout,
and soon joined with the *Cornish* Army, when it
was as soon resolved to give Battle to *Waller* ; and,
give him his due, he was as forward to fight as
we. As it is easy to meet when both Sides are
willing to be found, Sir *William Waller* met us upon *Roundway-down*, where we had a fair Field
on both Sides, and Room enough to draw up
our Horse. In a Word, there was little Ceremony to the Work ; the Armies joined, and we
charged his Horse with so much Resolution, that
they quickly fled, and quitted the Field ; for
we over-matched him in Horse, and this was
the entire Destruction of their Army : For their
Infantry, which out-numbered ours by 1500,
were now at our Mercy ; some faint Resistance
they made, just enough to give us Occasion to
break into their Ranks with our Horse, where

we

we gave Time to our Foot to defeat others that
ftood to their Work: Upon which they began
to disband, and run every Way they could;
but our Horfe having furrounded them, we
made a fearful Havock of them.

We loft not above 200 Men in this Action;
Waller loft above 4000 killed and taken, and as
many difperfed that never returned to their
Colours: Thofe of Foot that efcaped got into
Briftol, and *Waller*, with the poor Remains of his
routed Regiments, got to *London*; fo that it is
plain fome run Eaft, and fome run Weft, that
is to fay, they fled every Way they could.

My going with this Detachment prevented
my being at the Siege of *Briftol*, which Prince
Rupert attacked much about the fame Time, and
it furrendered in three Days. The Parliament
queftioned Collonel *Nathaniel Fienns*, the Governor,
and had him tried as a Coward by a Court Martial,
and condemned to die, but fufpended the Execution alfo, as the King did the Governor of *Reading*.
I have often heard Prince *Rupert* fay, they did Collonel *Fienns* wrong in that Affair; and that if the Collonel would have fummoned him, he would have
demanded a Paffport of the Parliament, and have
come up and convinced the Court, that Collonel
Fienns had not misbehaved himfelf; and that he had
not a fufficient Garrifon to defend a City of that
Extent; having not above 1200 Men in the Town,
excepting fome of *Waller*'s Runaways, moft of whom
were unfit for Service, and without Arms; and that
the Citizens in general being difaffected to him,
and ready on the firft Occafion to open the Gates
to the King's Forces, it was impoffible for him
to have kept the City; and *when I had farther informed them*, faid the Prince, *of the Meafures I had
taken for a general Affault the next Day, I am confi-

dent I should have convinc'd them, that I had taken the City by Storm, if he had not surrendered.

The King's Affairs were now in a very good Posture, and three Armies in the North, West, and in the Center, counted in the Musters above 70000 Men, besides small Garrisons and Parties abroad. Several of the Lords, and more of the Commons, began to fall off from the Parliament, and make their Peace with the King; and the Affairs of the Parliament began to look very ill. The City of *London* was their inexhaustible Support and Magazine, both for Men, Money, and all things necessary; and whenever their Army was out of Order, the Clergy of their Party in but one *Sunday* or two, would preach the young Citizens out of their Shops, the Labourers from their Masters, into the Army, and recruit them on a sudden: And all this was still owing to the Omission I first observed, of not marching to *London*, when it might have been so easily effected.

We had now another, or a fairer Oppottunity, than before, but, as ill Use was made of it. The King, as I have observed, was in a very good Posture; he had three large Armies roving at large over the Kingdom. The *Cornish* Army, Victorious and Numerous, had beaten *Waller*, secured and fortified *Exeter*, which the Queen had made her Residence, and was there delivered of a Daughter, the Princess *Henrietta Maria*, afterwards Dutchess of *Orleans*, and Mother of the Dutchess Dowager of *Savoy*, commonly known in the *French* Stile by the Title of *Madam Royal*. They had secured *Salisbury*, *Sherbon* Castle, *Weymouth*, *Winchester*, and *Basing-house*, and commanded the whole Country, except *Bridgewater* and *Taunton*, *Plymouth* and *Linn*; all which Places they

P 3　　　　held

held blocked up. The King was also entirely Master of all *Wales*, *Monmouthshire*, *Cheshire*, *Shropshire*, *Staffordshire*, *Worcestershire*, *Oxfordshire*, *Berkshire*, and all the Towns from *Windsor* up the *Thames* to *Cirencester*, except *Reading* and *Henly*; and of the whole *Severn*, except *Gloucester*.

The Earl of *Newcastle* had Garrisons in every strong Place in the *North*, from *Berwick* upon *Tweed*. to *Boston* in *Lincolnshire*, and *Newark* upon *Trent*, *Hull* only excepted, whither the Lord *Fairfax* and his Son Sir *Thomas* were retreated, their Troops being routed and broken, Sir *Thomas Fairfax* his Baggage with his Lady and Servants taken Prisoners, and himself hardly escaping.

And now a great Council of War was held in the King's Quarters, what Enterprize to go upon; and it happened to be the very same Day when the Parliament were in a serious Debate what should become of them, and whose Help they should seek? And indeed they had Cause for it; and had our Counsels been as ready and well grounded as theirs, we had put an End to the War in a Month's time.

In this Council the King proposed the Marching to *London*, to put an End to the Parliament; and encourage his Friends and loyal Subjects in *Kent*, who were ready to rise for him ; and shewed us Letters from the Earl of *Newcastle*, wherein he offered to join his Majesty with a Detachment of 4000 Horse, and 8000 Foot, if his Majesty thought fit to march Southward, and yet leave Forces sufficient to guard the *North* from any Invasion. I confess, when I saw the Scheme the King had himself drawn for this Attempt, I felt an unusual Satisfaction in my Mind, from the Hopes that we might bring this War to some tolerable End; for I professed my self

on

on all Occasions heartily weary of Fighting with Friends, Brothers, Neighbours, and Acquaintance: And I made no Question, but this Motion of the King's would effectually bring the Parliament to Reason.

All Men seemed to like the Enterprize but the Earl of *Worcester*, who on particular Views for securing the Country behind, as he called it, proposed the taking in the Town of *Gloucester* and *Hereford* first: He made a long Speech of the Danger of leaving *Massey*, an active, bold Fellow, with a strong Party in the Heart of all the King's Quarters, ready on all Occasions to sally out, and surprize the neighbouring Garrisons, as he had done *Sudley* Castle and others; and of the Ease and Freedom to all those Western Parts, to have them fully cleared of the Enemy. Interest presently backs this Advice, and all those Gentlemen whose Estates lay that way, or whose Friends lived about *Worcester*, *Shrewsbury*, *Bridgnorth*, or the Borders; and who, as they said, had heard the frequent Wishes of the Country to have the City of *Gloucester* reduced, fell in with this Advice, alledging the Consequence it was of for the Commerce of the Country, to have the Navigation of the *Severn* free, which was only interupted by this one Town from the *Sea* up to *Shrewsbury* &c.

I opposed this, and so did several others: Prince *Rupert* was vehemently against it; and we both offered, with the Troops of the County, to keep *Gloucester* blocked up during the King's March for *London*, so that *Massey* should not be able to stir.

This Proposal made the Earl of *Worcester*'s Party more eager for the Siege than before; for they had no Mind to a Blockade, which would

leave

leave the Country to maintain the Troops all
the Summer; and of all Men the Prince did not
pleafe them: For he having no extraordinary
Character for Difcipline, his Company was not
much defired even by our Friends. Thus, *in an
ill Hour* 'twas refolved to fit down before *Gloucefter*. The King had a gallant Army of 28000
Men, whereof 11000 Horfe, the fineft Body of
Gentlemen that ever I faw together in my Life;
their Horfes without Comparifon, and their
Equipages the fineft and the beft in the World,
and their Perfons *Englifhmen*, which I think is
enough to fay of them.

According to the Refolution taken in the
Council of War, the Army marched Weftward,
and fat down before *Gloucefter* the Beginning of
Auguft. There we fpent a Month to the leaft
Purpofe that ever Army did; our Men received
frequent Affronts from the defperate Sallies of
an inconfiderable Enemy. I cannot forbear re-
flecting on the the Misfortunes of this Siege:
Our Men were ftrangely difpirited in all the
Affaults they gave upon the Place; there was
fomething looked like Difafter and Mifmanagement, and our Men went on with an ill Will, and
no Refolution. The King defpifed the Place,
and the King, to carry it Sword in Hand, made
no regular Approaches, and the Garrifon being defperate, made therefore the greater Slaughter. In this Work our Horfe, who were fo numerous and fo fine, had no Employment: 2000
Horfe had been enough for this Bufinefs, and
the Enemy had no Garrifon or Party within
fourty Miles of us; fo that we had nothing to
do but look on with infinite Regret, upon the
Loffes of our Foot.

The

The Enemy made frequent and defperate Sallies, in one of which I had my Share. I was pofted upon a Parade, or Place of Arms, with Part of my Regiment, and Part of Collonel *Goring*'s Regiment of Horfe, in order to fupport a Body of Foot who were ordered to ftorm the Point of a Breaft-work which the Enemy had raifed to defend one of the Avenues to the Town. The Foot were beat off with Lofs, as they always were; and *Maffey* the Governor, not content to have beaten them from his Works, fallies out with near 400 Men, and falling in upon the Foot as they were rallying under the Cover of our Horfe, we put our felves in the beft Pofture we could to receive them. As *Maffey* did not expect, I fuppofe, to engage with any Horfe, he had no Pikes with him, which encouraged us to treat him the more rudley; but as to defperate Men Danger is no Danger, when he found he muft clear his Hands of us, before he could difpatch the Foot, he faces up to us, fires but one Volley of his fmall Shot, and fell to battering us with the Stocks of their Mufquets, in fuch a manner, that one would have thought they had been mad Men.

We at firft defpifed this way of Clubbing us, and charging through them, laid a great many of them upon the Ground; and in repeating our Charge, trampled more of them under our Horfes Feet: And wheeling thus continually, beat them off from our Foot, who were juft upon the Point of disbanding. Upon this they charged us again with their Fire, and at one Volley killed 33 or 34 Men and Horfes; and had they had Pikes with them, I know not what we fhould have done with them: But at laft charging through them again, we divided them;
one

one Part of them being hemmed in between us and our own Foot, were cut in Pieces to a Man; the reſt, as I underſtood afterwards, retreated into the Town, having loſt 3co of their Men.

In this laſt Charge I received a rude Blow from a ſtout Fellow on Foot, with the But End of his Muſquet, which perfectly ſtunned me, and fetched me off from my Horſe; and had not ſome near me took Care of me, I had been trod to Death by our own Men: But the Fellow being immediately killed, and my Friends finding me alive, had taken me up, and carried me off at ſome Diſtance, where I came to my ſelf again, after ſome time, but knew little of what I did or ſaid that Night. This was the Reaſon why I ſay I afterwards underſtood the Enemy retreated; for I ſaw no more what they did then; nor indeed was I well of this Blow for all the reſt of the Summer, but had frequent Pains in my Head, Dizzineſſes and Swimming, that gave me ſome Fears the Blow had injured the Scull, but it wore off again; nor did it at all hinder my attending my Charge.

This Action, I think, was the only one that looked like a Defeat given the Enemy at this Siege; we killed them near 300 Men, as I have ſaid, and loſt about 60 of our Troopers.

All this Time, while the King was harraſſing and weakening the beſt Army he ever ſaw together during the whole War, the Parliament Generals, or rather Preachers, were recruiting theirs; for the Preachers were better than Drummers to raiſe Voluntiers, zealouſly exhorting the London Dames to part with their Husbands, and the City to ſend ſome of their Trained Bands to join the Army for the Relief of Glouceſter; and now they began to advance towards us.

The

The King hearing of the Advance of *Effex's* Army, who by this time was come to *Alisbury*, had fummoned what Forces he had within Call, to join him; and accordingly he received 3000 Foot from *Somerfetfhire*: And having batter'd the Town for 36 Hours, and made a fair Breach, refolves upon an Affault, if poffible, to carry the Town before the Enemy came up: The Affault was begun about Seven in the Evening, and the Men boldly mounted the Breach; but after a very obftinate and bloody Difpute, were beaten out again by the befieged with great Lofs.

Being thus often repulfed, and the Earl of *Effex's* Army approaching, the King calls a Council of War, and propofed to fight *Effex's* Army. The Officers of the Horfe were for fighting; and without doubt we were fuperior to him both in Number and Goodnefs of our Horfe, but the Foot were not in an equal Condition: And the Collonels of Foot reprefenting to the King the Weaknefs of their Regiments, and how their Men had been bauked and difheartened at this curfed Siege, the graver Counfel prevailed, and it was refolved to raife the Siege, and retreat towards *Briftol*, till the Army was recruited. Purfuant to this Refolution, the 5th of *September*, the King having before fent away his heavy Cannon and Baggage, raifed the Siege, and marched to *Berkley* Caftle. The Earl of *Effex* came the next Day to *Birdlip Hills*; and underftanding by Meffengers from Collonel *Maffey*, that the Siege was raifed, fends a Recruit of 2500 Men into the City, and followed us himfelf with a great Body of Horfe.

This Body of Horfe fhewed themfelves to us once in a large Field fit to have entertained them in; and our Scouts having affured us they were not above 4000, and had no Foot with
them,

them, the King ordered a Detachment of about
the fame Number to face them. I defired his
Majefty to let us have two Regiments of Dragoons with us, which was then 800 Men in a
Regiment, left there might be fome Dragoons
among the Enemy, which the King granted;
and accordingly we marched, and drew up in
View of them. They ftood their Ground, having, as they fuppofed, fome Advantage of the
manner they were pofted in, and expected we
would charge them. The King who did us the
Honour to command this Party, finding they
would not ftir, calls me to him, and ordered
me with the Dragoons, and my own Regiment,
to take a Circuit round by a Village to a certain
Lane, where in their Retreat they muft have
paffed, and which opened to a fmall Common
on their Flank, with Orders, if they engaged,
to advance and charge them in the Flank.
I marched immediately; but though the Country about there was almoft all Enclofures, yet
their Scouts were fo vigilant, that they difcovered me, and gave Notice to the Body; upon
which their whole Party moved to the Left, as
if they intended to charge me, before the King
with his Body of Horfe could come; but the
King was too vigilant to be circumvented fo; and
therefore his Majefty perceiving this, fends away
three Regiments of Horfe to fecond me, and a
Meffenger before them, to order me to halt, and
expect the Enemy, for that he would follow with
the whole Body.

But before this Order reached me, I had halted for fome time; for, finding my felf difcovered, and not judging it fafe to be entirely cut
off from the main Body, I ftopt at the Village,
and caufing my Dragoons to alight, and line a
thick

thick Hedge on my Left. I drew up my Horfe juft at the Entrance into the Village opening to a Common; the Enemy came up on the Trot to charge me, but were faluted with a terrible Fire from the Dragoons out of the Hedge, which killed them near 100 Men. This being a perfect Surprize to them, they halted; and juft at that Moment they received Orders from their main Body to retreat; the King at the fame time appearing upon fome fmall Heights in their Rear, which obliged them to think of retreating, or coming to a general Battle, which was none of their Defign.

I had no Occafion to follow them, not being in a Condition to attack their whole Body; but the Dragoons coming out into the Common, gave them another Volley at a Diftance, which reached them effectually; for it killed about 20 of them, and wounded more; but they drew off, and never fired a Shot at us, fearing to be enclofed between two Parties, and fo marched away to their General's Quarters, leaving 10 or 12 more of their Fellows killed, and about 180 Horfes. Our Men, after the Country Fafhion, gave them a Shout at parting, to let them fee we knew they were afraid of us.

However, this Relieving of *Gloucefter* raifed the Spirits as well as the Reputation of the Parliament Forces, and was a great Defeat to us; and from this time things began to look with a melancholy Afpect; for the profperous Condition of the King's Affairs began to decline. The Opportunities he had let flip, were never to be recovered; and the Parliament, in their former Extremity, having voted an Invitation to the *Scots* to March to their Affiftance, we had now new Enemies to encounter; and indeed there began the

Ruine

Ruine of his Majefty's Affairs; for the Earl of
Newcaftle, not able to defend himfelf againft the
Scots on his Rear, the Earl of *Manchefter* in his
Front, and Sir *Thomas Fairfax* on his Flank, was
every where routed and defeated, and his Forces
obliged to quit the Field to the Enemy.

About this Time it was that we firft began to
hear of one *Oliver Cromwell*, who, like a little
Cloud, rofe out of the Eaft, and fpread firft into
the North, 'till it fhed down a Flood that over-
helmed the three Kindoms.

He firft was a private Captain of Horfe, but
now commanded a Regiment whom he armed
Cap-a-pee a la Curiaffier; and joining with the Earl
of *Manchefter*, the firft Action we heard of him,
that made him any thing famous, was about
Grantham, where, with only his own Regiment,
he defeated 24 Troops of Horfe and Dragoons
of the King's Forces: Then at *Gainsborough*, with
two Regiments, his own of Horfe, and one of
Dragoons, where he defeated near 3000 of the
Earl of *Newcaftle*'s Men, killed Lieutenant General *Cavendifh*, Brother to the Earl of *Devonfhire*,
who commanded them, and relieved *Gainf-
borough*; and though the whole Army came in
to the Refcue, he made good his Retreat to
Lincoln, with little Lofs; and the next Week he
defeated Sir *John Henderfon*, at *Winsby*, near *Horn
Caftle*, with fixteen Regiments of Horfe and
Dragoons, himfelf having not half that Number, killed the Lord *Widdrington*, Sir *Ingram Hopton*,
and feveral Gentlemen of Quality.

Thus this Firebrand of War began to blaze,
and he foon grew a Terror to the North; for
Victory attended him like a Page of Honour,
and he was fcarce ever known to be beaten, during the whole War.

Now

(223)

Now we began to reflect again on the Mif-
fortune of our Mafter's Counfels: Had we
marched to *London*, inftead of befieging *Gloucefter*,
we had finifhed the War with a Stroke. The
Parliament's Army was in a moft defpicable
Condition, and had never been recruited, had we
not given them a Month's time, which we linge-
red away at this fatal Town of *Gloucefter*: But
'twas too late to reflect; we were a difheartned
Army, but we were not beaten yet, nor broken;
we had a large Country to recruit in, and we loft
no time, but raifed Men apace. In the mean
time his Majefty, after a fhort Stay at *Briftol*,
makes back again towards *Oxford* with a part
of the Foot, and all the Horfe.

At *Cireneefter* we had a Brufh again with
Effex; that Town owed us a fhrewd Turn for
having handled them coarfly enough before,
when Prince *Rupert* feized the County Magazine. I happened to be in the Town that Night
with Sir *Nicholas Crifp*, whofe Regiment of Horfe
quartered there with Collonel *Spencer*, and fome
Foot; my own Regiment was gone before to
Oxford. About Ten at Night, a Party of *Effex*'s
Men beat up our Quarters by Surprize, juft as
we had ferved them before; they fell in with
us, juft as People were going to Bed, and having
beaten the Out-Guards, where gotten into the
Middle of the Town, before our Men could get
on Horfeback. Sir *Nicholas Crifp* hearing the
Alarm, gets up, and with fome of his Clothes on,
and fome off, comes into my Chamber: We are
all undone, *fays he*, the Roundheads are upon us.
We had but little time to confult; but being in
one of the principal Inns in theTown, we prefently ordered the Gates of the Inn to be fhut, and
fent to all the Inns where our Men were quartered,

to

to do the like, with Orders, if they had any
Back-doors, or Ways to get out, to come to us.
By this means however we got fo much time as
to get on Horfeback, and fo many of our Men
came to us by Back-ways, that we had near 300
Horfe in the Yards and Places behind the Houfe;
and now we began to think of Breaking out
by a Lane which led from the back Side of the
Inn; but a new Accident determined us another,
though a worfe Way. The Enemy being entered,
and our Men cooped up in the Yards of the Inns,
Collonel *Spencer* the other Collonel, whofe Regiment of Horfe lay alfo in the Town, had got on
Horfeback before us, and engaged with the Enemy, but being over-powered, retreated fighting,
and fends to Sir *Nicholas Crifp* for Help. Sir
Nicholas moved to fee the Diftrefs of his Friend,
turning to me, fays he *What can we do for him?*
I told him, I thought 'twas time to help him, if
poffible; upon which, opening the Inn Gates,
we fallied out in very good Order, about 300
Horfe; and feveral of the Troops from other
parts of the Town joining us, we recovered
Collonel *Spencer*, and charging home, beat back
the Enemy to their main Body: But finding
their Foot drawn up in the Church-yard,
and feveral Detachments moving to charge us,
we retreated in as good Order as we could. They
did not think fit to purfue us, but they took
all the Carriages which were under the Convoy
of this Party, and loaden with Provifions and
Ammunition, and above 500 of our Horfe. The
Foot fhifted away as well as they could: Thus we
made off in a fhattered Condition towards *Farrington*, and fo to *Oxford*, and I was very glad
my Regiment was not there.

We

We had fmall Reft at *Oxford*, or indeed any
where elfe; for the King was marched from
thence, and we followed him. I was fomething
uneafy at my Abfence from my Regiment, and
did not know how the King might refent it,
which caufed me to ride after them with all Expedition. But the Armies were engaged that
very Day at *Newberry*, and I came in too late.
I had not behaved my felf fo as to be fufpected
of a wilful Shunning the Action; but a Collonel
of a Regiment ought to avoid Abfence from his
Regiment in time of Fight, be the Excufe never
fo juft, as carefully as he would a Surprize in
his Quarters. The *Truth is,* 'twas an Error of
my own, and owing to two Days Stay I made at
the *Bath,* where I met with fome Ladies who
were my Relations: And this is far from being
an Excufe; for if the King had been a *Guftavus Adolphus,* I had certainly received a Check
for it.

This Fight was very obftinate, and could our
Horfe have come to Action as freely as the Foot,
the Parliament Army had fuffered much more;
for we had here a much better Body of Horfe
than they, and we never failed beating them
where the Weight of the Work lay upon the
Horfe.

Here the City Train-Bands, of which there
was two Regiments, and whom we ufed to de-
fpife, fought very well: They loft one of their
Collonels, and feveral Officers in the Action;
and I heard our Men fay, they behaved themfelves as well as any Forces the Parliament
had.

The Parliament cried Victory here too, *as they
always did;* and indeed where the Foot were
concerned they had fome Advantage; but our

Q   Horfe

Horfe defeated them evidently. The King drew
up his Army in Battalia, in Perfon, and faced
them all the next Day, inviting them to renew
the Fight; but they had no Stomach to come
on again.

It was a kind of a Hedge Fight, for neither
Army was drawn out in the Field; if it had,
'twould never have held from fix in the Morning
to ten at Night: But they fought for Advantages; fometimes one Side had the better, fometimes another. They fought twice through the
Town, in at one End, and out at the other; and in
the Hedges and Lanes, with exceeding Fury. The
King loft the moft Men, his Foot having fuffered for want of the Succour of their Horfe, who
on two feveral Occafions, could not come at
them. But the Parliament Foot fuffered alfo,
and two Regiments were entirely cut in Peices,
and the King kept the Field.

Effex, the Parliament General, had the Pillage
of the dead, and left us to bury them; for while
we ftood all Day to our Arms, having given them
a fair Field to fight us in, their Camp Rabble
ftript the dead Bodies, and they not daring to
venture a fecond Engagement with us, marched
away towards *London*.

The King Loft in this Action the Earls of
Carnarvon and *Sunderland*, the Lord *Falkland*, a
French Marquefs, and fome very gallant Officers,
and about 1200 Men. The Earl of *Carnarvon* was
brought into an Inn in *Newberry*, where the
King came to fee him. He had juft Life enough
to fpeak to his Majefty, and died in his Prefence.
The King was exceedingly concerned for him,
and was obferved to fhed Tears at the Sight of
it. We were indeed all of us troubled for the
Lofs of fo brave a Gentleman, but the Concern
our

our royal Mafter difcovered, moved us more than ordinary. Every body endeavoured to have the King out of the Room, but he would not ftir from the Bed Side, till he fee all Hopes of Life was gone.

The indefatigable Induftry of the King, his Servants and Friends, continually to fupply and recruit his Forces, and to harrafs and fatigue the Enemy, was fuch, that we fhould ftill have given a good Account of the War had the Scots ftood neuter. But bad News came every Day out of the North; as for other Places, Parties were always in Action: Sir *William Waller* and Sir *Ralph Hopton* beat one another by Turns; and Sir *Ralph* had extended the King's Quarters from *Launcefton* in *Cornwal* to *Farnham* in *Surry*, where he gave Sir *William Waller* a Rub, and drove him into the Caftle.

But in the North, the Storm grew thick, the *Scots* advanced to the Borders, and entered *England* in Confederacy with the Parliament, againft their King; for which the Parliament requited them afterwards as they deferved.

Had it not been for this *Scotch* Army, the Parliament had eafily been reduced to Terms of Peace: But after this they never made any Propofals fit for the King to receive. Want of Succefs before had made them differ among themfelves: *Effex* and *Waller* could never agree; the Earl of *Manchefter* and the Lord *Willoughby* differed to the higheft Degree; and the King's Affairs went never the worfe for it. But this Storm in the North ruined us all; for the *Scots* prevailed in *Yorkfhire*, and being joined with *Fairfax*, *Manchefter*, and *Cromwell*, carried all before them; fo that the King was obliged to fend Prince *Rupert* with a Body of 4000 Horfe, to

the

the Affiftance of the Earl of *Newcaftle*, where
that Prince finifhed the Deftruction of the King's
Intereft, by the rafheft and unaccountableft Action
in the World, of which I fhall fpeak in its Place.

Another Action of the King's, though in it
felf no greater a Caufe of Offence than the calling the *Scots* into the Nation, gave great Offence
in general, and even the King's own Friends
difliked it; and was carefully improved by his
Enemies to the Difadvantage of the King, and
of his Caufe.

The Rebels in *Ireland* had, ever fince the
bloody Maffacre of the Proteftants, maintained
a War againft the *Englifh*, and the Earl of *Ormond* was General and Governour for the King.
The King finding his Affairs pinch him at home,
fends Orders to the Earl of *Ormond* to confent
to a Ceffation of Arms with the Rebels, and to
fhip over certain of his Regiments hither to his
Majefty's Affiftance. 'Tis true, the *Irifh* had deferved to be very ill treated by the *Englifh*; but
while the Parliament preffed the King with a
cruel and unnatural War at home, and called
in an Army out of *Scotland* to fupport their
Quarrel with their King, I could never be convinced, that it was fuch a difhonourable Action
for the King to fufpend the Correction of his
Irifh Rebls, 'till he was in a Capacity to do it
with Safety to himfelf; or to delay any farther
Affiftance to preferve himfelf at home; and the
Troops he recalled being his own, it was no
Breach of his Honour to make ufe of them, fince
he now wanted them for his own Security,
againft thofe who fought againft him at home.

But the King was perfwaded to make one
Step farther; and that, I confefs, was unpleafing
to us all; and fome of his beft and moft faithful
Servants

Servants took the Freedom to fpeak plainly to him of it; and that was bringing fome Regiments of the *Irifh* themfelves over. This caft, as we thought an *Odium* upon our whole Nation, being fome of thofe very Wretches who had dipt their Hands in the innocent Blood of the Proteftants, and with unheard of Butcheries, had maffacred fo many Thoufands of *Englifh* in cool Blood.

Abundance of Gentlemen forfook the King upon this Score; and feeing they could not brook the Fighting in Conjunction with this wicked Generation, came into the Declaration of the Parliament, and making Compofition for their Eftates, lived retired Lives all the reft of the War, or went abroad.

But as Exigences and Neceffities oblige us to do things which at other times we would not do, and is, as to Man, fome Excufe for fuch things; fo I cannot but think the Guilt and Difhonour of fuch an Action muft lye, very much of it, at leaft, at their Doors, who drove the King to thefe Neceffities and Diftreffes by calling in an Army of his own Subjects whom he had not injured, but had complied with them in every thing, to make War upon him without any Provocation.

As to the Quarrel between the King and his Parliament, there may fomething be faid on both Sides; and the King faw Caufe himfelf, to difown and diflike fome things he had done, which the Parliament objected againft, fuch as levying Money without Confent of Parliament, Infractions on their Privileges, *and the like*: Here I fay, was fome room for an Argument at leaft, and Conceffions on both Sides were needful to come to a Peace; but for the *Scots*, all their

Demands

Demands had been anfwered, all their Grievances had been redreffed, they had made Articles with their Sovereign, and he had performed thofe Articles; their capital Enemy Epifcopacy was abolifhed; they had not one thing to demand of the King which he had not granted: And therefore they had no more Caufe to take up Arms againft their Sovereign, than they had againft the *Grand Senior*. But it muft for ever lye againft them as a Brand of Infamy, and as a Reproach on their Whole Nation that, *purchafed by the Parliament's Money*, they fold their *Honefty*, and rebelled againft their King *for Hire*; and it was not many years before, as I have faid already, they were fully paid the Wages of their Unrighteoufnefs, and chaftifed for their Treachery by the very fame People whom they thus bafely affifted: Then they would have retrieved it, if it had not been too late.

But I could not but accufe this Age of Injuftice and Partiality, who while they reproached the King for his Ceffation of Arms with the *Irifh* Rebls, and not profecuting them with the utmoft Severity, though he was conftrained by the Neceffities of the War to do it, could yet, at the fame time, juftify the *Scots* taking up Arms in a Quarrel they had no Concern in, and againft their own King, with whom they had articled and capitulated, and who had fo punctually complied with all their Demands, that they had no Claim upon him, no Grievances to be redreffed, no Oppreffion to cry out of, nor could ask any thing of him which he had not granted.

But as no Action in the World is fo vile, but the Actors can cover with fome fpecious Pretence, fo the *Scots* now paffing into *England*, publifh a Declaration to juftify their Affifting the

Parlia-

Parliament: To which I shall only say, in my Opinion, it was no Justification at all; for admit the Parliament's Quarrel had been never so just, it could not be just in them to aid them, because 'twas against their own King too, to whom they had sworn Allegiance, or at least had crowned him; and thereby had recognized his Authority: For if Male-Administration be, according to *Prynn's* Doctrine, or according to their own *Buchanan*, a sufficient Reason for Subjects to take up Arms against their Prince, the Breach of his Coronation Oath being supposed to dissolve the Oath of Allegiance, which *however I cannot believe*; yet this can never be extended to make it lawful, that because a King of *England* may, by Male-Administration discharge the Subjects of *England* from their Allegiance, that therefore the Subjects of *Scotland* may take up Arms against the King of *Scotland*, he having not infringed the Compact of Government as to them, and they having nothing to complain of for themselves: Thus I thought their own Arguments were against them, and Heaven seemed to concur with it; for although they did carry the Cause for the *English* Rebels, yet the most of them left there Bones here in the Quarrel.

But what signifies Reason to the Drum and the Trumpet. The Parliament had the supream Argument with those Men, (*viz.*) the Money; and having accordingly advanced a good round Sum, upon Payment of this, (*for the Scots would not stir a Foot without it*) they entred *England* on the 15th of *January* 1643, with an Army of 12000 Men, under the Command of old *Lesley* now Earl of *Leven*, an old Soldier of great Experience, having been bred to Arms from a Youth in the Service of the Prince of *Orange*.

Q 4 The

The *Scots* were no fooner entred *England*, but
they were joined by all the Friends to the Parliament Party in the North; and firft, Collonel
Grey, Brother to the Lord *Gray*, joined them
with a Regiment of Horfe, and feveral out of
Weftmoreland and *Cumberland*, and fo they advanced to *Newcaftle*, which they fummoned to furrender. The Earl of *Newcaftle*, who rather faw,
than was able to prevent this Storm, was in
Newcaftle, and did his beft to defend it; but the
Scots encreafed by this time to above 20000,
lay clofe Siege to the Place, which was but
meanly fortified; and having repulfed the Garrifon upon feveral Sallies, and preffing the Place
very Clofe; after a Siege of 12 Days, or thereabouts, they enter the Town Sword in Hand.
The Earl of *Newcaftle* got away, and afterwards
gathered what Forces together he could; but
not ftrong enough to hinder the *Scots* from advancing to *Durham* which he quitted to them, nor
to hinder the Conjunction of the *Scots* with the
Forces of *Fairfax*, *Manchefter*, and *Cromwell*. Whereupon the Earl feeing all things thus going to
wreck, he fends his Horfe away, and retreats
with his Foot into *York*, making all neceffary
Preparations for a vigorous Defence there, in
cafe he fhould be attacked, which he was pretty
fure of, as indeed afterwards happened. *York* was
in a very good Pofture of Defence: The Fortifications very regular, and exceeding ftrong;
well furnifhed with Provifions, and had now a
Garrifon of 12000 Men in it. The Governour
under the Earl of *Newcaftle* was Sir *Thomas Glemham*, a good Souldier, and a Gentleman brave
enough.

The *Scots*, as I have faid, having taken *Durham*, *Tinmouth* Caftle and *Sunderland*, and being
joined

joined by Sir *Thomas Fairfax*, who had taken *Selby*, resolve, with their united Strength, to besiege *York*; but when they came to view the City, and saw a Plan of the Works, and had Intelligence of the Strength of the Garrison, they sent Expreffes to *Manchester* and *Cromwell* for Help, who came on, and join them with 9000, making together about 30000 Men, rather more than less.

Now had the Earl of *Newcastle's* repeated Meffengers convinced the King, that it was abfolutely neceffary to send some Forces to his Affiftance, or else all would be loft in the North. Whereupon Prince *Rupert* was detached with Orders firft to go into *Lancashire*, and relieve *Latham-Houfe*, defended by the brave Countefs of *Derby*; and then taking all the Forces he could collect in *Cheshire*, *Lancashire*, and *Yorkshire*, to march to relieve *York*.

The Prince marched from *Oxford* with but three Regiments of Horse, and one of Dragoons, making in all about 2800 Men. The Collonels of Horse were Collonel *Charles Goring*, the Lord *Biron*, and my felf; the Dragoons were of Collonel *Smith*. In our March we were joined by a Regiment of Horse from *Banbury*, one of Dragoons from *Bristol*, and three Regiments of Horse from *Chester*: So that when we came into *Lancashire*, we were about 5000 Horse and Dragoons. Thefe Horse we received from *Chester*, were thofe who having been at the Siege of *Nantwich*, were obliged to raife the Siege by Sir *Thomas Fairfax*; and the Foot having yielded, the Horse made good their Retreat to *Chester*, being about 2000; of whom three Regiments now joined us.

We

We received alfo 2000 Foot from *Weſt Cheſter*, and 2000 more out of *Wales*; and with this Strength we entered *Lancaſhire*. We had not much time to ſpend, and a great deal of Work to do.

Bolton and *Leverpool* felt the firſt Fury of our Prince: At *Bolton* indeed he had ſome Provo-cation; for here we were like to be beaten off. When firſt the Prince came to the Town, he ſent a Summons to demand the Town for the King, but received no Anſwer but from their Guns, commanding the Meſſenger to keep off at his Peril. They had raiſed ſome Works about the Town, and having by their Intelligence, learnt that we had no Artillery, and were only a flying Party, *ſo they called us*, they contemned the Summons, and ſhewed themſelves upon their Ramparts ready for us. The Prince was reſolved to humble them, if poſſible, and takes up his Quarters cloſe to the Town. In the Evening he orders me to advance with one Regiment of Dragoons, and my Horſe to bring them off, if Occaſion was, and to poſt my ſelf as near as poſſibly I could to the Lines, yet ſo as not to be diſcovered; and at the ſame time having concluded what Part of the Works to fall upon, he draws up his Men on two other Sides, as if he would Storm them there; and on a Signal I was to begin the real Aſſault on my Side, with my Dragoons. I had got ſo near the Town with my Dragoons, making them creep upon their Bellies a great way, that we could hear the Soldiers talk on the Walls, when the Prince believing one Regiment would be too few, ſends we Word, that he had ordered a Regiment of Foot to help, and that I ſhould not diſcover my ſelf till they were come up to me. This broke
our

our Measures; for the March of this Regiment was discovered by the Enemy, and they took the Alarm. Upon this I sent to the Prince, to desire he would put off the Storm for that Night, and I would answer for it the next Day; but the Prince was impatient, and sent Orders we should fall on as soon as the Foot came up to us. The Foot marching out of the Way, missed us, and fell in with a Road that leads to another Part of the Town; and being not able to find us, make an Attack upon the Town themselves; but the Defendants being ready for them, received them very warmly, and beat them off with great Loss. I was at a Loss now what to do; for hearing the Guns, and by the Noise knowing it was an Assault upon the Town, I was very uneasy to have my Share in it; but as I had learnt under the King of *Sweden* punctually to adhere to the Exccecution of Orders; and my Orders being to lye still till the Foot came up with me; I would not stir if I had been sure to have done never so much Service; but however to satisfy my self, I sent to the Prince to let him know that I continued in the same Place expecting the Foot, and none being yet come, I desired farther Orders. The Prince was a little amazed at this, and finding there must be some Mistake, came galloping away in the Dark to the Place, and drew off the Men, which was no hard Matter, for they were willing enough to give it over.

As for me, the Prince ordered me to come off so privately, as not to be discovered, if possible, which I effectually did; and so we were baulked for that Night. The next Day the Prince fell on upon another Quarter with three Regiments of Foot, but was beaten off with Loss; and

the

the like a third time. At laft, the Prince, *re-folved to carry it*, doubled his Numbers, and renewing the Attack with frefh Men, the Foot entred the Town over their Works, killing in the firft Heat of the Action, all that came in their way; fome of the Foot at the fame time letting in the Horfe ; and fo the Town was entirely won. There was about 600 of the Enemy killed, and we loft above 400 in all which was owing to the foolifh Miftakes we made. Our Men got fome Plunder here, which the Parliament made a great Noife about ; but it was their due, and they bought it dear enough.

Leverpool did not coft us fo much, nor did we get fo much by it, the People having fent their Women and Children, and beft Goods on board the Ships in the Road; and as we had no Boats to board them with, we could not get at them. Here, as at *Bolton*, the Town and Fort was taken by Storm, and the Garrifon were many of them cut in Pieces, which by the way was their own Faults.

Our next Stop was *Lathan-Houfe*, which the Countefs of *Derby* had gallantly defended above 18 Weeks, againft the Parliament Forces; and this Lady not only encouraged her Men by her chearful and noble Maintenance of them, but by Examples of her own undaunted Spirit, expofing her felf upon the Walls in the midft of the Enemy's Shot, would be with her Men in the greateft Dangers; and fhe well deferved our Care of her Perfon; for the Enemy were prepaired to ufe her very rudely if fhe fell into their Hands.

Upon our Approach, the Enemy drew off; and the Prince not only effectually relieved this
vigorous

vigorous Lady, but left her a good Quantity
of all Sorts of Ammunition, three great Guns,
500 Arms, and 200 Men, commanded by a Major, as her extraordinary Guard.

Here the Way being now opened, and our
Succefs anfwering our Expectation, feveral Bodies of Foot came in to us from *Weftmoreland*, and
from *Cumberland*; and here it was that the Prince
found Means to furprize the Town of *Newcaftle
upon Tyne*, which was recovered for the King, by
the Management of the Mayor of the Town, and
fome loyal Gentlemen of the County, and a Garrifon placed there again for the King.

But our main Defign being the Relief of *York*,
the Prince advanced that Way a-pace, his Army ftill increafing; and being joined by the
Lord *Goring* from *Richmondfhire* with 4000 Horfe,
which were the fame the Earl of *Newcaftle* had
fent away when he threw himfelf into *York* with
the Infantry. We were now 18000 effective Men,
whereof 10000 Horfe and Dragoons; fo the
Prince, full of Hopes, and his Men in good
Heart, boldly marched directly for *York*.

The *Scots*, as much furprized at the taking
of *Newcaftle*, as at the coming of their Enemy,
began to enquire which Way they fhould get
home, if they fhould be beaten; and calling a
Council of War, they all agreed to raife the
Siege. The Prince, who drew with him a great
Train of Carriages charged with Provifion and
Ammunition, for the Relief of the City, like a
wary General, kept at a Diftance from the Enemy, and fetching a great Compafs about, brings
all fafe into the City, and enters into *York* himfelf with all his Army.

No Action of this whole War had gained
the Prince fo much Honour, or the King's Affairs

fairs fo much Advantage as this, had the Prince
but had the Power to have reftrained his Courage after this, and checked his fatal Eagernefs
for Fighting. Here was a Siege raifed, the Reputation of the Enemy juftly flurred, a City
relieved and furnifhed, with all things neceffary
in the Face of an Army fuperior in Number
by near 10000 Men, and commanded by a Tri-
umvirate of Generals *Leven*, *Fairfax* and *Manchefter*. Had the Prince but remembered the
Proceeding of the great Duke of *Parma* at the
Relief of *Paris*, he would have feen the relieving
the City was his Bufinefs; 'twas the Enemy's
Bufinefs to fight, if poffible, 'twas his to avoid
it; for, having delivered the City, and put
the Difgrace of raifing the Siege upon the Enemy, he had nothing farther to do, but to have
waited till he had feen what Courfe the Enemy
would take, and taken his farther Meafures
from their Motion.

But *the Prince*, a continual Friend to precipitant Counfels, would hear no Advice: I entreated
him not to put it to the Hazard; I told him,
that he ought to confider if he loft the Day, he
loft the Kingdom, and took the Crown off from
the King's Head. I put him in mind that it
was impoffible thofe three Generals fhould continue long together; and that if they did, they
would not agree long in their Counfels: Which
would be as well for us as their feparating.
'Twas plain *Manchefter* and *Cromwell* muft return
to the affociated Counties, who would not
fuffer them to ftay, for fear the King fhould
attempt them; That he could fubfift well
enough, having *York* City and River at his
Back; but the *Scots* would eat up the Country,
make themfelves odious, and dwindle away to
nothing

nothing, if he would but hold them at Bay a
little; other General Officers were of the same
Mind; but all I could say, or they either, to a
Man deaf to any thing but his own Courage,
signified nothing. He would draw out and fight,
there was no perswading him to the contrary,
unless a Man would run the Risque of being
upbraided with being a Coward, and afraid of
the Work. The Enemy's Army lay on a large
Common, called *Marston-Moor*, doubtful what to
do: Some were for fighting the Prince, the
Scots were against it, being uneasy at having the
Garrison of *Newcastle* at their Backs; but the
Prince brought their Councils of War to a Result; for he let them know, they must fight
him, whether they would or no; for the Prince
being, *as before*, 18000 Men, and the Earl of
Newcastle having joined him with 8000 Foot out
of the City, were marched in Quest of the Enemy, had entered the Moor in View of their Army, and began to draw up in Order of Battle;
but the Night coming on, the Armies only
viewed each other at a Distance for that time.
We lay all Night upon our Arms, and with the
first of the Day were in Order of Battle; the
Enemy was getting ready, but part of *Manchester*'s Men were not in the Field, but lay about
three Miles off, and made a hasty March to
come up.

The Prince his Army was exceedingly well
managed; he himself commanded the Left Wing,
the Earl of *Newcastle* the Right Wing; and the
Lord *Goring*, as General of the Foot, assisted by
Major General *Porter*, and Sir *Charles Lucas*, led
the main Battle. I had prevailed with the
Prince, according to the Method of the King of
Sweden, to place some small Bodies of Musqueteers

in

in the Intervals of his Horfe, in the Left Wing,
but could not prevail upon the Earl of _New-
caftle_ to do it in the Right; which he afterwards repented. In this Pofture we ftood facing the Enemy, expecting they would advance
to us, which at laft they did; and the Prince
began the Day by faluting them with his Artillery, which being placed very well, galled
them terribly for a Quarter of an Hour ; they
could not fhift their Front, fo they advanced
the haftier to get within our great Guns,
and confequently out of their Danger, which
brought the Fight the fooner on.

The Enemy's Army was thus ordered; Sir
Thomas Fairfax had the Right Wing, in which
was the _Scots_ Horfe, and the Horfe of his own
and his Father's Army; _Cromwell_ led the Left
Wing, with his own and the Earl _Manchefter's_
Horfe, and the three Generals _Lefley_, old _Fair-
fax_, and _Manchefter_, led the main Battle.

The Prince, with our Left Wing, fell on firft,
and, with his ufual Fury, broke, like a Clap
of Thunder, into the Right Wing of the _Scots_
Horfe, led by Sir _Thomas Fairfax_; and, as nothing could ftand in his Way, he broke through
and through them, and entirely routed them,
purfuing them quite out of the Field. Sir _Tho-
mas Fairfax_, with a Regiment of Lances, and
about 500 of his own Horfe, made good the
Ground for fome time; but our Mufqueteers,
which, as I faid, were placed among our Horfe
were fuch an unlooked for fort of an Article
in a Fight among the Horfe, that thofe Lances, which otherwife were brave Fellows, were
mowed down with their Shot, and all was
put into Confufion. Sir _Thomas Fairfax_ was
wounded in the Face, his Brother killed, and a
great

great Slaughter was made of the *Scots*, to whom I confefs we fhewed no Favour at all.

While this was doing on our Left, the Lord *Goring* with the main Battle charged the Enemy's Foot, and particulary one Brigade commanded by Major General *Porter*, being moftly Pikemen, not regarding the Fire of the Enemy, charged with that Fury in a clofe Body of Pikes, that they overturned all that came in their Way, and breaking into the Middle of the Enemy's Foot, filled all with Terror and Confufion, infomuch that the three Generals thinking all had been loft, fled, and quitted the Field.

But Matters went not fo well with that *always Unfortunate* Gentleman the Earl of *Newcaftle*, and our Right Wing of Horfe; for *Cromwell* charged the Earl of *Newcaftle* with a powerful Body of Horfe; and though the Earl, and thofe about him, did what Men could do, and behaved themfelves with all poffible Gallantry, yet there was no withftanding *Cromwell's* Horfe; but, like Prince *Rupert*, they bore down all before them; and now the Victory was wrung out of our Hands by our own grofs Mifcarriage; for the Prince, as 'twas his Cuftom, too eager in the Chafe of the Enemy, was gone, and could not be heard of: The Foot in the Center, the Right Wing of the Horfe being routed by *Cromwell*, was left, and without the Guard of his Horfe; *Cromwell* having routed the Earl of *Newcaftle*, and beaten him quite out of the Field, and Sir *Thomas Fairfax* rallying his difperfed Troops, they fall all together upon the Foot. General Lord *Goring*, like himfelf, fought like a Lion, but, forfaken of his Horfe, was hemmed in on all Sides, and overthrown; and an Hour

R   after

after this, the Prince returning too late to recover
his Friends, was obliged with the reft to quit
the Field to Conquerors.

This was a fatal Day to the King's Affairs,
and the Rifque too much for any Man in his
Wits to run; we loft 4000 Men on the Spot,
3000 Prifoners, amongft whom was Sir *Charles
Lucas*, Major General *Porter*, Major General
Telier, and about 170 Gentlemen of Quality.
We loft all our Baggage, 25 Pieces of Cannon,
300 Carriages, 150 Barrels of Powder, and
10000 Arms.

The Prince got into *York* with the Earl of
Newcaftle, and a great many Gentlemen, and 7
or 8000 of the Men, as well Horfe as Foot.

I had but very courfe Treatment in this
Fight; for returning with the Prince from
the Purfuit of the Right Wing, and finding
all loft, I halted with fome other Officers, to
confider what to do: At firft we were for making our Retreat in a Body, and might have
done fo well enough, if we had known what had
happened, before we faw our felves in the Middle of the Enemy; for Sir *Thomas Fairfax*, who
had got together his fcattered Troops, and joined by fome of the Left Wing, knowing who we
were, charged us with great Fury. 'Twas not
a Time to think of any thing but getting away,
or dying upon the Spot; the Prince kept on
in the Front, and Sir *Thomas Fairfax*, by this
Charge cut off about three Regiments of us
from our Body; but bending his main Strength
at the Prince, left us, as it were, behind him,
in the Middle of the Field of Battle. We took
this for the only Opportunity we could have
to get off, and joining together, we made crofs
the Place of Battle in as good Order as we could,
with

with our Carabines prefented. In this Pofture we paffed by feveral Bodies of the Enemy's Foot, who ftood with their Pikes charged to keep us off; but they had no Occafion, for we had no Defign to meddle with them, but to get from them. Thus we made a fwift March, and thought our felves pretty fecure, but our Work was not done yet; for, on a fudden, we faw our felves under a Neceffity of Fighting our Way through a great Body of *Manchefter*'s Horfe, who came galloping upon us over the Moor. They had as, we fuppofe, been purfuing fome of our broken Troops, which were fled before, and feeing us, they gave us a home Charge. We received them as well as could, but pufhed to get through them, which at laft we did with a confiderable Lofs to them. However, we loft fo many Men, either killed or feparated from us, (for all could not follow the fame Way) that of our three Regiments we could not be above 400 Horfe together, when we got quite clear, and thefe were mixt Men, fome of one Troop and Regiment, fome of another. Not that I believe many of us were killed in the laft Attack; for we had plainly the better of the Enemy; but our Defign being to get off, fome fhifted for themfelves one Way, and fome another, in the beft Manner they could, and as their feveral Fortunes guided them. 400 more of this Body, as I afterwards underftood, having broke through the Enemy's Body another Way, kept together, and got into *Pontfract* Caftle, and 300 more, made Northward, and to *Skippon*, were the Prince afterwards fetched them off.

Thofe few of us that were left together, with whom I was, being now pretty clear of Pur-

fuit,

fuit, halted, and began to enquire who and
who we were, and what we fhould do; and on
a fhort Debate, I propofed we fhould make to
the firft Garrifon of the King's that we could
recover; and that we fhould keep together,
left the Country People fhould infult us upon
the Roads. With this Refolution we pufhed
on Weftward for *Lancafhire*; but our Misfortunes were not yet at an End: We travelled
very hard, and got to a Village upon the River
Wharf, near *Wetherby*. At *Wetherby* there was
a Bridge, but we underftood that a Party from
Leeds had fecured the Town and the Poft, in
order to ftop the flying Cavaliers; and that
'twould be very hard to get through there;
though, as we underftood afterwards, there
were no Soldiers there but a Guard of the
Townfmen. In this Pickle we confulted what
Courfe to take; to ftay where we were till
Morning, we all concluded would not be fafe;
fome advifed to take the Stream with our
Horfes; but the River, which is deep, and the
Current ftrong, feemed to bid us have a care
what we did of that Kind, efpecially in the
Night. We refolved therefore to refrefh our
felves and our Horfes, *which indeed is more than
we did*, and go on till we might come to a Ford
or Bridge, where we might get over. Some
Guides we had, but they either were foolifh
or falfe; for after we had rid eight or nine Miles,
they plunged us into a River, at a Place they
called a Ford, but 'twas a very ill one; for moft
of our Horfes fwam, and feven or eight were
loft, but we faved the Men; however, we got
all over.

We made bold with our firft Convenience to
trefpafs upon the Country for a few Horfes,
where

where we could find them, to remount our Men, whofe Horfes were drowned, and continued our March; but being obliged to refrefh our felves at a fmall Village on the Edge of *Bramham-moor*, we found the Country alarmed by our. taking fome Horfes, and we were no fooner got on Horfeback in the Morning, and entering on the Moor, but we underftood we were purfued by fome Troops of Horfe: There was no Remedy but we muft pafs this Moor; and though our Horfes were exceedingly tired, yet we preffed on upon a round Trot, and recovered an enclofed Country on the other Side, where we halted. And here, Neceffity putting us upon it, we were obliged to look out for more Horfes, for feveral of our Men were difmounted, and others Horfes difabled by carrying double, thofe who loft their Horfes getting up behind them; but we were fupplied by our Enemies againft their Will.

The Enemy followed us over the Moor, and we having a woody enclofed Country about us, where we were, I obferved by their moving, they had loft Sight of us; upon which I propofed concealing our felves till we might judge of their Numbers. We did fo, and lying clofe in a Wood, they paft haftily by us, without skirting or fearching the Wood, which was what on another Occafion they would not have done. I found they were not above 150 Horfe, and confidering, that to let them go before us, would be to alarm the Country, and ftop our Defign; I thought, fince we might be able to deal with them, we fhould not meet with a better Place for it, and told the reft of our Officers my Mind, which all our Party prefently, (for we not had Time for a long Debate) agreed

to

to. Immediately upon this I caused two Men to fire their Piftols in the Wood, at two different Places, as far asunder as I could. This I did to give them an Alarm, and amuse them; for being in the Lane, they would otherwise have got through before we had been ready, and I resolved to engage them there, as soon as 'twas possible. After this Alarm, we rushed out of the Wood, with about 100 Horse, and charged them on the Flank in a broad Lane, the Wood being on their Right. Our Passage into the Lane being narrow, gave us some Difficulty in our getting out; but the Surprize of the Charge did our Work; for the Enemy thinking we had been a Mile or two before, had not the least Thoughts of this Onset, till they heard us in the Wood, and then they who were before could not come back. We broke into the Lane juft in the Middle of them, and by that means divided them; and facing to the Left, charged the Rear. First our difmounted Men, which were near 50, lined the Edge of the Wood, and fired with their Carabines upon those which were before, so warmly, that they put them into a great Diforder: Mean while 50 more of our Horse from the farther Part of the Wood shewed themselves in the Lane upon their Front; this put them of the foremoft Party into a great Perplexity, and they began to face about, to fall upon us who were engaged in the Rear: But their facing about in a Lane where there was no Room to wheel, and one who underftands the Manner of wheeling a Troop of Horse, muft imagine, put them into a great Diforder. Our Party in the Head of the Lane taking the Advantage of this Mistake of the Enemy, charged in upon them,

them, and routed them entirely. Some found means to break into the Enclosures on the other Side of the Lane, and get away. About 30 were killed, and about 25 made Prisoners, and 40 very good Horses were taken; all this while not a Man of ours was lost, and not above seven or eight wounded. Those in the Rear behaved themselves better ; for they stood our Charge with a great deal of Resolution, and all we could do, could not break them; but at last our Men who had fired on Foot through the Hedges at the other Party, coming to do the like here, there was no standing it any longer. The Rear of them faced about, and retreated out of the Lane, and drew up in the open Field to receive and rally their Fellows. We killed about 17 of them, and followed them to the End of the Lane, but had no mind to have any more fighting than needs must; our Condition at that time not making it proper, the Towns round us being all in the Enemy's Hands; and the Country but indifferently pleased with us; however, we stood facing them till they thought fit to march away. Thus we were supplied with Horses enough to remount our Men, and pursued our first Design of getting into *Lancashire*. As for our Prisoners, we let them go off on Foot.

But the Country being by this time alarmed, and the Rout of our Army every where known, we foresaw Abundance of Difficulties before us; we were not strong enough to venture into any great Towns, and we were too many to be concealed in small ones. Upon this we resolved to halt in a great Wood about three Miles beyond the Place, where we had the last Skirmish, and sent out Scouts to discover the

Country

Country, and learn what they could, either of
the Enemy, or of our Friends.

Any Body may suppose we had but indifferent Quarters here, either for our selves or for
our Horses ; but however, we made shift to lye
here two Days and one Night. In the interim
I took upon me, with two more, to go to *Leeds* to
learn some News ; we were disguised like Country Ploughmen ; the Clothes we got at a Farmer's
House, which for that particular Occasion we
plundered ; and I cannot say no Blood was shed
in a Manner too rash, and which I could not
have done at another Time ; but our Case was
desperate, and the People too surly, and shot
at us out the Window, wounded one Man and
shot a Horse, which we counted as great a Loss
to us as a Man, for our Safety depended upon our
Horses. Here we got Clothes of all Sorts enough
for both Sexes, and thus dressing my self up *a
la Paisant*, with a white Cap on my Head, and
a Fork on my Shoulder, and one of my Comerades in the Farmer's Wife's Russet Gown and
Petticoat, like a Woman ; the other with an old
Crutch like a lame Man, and all mounted on
such Horses as we had taken the Day before
from the Country. Away we go to *Leeds* by
three several Ways, and agreed to meet upon
the Bridge. My pretended Country Woman
acted her Part to the Life, though the Party
was a Gentleman of good Quality of the Earl
of *Worcester*'s Family, and the Cripple did as
well he ; but I thought my self very awkward
in my Dress, which made me very shy, especially among the Soldiers. We passed their Centinels and Guards at *Leeds* unobserved, and put
up our Horses at several Houses in the Town,
from whence we went up and down to make

our

our Remarks. My Cripple was the fitteſt to go among the Soldiers, becauſe there was leſs Danger of being preſſed : There he informed himſelf of the Matters of War, particularly that the Enemy ſat down again to the Siege of *York*; that flying Parties were in Purſuit of the Cavaliers; and there he heard that 500 Horſe of the Lord *Mancheſter*'s Men had followed a Party of Cavaliers over *Bramham Moor*; and, that entering a Lane, the Cavaliers, who were 1000 ſtrong, fell upon them, and killed them all but about 50. This, though it was a Lie, was very pleaſant to us to hear, knowing it was our Party, becauſe of the other part of the Story, which was thus; that the Cavaliers had taken Poſſeſſion of ſuch a Wood, where they rallied all the Troops of their flying Army; that they had plundered the Country as they came, taking all the Horſes they could get ; that they had plundered Goodman *Thompſon*'s Houſe, which was the Farmer I mentioned, and killed Man, Woman and Child; and that they were about 2000 ſtrong.

My other Friend in Woman's Clothes got among the good Wives at an Inn, where ſhe ſet up her Horſe, and there ſhe heard the ſame ſad and dreadful Tidings; and that this Party was ſo ſtrong, none of the neighbouring Garriſons durſt ſtir out; but that they had ſent Expreſſes to *York* for a Party of Horſe to come to their Aſſiſtance.

I walked up and down the Town, but fancied my ſelf ſo ill diſguiſed, and ſo eaſy to be known, that I cared not to talk with any Body. We met at the Bridge exactly at our Time, and compared our Intelligence, found it anſwered our End of coming, and that we had nothing

thing to do but to get back to our Men; but
my Cripple told me, he would not ftir till he
bought fome Victuals: So away he hops with
his Crutch, and buys four or five great Pieces
of Bacon, as many of hung Beef, and two or
three Loaves; and, borrowing a Sack at the
Inn (which I fuppofe he never reftored,) he
loads his Horfe, and, getting a large Leather
Bottle, he filled that of *Aquavitæ* inftead of fmall
Beer; my Woman Comerade did the like. I was
uneafy in my Mind, and took no Care but to
get out of the Town; however, we all came off
well enough; but 'twas well for me that I had
no Provifions with me, as you will hear prefently. We came, as I faid, into the Town by
feveral Ways, and fo we went out; but about
three Miles from the Town we met again exactly where we had agreed: I being about a
Quarter of a Mile from the reft, I meets three
Country Fellows on Horfeback; one had a long
Pole on his Shoulder, another a Fork, the third
no Weapon at all, that I faw; I gave them the
Road very orderly, being habited like one of
their Brethren; but one of them ftopping fhort
at me, and looking earneftly, calls out, *Hark
thee, Friend,* fays he, in a broad North Country
Tone, *whar haſt thou thilk Horfe?* I muft confefs
I was in the utmoft Confufion at the Queftion,
neither being able to anfwer the Queftion, nor
to fpeak in his Tone; fo I made as if I did not
hear him, and went on. *Na, but ye's not gang foa,*
fays the Boor, and comes up to me, and takes
hold of the Horfe's Bridle to ftop me; at which,
vexed at Heart that I could not tell how to talk
to him, I reached him a great Knock on the Pate
with my Fork, and fetched him off of his Horfe,
and then began to mend my Pace. The other
Clowns

Clowns, though it feems they knew not what
the Fellow wanted, purfued me, and, finding
they had better Heels than I, I faw there was
no Remedy but to make ufe of my Hands, and
faced about. The firft that came up with me
was he that had no Weapons, fo I thought I might
parley with him; and, fpeaking as Country like
as I could, I asked him what he wanted? *Thou'ft
know that foon,* fays *Yorkfhire, and Ife but come at
thee. Then keep awa' Man,* faid I, *or Ife brain thee.*
By this Time the third Man came up, and the
Parley ended; for he gave me no Words but
laid at me with his long Pole, and that with
fuch Fury, that I began to be doubtful of him:
I was loath to fhoot the Fellow, though I had
Piftols under my grey Frock, as well for that
the Noife of a Piftol might bring more People
in, the Village being on our Rear; and alfo becaufe I could not imagine what the Fellow
meant, or would have; but at laft finding he
would be too many for me with that long Weapon, and a hardy ftrong Fellow, I threw
my felf off of my Horfe, and running in with
him, ftabbed my Fork into his Horfe; the Horfe
being wounded, ftaggered a while, and then fell
down, and the Booby had not the Senfe to get
down in time, but fell with him; upon which,
giving him a knock or two with my Fork, I
fecured him. The other, by this Time, had furnifhed himfelf with a great Stick out of a Hedge,
and, before I was difingaged from the laft Fellow,
gave me two fuch Blows, that if the laft had
not miffed my Head, and hit me on the Shoulder, I had ended the Fight and my Life together. 'Twas time to look about me now,
for this was a mad Man; I defended my felf
with my Fork, but 'twould not do; at laft, in
short

short, I was forced to Piftol him, and get on
Horfeback again, and, with all the Speed I
could make get away to the Wood to our Men.

If my two Fellow Spies had not been behind,
I had never known what was the Meaning of
this Quarrel of the three Countrymen, but
my Cripple had all the Particulars; for he being behind us, as I have already obferved,
when he came up to the firft Fellow, who began the Fray, he found him beginning to come
to himfelf; fo he gets off, and pretends to help
him, and fets him up upon his Breech, and being a very merry Fellow, talked to him, *Well
and what's the Matter now*, fays he to him, *ah
wae's me*, fays the Fellow, *I is killed: Not quite
Mon*, fays the Cripple. O that's *a fau Thief*,
fays he, and thus they parlied. My Cripple
got him on's Feet, and gave him a Dram of
his *Aqua Vitæ* Bottle, and made much of him,
in order to know what was the Occafion of the
Quarrel. Our difguifed Woman pitied the Fellow too, and together they fet him up again
upon his Horfe, and then he told him that
that Fellow was got upon one of his Brother's
Horfes who lived at *Wetherby*: They faid the
Cavaliers ftole him, but 'twas like fuch Rogues;
no Mifchief could be done in the Country, but
'twas the poor Cavaliers muft bear the Blame,
and the like; and thus they jogged on till they
came to the Place where the other two lay.
The firft Fellow they affifted as they had done
t'other, and gave him a Dram out of the Leather Bottle; but the laft Fellow was paft their
Care; fo they came away: For when they underftood that 'twas my Horfe, they claimed,
they began to be affraid that their own Horfes
might be known too, and then they had been
betraid

betraid in a worſe Pickle than I, and muſt
have been forced to have done ſome Miſchief
or other to have got away.

I had ſent out two Troopers to fetch them
off, if their was any Occaſion; but their Stay
was not long, and the two Troopers ſaw
them at a Diſtance coming towards us, ſo they
returned.

I had enough of going for a Spy, and my
Companions had enough of ſtaying in the Wood;
for other Intelligences agreed with ours, and all
concurred in this, that it was time to be going;
however, this Uſe we made of it, that while
the Country thought us ſo ſtrong we were in
the leſs Danger of being attacked, though in
the more of being obſerved; but all this while
we heard nothing of our Friends, till the next
Day. We heard Prince *Rupert*, with about 1000
Horſe, was at *Skipton*, and from thence marched
away to *Weſtmoreland*.

We concluded now we had two or three Days
time good; for, ſince Meſſengers were ſent to
Tork for a Party to ſuppreſs us, we muſt have
at leaſt two Days March of them, and therefore all concluded we were to make the beſt of
our Way; early in the Morning therefore we
decamped from thoſe dull Quarters; and as we
marched through a Village, we found the People very civil to us, and the Woman cried out,
*God bleſs them, 'tis pity the Roundheads ſhould make
ſuch Woork with ſuch brave Men*, and the like. Finding we were among our Friends, we reſolved to
halt a little and refreſh our ſelves; and, indeed,
the People were very kind to us, gave us Victuals
and Drink, and took Care of our Horſes. It
happened to be my Lot to ſtop at a Houſe where
the good Woman took a great deal of Pains

to

to provide for us; but I obferved the good Man walked about with a Cap upon his Head, and very much out of Order, I took no great Notice of it, being very fleepy, and having asked my Landlady to let me have a Bed, I lay down and flept heartily: When I waked I found my Landlord on another Bed groaning very heavily.

When I came down Stairs, I found my Cripple talking with my Landlady; he was now out of his Difguife, but we called him Cripple ftill; and the other, who put on the Woman's Clothes, we called Goody *Thompfon*. As foon as he faw me, he called me out, *Do you know*, fays he *the Man of the Houfe you are quartered in? No, not I*, fays I. *No, fo I believe, nor they you*, fays he, *if they did, the good Wife would not have made you a Poffet, and fetched a white Loaf for you. What do you mean*, fays I. *Have you feen the Man* fays he? *Seen him*, fays I, *yes, and heard him too; the Man's Sick, and groans fo heavily*, fays I, *that I could not lye upon the Bed any longer for him. Why, this is the poor Man*, fays he, *that you knocked down with your Fork Yefterday, and I have had all the Story out yonder at the next Door.* I confefs it grieved me to have been forced to treat one fo roughly who was one of our Friends, but to make fome amends, we contrived to give the poor Man his Brother's Horfe; and my Cripple told him a formal Story, that he believed the Horfe was taken away from the Fellow by fome of our Men; and, if he knew him again, if 'twas his Friend's Horfe, he fhould have him. The Man came down upon the News, and I caufed fix or feven Horfes, which were taken at the fame time, to be fhewn him; he immediately chofe the right; fo I gave him the Horfe, and we

preten-

pretended a great deal of Sorrow for the Man's
Hurt; and that we had not knocked the Fellow
on the Head as well as took away the Horfe.
The Man was fo over-joyed at the Revenge he
thought was taken on the Fellow, that we heard
him groan no more. We ventured to ftay all
Day at this Town, and the next Night, and got
Guides to lead us to *Blackftone Edge*, a Ridge of
Mountains which part this Side of *Yorkfhire* from
Lancafhire. Early in the Morning we marched,
and kept our Scouts very carefully out every
Way, who brought us no News for this Day;
we kept on all Night, and made our Horfes do
Penance for that little Reft they had, and the
next Morning we paffed the Hills, and got into
Lancafhire, to a Town called *Littlebury*; and from
thence to *Rochedale*, a little Market-Town. And
now we thought our felves fafe as to the Purfuit
of Enemies from the Side of *York*; our Defign
was to get to *Bolton*, but all the County was
full of the Enemy in flying Parties, and how to
get to *Bolton* we knew not. At laft we refolved
to fend a Meffenger to *Bolton*; but he came back
and told us, he had with lurking and hiding,
tried all the Ways that he thought poffible, but
to no Purpofe; for he could not get into the
Town. We fent another, and he never returned; and fome time after we underftood he was
taken by the Enemy. At loft one got into the
Town, but brought us Word, they were tired
out with conftant Alarms, had been ftraitly
blocked up, and every Day expected a Siege,
and therefore advifed us either to go Northward, where Prince *Rupert*, and the Lord *Goring* ranged at Liberty; or to get over *Warrington* Bridge, and fo fecure our Retreat to *Chefter*.
This double Direction divided our Opinions; I

I was

was for getting into *Chester*, both to recruit my
self with Horses and with Money, both which
I wanted, and to get Refreshment, which we all
wanted; but the major Part of our Men were
for the North. First they said, there was their
General, and 'twas their Duty to the Cause,
and the King's Interest obliged us to go
where we could do best Service; and there
was their Friends, and every Man might hear
some News of his own Regiment, for we belonged
to several Regiments; besides, all the Towns to
to the Left of us, were possessed by Sir *William
Brereton*, *Warrington* and *Northwich*, Garrisoned by
the Enemy, and a strong Party at *Manchester*; so
that 'twas very likely we should be beaten and
dispersed before we could get to *Chester*. These
Reasons, and especially the last, determined us
for the North, and we had resolved to march
the next Morning, when other Intelligence
brought us to more speedy Resolutions. We kept
our Scouts continually abroad, to bring us Intelligence of the Enemy, whom we expected on
our Backs, and also to keep an Eye upon the
Country; for as we lived upon them something
at large, they were ready enough to do us any
ill Turn, as it lay in their Power.

The first Messenger that came to us, was from
our Friends at *Bolton*, to inform us, that they
were preparing at *Manchester* to attack us: One
of our Parties had been as far as *Stockport*, on
the Edge of *Cheshire*, and was pursued by a Party
of the Enemy, but got off by the Help of the
Night. Thus all things looking black to the
South, we had resolved to march Northward
in the Morning, when one of our Scouts from
the Side of *Manchester* assured us, Sir *Thomas Middleton*, with some of the Parliament Forces, and
the

the Country Troops, making above 1200 Men, were on their March to attack us, and would certainly beat up our Quarters that Night. Upon this Advice we refolved to be gone; and getting all things in Readinefs, we began to march about two Hours before Night: And having gotten a trufty Fellow for a Guide, a Fellow that we found was a Friend to our Side, he put a Project into my Head, which faved us all for that time; and that was, to give out in the Village, that we were marched back to *York-shire*, refolving to get into *Pontfract* Caftle; and accordingly he leads us out of the Town the fame way we came in; and taking a Boy with him, he fends the Boy back juft at Night, and bad him fay he faw us go up the Hills at *Black-ftone-Edge*; and it happened very well; for this Party were fo fure of us, that they had placed 400 Men on the Road to the Northward, to intercept our Retreat that Way, and had left no Way for us, as they thought, to get away, but back again.

About Ten a Clock at Night, they affaulted our Quarters, but found we were gone; and being informed which way, they followed upon the Spur, and travelling all Night, being Moon-Light, they found themfelves the next Day about 15 Miles Eaft, juft out of their Way; for we had by the Help of our Guide, turned fhort at the Foot of the Hills, and through blind, untrodden Paths, and with Difficulty enough, by Noon the next Day, had reached almoft 25 Miles North near a Town called *Clithero*. Here we halted in the open Field, and fent out our People to fee how things were in the Country. This Part of the Country almoft unpaffable, and walled round with Hills, was indifferent quiet, and we got fome Refrefhment for our

S felves,

felves, but very little Horfemeat, and fo went on; but we had not marched far before we found our felves difcovered; and the 400 Horfe fent to lye in wait for us as before, having underftood which way we went, followed us hard; and by Letters to fome of their Friends at *Prefton*, we found we were befet again. Our Guide began now to be out of his Knowledge, and our Scouts brought us Word, the Enemy's Horfe was pofted before us, and we knew they were in our Rear. In this Exigence, we refolved to divide our fmall Body, and fo amufing them, at leaft one might get off, if the other mifcarried. I took about 80 Horfe with me, among which were all that I had of our own Regiment, amounting to above 32, and took the hills towards *York-fhire*. Here we met with fuch unpaffable Hills, vaft Moors, Rocks, and ftony Ways, as lamed all our Horfes, and tired our Men; and fometimes I was ready to think we fhould never be able to get over them, till our Horfes failing, and Jack-boots being but indifferent things to travel in, we might be ftarved before we fhould find any Road, or Towns, (for Guide we had none) but a Boy who knew but little, and would cry, when we asked him any Queftions. I believe neither Men nor Horfes ever paffed in fome Places where we went, and for 20 Hours we faw not a Town nor a Houfe, excepting fometimes from the Top of the Mountains, at a vaft Diftance. I am perfwaded we might have encamped here, if we had had Provifions, till the War had been over, and have met with no Difturbance; and I have often wondered fince, how we got into fuch horrible Places, as much as how got out. That which was worfe to us than all the reft, was, that we knew not where we were going,

nor

nor what Part of the Country we should come into, when we came out of those desolate Craggs. At last, after a terrible Fatigue, we began to see the Western Parts of *Yorkshire*, some few Villages, and the Country at a Distance, looked a little like *England*; for I thought before it looked like old *Brennus* Hill, which the *Grisons* call the Grandfather of the *Alps*. We got some Relief in the Villages, which indeed some of us had so much need of, that they were hardly able to sit their Horses, and others were forced to help them off, they were so faint. I never felt so much of the Power of Hunger in my Life; for having not eaten in 30 Hours, I was as ravenous as a Hound; and if I had had a Piece of Horse-flesh, I believe I should not have had Patience to have staid Dressing it, but have fallen upon it raw, and have eaten it as greedily as a *Tartar*.

However, I eat very cautiously, having often seen the Danger of Mens eating heartily after long Fasting. Our next Care was to enquire our Way. *Hallifax*, they told us, was on our right; there we durst not think of going; *Skippon* was before us, and there we knew not how it was; for a Body of 3000 Horse, sent out by the Enemy in Pursuit of Prince *Rupert*, had been there but two Days before, and the Country People could not tell us, whether they were gone, or no: And *Manchefter*'s Horse, which were sent out after our Party, were then at *Hallifax*, in Quest of us, and afterwards marched into *Chefhire*. In this Distress we would have hired a Guide, but none of the Country People would go with us; for the Roundheads would hang them, they said, when they came there. Upon this I called a Fellow to me, *Harke ye friend*, says I, *dost thee*

know

know the Way fo as to bring us into Weſtmoreland, *and not keep the great Road from* York? *Ay merry,* ſays *he, I ken the Ways weel enou; and you would go and guide us,* ſaid I, *but that you are afraid the Roundheads will hang you?* Indeed would I, ſays the Fellow. *Why then,* ſays I, *thou hadſt as good be hanged by a Roundhead as a Cavalier; for if thou wilt not go, I'll hang thee juſt now. Na, and ye ſerve me ſoa,* ſays the Fellow, *Iſe ene gang with ye; for I care not for Hanging; and ye'l get me a good Horſe, Iſe gang and be one of ye, for I'll nere come heame mere.* This pleaſed us ſtill better, and we mounted the Fellow; for three of our Men died that Night with the extreme Fatigue of the laſt Service.

Next Morning, when our new Trooper was mounted and cloathed, we hardly knew him; and this Fellow led us by ſuch Ways, ſuch Wilderneſſes, and yet with ſuch Prudence, keeping the Hills to the left, that we might have the Villages to refreſh our ſelves, that without him, we had certainly either periſhed in thoſe Mountains, or fallen into the Enemy's Hands. We paſſed the great Road from *York* ſo critically as to time, that from one of the Hills he ſhewed us a Party of the Enemy's Horſe, who were then marching into *Weſtmoreland.* We lay ſtill that Day, finding we were not diſcovered by them; and our Guide proved the beſt Scout that we could have had; for he would go out ten Miles at a time, and bring us in all the News of the Country: Here he brought us word, that *York* was ſurrendered upon Articles, and that *Newcaſtle,* which had been ſurprized by the King's Party, was beſieged by another Army of *Scots* advanced to help their Brethren.

Along the Edges of thoſe vaſt Mountains we paſt with the Help of our Guide, till we came
into

into the Foreft of *Swale*; and finding our felves
perfectly concealed here, for no Soldier had
ever been here all the War, nor perhaps would
not, if it had lafted 7 Years; we thought we
wanted a few Days Reft, at leaft for our Horfes,
fo we refolved to halt, and, while we did fo,
we made fme Difguifes, and fent out fome
Spies into the Country; but as here were no
great Towns, nor no Poft Road, we got very little
Intelligence. We refted four Days, and then
marched again; and indeed having no great
Stock of Money about us, and not very free of
that we had, four Days was enough for thofe
poor Places to be able to maintain us.

We thought our felves pretty fecure now;
but our chief Care was how to get over thofe
terrible Mountains; for having paffed the great
Road that leads from *York* to *Lancafter*, the
Craggs, the farther Northward we looked,
look'd ftill the worfe, and our Bufinefs was all
on the other Side. Our Guide told us, he would
bring us out, if we would have Patience, which
we were obliged to, and kept on this flow
March, till he brought us to *Stanhope*, in the
County of *Durham*; where fome of *Goring*'s
Horfe, and two Regiments of Foot, had their
Quarters: This was 19 Days from the Battle
of *Marfton-Moor*. The Prince who was then at
Kendal in *Weftmoreland*, and who had given me
over as loft, when he had News of our Arrival,
fent an Exprefs to me, to meet him at *Appleby*.
I went thither accordingly, and gave him an
Account of our Journey, and there I heard the
fhort Hiftory of the other Part of our Men,
whom we parted from in *Lancafhire*. They made
the beft of their way North; they had two
refolute Gentlemen who commanded; and be-

ing

ing fo clofely purfued by the Enemy, that they
found themfelves under a Neceffity of Fighting,
they halted, and faced about, expecting the
Charge. The Boldnefs of the Action made the
Officer who led the Enemy's Horfe (which it
feems were the County Horfe only) afraid of
them ; which they perceiving, taking the Advantage of his Fears, bravely advance, and charge
them; and, though they were above 200 Horfe,
they routed them, killed about 30 or 40, got
fome Horfes, and fome Money, and pufhed on
their March Night and Day; but coming near
Lancafter, they were fo way-laid and purfued,
that they agreed to feparate, and fhift every
Man for himfelf; many of them fell into the
Enemy's Hands ; fome were killed attempting
to pafs through the River *Lune*; fome went
back again, fix or feven got to *Bolton*, and about
18 got fafe to Prince *Rupert*.

The Prince was in a better Condition here-
abouts than I expected; he and my Lord *Goring*,
with the Help of Sir *Marmaduke Langdale*, and
the Gentlemen of *Cumberland*, had gotten a Body
of 4000 Horfe, and about 6000 Foot; they had
retaken *Newcaftle*, *Tinmouth*, *Durham*, *Stockton*,
and feveral Towns of Confequence from the
Scots, and might have cut them out Work
enough ftill, if that bafe People, refolved to
engage their whole Intereft to ruine their Sovereign, had not fent a fecond Army of 10000 Men,
under the Earl of *Calender*, to help their firft.
Thefe came and laid Siege to *Newcaftle*, but
found more vigorous Refiftance now than they
had done before.

There were in the Town Sir *John Morley*, the
Lord *Crawford*, Lord *Rea*, and *Maxwell*, *Scots*;
and old Soldiers, who were refolved their Countrymen

trymen fhould buy the Town very dear if they had it; and had it not been for our Difafter at *Marfton-Moor*, they had never had it; for *Calender*, finding he was not able to carry the Town, fends to General *Leven* to come from the Siege of *York* to help him.

Mean time the Prince forms a very good Army, and the Lord *Goring*, with 10000 Men fhews himfelf on the Borders of *Scotland*, to try if that might not caufe the *Scots* to recal their Forces; and, I am perfwaded had he entered *Scotland*, the Parliament of *Scotland* had recalled the Earl of *Calender*, for they had but 5000 Men left in Arms to fend againft him; but they were loath to venture.

However, this Effect it had, that it called the *Scots* Northward again, and found them Work there for the reft of the Summer, to reduce the feveral Towns in the Bifhoprick of *Durham*.

I found with the Prince the poor Remains of my Regiment, which when joined with thofe that had been with me, could not all make up three Troops, and but two Captains, three Lieutenants, and one Cornet; the reft were difperfed, killed, or taken Prifoners.

However, with thofe, which we ftill called a Regiment, I joined the Prince, and after having done all we could on that Side, the *Scots* being returned from *York*, the Prince returned through *Lancafhire* to *Chefter*.

The Enemy often appeared and alarmed us, and once fell on one of our Parties, and killed us about a hundred Men; but we were too many for them to pretend to fight us, fo we came to *Bolton*, beat the Troops of the Enemy near *Warrington*, where I got a Cut with a Halbard in

my

my Face, and arrived at *Chefter* the beginning of *Auguft*.

The Parliament, upon their great Succefs in the North, thinking the King's Forces quite broken, had fent their General *Effex* into the Weft, where the King's Army was commanded by Prince *Maurice*, Prince *Rupert*'s elder Brother, but not very ftrong ; and the King being, as they fuppofed, by the Abfence of Prince *Rupert*, weakened fo much as, that he might be checked by Sir *William Waller*, who, with 4500 Foot, and 1500 Horfe, was at that Time about *Winchefter*, having lately beaten Sir *Ralph Hopton*. Upon all thefe Confiderations, the Earl of *Effex* marches Weftward.

The Forces in the Weft being too weak to oppofe him, every thing give way to him, and all People expected he would befiege *Exeter*, where the Queen was newly lying in, and fent a Trumpet to defire he would forbear the City, while fhe could be removed; which he did, and paffed on Weftward, took *Tiverton*, *Biddeford*, *Barnftable*, *Lancefton*, relieved *Plymouth*, drove Sir *Richard Greenvil* up into *Cornwall*, and followed him thither, but left Prince *Maurice* behind him with 4000 Men about *Barnftable* and *Exeter*. The King, in the mean time, marches from *Oxford* into *Worcefter*, with *Waller* at his Heels; at *Edgehill* his Majefty turns upon *Waller*, and gave him a Brufh, to put him in mind of the Place; the King goes on to *Worcefter*, fends 300 Horfe to relieve *Durley* Caftle, befieged by the Earl of *Denby*, and fending Part of his Forces to *Briftol*, returns to *Oxford*.

His Majefty had now firmly refolved to march into the Weft, not having yet any Account of

our

our Misfortunes in the North. *Waller* and *Middleton* way-lay the King at *Cropedy* Bridge: The King aſſaults *Middleton* at the Bridge; *Waller's* Men were poſted with ſome Canr on to guard a Paſs; *Middleton's* Men put a Regiment of the King's Foot to the Rout, and purſued them: *Waller's* Men, willing to come in for the Plunder, a thing their General had often uſed them to, quit their Poſt at the Paſs, and their great Guns, to have Part in the Victory. The King coming in ſeaſonably to the Relief of his Men, routs *Middleton*, and at the ſame time ſends a Party round, who clapt in between Sir *William Waller's* Men and their great Guns, and ſecured the Paſs and the Cannon too.

The King took three Collonels, beſides other Officers, and about 300 Men Priſoners, with eight great Guns, 19 Carriages of Ammunition, and killed about 200 Men.

Waller loſt his Reputation in this Fight, and was exceedingly ſlighted ever after, even by his own Party; but eſpecially by ſuch as were of General *Eſſex's* Party, between whom and *Waller* there had been Jealouſies and Miſunderſtandings for ſome time.

The King, about 8000 ſtrong, marched on to *Briſtol*, where Sir *William Hopton* joined him; and from thence he follows *Eſſex* into *Cornwall*; *Eſſex* ſtill following *Greenvil*, the King comes to *Exeter*, and joining with Prince *Maurice*, reſolves to purſue *Eſſex*; and now the Earl of *Eſſex* began to ſee his Miſtake, being cooped up between two Seas, the King's Army in his Rear, the Country his Enemy, and Sir *Richard Grenvil* in his Van.

The King, who always took the beſt Meaſures, when he was left to his own Counſel, wiſely
refuſes

refuses to engage, though superior in Number, and much stronger in Horse. *Essex* often drew out to fight, but the King fortifies, takes the Passes and Bridges, Plants Cannon, and secures the Country to keep off Provisions, and continually streightens their Quarters, but would not fight.

Now *Essex* sends away to the Parliament for Help, and they write to *Waller*, and *Middleton*, and *Manchester*, to follow, and come up with the King in his Rear; but some were too far off, and could not, as *Manchester* and *Fairfax*; others made no Haste, as having no mind to it, as *Waller* and *Middleton*, and if they had, it had been too late.

At last the Earl of *Essex* finding nothing to be done, and unwilling to fall into the King's Hands, takes Shipping, and leaves his Army to shift for themselves. The Horse, under Sir *William Balfour*, the best Horse-Officer, and, without Comparison, the bravest in all the Parliament Army, advanced in small Parties, as if to Skirmish, but following in with the whole Body, being 3500 Horse, broke through, and got off. Though this was a Loss to the King's Victory, yet the Foot were now in a Condition so much the worse. Brave old *Skippon* proposed to fight through with the Foot and die, as he called, it, like *English* Men, with Sword in Hand; but the rest of the Officers shook their Heads at it; for, being well paid, they had at present no Occasion for dying.

Seeing it thus, they agreed to treat, and the King grants them Conditions, upon laying down their Arms, to march off free. This was too much; had his Majesty but obliged them upon Oath not to serve again for a certain Time, he

had

had done his Bufinefs; but this was not thought of; fo they paffed free, only difarmed, the Soldiers not being allowed fo much as their Swords.

The King gained by this Treaty 40 Pieces of Cannon, all of Brafs, 300 Barrels of Gunpowder, 9000 Arms, 8000 Swords, Match and Bullet in Proportion, 200 Waggons, 150 Colours and Standards, all the Bag and Baggage of the Army, and about 1000 of the Men lifted in his Army. This was a compleat Victory without Bloodfhed; and, had the King but fecured the Men from ferving but for fix Months, it had moft effectually anfwered the Battle of *Marfton-Moor*.

As it was, it infufed new Life into all his Majefty's Forces and Friends, and retrieved his Affairs very much; but efpecially it encouraged us in the North, who were more fenfible of the Blow received at *Marfton-Moor*, and of the Deftruction the *Scots* were bringing upon us all.

While I was at *Chefter*, we had fome fmall Skirmifhes with Sir *William Brereton*. One Morning in particular Sir *William* drew up, and faced us, and one of our Collonels of Horfe obferving the Enemy to be not, as he thought, above 200, defires Leave of Prince *Rupert* to attack them with the like Number, and accordingly he fallied out with 200 Horfe. I ftood drawn up without the City with 800 more, ready to bring him off, if he fhould be put to the worft, which happened accordingly; for, not having difcovered neither the Country nor the Enemy as he ought, Sir *William Brereton* drew him into an Ambufcade; fo that before he came up with Sir *William*'s Forces, near enough to charge, he finds about 300 Horfe

in

in his Rear: Though he was furprized at this, yet, being a Man of a ready Courage, he boldly faces about with 150 of his Men, leaving the other 50 to face Sir *William*. With this fmall Party, he defperately charges the 300 Horfe in his Rear, and putting them into Diforder, breaks through them, and, had there been no greater Force, he had cut them all in Pieces. Flufhed with this Succefs, and loath to defert the 50 Men he had left behind, he faces about again, and charges through them again, and with thefe two Charges entirely routs them. Sir *William Brereton* finding himfelf a little difappointed, advances, and falls upon the 50 Men juft as the Collonel came up to them; they fought him with a great deal of Bravery, but the Collonel being unfortunately killed in the firft Charge, the Men gave Way, and came flying all in Confufion, with the Enemy at their Heels. As foon as I faw this, I advanced, according to my Orders, and the Enemy, as foon as I appeared, gave over the Purfuit. This Gentleman, as I remember, was Collonel *Morrough*; we fetched off his Body, and retreated into *Chefter*.

The next Morning the Prince drew out of the City with about 1200 Horfe and 2000 Foot, and attacked Sir *William Brereton* in his Quarters. The Fight was very fharp for the time, and near 700 Men, on both Sides, were killed; but Sir *William* would not put it to a general Engagement, fo the Prince drew off, contenting himfelf to have infulted him in his Quarters.

We now had received Orders from the King to join him; but I reprefenting to the Prince the Condition of my Regiment, which was now 100 Men, and, that being within 25 Miles

of

of my Father's Houſe, I might ſoon recruit it, my Father having got ſome Men together already, I deſired Leave to lye at *Shrewsbury* for a Month, to make up my Men. Accordingly having obtained his Leave, I marched to *Wrexham*, where, in two Days time I got 20 Men, and ſo on to *Shrewsbury*. I had not been here above 10 Days, but I received an Expreſs to come away with what Recruits I had got together, Prince *Rupert* having poſitive Orders to meet the King by a certain Day. I had not mounted 100 Men, though I had liſted above 200, when theſe Orders came ; but leaving my Father to compleat them for me, I marched with thoſe I had, and came to *Oxford*.

The King, after the Rout of the Parliament Forces in the Weſt, was marched back, took *Barnſtable*, *Plympton*, *Lanccſton*, *Tiverton*, and ſeveral other Places, and left *Plymouth* beſieged by Sir *Richard Grenvil*, met with Sir *William Waller* at *Shaftsbury*, and again at *Andover*, and boxed him at both Places, and marched for *Newberry*. Here the King ſent for Prince *Rupert* to meet him, who with 3000 Horſe made long Marches to join him; but the Parliament having joined their three Armies together, *Manchcſter* from the North, *Waller* and *Eſſex*, the Men being cloathed and armed, from the Weſt, had attacked the King, and obliged him to fight the Day, before the Prince came up.

The King had ſo poſted himſelf, as that he could not be obliged to fight but with Advantage; the Parliament's Forces being ſuperior in Number, and therefore, when they attacked him, he galled them with his Cannon, and declining to come to a general Battle, ſtood upon
the

the Defenſive, expecting Prince *Rupert* with the Horſe.

The Parliament's Forces had ſome Advantage over our Foot, and took the Earl of *Cleveland* Priſoner; but the King, whoſe Foot were not above one to two, drew his Men under the Cannon of *Dennington* Caſtle, and having ſecured his Artillery and Baggage, made a Retreat with his Foot in very good Order, having not loſt in all the Fight above 300 Men, and the Parliament as many: We loſt five Pieces of Cannon and took two, having repulſed the Earl of *Mancheſter*'s Men on the North Side of the Town, with conſiderable Loſs.

The King, having lodged his Train of Artillery and Baggage in *Dennington* Caſtle, marched the next Day for *Oxford*; there we joined him with 3000 Horſe, and 2000 Foot. Encouraged with this Reinforcement, the King appears upon the Hills on the North-weſt of *Newberry*, and faces the Parliament Army. The Parliament having too many Generals as well as Soldiers, they could not agree whether they ſhould fight or no. This was no great Token of the Victory they boaſted of; for they were now twice our Number in the whole, and their Foot three for one. The King ſtood in Battalia all Day, and finding the Parliament Forces had no Stomach to engage him, he drew away his Cannon and Baggage out of *Dennington* Caſtle, in View of their whole Army, and marched away to *Oxford.*

This was ſuch a falſe Step of the Parliament's Generals, that all the People cried ſhame of them: The Parliament appointed a Committee to enquire into it. *Cromwell* accuſed *Mancheſter,*
and

and he *Waller*, and ſo they laid the Fault upon
one another. *Waller* would have been glad to
have charged it upon *Eſſex* ; but as it happened
he was not in the Army, having been taken ill
ſome Days before ; but, as it generally is when
a Miſtake is made, the Actors fall out among
themſelves, ſo it was here. No doubt it was
as falſe a Step as that of *Cornwall*, to let the King
fetch away his Baggage and Cannon in the
Face of three Armies, and never fire a Shot
at them.

The King had not above 8000 Foot in his
Army, and they above 25000 : 'Tis true, the
King had 8000 Horſe, a fine Body, and much
ſuperior to theirs ; but the Foot might, with
the greateſt Eaſe in the World, have prevented
the removing the Cannon, and in three Days
time have taken the Caſtle, with all that was
in it.

Thoſe Differences produced their Self-deny-
ing Ordinance, and the putting by moſt of their
old Generals, as *Eſſex*, *Waller*, *Mancheſter*, and the
like ; and Sir *Thomas Fairfax*, a terrible Man in
the Field, though the mildeſt of Men out of it,
was voted to have the Command of all their
Forces, and *Lambert* to take the Command of
Sir *Thomas Fairfax*'s Troops in the North, old
Skippon being Major General.

This Winter was ſpent on the Enemy's Side
in modelling, as they called it, their Army ;
and, on our Side, in recruiting ours, and ſome
petty Excurſions. Amongſt the many Addreſ-
ſes, I obſerved one from *Suſſex* or *Surrey*, complaining of the Rudeneſs of their Soldiers, and particularly of the raviſhing of Women, and the
murthering of Men ; from which I only obſerved, that there were Diſorders among them, as
well

well as among us, only with this Difference, that they, for Reasons I mentioned before, were under Circumstances to prevent it better than the King: But I must do the King's Memory that Justice, that he used all possible Methods, by Punishment of Soldiers, charging, and sometimes entreating, the Gentlemen not to suffer such Disorders and such Violences in their Men; but it was to no Purpose for his Majesty to attempt it, while his Officers, Generals, and Great Men, winked at it ; for the Licentiousness of the Soldier is supposed to be approved by the Officer, when it is not corrected.

The Rudeness of the Parliament Soldiers began from the Divisions among their Officers ; for, in many Places, the Soldiers grew so out of all Discipline, and so unsufferably rude, that they in particular refused to march when Sir *William Waller* went to *Weymouth.* This had turned to good Account for us, had these cursed *Scots* been out of our way, but they were the Staff of the Party ; and now they were daily follicited to march Southward, which was a very great Affliction to the King, and all his Friends.

One Booty the King got at this time, which was a very seasonable Assistance to his Affairs, *(viz.)* a great Merchant Ship richly laden at *London,* and bound to the *East-Indies,* was, by the Seamen, brought into *Bristol,* and delivered up to the King. Some Merchants in *Bristol* offered the King 40000 l. for her, which his Majesty ordered should be accepted, reserving only 30 great Guns for his own Use.

The Treaty at *Uxbridge* now was begun, and we that had been well beaten in the War, heartily wished the King would come to a Peace ; but

e

but we all forefaw the Clergy would ruine it all.
The Commons were for Presbytery, and would
never agree the Bifhops fhould be reftored ; the
King was willinger to comply with any thing than
this, and we forefaw it would be fo; from whence
we ufed to fay among our felves, *That the Clergy
was refolved if there fhould be no Bifhop, there fhould
be no King.*

This Treaty at *Uxbridge* was a perfect War
between the Men of the Gown, ours was between thofe of the Sword ; and I cannot but
take Notice how the Lawyers, Statefmen, and
the Clergy of every Side beftirred themfelves,
rather to hinder than promote the Peace.

There had been a Treaty at *Oxford* fome time
before, where the Parliament infifting that the
King fhould pafs a Bill to abolifh Epifcopacy,
quit the Militia, abandon feveral of his faithful
Servants to be exempted from Pardon, and making feveral other moft extravagant Demands.
Nothing was done, but the Treaty broke off, both
Parties being rather farther exafperated, than
nclined to hearken to Conditions.

However, foon after the Succefs in the Weft,
his Majefty, to let them fee that Victory had
not puffed him up fo as to make him reject the
Peace, fends a Meffage to the Parliament, to
put them in Mind of Meffages of like Nature
which they had flighted ; and to let them know,
that notwithftanding he had beaten their Forces,
he was yet willing to hearken to a reafonable
Propofal for putting an End to the War.

The Parliament pretended the King, in his
Meffage, did not treat with them as a legal Par-
liament, and fo made Hefitations ; but after long
Debates and Delays they agreed to draw up
Propofitions for Peace to be fent to the King.

T As

As this Meſſage was ſent to the Houſes about *Auguſt*, I think they made it the middle of *No-vember* before they brought the Propoſitions for Peace ; and, when they brought them, they had no Power to enter either upon a Treaty, or ſo much as Preliminaries for a Treaty, only to de-liver the Letter, and receive an Anſwer.

However, ſuch were the Circumſtances of Af-fairs at this Time, that the King was uneaſy to ſee himſelf thus treated, and take no Notice of it: The King returned an Anſwer to the Propoſitions, and propoſed a Treaty by Commiſ-ſioners which the Parliament appointed.

Three Months more were ſpent in naming Commiſſioners. There was much Time ſpent in this Treaty, but little done ; the Commiſſio-ners debated chiefly the Article of Religion, and of the Militia ; in the latter they were very likely to agree, in the former both Sides ſee-med too poſitive. The King would by no Means abandon Epiſcopacy, nor the Parliament Pre-sbytery ; for both in their Opinion were *Jure Divino.*

The Commiſſioners finding this Point hardeſt to adjuſt, went from it to that of the Militia ; but the Time ſpinning out, the King's Commiſ-ſioners demanded longer Time for the Treaty ; the other ſent up for Inſtructions, but the Houſe refuſed to lengthen out the Time.

This was thought an Inſolence upon the King, and gave all good People a Deteſtation of ſuch haughty Behaviour ; and thus the Hopes of Peace vaniſhed, both Sides prepared for War with as much Eagerneſs as before.

The Parliament was employed at this Time in what they called a Modelling their Army ; that is to ſay, that now the Independent Party be-ginning

ginning to prevail; and, as they outdid all the
others in their Refolution of carrying on the
War to all Extremities, fo they were both the
more vigorous and more politick Party in carrying it on.

Indeed the War was after this carried on with
greater Annimofity than ever, and the Generals
pufhed forward with a Vigour, that, as it had
fomething in it unufual, fo it told us plainly
from this Time, whatever they did before, they
now pufhed at the Ruine even of Monarchy
it felf.

All this while alfo the War went on, and
though the Parliament had no fettled Army, yet
their Regiments and Troops were always in
Aftion; and the Sword was at work in every Part
of the Kingdom.

Among an infinite Number of Party Skir-
mifhings and Fights this Winter, one happened
which nearly concerned me, which was the Surprize of the Town and Caftle of *Shrewsbury*. Collonel *Mitton*, with about 1200 Horfe and Foot,
having Intelligence with fome People in the Town,
on a *Sunday* Morning early broke into the Town,
and took it, Caftle and all. The Lofs for the Quality, more than the Number, was very great to
the King's Affairs. They took there 15 Pieces
of Cannon, Prince *Maurice*'s Magazine of Arms
and Ammunition, Prince *Rupert*'s Baggage, above
50 Perfons of Quality and Officers: There was
not above 8 or 10 Men killed on both Sides;
for the Town was furprized, not ftormed. I had
a particular Lofs in this Aftion; for, all the
Men and Horfes my Father had got together
for the recruiting my Regiment, were here loft
and difperfed; and, which was the worfe, my
Father happening to be then in the Town, was

taken

taken Prifoner, and carried to *Beefton* Caftle in *Chefhire*.

I was quartered all this Winter at *Banbury*, and went little abroad; nor had we any Action till the latter end of *February*, when I was ordered to march to *Leicefter* with Sir *Marmaduke Langdale*, in order, as we thought, to raife a Body of Men in that County and *Staffordfhire*, to join the King.

We lay at *Daventry* one Night, and continuing our March to pafs the River above *Northampton*, that Town being poffeffed by the Enemy, we underftood a. Party of *Northampton* Forces were abroad, and intended to attack us : Accordingly in the Afternoon our Scouts brought us Word, the Enemy were quartered in fome Villages on the Road to *Coventry*; our Commander thinking it much better to fet upon them in their Quarters, than to wait for them in the Field, refolves to attack them early in the Morning, before they were aware of it. We refrefhed our felves in the Field for that Day, and getting into a great Wood near the Enemy, we ftayed there all Night, till almoft break of Day, without being difcovered.

In the Morning very early we heard the Enemy's Trumpets found to Horfe; this roufed us to look abroad; and, fending out a Scout, he brought us Word a Party of the Enemy was at Hand. We were vexed to be fo difappointed, but finding their Party fmall enough to be dealt with, Sir *Marmaduke* ordered me to charge them with 300 Horfe and 200 Dragoons, while he at the fame Time entered the Town. Accordingly I lay ftill till they came to the very Skirt of the Wood where I was pofted, when I faluted them with a Volley from my Dragoons out of the Wood,

Wood, and immediately ſhewed my ſelf with
my Horſe on their Front, ready to charge them ;
they appeared not to be ſurprized, and received
our Charge with great Reſolution ; and, being
above 400 Men, they puſhed me vigorouſly in
their Turn, putting my Men into ſome Diſorder. In this Extremity I ſent to order the Dragoons to charge them in the Flank, which they
did with great Bravery, and the other ſtill maintained the Fight with deſperate Reſolution.
There was no want of Courage in our Men on
both Sides; but our Dragoons had the Advan-.
tage, and at laſt routed them, and drove them
back to the Village. Here Sir *Marmaduke Langdale* had his Hands full too ; for my firing had
alarmed the Towns adjacent, that when he came
into the Town, he found them all in Arms ; and,
contrary to his Expectation, two Regiments of
Foot, with about 500 Horſe more. As Sir *Marmaduke* had no Foot, only Horſe and Dragoons,
this was a Surprize to him ; but he cauſed his
Dragoons to enter the Town, and charge the
Foot, while his Horſe ſecured the Avenues of
the Town.

The Dragoons bravely attacked the Foot, and
Sir *Marmaduke* falling in with his Horſe, the
Fight was obſtinate and very bloody, when the
Horſe that I had routed came flying into the
Street of the Village, and my Men at their Heels.
Immediately I left the Purſuit, and fell in with
all my Force to the Aſſiſtance of my Friends,
and, after an obſtinate Reſiſtance, we routed the
whole Party ; we killed about 700 Men, took
350, 27 Officers, 100 Arms, all their Baggage,
and 200 Horſes, and continued our March to
Harborough, where we halted to refreſh our ſelves.

Between

Between *Harborough* and *Leicester* we met with
a Party of 800 Dragoons of the Parliament
Forces. They found themselves too few to attack us, and therefore to avoid us, they had
gotten into a small Wood; but perceiving themselves discovered, they came boldly out, and
placed themselves at the Entrance into a Lane,
lining both Sides of the Hedges with their
Shot. We immediately attacked them, beat
them from their Hedges, beat them into the
Wood, and out of the Wood again, and forced
them at last to a down right *Run-away*, on Foot,
among the Enclosures, where we could not follow them, killed about 100 of them, and took
250 Prisoners, with all their Horses, and came
that Night to *Leicester*. When we came to
Leicester, and had taken up our Quarters, Sir *Marmaduke Langdale* sent for me to sup with him,
and told me, that he had a secret Commission
in his Pocket, which his Majesty had commanded
him not to open 'till he came to *Leicester*; that
now he had sent for me to open it together,
that we might know what it was we were to do,
and to consider how to do it; so pulling out his
sealed Orders, we found we were to get what
Force we could together, and a certain Number of Carriages with Ammunition which the
Governour of *Leicester* was to deliver us, and a
certain Quantity of Provision, especally Corn
and Salt, and to relieve *Newark*. This Town had
been long besieged: The Fortifications of the
Place, together with its Situation, had rendered
it the strongest Piece in *England*; And, as it was
the greatest Pass in *England*, so it was of vast
Consequence to the King's Affairs. There was
in it a Garrison of brave old rugged Boys, Fellows, that, like Count *Tily*'s *Germans*, had Iron
Faces,

Faces, and they had defended themfelves with extraordinary Bravery a great while, but were reduced to an exceeding Streight for want of Provifions.

Accordingly we received the Ammunition and Provifion, and away we went for *Newark*; about *Melton Mowbray*, Collonel *Rofeter* fet upon us, with above 3000 Men; we were about the fame Number, having 2500 Horfe, and 800 Dragoons. We had fome Foot, but they were ftill at *Harborough*, and were ordered to come after us.

Rofeter, like a brave Officer, as he was, charged us with great Fury, and rather outdid us in Number, while we defended our felves with all the Eagernefs we could, and withal gave him to underftand we were not fo foon to be beaten as he expected. While the Fight continued doubtful, efpecially on our Side, our People, who had charge of the Carriages and Provifions, began to enclofe our Flanks with them, as if we had been marching; which, though it was done without Orders, had two very good Effects, and which did us extraordinary Service. Firft, it fecured us from being charged in the Flank, which *Rofeter* had twice attempted; and, Secondly, it fecured our Carriages from being plundered, which had fpoiled our whole Expedition. Being thus enclofed, we fought with great Security; and though *Rofeter* made three defperate Charges upon us, he could never break us. Our Men received him with fo much Courage, and kept their Order fo well, that the Enemy finding it impoffible to force us, gave it over, and left us to purfue our Orders. We did not offer to chafe them, but contented enough to have repulfed and beaten them off,

T 4   and

and our Bufinefs being to relieve *Newark*, we proceeded.

If we are to reckon by the Enemy's ufual Method, we got the Victory, becaufe we kept the Field, and had the Pillage of their Dead; but otherwife, neither Side had any great Caufe to boaft. We loft about 150 Men, and near as many hurt; they left 170 on the Spot, and carried off fome. How many they had wounded we could not tell; we got 70 or 80 Horfe, which helped to remount fome of our Men that had loft theirs in the Fight. We had, however, this Difadvantage, that we were to march on immediately after this Service; the Enemy only to retire to their Quarters, which was but hard by. This was an Injury to our wounded Men, who we were after obliged to leave at *Belvoir* Caftle, and from thence we advanced to *Newark*.

Our Bufinefs at *Newark* was to relieve the Place, and this we refolved to do, whatever it coft, though, at the fame Time, we refolved not to fight, unlefs we were forced to it. The Town was rather blocked up than befieged; the Garrifon was ftrong, but ill provided; we had fent them word of our coming to them, and our Orders to relieve them, and they propofed fome Meafures for our doing it. The chief Strength of the Enemy lay on the other Side of the River; but they having alfo fome Notice of our Defign, had fent over Forces to ftrengthen their Leaguer on this Side. The Garrifon had often furprized them by Sallies, and indeed had chiefly fubfifted for fome time by what they brought in on this Manner.

Sir *Marmaduke Langdale*, who was our General for the Expedition, was for a general Attempt

to

to raife the Siege; but I had perfwaded him off of that: Firft, Becaufe if we fhould be beaten, as might be probable, we then loft the Town. Sir *Marmaduke* briskly replied, *A Soldier ought never to fuppofe he fhall be beaten.* But, Sir, fays I, *you'll get more Honour by relieving the Town, than by beating them: One will be a Credit to your Conduct, as the other will be to your Courage; and, if you think you can beat them, you may do it afterward, and then if you are miftaken, the Town is neverthelefs fecured, and half your Victory gained.*

He was prevailed with to adhere to this Advice, and accordingly we appeared before the Town about two Hours before Night. The Horfe drew up before the Enemy's Works; the Enemy drew up within their Works, and feeing no Foot, expected when our Dragoons would difmount and attack them. They were in the right to let us attack them, becaufe of the Advantage of their Batteries and Works, if that had been our Defign; but, as we intended only to amufe them, this Caution of theirs effected our Defign; for, while we thus faced them with our Horfe, two Regiments of Foot, which came up to us but the Night before, and was all the Infantry we had, with the Waggons of Provifions, and 500 Dragoons, taking a Compafs clean round the Town, pofted themfelves on the lower Side of the Town by the River. Upon a Signal the Garrifon agreed on before, they fallied out at this very Juncture, with all the Men they could fpare, and dividing themfelves in two Parties, while one Party moved to the Left to meet our Relief, the other Party fell on upon Part of that Body which faced us. We kept in Motion, and upon this Signal advanced to their Works, and our Dragoons fired upon

them

them; and the Horse wheeling and counter-marching often, kept them continually expecting to be attacked. By this Means the Enemy were kept employed, and our Foot with the Waggons, appearing on that Quarter where they were least expected, easily defeated the advanced Guards, and forced that Post, where entring the Leaguer, the other Part of the Garrison, who had sallied that way, came up to them, received the Waggons, and the Dragoons entered with them into the Town. That Party which we faced on the other Side of the Works; knew nothing of what was done till all was over; the Garrison retreated in good Order, and we drew off, having finished what we came for without fighting.

Thus we plentifully stored the Town with all things wanting, and with an Addition of 500 Dragoons to their Garrison; after which we marched away without fighting a Stroke. Our next Orders were to relieve *Pontfract* Castle, another Garrison of the King's, which had been besieged ever since a few Days after the Fight at *Marston-Moor*, by the Lord *Fairfax*, Sir *Thomas Fairfax*, and other Generals in their Turn.

By the Way, we were joined with 800 Horse out of *Derbyshire*, and some Foot, so many as made us, about 4500 Men in all.

Collonel *Forbes*, a *Scotchman*, commanded at the Siege, in the Absence of the Lord *Fairfax*; the Collonel had sent to my Lord for more Troops, and his Lordship was gathering his Forces to come up to him; but he was pleased to come too late. We came up with the Enemy's Leaguer about Break of Day, and having been discovered by their Scouts, they, with more

Courage

Courage than Difcretion, drew out to meet us. We faw no Reafon to avoid them, being ftronger in Horfe than they; and though we had but a few Foot, we had 1000 Dragoons, which helped us out. We had placed our Horfe and Foot throughout in one Line, with two Referves of Horfe, and between every Divifion of Horfe, a Divifion of Foot, only that on the Extremes of our Wings, there were two Parties of Horfe on each Point by themfelves, and the Dragoons in the Center, on Foot. Their Foot charged us home, and ftood with Pufh of Pike a great while; but their Horfe charging our Horfe and Mufqueteers, and being clofed on the Flanks with thofe two extended Troops on our Wings, they were prefently difordered, and fled out of the Field. The Foot thus deferted, were charged on every Side, and broken. They retreated ftill fighting, and in good Order, for a while; but the Garrifon fallying upon them at the fame Time, and being followed clofe by our Horfe, they were fcattered, entirely routed, and moft of them killed. The Lord *Fairfax* was come with his Horfe as far as *Ferribridge*, but the Fight was over; and all he could do was to rally thofe that fled, and fave fome of their Carriages, which elfe had fallen into our Hands. We drew up our little Army in Order of Battle the next Day, expecting the Lord *Fairfax* would have charged us; but his Lordfhip was fo far from any fuch Thoughts, that he placed a Party of Dragoons, with Orders to fortify the Pafs at *Ferribridge*, to prevent our falling upon him in his Retreat, which he needed not have done; for, having raifed the Siege of *Pontfract*, our Bufinefs was done, we had nothing to fay to him, unlefs we had been ftrong enough to ftay.

We

We loft not above 30 Men in this Action, and the Enemy 300, with about 150 Prifoners, one Piece of Cannon, all their Ammunition, 1000 Arms, and moft of their Baggage, and Collonel *Lambert* was once taken Prifoner, being wounded, but got off again.

We brought no Relief for the Garrifon, but the Opportunity to furnifh themfelves out of the Country, which they did very plentifully. The Ammunition taken from the Enemy was given to them, which they wanted, and was their Due, for they had fiezed it in the Sally they made, before the Enemy was quite defeated.

I cannot omit taking Notice, on all Occafions, how exceeding ferviceable this Method was of pofting Mufqueteers in the Intervals, among the Horfe, in all this War: I perfwaded our Generals to it, as much as poffible, and I never knew a Body of Horfe beaten that did fo; yet I had great Difficulty to prevail upon our People to believe it, though it was taught me by the greateft General in the World, (viz.) the King of *Sweden.* Prince *Rupert* did it at the Battle *Marfton-Moor* ; and had the Earl of *Newcaftle* not been obftinate againft it in his Right Wing, as I obferved before, the Day had not been loft. In difcourfing this with Sir *Marmaduke Langdale*, I had related feveral Examples of the Serviceablenefs of thefe fmall Bodies of Firemen, and, with great Difficulty, brought him to agree, telling him, I would be anfwerable for the Succefs; but, after the Fight, he told me plainly he faw the Advantage of it, and would never fight otherwife again, if he had any Foot to place. So having relieved thefe two Places, we haftened, by long Marches, through *Derbyfhire*, to join Prince *Rupert* on the Edge of *Shropfhire* and *Chefhire*. We found
Collonel

Collonel *Rofeter* had followed us at a Diftance, ever fince the Bufinefs at *Melton Mowbray*, but never cared to attack us, and we found he did the like ftill. Our General would fain have been doing with him again, but we found him too fhy. Once we laid a Trap for him at *Dove-Bridge*, between *Derby* and *Burton upon Trent*, the Body being marched two Days before; 300 Dragoons were left to guard the Bridge, as if we were afraid he fhould fall upon us. Upon this we marched, as I faid, on to *Burton*, and, the next Day, fetching a Compafs round, came to a Village near *Titbury* Caftle, whofe Name I forgot, were we lay ftill expecting our Dragoons would be attacked.

Accordingly the Collonel, ftrengthned with fome Troops of Horfe from *Yorkfhire*, comes up to the Bridge, and finding fome Dragoons pofted, advances to charge them: The Dragoons immediately get a Horfeback, and run for it, as they were ordered; but the old Lad was not to be caught fo; for he halts immediately at the Bridge, and would not come over till he had fent three or four flying Parties abroad, to difcover the Country. One of thefe Parties fell into our Hands, and received but coarfe Entertainment. Finding the Plot would not take, we appeared, and drew up in View of the Bridge but he would not ftir: So we continued our March into *Chefhire*, where we joined Prince *Rupert*, and Prince *Maurice*, making together a fine Body, being above 8000 Horfe and Dragoons.

This was the beft and moft fuccefsful Expedition I was in during this War. 'Twas well concerted, and executed with as much Expedition and Conduct as could be defired, and the Succefs was anfwerable to it: And indeed, confidering

fidering the Seafon of the Year (for we fet out from *Oxford* the latter end of *February*) the Ways bad, and the Seafon wet, it was a terrible March of above 200 Miles, in continual Action, and continually dodged and obferved by a vigilant Enemy, and at a Time when the North was over-run by their Armies, and the *Scots* wanting Employment for their Forces; yet in lefs than 23 Days, we marched 200 Miles, fought the Enemy in open Field four Times, relieved one Garrifon befieged, and raifed the Siege of another, and joined our Friends at laft in Safety.

The Enemy was in great Pain for Sir *William Brereton* and his Forces, and Expreffes rid Night and Day to the *Scots* in the North, and to the Parties in *Lancafhire*, to come to his Help. The Prince, who ufed to be rather too forward to fight than otherwife, could not be perfwaded to make ufe of this Opportunity, but loitered, if I may be allowed to fay fo, till the *Scots*, with a Brigade of Horfe and 2000 Foot, had joined him; and then 'twas not thought proper to engage them.

I took this Opportunity to go to *Shrewsbury* to vifit my Father, who was a Prifoner of War there, getting a pafs from the Enemy's Governour. They allowed him the Liberty of the Town, and fometimes to go to his own Houfe, upon his Parole, fo that his Confinement was not very much to his perfonal Injury; but this, together with the Charges he had been at in raifing the Regiment, and above 20000 l. in Money and Plate, which at feveral Times he had lent, or given rather, to the King, had reduced our Family to very ill Circumftances; and now they talked of cutting down his Woods.

I had

I had a great deal of Difcourfe with my Father on this Affair; and finding him extremely concerned, I offered to go to the King, and defire his Leave to go to *London*, and treat about his Compofition, or to render my felf a Prifoners in his ftead, while he went up himfelf. In this Difficulty I treated with the Governour of the Town, who very civilly offered me his Pafs to go for *London*, which I accepted; and waiting on Prince *Rupert*, who was then at *Worcefter*, I acquainted him with my Defign. The Prince was unwilling I fhould go to *London*; but told me, he had fome Prifoners of the Parliament's Friends in *Cumberland*, and he would get an Exchange for my Father. I told him, if he would give me his Word for it, I knew I might depend upon it, otherwife there was fo many of the King's Party in their Hands, that his Majefty was tired with Sollicitations for Exchanges; for we never had a Prifoner but there was ten Offers of Exchanges for him. The Prince told me, I fhould depend upon him; and he was as good as his Word quickly after.

While the Prince lay at *Worcefter* he made an Incurfion into *Herefordfhire*, and having made fome of the Gentlemen Prifoners, brought them to *Worcefter*; and though it was an Action which had not been ufual, they being Perfons not in Arms, yet the like being my Father's Cafe, who was really not in Commiffion, nor in any Military Service, having refigned his Regiment three Years before to me, the Prince infifted on exchanging them for fuch as the Parliament had in Cuftody in like Circumftances. The Gentlemen feeing no Remedy, follicited their own Cafe at the Parliament, and got it paffed in their behalf; and by this Means

my

my Father got his Liberty; and, by the Affiftance of the Earl of *Denbigh*, got Leave to come to *London* to make a Compofition, as a Delinquent, for his Eftate. This they charged at 7000 l. but by the Affiftance of the fame noble Perfon, he got off for 4000 l. Some Members of the Committee moved very kindly, that. my Father fhould oblige me to quit the King's Service; but that, as a thing which might be out of his Power, was not infifted on.

The Modelling the Parliament Army took them up all this Winter, and we were in great Hopes the Divifions which appeared amongft them might have weakened their Party; but when they voted Sir *Thomas Fairfax* to be General, I confefs I was convinced the King's Affairs were loft and defperate. Sir *Thomas*, abating the Zeal of his Party, and the miftaken Opinion of his Caufe, was the fitteft Man amongft them to undertake the Charge: He was a compleat General, ftrict in his Difcipline, wary in Conduct, fearlefs in Action, unwearied in the Fatigue of the War, and withal, of a modeft, noble, generous Difpofition. We all aprehended Danger from him, and heartily wifhed him of our own Side; and the King was fo fenfible, though he would not difcover it, that when an Account was brought him of the Choice they had made, he replied, *he was forry for it; he had rather it had been any Body than he.*

The firft Attempts of this new General and new Army were at *Oxford*, which, by the Neighbourhood of a numerous Garrifon in *Abingdon*, began to be very much ftreightned for Provifions; and the new Forces under *Cromwell* and *Skippon*, one Lieutenant General, the other Major General to *Fairfax*, approaching with a
Defign

Defign to block it up, the King left the Place, fuppofing his Abfence would draw them away, as it foon did.

The King refolving to leave *Oxford*, marches from thence with all his Forces, the Garrifon excepted, with Defign to have gone to *Briftol*, but the Plague was in *Briftol*, which altered the Meafures, and changed the Courfe of the King's Defigns, fo he marched for *Worcefter* about the begining of *June* 1645. The Foot with a Train of 40 Pieces of Cannon, marching into *Worcefter*, the Horfe ftayed behind fome time in *Gloucefterfhire*.

The firft Action our Army did, was to raife the Siege of *Chefter*; Sir *William Brereton* had befieged it, or rather blocked it up, and when his Majefty came to *Worcefter*, he fent Prince *Rupert*, with 4000 Horfe and Dragoons, with Orders to join fome Foot out of *Wales*, to raife the Siege; but Sir *William* thought fit to withdraw, and not ftay for them, and the Town was freed without fighting. The Governour took Care in this Interval to furnifh himfelf with all things neceffary for another Siege; and, as for Ammunition and other Neceffaries, he was in no Want.

I was fent with a Party into *Staffordfhire*, with Defign to intercept a Convoy of Stores coming from *London*, for the Ufe of Sir *William Brereton*; but they having fome Notice of the Defign, ftopt, and went out of the Road to *Burton upon Trent*, and fo I miffed them; but that we might not come back quite empty, we attacked *Hawkefly* Houfe, and took it; where we got good Booty, and brought 80 Prifoners back to *Worcefter*. From *Worcefter* the King advanced into *Shropfhire*, and took his Head Quar-

U   ters

ters at *Bridgenorth*. This was a very happy
March of the King's, and had his Majefty proceeded, he had certainly cleared the North
once more of his Enemies, for the Country was
generally for him. At his advancing fo far as
Bridgenorth, Sir *William Brereton* fled up into
Lancafhire; the *Scots* Brigades who were with
him retreated into the North, while yet the
King was above 40 Miles from them, and all
things lay open for Conqueft. The new Generals, *Fairfax* and *Cromwell*, lay about *Oxford*
preparing as if they would befiege it, and gave
the King's Army fo much Leifure, that his
Majefty might have been at *Newcaftle* before
they could have been half Way to him. But
Heaven, when the Ruine of a Perfon or Party is
determined, always fo infatuates their Counfels,
as to make them inftrumental to it themfelves.

The King let flip this great Opportunity, as
fome thought, intending to break into the
Affociated Counties, of *Northampton*, *Cambridge*,
Norfolk, where he had fome Interefts forming.
What the Defign was, we knew not, but the
King turns Eaftward, and Marches into *Leicefter-
fhire*, and having treated the Country but very
indifferently, as having deferved no better of us,
laid Siege to *Leicefter*.

This was but a fhort Siege; for the King, refolving not to lofe Time, fell on with his great
Guns, and having beaten down their Works,
our Foot entered, after a vigorous Refiftance,
and took the Town by Storm. There was fome
Blood fhed here, the Town being carried
by Affault; but it was their own Faults; for after
the Town was taken, the Soldiers and Townfmen obftinately fought us in the Market-Place;
infomuch that the Horfe was called to enter
the

the Town to clear the Streets. But this was not all; I was commanded to advance with thefe Horfe, being three Regiments, and to enter the Town; the Foot, who were engaged in the Streets, crying out, *Horfe, Horfe*. Immediately I advanced to the Gate, for we were drawn up about Mufquet Shot from the Works, to have fupported our Foot, in Cafe of a Sally. Having fiezed the Gate, I placed a Guard of Horfe there, with Orders to let no Body pafs in or out, and dividing my Troops, rode up by two Ways towards the Market-Place; the Garrifon defending themfelves in the Market-Place, and in the Church-yard with great Obftinancy, killed us a great many Men; but, as foon as our Horfe appeared, they demanded Quarter, which our Foot refufed them in the firft Heat; as is frequent in all Nations, in like Cafes; 'till at laft, they threw down their Arms, and yielded at Difcretion; and then I can teftify to the World, that fair Quarter was given them. I am the more particular in this Relation, having been an Eye-witnefs of the Action, becaufe the King was reproached in all the publick Libels, with which thofe Times abounded, for having put a great many to Death, and hanged the Committee of the Parliament, and fome *Scots*, in cold Blood, which was a notorious Forgery; and as I am fure there was no fuch thing done, fo I muft acknowledge I never faw any Inclination in his Majefty to Cruelty, or to act any thing which was not practifed by the General Laws of War, and by Men of Honour in all Nations.

But the Matter of Fact, in Refpect to the Garrifon, was as I have related; and, if they had thrown down their Arms fooner, they had had Mercy fooner; but it was not for a conquering

Army,

Army, entered a Town by Storm, to offer Conditions of Quarter in the Streets.

Another Circumftance was, that a great many of the Inhabitants, both Men and Women,
were killed, which is moft true; and the Cafe
was thus: The Inhabitants, to fhew their over-
forward Zeal to defend the Town, fought in
the Breach; nay, the very Women, to the Honour of the *Leicefter* Ladies, if they like it, of-
ficioufly did their Parts; and after the Town was
taken, and when, if they had had any Brains in
their Zeal, they would have kept their Houfes,
and been quiet, they fired upon our Men out
of their Windows, and from the Tops of their
Houfes, and threw Tiles upon their Heads; and
I had feveral of my Men wounded fo, and 7
or 8 killed. This exafperated us to the laft
Degree; and, finding one Houfe better manned
than ordinary, and many Shot fired at us out
of the Windows, I caufed my Men to attack it,
refolved to make them an Example for the reft;
which they did, and breaking open the Doors,
they killed all they found there, without Diftinction; and I appeal to the World if they were
to blame. If the Parliament Committee, or the
Scots Deputies were here, they ought to have
been quiet, fince the Town was taken; but they
began with us, and, I think, brought it upon
themfelves. This is the whole Cafe, fo far as
came within my Knowledge, for which his Majefty was fo much abufed.

We took here Collonel *Gray* and Captain
Hacker, and about 300 Prifoners, and about 300
more were killed. This was the laft Day of
May 1645.

His Majefty having given over *Oxford* for loft,
continued here fome Days, viewed the Town,
ordered

ordered the Fortifications to be augmented, and prepares to make it the Seat of War. But the Parliament, rouzed at this Appearance of the King's Army, order their General to raife the Siege of *Oxford*, where the Garrifon had, in a Sally, ruined fome of their Works, and killed them 150 Men, taking feveral Prifoners, and carrying them with them into the City; and orders him to march towards *Leicefter*, to obferve the King.

The King had now a fmall, but gallant Army, all brave tried Soldiers, and feemed eager to engage the new-modelled Army; and his Majefty, hearing that Sir *Thomas Fairfax* having raifed the Siege of *Oxford*, advanced towards him, fairly faves him the Trouble of a long March, and meets him half Way.

The Army lay at *Daventry*, and *Fairfax* at *Towcefter*, about 8 Miles off. Here the King fends away 600 Horfe, with 3000 Head of Cattle, to relieve his People in *Oxford*; the Cattle he might have fpared better than the Men. The King having thus victualled *Oxford*, changes his Refolution of fighting *Fairfax*, to whom *Cromwell* was now joined with 4000 Men, or was within a Day's March, and marches Northward. This was unhappy Counfel, becaufe late given: Had we marched Northward at firft, we had done it; but thus it was. Now we marched with a triumphing Enemy at our Heels, and at *Nafeby* their advanced Parties attacked our Rear. The King, upon this, alters his Refolution again, and refolves to fight, and at Midnight calls us up at *Harborough* to come to a Council of War. Fate and the King's Opinion determined the Council of War; and 'twas refolved to fight. Accordingly the Van, in which was Prince *Rupert's* Bri-

gade

gade of Horfe, of which my Regiment was a Part, countermarched early in the Morning.

By five a Clock in the Morning, the whole Army, in Order of Battle, began to defcry the Enemy from the rifing Grounds, about a Mile from *Nafeby*, and moved towards them. They were drawn up on a little Afcent in a large Common Fallow Field, in one Line extended from one Side of the Field to the other, the Field fomething more than a Mile over, our Army in the fame Order, in one Line, with the Referves.

The King led the main Battle of Foot, Prince *Rupert* the Right Wing of the Horfe, and Sir *Marmaduke Langdale* the Left. Of the Enemy *Fairfax* and *Skippen* led the Body, *Cromwell* and *Rofeter* the Right, and *Ireton* the Left. The Numbers of both Armies fo equal, as not to differ 500 Men, fave that the King had moft Horfe by about 1000, and *Fairfax* moft Foot by about 500. The Number was in each Army about 18000 Men.

The Armies coming clofe up, the Wings engaged firft. The Prince with his Right Wing charged with his wanted Fury, and drove all the Parliament's Wing of Horfe, one Divifion excepted, clear out of the Field. *Ireton*, who commanded this Wing, give him his due, rallied often, and fought like a Lion; but our Wing bore down all before them, and purfued them with a terrible Execution.

Ireton feeing one Divifion of his Horfe left, repaired to them, and keeping his Ground, fell foul of a Brigade of our Foot, who coming up to the Head of the Line; he like mad Man charges them with his Horfe: But they with their Pikes tore him to Pieces; fo that this

Divifion

Divifion was entirely ruined. *Ireton* himfelf thruft through the Thigh with a Pike, wounded in the Face with a Halberd, was unhorfed and taken Prifoner.

Cromwell, who commanded the Parliament's Right Wing, charged Sir *Marmaduke Langdale* with extraordinary Fury; but he an old tried Soldier, ftood firm, and received the Charge with equal Gallantry, exchanging all their Shot, Carabines and Piftols, and then fell on Sword in Hand. *Rofeter* and *Whaley* had the better on the Point of the Wing, and routed two Divifions of Horfe, pufhing them behind the Referves, where they rallied, and charged again, but were at laft defeated; the reft of the Horfe now charged in the Flank retreated fighting, and were pufhed behind the Referves of Foot.

While this was doing, the Foot engaged with equal Feircenefs, and for two Hours there was a terrible Fire. The King's Foot backed with gallant Officers, and full of Rage at the Rout of their Horfe, bore down the Enemy's Brigade led by *Skippon*. The old Man wounded, bleeding retreats to their Referves. All the Foot, except the General's Brigade, were thus driven into the Referves, where their Officers rallied them, and bring them on to a frefh Charge; and here the Horfe having driven our Horfe about a Quarter of a Mile from the Foot, face about, and fall in on the Rear of the Foot.

Had our Right Wing done thus, the Day had been fecured; but Prince *Rupert* according to his Cuftom, following the flying Enemy, never concerned himfelf with the Safety of thofe behind; and yet he returned fooner than he had done in like Cafes too. At our Return we

found

found all in Confufion, our Foot broken, all
but one Brigade, which though charged in
Front, Flank and Rear, could not be broken,
till Sir *Thomas Fairfax* himfelf came up to the
Charge with frefh Men, and then they were
rather cut in Pieces then beaten; for they
ftood with their Pikes charged every Way to
the laft Extremity.

In this Condition, at the Diftance of a Quarter of a Mile, we faw the King rallying his
Horfe, and preparing to renew the Fight; and
our Wing of Horfe coming up to him, gave
him Opportunity to draw up a large Body of
Horfe, fo large, that all the Enemy's Horfe
facing us, ftood ftill and looked on, but did
not think fit to charge us, till their Foot, who
had entirely broken our main Battle, were put
into Order again, and brought up to us.

The Officers about the King advifed his
Majefty rather to draw off; for, fince our Foot
were loft, it would be too much Odds to expofe
the Horfe to the Fury of their whole Army,
and would but be facrificing his beft Troops,
without any Hopes of Succefs.

The King, though with great .Regret; at the
Lofs of his Foot, yet feeing there was no other
Hope, took this advice, and retreated in good
Order to *Harborough*, and from thence to *Lei-
cefter.*

This was the Occafion of the Enemy having
fo great a Number of Prifoners; for the Horfe
being thus gone off, the Foot had no Means to
make their Retreat, and were obliged to yield
themfelves. Commiffary General *Ireton* being
taken by a Captain of Foot, makes the Captain
his Prifoner, to fave his Life, and gives him his
Liberty for his Courtefy before.

Cromwell

Cromwell and *Roſeter*, with all the Enemy's Horſe, followed us as far as *Leiceſter*, and killed all that they could lay hold on ſtraggling from the Body, but durſt not attempt to charge us in a Body. The King expecting the Enemy would come to *Leiceſter*, removes to *Aſhby de la Zouch*, where we had ſome Time to recollect our ſelves.

This was the moſt fatal Action of the whole War; not ſo much for the Loſs of our Cannon, Ammunition, and Baggage, of which the Enemy boaſted ſo much, but as it was impoſſible for the King ever to retrieve it: The Foot, the beſt that ever he was Maſter of, could never be ſupplied; his Army in the Weſt was expoſed to certain Ruin, the North over-run with the *Scots*; *in ſhort*, the Caſe grew deſperate, and the King was once upon the Point of bidding us all disband, and ſhift for our ſelves.

We loſt in this Fight not above 2000 ſlain, and the Parliament near as many, but the Priſoners were a great Number; the whole Body of Foot being, as I have ſaid, diſperſed, there were 4500 Priſoners, beſides 400 Officers, 2000 Horſes, 12 Pieces of Cannon, 40 Barrels of Powder, all the King's Baggage, Coaches, moſt of his Servants, and his Secretary, with his Cabinet of Letters, of which the Parliament made great Improvement, and, baſely enough cauſed his private Letters between his Majeſty and the Queen, her Majeſty's Letters to the King, and a great deal of ſuch Stuff to be printed.

After this fatal Blow, being retreated, as I have ſaid, to *Aſhby de la Zouch* in *Leiceſterſhire*, the King ordered us to divide; his Majeſty, with a Body of Horſe, about 3000, went to *Litchfield*, and through *Cheſhire* into North *Wales* and

and Sir *Marmaduke Langdale*, with about 2500 went to *Newark*.

The King remained in *Wales* for several Months; and though the Length of the War had almost drained that Country of Men, yet the King raised a great many Men there, recruited his Horse Regiments, and got together six or seven Regiments of Foot, which seemed to look like the Beginning of a New Army.

I had frequent Discourses with his Majesty in this low Ebb of his Affairs, and he would often wish he had not exposed his Army at *Naseby*. I took the Freedom once to make a Proposition to his Majesty, which if it had taken Effect, I verily believe would have given a new Turn to his Affairs; and that was, at once to slight all his Garrisons in the Kingdom, and give private Orders to all the Soldiers in every Place, to join in Bodies, and meet at two General Rendezvous, which I would have appointed to be, one at *Bristol*, and one at *West-chester*. I demonstrated how easily all the Forces might reach these two Places; and both being strong and wealthy Places, and both Sea-Ports, he would have a free Communication by Sea, with *Ireland*, and with his Friends abroad; and having *Wales* entirely his own, he might yet have an Opportunity to make good Terms for himself, or else have another fair Field with the Enemy.

Upon a fair Calculation of his Troops in several Garrisons and small Bodies dispersed about, I convinced the King, by his own Accounts, that he might have two compleat Armies, each of 25000 Foot, 8000 Horse, and 2000 Dragoons; that the Lord *Goring* and the Lord *Hopton* might Ship all their Forces, and come by by Sea in two Tides, and be with him in a shorter Time than the Enemy could follow.

With two such Bodies he might face the Enemy, and make a Day of it; but now his Men were only sacrificed, and eaten up by Piece-meal in a Party-War, and spent their Lives and Estates to do him no Service: That if the Parliament garrisoned the Towns and Castles he should quit, they would lessen their Army, and not dare to see him in the Field; and if they did not, but left them open, then 'twould be no Loss to him, but he might possess them as often as he pleased.

This Advice I pressed with such Arguments, that the King was once going to dispatch Orders for the doing it; but to be irresolute in Counsel, is always the Companion of a declining Fortune; the King was doubtful, and could not resolve till it was too late.

And yet, though the King's Forces were very low, his Majesty was resolved to make one Adventure more, and it was a strange one; for, with but a Handful of Men he made a desperate March, almost 250 Miles in the Middle of the whole Kingdom, compassed about with Armies and Parties innumerable, traversed the Heart of his Enemy's Country, entered their associated Counties, where no Army had ever yet come, and in spight of all their victorious Troops facing and following him, alarmed even *London* it self, and returned safe to *Oxford*.

His Majesty continued in *Wales* from the Battle at *Naseby* till the 5th or 6th *August*, and till he had an Account from all parts of the Progress of his Enemies, and the Posture of his own Affairs.

Here

Here he found, that the Enemy being hard preſſed in *Somerſetſhire* by the Lord *Goring,* and Lord *Hopton's* Forces, who had take *Bridgewater,* and diſtreſſed *Taunton,* which was now at the Point of Surrender, they had ordered *Fairfax* and *Cromwell,* and the whole Army to march Weſtward, to relieve the Town; which they did, and *Goring's* Troops were worſted, and himſelf wounded at the Fight at *Langport.*

The *Scots,* who were always the dead Weight upon the King's Affairs, having no more Work to do in the North, were, at the Parliament's Deſire, advanced Southward, and then ordered away towards South *Wales,* and were ſet down to the Siege of *Hereford.* Here this famous *Scotch* Army ſpent ſeveral Months in a fruitleſs Siege, ill provided of Ammunition, and worſe with Money; and having ſat near three Months before the Town, and done little but eaten up the Country round them; upon the repeated Accounts of the Progreſs of the Marqueſs of *Montroſe* in that Kingdom, and preſſing Inſtances of their Countrymen, they reſolved to raiſe their Siege, and go home to relieve their Friends.

The King, who was willing to be rid of the *Scots,* upon good Terms; and therefore to haſten them, and leaſt they ſhould pretend to puſh on the Siege to take the Town firſt, gives it out, that he was reſolved with all his Forces to go into *Scotland,* and join *Montroſe*; and ſo having ſecured *Scotland,* to renew the War from thence.

And accordingly his Majeſty marches Northwards, with a Body of 4000 Horſe; and, had the King really done this, and with that Body of Horſe marched away, (for he had the Start of all his Enemies, by above a Fortnight's March)

lio

he had then had the faireſt Opportunity for a general Turn of all his Affairs, that he ever had in all the latter Part of this War: For *Montroſe*, a gallant daring Soldier, who from the leaſt Shadow of Force in the fartheſt Corner of his Country, had, rowling like a Snow Ball, ſpread all over *Scotland*, was come into the South Parts, and had ſummoned *Edinburgh*, frighted away their Stateſmen, beaten their Soldiers at *Dundee* and other Places, and Letters and Meſſengers in the Heels of one another, repeated their Cries to their Brethren in *England*, to lay before them the ſad Condition of the Country, and to haſten the Army to their Relief. The *Scots* Lords of the Enemy's Party fled to *Berwick*, and the Chancellor of *Scotland* goes himſelf to General *Leſly*, to preſs him for help.

In this Extremity of Affairs *Scotland* lay, when we marched out of *Wales*. The *Scots* at the Siege of *Hereford* hearing the King was gone Northward with his Horſe, conclude he was gone directly for *Scotland*, and immediately ſend *Leſly* with 4000 Horſe and Foot to follow, but did not yet raiſe the Siege.

But the King ſtill irreſolute, turns away to the Eaſtward, and comes to *Litchfield*, where he ſhewed his Reſentments at Collonel *Haſtings*, for his eaſy Surrender of *Leiceſter*.

In this March the Enemy took Heart; we had Troops of Horſe on every Side upon us, like Hounds ſtarted at a freſh Stag. *Leſly*, with the *Scots*, and a ſtrong Body followed in our Rear, Major General *Points*, Sir *John Gell*, Collonel *Roſeter*, and others, in our Way; they pretended to be 10000 Horſe, and yet never durſt face us. The *Scots* made one Attempt upon a Troop which
ſtayed

ſtayed a little behind, and took ſome Priſoners; but when a Regiment of our Horſe faced them, they retired. At a Village near *Litchfield*, another Party of about 1000 Horſe attacked my Regiment; we were on the left of the Army, and, at a little too far a Diſtance. I happened to be with the King at that time, and my Lieutenant Collonel with me; ſo that the Major had Charge of the Regiment; he made a very handſome Defence, but ſent Meſſengers for ſpeedy Relief; we were on a March, and therefore all ready, and the King orders me a Regiment of Dragoons and 300 Horſe, and the Body halted to bring us off, not knowing how ſtrong the Enemy might be. When I came to the Place I found my Major hard layed to, but fighting like a Lion; the Enemy had broke in upon him in two Places, and had routed one Troop, cutting them off from the Body, and had made them all Priſoners. Upon this I fell in with the 300 Horſe, and cleared my Major from a Party who charged him in the Flank; the Dragoons immediately lighting, one Party of them comes up on my Wing, and ſaluting the Enemy with their Muſquets, put them to a ſtand; the other Party of Dragoons wheeling to the Left, endeavoured to get behind them. The Enemy perceiving they ſhould be over-powered, retreated in as good Order as they could, but left us moſt of our Priſoners, and about 30 of their own. We loſt about 15 of our Men, and the Enemy about 40, chiefly by the Fire of our Dragoons in their Retreat.

In this Poſture we continued our March; and though the King halted at *Litchfield*, which was a dangerous Article, having ſo many of the Enemy's Troops upon his Hands, and this Time gave

gave them Opportunity to get into a Body; yet the *Scots*, with their General *Lesly*, resolving for the North, the rest of the Troops were not able to face us, till having ravaged the Enemy's Country through *Staffordshire*, *Warwick*, *Leicester*, and *Nottinghamshire*, we came to the Leaguer before *Newark*.

The King was once more on the Mind to have gone into *Scotland*, and called a Council of War to that Purpose; but then it was resolved by all Hands, that it would be too late to attempt it; for the *Scots* and Major General *Pointz* were before us, and several strong Bodies of Horse in our Rear; and there was no venturing now, unless any Advantage presented to rout one of those Parties which attended us.

Upon these and like Considerations we resolved for *Newark*; on our Approach the Forces which blocked up that Town drew off, being too weak to oppose us; for the King was now above 5000 Horse and Dragoons, besides 300 Horse and Dragoons he took with him from *Newark*.

We halted at *Newark* to assist the Garrison, or give them Time rather to furnish themselves from the Country with what they wanted, which they were very diligent in doing; for in two Days time they filled a large Island which lies under the Town, between the two Branches of the *Trent*, with Sheep, Oxen, Cows and Horses, an incredible Number; and our Affairs being now something desperate, we were not very nice in our Usage of the Country; for really if it was not with a Resolution, both to punish the Enemy and enrich our selves, no Man can give any rational Account why this desperate Journey was undertaken.

'Tis

'Tis certain the *Newarkers*, in the Refpite they
gained by our coming, got above 50000 l. from
the Country round them, in Corn, Cattle, Money, and other Plunder.

From hence we broke into *Lincolnfhire*, and
the King lay at *Belvoir* Caftle, and from *Belvoir*
Caftle to *Stamford*. The Swiftnefs of our March
was a terrible Surprize to the Enemy ; for our
Van being at a Village on the great Road called
Stilton, the Country People fled into the Ifle of
Ely, and every Way, as if all was loft. Indeed
our Dragoons treated the Country very coarfly ;
and all our Men in general made themfelves rich.
Between *Stilton* and *Huntingdon* we had a fmall
Buftle with fome of the Affociation Troops of
Horfe, but they were foon routed, and fled to
Huntingdon, where they gave fuch an Account
of us to their Fellows, that they did not think
fit to ftay for us, but left their Foot to defend
themfelves as well as they could.

While this was doing in the Van, a Party
from *Burleigh* Houfe, near *Stamford*, the Seat of
the Earl of *Exeter*, purfued four Troops of our
Horfe, who ftraggling towards *Peterborough*, and
committing fome Diforders there, were furprized before they could get into a Pofture of
Fighting ; and encumbered, as I fuppofe, with
their Plunder, they were entirely routed, loft
moft of their Horfes, and were forced to come
away on Foot ; but finding themfelves in this
Condition, they got into a Body in the Enclofures, and in that Pofture turning Dragoons, they
lined the Hedges, and fired upon the Enemy
with their Carabines. This way of Fighting,
though not very pleafant to Troopers, put the
Enemy's Horfe to fome Stand, and encouraged
our Men to venture into a Village, where the

e   Enemy

Enemy had fecured 40 of their Horfe; and boldly charging the Guard, they beat them off and recovered thofe Horfes; the reft made their Retreat good to *Wandsford* Bridge; but we loft near 100 Horfes, and about 12 of our Men taken Prifoners.

The next Day the King took *Huntington*; the Foot which were left in the Town, as I obferved by their Horfe, had pofted themfelves at the Foot of the Bridge, and fortified the Pafs, with fuch Things as the Hafte and Shortnefs of the Time would allow; and in this Pofture they feemed refolute to defend themfelves. I confefs, had they in Time planted a good Force here, they might have put a full Stop to our little Army; for the River is large and deep, the Country on the left marfhy, full of Drains and Ditches, and unfit for Horfe, and we muft have either turned back, or took the Right Hand into *Bedfordfhire*; but here not being above 400 Foot, and they forfaken of their Horfe, the Refiftance they made was to no other Purpofe than to give us Occafion to knock them in the Head, and plunder the Town.

However, they defended the Bridge, as I have faid, and oppofed our Paffage. I was this Day in the Van, and our Forelorn having entered *Huntington* without any great Refiftance till they came to the Bridge, finding it barricaded, they fent me Word; I caufed the Troops to halt, and rid up to the Forelorn, to view the Countenance of the Enemy, and found by the Pofture they had put themfelves in, that they refolved to fell us the Paffage as dear as they could.

I fent to the King for fome Dragoons, and gave him Account of what I obferved of the Enemy, and

X   that

that I judged them to be 1000 Men; for I could not particularly fee their Numbers. Accordingly the King ordered 500 Dragoons to attack the Bridge, commanded by a Major; the Enemy had 200 Mufqueteers placed on the Bridge, their Barricade ferved them for a Breaft-work on the Front, and the low Walls on the Bridge ferved to fecure their Flanks: Two Bodies of their Foot were placed on the oppofite Banks of the River, and a Referve ftood in the High-way on the Rear. The Number of their Men could not have been better ordered, and they wanted not Courage anfwerable to the Conduct of the Party. They were commanded by one *Bennet*, a refolute Officer, who ftood in the Front of his Men on the Bridge with a Pike in his Hand.

Before we began to fall on, the King ordered to view the River, to fee if it was no where paffable, or any Boat to be had; but the River being not fordable, and the Boats all fecured on the other Side, the Attack was refolved on, and the Dragoons fell on with extraordinary Bravery. The Foot defended themfelves obftinately, and beat off our Dragoons twice; and though *Bennet* was killed upon the Spot, and after him him his Lieutenant, yet their Officers relieving them with frefh Men, they would certainly have beat us all off, had not a venturous Fellow, one of our Dragoons thrown himfelf into the River, fwum over, and, in the midft of a Shower of Mufquet Bullets, cut the Rope which tied a great flat-bottom Boat, and brought her over: With the Help of this Boat, I got over 100 Troopers firft, and then their Horfes, and then 200 more without their Horfes; and with this Party fell in with one of the fmall Bodies of Foot that were pofted on that Side, and

and having routed them, and after them the Reserve which stood in the Road, I made up to the other Party; they stood their Ground, and having rallied the Run-aways of both the other Parties, charged me with their Pikes, and brought me to a Retreat; but by this time the King had sent over 300 Men more, and they coming up to me, the Foot retreated. Those on the Bridge finding how 'twas and having no Supplies sent them, as before, fainted, and fled; and the Dragoons rushing forward, most of them were killed; about 150 of the Enemy were killed, of which all the Officers at the Bridge, the rest run away.

The Town suffered for it; for our Men left them little of any thing they could carry. Here we halted, and raised Contributions, took Money of the Country, and of the open Towns, to exempt them from Plunder. Twice we faced the Town of *Cambridge*, and several of our Officers advised his Majesty to storm it; but having no Foot, and but 1200 Dragoons, wiser Heads diverted him from it; and, leaving *Cambridge* on the left, we marched to *Wooburn*, in *Bedfordshire*, and our Parties raised Money all over the County quite into *Hertfordshire*, within 5 Miles of St. *Alban*'s.

The Swiftness of our March, and Uncertainty which Way we intended, prevented all possible Preparation to oppose us, and we met with no Party able to make Head against us. From *Wooburn* the King went through *Buckingham* to *Oxford*; some of our Men straggling in the Villages for Plunder, were often picked up by the Enemy; but in all this long March we did not loose 200 Men, got an incredible Booty, and

X 2

brought

brought 6 Waggons loaden with Money, besides 2000 Horses, and 3000 Head of Cattle into *Oxford.*

From *Oxford* his Majesty moves again into *Gloucestershire* having left about 1500 of his Horse at *Oxford*, to scour the Country, and raise Contributions, which they did as far as *Reading.*

Sir *Thomas Fairfax* was returned from taking *Bridgewater*, and was sat down before *Bristol*, in which Prince *Rupert* commanded with a strong Garrison, 2500 Foot and 1000 Horse. We had not Force enough to attempt any thing there ; but the *Scots*, who lay still before *Hereford*, were afraid of us, having before parted with all their Horse under Lieutenant General *Lesly*, and but ill stored with Provisions; and, if we came on their Backs, were in a fair way to be starved, or made to buy their Provisions at the Price of their Blood.

His Majesty was sensible of this, and had we had but 10 Regiments of Foot, would certainly have fought the *Scots*; but we had no Foot, or so few as was not worth while to march them. However, the King marched to *Worcester*, and the *Scots* apprehending they should be blocked up, immediately raised the Siege, pretending it was to go help their Brethren in *Scotland*, and away they marched Northwards.

We picked up some of their Stragglers, but they were so poor, had been so ill paid, and so harrassed at the Siege, that they had neither Money nor Clothes ; and the poor Soldiers fed upon Apples and Roots, and eat the very green Corn as it grew in the Fields, which reduced them to a very sorry Condition of Health, for they died like People infected with the Plague.

'Twas

'Twas now debated whether we should yet march for *Scotland*, but two Things prevented. 1. The Plague was broke out there, and Multitudes died of it, which made the King backward, and the Men more backward. 2. The Marquefs of *Montrofe* having routed a whole Brigade of *Lefly*'s beft Horfe, and carried all before him, wrote to his Majefty, that he did not now want Affiftance, but was in Hopes in a few Days to fend a Body of Foot into *England*, to his Majefty's Affiftance. This over Confidence of his was his Ruine; for, on the contrary, had he earneftly preffed the King to have marched, and fallen in with his Horfe, the King had done it, and been abfolutely Mafter of *Scotland* in a Fortnight's time; but *Montrofe* was too confident, and defied them all, till at laft they got their Forces together, and *Lefly*, with his Horfe out of *England*, and worfted him in two or three Encounters, and then never left him till they drove him out of *Scotland*.

While his Majefty ftayed at *Worcefter* feveral Meffengers came to him from *Chefhire* for Relief, being exceedingly ftreightened by the Forces of the Parliament: In order to which, the King marched, but *Shrewsbury* being in the Enemy's Hands, he was obliged to go round by *Ludlow*, where he was joined by fome Foot out of *Wales*. I took this Opportunity to ask his Majefty's Leave to go by *Shrewsbury* to my Father's, and taking only two Servants, I left the Army two Days before they marched.

This was the moft Unfoldier-like Action that ever I was guilty of, to go out of the Army to pay a Vifit, when a Time of Action was juft at Hand; and, though I proteft I had not the leaft Intimation, no not from my own Thoughts, that the

X 3　　　　　Army

Army would engage, at leaſt before they came to *Cheſter*, before which I intended to meet them; yet it looked ſo ill, ſo like an Excuſe, or a Sham of Cowardiſe, or Diſaffection to the Cauſe, and to my Maſter's Intereſt, or ſomething I know not what, that I could not bear to think of it, nor never had the Heart to ſee the King's Face after it.

From *Ludlow* the King marched to relieve *Cheſter*; *Poyntz*, who commanded the Parliament's Forces, follows the King, with Deſign to join with the Forces before *Cheſter*, under Collonel *Jones*, before the King could come up. To that End *Poyntz* paſſes through *Shrewsbury* the Day that the King marched from *Ludlow*; yet the King's Forces got the Start of him, and forced him to engage: Had the King engaged him but three Hours ſooner, and conſequently farther off from *Cheſter*, he had ruined him; for *Poyntz*'s Men not able to ſtand the Shock of the King's Horſe, gave Ground, and would in half an Hour more been beaten out of the Field; but Collonel *Jones*, with a ſtrong Party from the Camp, which was within two Miles, comes up in the Heat of the Action, falls on in the King's Rear, and turned the Scale of the Day: The Body was, after an obſtinate Fight defeated, and a great many Gentlemen of Quality killed and taken Priſoners; the Earl of *Litchfield* was of the Number of the former, and 67 Officers of the latter, with 1000 others.

The King with about 500 Horſe got into *Cheſter*, and from thence into *Wales*, whither all that could get away made up to him as faſt as they could, but in a bad Condition.

This was the laſt Stroke they ſtruck, the reſt of the War was nothing but taking all his Garrifons

rifons from him, one by one, till they finifhed the War, with the captivating his Perfon, and then, for want of other Bufinefs, fell to fighting with one another.

I was quite difconfolate at the News of this laft Action, and the more becaufe I was not there; my Regiment was wholly difperfed, my Lieutenant Collonel, a Gentleman of a good Family, and a near Relation to my Mother, was Prifoner, my Major and three Captains killed, and moft of the reft Prifoners.

The King, hopelefs of any confiderable Party in *Wales*, *Briftol* being furrendered, fends for Prince *Rupert* and Prince *Maurice*, who came to him. With them, and the Lord *Digby*, Sir *Marmaduke Langdale*, and a great Train of Gentlemen, his Majefty marches to *Newark* again, leaves a Thoufand Horfe with Sir *William Vaughan*, to attempt the Relief of *Chefter*, in doing whereof he was routed the fecond time by *Jones* and his Men, and entirely difperfed.

The chief Strength the King had in thefe Parts was at *Newark*, and the Parliament were very earneft with the *Scots* to march Southward, and to lay Siege to *Newark*; and while the Parliament preffed them to it, and they fat ftill, and delayed it, feveral Heats began, and fome ill blood between them, which afterwards broke out into open War. The *Englifh* reproached the *Scots* with pretending to help them, and really hindering their Affairs. The *Scots* returned, that they come to fight for them, and are left to be ftarved, and can neither get Money nor Clothes. At laft they came to this, the *Scots* will come to the Siege, if the Parliament will fend them Money, but not before: However, as People fooner agree in doing ill,

X 4   than

than in doing well, they came to Terms, and the *Scots* came with their whole Army to the Siege of *Newark*.

The King, foreseeing the Siege, calls his Fiends about him, tells them, he sees his Circumstances are such, that they can help him but little, nor he protect them, and advises them to separate. The Lord *Digby*, with Sir *Marmaduke Langdale*, with a strong Body of Horse, attempt to get into *Scotland*, to join with *Montrose*, who was still in the Highlands, though reduced to a low Ebb; but these Gentlemen are fallen upon on every Side and routed, and at last being totally broken and dispersed, they fly to the Earl of *Derby*'s Protection in the Isle of Man.

Prince *Rupert*, Prince *Maurice*, Collonel *Gerrard*, and above 400 Gentlemen, all Officers of Horse, lay their Commissions down, and siezing, upon *Wooton* House for a Retreat, make Proposals to the Parliament to leave the Kingdom, upon their Parole not to return again in Arms against the Parliament, which was accepted, though afterwards the Princes declined it. I sent my Man Post to the Prince to be included in this Treaty, and for Leave for all that would accept of like Conditions, but they had given in the List of their Names, and could not alter it.

This was a sad Time; the poor Remains of the King's Fortunes went every where to wreck; every Garrison of the Enemy was full of the Cavalier Prisoners, and every Garrison the King had was beset with Enemies, either blocked up or besieged. *Goring* and the Lord *Hopton* were the only Remainders of the King's Forces, which kept in a Body, and *Fairfax* was

pushing

pushing them with all imaginable Vigour with his whole Army, about *Exeter*, and other Parts of *Devonshire* and *Cornwall*.

In this Condition the King left *Newark* in the Night, and got to *Oxford*. The King had in *Oxford* 8000 Men, and the Towns of *Banbury*, *Farrington*, *Dunnington* Castle, and such Places as might have been brought together in 24 Hours, 15 or 20000 Men, with which if he had then resolved to have quitted the Place, and collected the Forces in *Worcester*, *Hereford*, *Lichfield*, *Ashby de la Zouch*, and all the small Castles and Garrisons he had thereabouts, he might have had near 40000 Men, might have beaten the *Scots* from *Newark*, Collonel *Jones* from *Chester*, and all, before *Fairfax* who was in the West, could be able to come to their Relief, and this his Majesty's Friends in North *Wales* had concerted; and, in order to it, Sir *Jacob Ashby* gathered what Forces he could, in our Parts, and attempted to join the King at *Oxford*, and to have proposed it to him; but Sir *Jacob* was entirely routed at *Stow on the Would*, and taken Prisoner, and of 3000 Men not above 600 came to *Oxford*.

All the King's Garrisons dropt one by one; *Hereford* which had stood out against the whole Army of the *Scots* was surprized by six Men and a Lieutenant dressed up for Country Labourers, and a Constable pressed to work, who cut the Guards in Pieces, and let in a Party of the Enemy.

Chester was reduced by Famine, all the Attempts the King made to relieve it being frustrated.

Sir *Thomas Fairfax* routed the Lord *Hopton* at *Torrington*, and drove him to such Extremities, that

that he was forced up into the fartheft Corner of *Cornwall*. The Lord *Hopton* had a gallant Body of Horfe with him of nine Brigades, but no Foot; *Fairfax*, a great Army.

Heartlefs, and tired out with continual ill News, and ill Succefs, I had frequent Meetings with fome Gentlemen, who had efcaped from the Rout of Sir *William Vaughan*, and we agreed upon a Meeting at *Worcefter* of all the Friends we could get, to fee if we could raife a Body fit to do any Service; or, if not, to confider what was to be done. At this Meeting we had almoft as many Opinions as People; our Strength appeared too weak to make any Attempt, the Game was too far gone in our Parts to be retrieved; all we could make up did not amount to above 800 Horfe.

'Twas unanimoufly agreed not to go into the Parliament as long as our Royal Mafter did not give up the Caufe; but in all Places, and by all poffible Methods, to do him all the Service we could. Some propofed one thing, fome another; at laft we propofed getting Veffels to carry us to the Ifle of *Man* to the Earl of *Derby*, as Sir *Marmaduke Langdale*, Lord *Digby*, and others had done. I did not forefee any Service it would be to the King's Affairs, but I ftarted a Propofal, that marching to *Pembrook* in a Body, we fhould there fieze upon all the Veffels we could, and embarking our felves, Horfes, and what Foot we could get, crofs the *Severn* Sea, and land in *Cornwall* to the Affiftance of Prince *Charles*, who was in the Army of the Lord *Hopton*, and where only there feemed to be any Poffibility of a Chance for the remaining part of our Caufe.

This Propofal was not without its Difficulties, as how to get to the Sea-fide, and, when there, what

what Affurance of Shipping. The Enemy, under Major General *Langhorn* had over-run *Wales,* and 'twould be next to impoffible to effect it.

We could never carry our Propofal with the whole Affembly; but however, about 200 of us refolved to attempt it, and Meeting being broke up without coming to any Conclufion, we had a private Meeting among our felves to effect it. .

We difpatched private Meffengers to *Swanzey* and *Pembrock*, and other Places; but they all difcouraged us from the Attempt that way, and advifed us to go higher towards North *Wales,* where the King's Intereft had more Friends, and the Parliament no Forces. Upon this we met, and refolved, and having fent feveral Meffengers that Way, one of my Men provided us two fmall Veffels in a little Creek near *Harlegh* Caftle, in *Merionethſhire*. We marched away with what Expedition we could, and embarked in the two Veffels accordingly. It was the worft Voyage fure that ever Man went; for firft, we had no Manner of Accomodation for fo many People, Hay for our Horfes we got none, or very little, but good Store of Oats, which ferved us for our own Bread as well as Provender for the Horfes.

In this Condition we put off to Sea, and had a fair Wind all the firft Night, but early in the Morning a fudden Storm drove us within two or three Leagues of *Ireland.* In this Pickle Sea-Sick our Horfes rouling about upon one another, and our felves ftifled for want of Room, no Cabins nor Beds, very cold Weather, and very indifferent Diet, we wifhed our felves afhore again a thoufand times; and yet we were not willing to go on Shore in *Ireland*, if we could

help

help it; for the Rebels having Poſſeſſion of every Place, that was juſt having our Throats cut at once. Having rouled about at the Mercy of the Winds all Day, the Storm ceaſing in the Evening, we had fair Weather again, but Wind enough, which being large, in two Days and a Night we came upon the Coaſt of *Cornwall*, and, to our no ſmall Comfort, landed the next Day at St. *Ives* in the County of *Cornwall*.

We reſted our ſelves here, and ſent an Expreſs to the Lord *Hopton*, who was then in *Devonſhire*, of our Arrival, and deſired him to aſſign us Quarters, and ſend us his farther Orders. His Lordſhip expreſſed a very great Satisfaction at our Arrival, and left it to our own Conduct to join him as we ſaw convenient.

We were marching to join him, when News came, that *Fairfax* had given him an entire Defeat at *Terrington*. This was but the old Story over again; we had been uſed to ill News a great while, and 'twas the leſs Surprize to us.

Upon this News we halted at *Bodmin*, till we ſhould hear farther; and it was not long before we ſaw a Confirmation of the News before our Eyes; for the Lord *Hopton*, with the Remainder of his Horſe, which he had brought off at *Torrington* in a very ſhattered Condition, retreated to *Lanceſton*, the firſt Town in *Cornwall*, and hearing that *Fairfax* purſued him, came on to *Bodmin*. Hither he ſummoned all the Troops which he had left, which when he had got together, were a fine Body indeed of 5000 Horſe, but few Foot but what were at *Pendennis*, *Barnſtable*, and other Garriſons; theſe were commanded by the Lord *Hopton*; the Lord *Goring* had taken ſhipping for *France*, to get Relief, a few Days before.

Here

Here a Grand Council of War was called, and
several things were proposed, but as it always
is in Distress, People are most irresolute, so
'twas here: Some were for breaking through by
Force, our Number being superiour to the
Enemy's Horse. To fight them with their Foot
would be Desperation, and ridiculous; and to
retreat, would but be to coop up themselves in
a narrow Place, where at last they must be
forced to fight upon Disadvantage, or yield at
Mercy. Others opposed this as a desperate Action, and without Probability of Success; and all
were of different Opinions: I confess, when I
saw how things were, I saw 'twas a lost Game,
and I was for the Opinion of breaking through,
and doing it now, while the Country was open
and large, and not being forced to it when it
must be with more Disadvantage; but nothing
was resolved on, and so we retreated before the
Enemy. Some small Skirmishes there happened near *Bodmin*, but none that were very considerable.

'Twas the 1st of *March* when we quitted
Bodmin, and quartered at large at *Columb, St.
Denis* and *Truro*, and the Enemy took his Quarters at *Bodmin*, posting his Horse at the Passes
from *Padstow* on the North, to *War-bridge Lesti-
thel* and *Foy*, spreading so from Sea to Sea, that
now breaking through was impossible. There
was no more Room for Counsel; for unless we had
Ships to carry us off, we had nothing to do but
when we were fallen upon, to defend our selves,
and sell Victory as dear as we could to the
Enemies.

The Prince of *Wales* seeing the Distress we
were in, and loath to fall into the Enemy's Hands,
ships himself on board some Vessels at *Falmouth*,

with

with about 400 Lords and Gentlemen; and, as I
had no Command here, to oblige my Attendance, I
was once going to make one; but my Comerades, whom I had been the principal Occasion
of bringing hither, began to take it ill, that I
would leave them; and so I resolved we would
take our Fate together.

While thus we had nothing before us but a
Soldier's Death, a fair Field, and a strong Enemy,
and People began to look one upon another : The
Soldiers asked how their Officers looked, and the
Officers asked how their Soldiers looked, and
every Day we expected to be our last, when
unexpectedly the Enemy's General sent a Trumpet to *Truro* to my Lord *Hopton* with a very
handsom Gentleman-like Offer.

That since the General could not be ignorant of his present Condition, and that the Place
he was in could not afford him Subsistance or
Defence ; and especially considering that the
State of our Affairs were such, that if we should
escape from thence, we could not remove to
our Advantage, he had thought good to let us
know, *That if we would deliver up our Horses and
Arms, he would, for avoiding the Effusion of Christian
Blood, or the putting any unsoldiery Extremities upon
us, allow such honourable and safe Conditions, as were
rather better than our present Circumstances could demand, and such as should discharge him to all the
World, as a Gentleman, as a Soldier, and as a
Christian.*

After this followed the Conditions he would
give us, which were as follows, (*viz.*) *That all
the Soldiery, as well* English *as Foreigners, should have
Liberty to go beyond the Seas, or to their own Dwellings, as they pleased ; and to such as shall chuse to live
at home, Protection for their Liberty, and from all*
Vio-

Violence, and plundering of Soldiers, and to give them Bag and Baggage, and all their Goods, except Horses and Arms.

That for *Officers* in *Commission,* and *Gentlemen* of *Quality,* he would allow them *Horses* for themselves and one *Servant,* or more, suitable to their *Quality,* and such *Arms* as are suitable to *Gentlemen* of such *Quality* travelling in *Times of Peace* ; and such *Officers* as would go *beyond Sea,* should take with them their full *Arms* and *Number* of *Horses* as are allowed in the *Army* to such *Officers.*

That all the *Troopers* should receive on the *Delivery* of their *Horses,* 20 s. a *Man,* to carry them home ; and the *General's Pass* and *Recommendation* to any *Gentleman* who defires to go to the *Parliament* to settle the *Composition* for their *Estates.*

Lastly, A very honourable *Mention* of the *General,* and *Offer* of their *Mediation* to the *Parliament,* to treat him as a *Man* of *Honour,* and one who has been tender of the *Country,* and behaved himself with all the *Moderation* and *Candor* that could be expected from an *Enemy.*

Upon the unexpected Receipt of this Message, a Council of War was called, and the Letter read; no Man offered to speak a Word; the General moved it, but every one was loath to begin.

At last, an old Collonel starts up, and asked the General what he thought might occasion the writing this Letter.? The General told him, *he could not tell*; but he could tell he was sure of one thing, that he knew what was not the Occasion of it *(viz.)* That is, not any want of Force in their Army to oblige us to other Terms. Then a Doubt was started, whether the King and Parliament were not in any Treaty, which this Agreement might be prejudicial to.

This

This occafioned a Letter to my Lord *Fairfax,* wherein our General returning the Civilities, and neither accepting nor refufing his Propofal, put it upon his Honour, whether there was not fome Agreement or Conceffion between his Majefty and the Parliament, in order to a General Peace, which this Treaty might be prejudicial to, or thereby be prejudicial to us.

The Lord *Fairfax* ingenuoufly declared, he had heard the King had made fome Conceffions, and he heartily wifhed he would make fuch as would fettle the Kingdom in Peace, that *Englifhmen* might not wound and deftroy one another; *but that he declared he knew of no Treaty commenced, nor any Thing paft which could give us the leaft Shadow of hope for any Advantage in not accepting his Conditions.* At laft telling us, *That though he did not infult over our Circumftances, yet if we thought fit, upon any fuch Suppofition, to refufe his Offers, he was not to feek in his Meafures.*

And it appeared fo, for he immediately advanced his Forlorns, and difpoffeffed us of two advanced Quarters, and thereby ftreightened us yet more.

We had now nothing to fay, but treat, and our General was fo fenfible of our Condition, that he returned the Trumpet with a fafe Conduct for Commiffioners at 12 a Clock that Night; upon which a Ceffation of Arms was agreed on, we quitting *Truro* to the Lord *Fairfax,* and he left St *Allan's* to us to keep our head Quarter.

The Conditions were foon agreed on, we difbanded nine full Brigades of Horfe, and all the Conditions were obferved with the moft Honour and Care by the Enemy that ever I faw in my Life.

Nor

Nor can I omit to make very honourable Mention of this noble Gentleman, though I did not like his Cause; but I never saw a Man of a more pleasant, calm, courteous, down-right, honest Behaviour in my Life; and, for his Courage and personal Bravery in the Field, that we had felt enough of. No Man in the World had more Fire and Fury in him while in Action, or more Temper and Softness out of it. In short, and I cannot do him greater Honour, he excedingly came near the Character of my Foreign Heroe *Gustavus Adolphus,* and in my Account, is, of all the Soldiers in *Europe,* the fittest to be reckoned in the second Place of Honour to him.

I had particular Occasion to see much of his Temper in all this Action, being one of the Hostages given by our General for the Performance of the Conditions, in which Circumstance the General did me several times the Honour to send to me to dine with him; and was exceedingly pleased to discourse with me about the Passages of the Wars in *Germany,* which I had served in; he having been at the same time in the *Low Countries,* in the Service of Prince *Maurice;* but I observed if at any time my Civilities extended to Commendations of his own Actions, and especially to comparing him to *Gustavus Adolphus,* he would blush like a Woman, and be uneasy, declining the Discourse, and in this he was still more like him.

Let no Man scruple my honourable Mention of this noble Enemy, since no Man can suspect me of favouring the Cause he embarked in, which I served as heartily against as any Man in the Army; but I cannot conceal extraordinary Merit for its being placed in an Enemy.

Y   This

This was the End of our making War; for now we were all under Parole never to bear Arms againſt the Parliament; and though ſome of us did not keep our Word, yet I think a Soldier's Parole ought to be the moſt ſacred in ſuch Caſe, that a Soldier may be the eaſier truſted at all Times upon his Word.

For my Part I went home fully contented, ſince I could do my Royal Maſter no better Service, that I had come off no worſe.

The Enemy going now on in a full Current of Succeſs, and the King reduced to the laſt Extremity, and *Fairfax*, by long Marches, being come back within five Miles of *Oxford*; his Majeſty loath to be cooped up in a Town which could on no Account hold long out, quits the Town in a Diſguiſe, leaving Sir *Thomas Glemham* Governour, and being only attended with Mr. *Aſhburnham* and one more, rides away to *Newark* and there fatally committed himſelf to the Honour and Fidelity of the *Scots*, under General *Leven*.

There had been ſome little Bickering between the Parliament and the *Scots* Commiſſioners, concerning the Propoſitions which the *Scots* were for a Treaty with the King upon, and the Parliament refuſed it. The Parliament, upon all Propoſals of Peace, had formerly invited the King to come and throw himſelf upon the Honour, Fidelity and Affection of his Parliament; and now the King from *Oxford* offering to come up to *London*, on the Protection of the Parliament for the Safety of his Perſon, they refuſed him, and the *Scots* differed from them in it, and were for a perſonal Treaty.

This, in our Opinion, was the Reaſon which prompted the King to throw himſelf upon the Fidelity

delity of the *Scots*, who really by their Infidelity had been the Ruine of all his Affairs, and now, by their perfidious Breach of Honour and Faith with him, will be virtually and mediately the Ruine of his Perſon.

The *Scots* were, as all the Nation beſides them was, ſurprized at the King's coming among them; the Parliament began very high with them, and ſend an Order to General *Leven* to ſend the King to *Warwick* Caſtle; but he was not ſo haſty to part with ſo rich a Prize. As ſoon as the King came to the General, he ſigns an Order to Collonel *Ballaſis*, the Governour of *Newark*, to ſurrender it, and immediately the *Scots* de-camp homewards, carrying the King in the Camp with them, and marching on, a Houſe was ordered to be provided for the King at *Newcaſtle*.

And now the Parliament ſaw their Error, in refuſing his Majeſty a Perſonal Treaty, which if they had accepted, (their Army was not yet taught the way of huffing their Maſters,) the Kingdom might have been ſettled in Peace. Upon this the Parliament ſend to General *Leven* to have his Majeſty not *be ſent*, which was their firſt Language, but *be ſuffered to come* to *London*, to treat with his Parliament; before it was, *Let the King be ſent to* Warwick *Caſtle*; now 'tis, *To let his Majeſty come to* London *to treat with his People*.

But neither one or the other would do with the *Scots*; but we who knew the *Scots* beſt, knew that there was *one Thing* would do with them, if the other would not, and that was Money; and therefore our Hearts aked for the King.

The *Scots*, as I ſaid, had retreated to *New-caſtle* with the King, and there they quartered

their

their whole Army at large upon the Country; the Parliament voted they had no farther Occasion for the *Scots,* and defired them to go home about their Bufinefs. I do not fay it was in thefe Words, but in whatfoever good Words their Meffages might be expreffed, this and nothing lefs was the *Englifh* of it. The *Scots* reply, by fetting forth ther Loffes Damages, and Dues, the Subftance of which was, *Pay us our Money, and we will be gone, or elfe we won't ftir.* The Parliament call for an Account of their Demands, which the *Scots* give in, amounting to a Million; but, according to their Cuftom, and efpecially finding that the Army under *Fairfax* inclined gradually that Way, fall down to 500000 l. and at laft to four; but all the while this is tranfacting, a feparate Treaty is carried on at *London* with the Commiffioners of *Scotland,* and afterwards at *Edinburgh,* by which it is given them to underftand, that whereas upon Payment of the Money, the *Scots* Army is to march out of *England,* and to give up all the Towns and Garrifons which they hold in this Kingdom, fo they are to take it for granted, that 'tis the meaning of the Treaty, that they fhall leave the King in the Hands of the *Englifh* Parliament.

To make this go down the better, the *Scotch* Parliament, upon his Majefty's Defire to go with their Army into *Scotland,* fend him for Anfwer, that it cannot be for the Safety of his Majefty or of the State, to come into *Scotland,* ..ot having taken the Covenant, and this was carried in their Parliament but by two Voices.

The *Scots* having refufed his coming into *Scotland,* as was concerted between the two Houfes, and their Army being to march out of *England,* the delivering up the King became
a Con-

a Confequence of the Thing unavoidable, and of Neceffity.

His Majefty thus deferted of thofe into whofe Hands he had thrown himfelf, took his Leave of the *Scots* General at *Newcaftle*, telling him only, in few Words, this fad Truth, *That he was Bought and Sold.* The Parliament Commiffioners received him at *Newcaftle* from the *Scots*, and brought him to *Holmby* Houfe, in *Northamton-fhire*; from whence, upon the Quarrels and Feuds of Parties, he was fetched by a Party of Horfe, commanded by one Cornet *Joyce*, from the Army, upon their mutinous Rendez-vous at *Triplow-Heath*; and, after this, fuffering many Violences, and Varieties of Circumftances among the Army, was carried to *Hampton-Court*, from whence his Majefty very readily made his Efcape; but not having Notice enough to pro-vide effectual Means for his more effectual Deli-verance was obliged to deliver himfelf to Collo-nel *Hammond* in the Ifle of *Wight*. Here, after fome very indifferent Ufage, the Parliament purfued a farther Treaty with him, and all Points were agreed but two. The entire Abo-lifhing Epifcopacy, which the King declared to be againft his Confcience, and his Coronation Oath; and the Sale of the Church-Lands, which he declared, being moft of them Gifts to God and the Church, by Perfons deceafed, his Majefty thought could not be alienated without the higheft Sacrilege, and if taken from the Ufes to which they were appointed by the Wills of the Donors, ought to be reftored back to the Heirs and Families of the Perfons who bequeathed them.

And thefe two Articles fo ftuck with his Majefty, that he ventured his Fortune and

Royal

Royal Family, and his own Life for them:
However, at laſt, the King condeſcended ſo far
in theſe, that the Parliament voted his Majeſty's Conceſſions to be ſufficient to ſettle and
eſtabliſh the Peace of the Nation.

This Vote diſcovered the bottom of all the
Counſels which then prevailed; for the Army, who
knew if Peace were once ſettled, they ſhould
be undone, took the Alarm at this, and clubbing
together in Committees and Councils, at laſt
brought themſelves to a Degree of Hardneſs
above all that ever this Nation ſaw; for, calling into Queſtion the Proceedings of their
Maſters who employed them, they immediately
fall to Work upon the Parliament, remove Collonel *Hammond*, who had the Charge of the
King, and uſed him honourably, place a new
Guard upon him, diſmiſs the Commiſſioners,
and put a Stop to the Treaty; and, following
their Blow, march to *London*, place Regiments
of Foot at the Parliament Houſe Door, and,
as the Members came up, ſieze upon all thoſe
whom they had down in a Liſt as Promoters of
the Settlement and Treaty, and would not
ſuffer them to ſit; but the reſt, who being of
their own Stamp, are permitted to go on, carry
on the Deſigns of the Army, revive their
Votes of Non-Addreſſes to the King, and then,
upon the Army's Petition, to bring all Delin-
quents to Juſtice; the Maſque was thrown off,
the Word all is declared to be meant the King,
as well as every Man elſe they pleaſed. 'Tis
too ſad a Story, and too much a Matter of Grief
to me, and to all good Men, to renew the Black-
reſs of thoſe Days, when Law and Juſtice was
under the Feet of Power; the Army ruled the
Parliament, the private Officers their Generals,
the

the common Soldiers their Officers, and Confusion was in every Part of the Government: In this Hurry they sacrificed their King, and shed the Blood of the *English* Nobility without Mercy.

The History of the Times will supply the Paticulars which I omit, being willing to confine my self to my own Accounts and Observations; I was now no more an Actor, but a melancholly Observator of the Misfortunes of the Times. I had given my Parole not to take up Arms against the Parliament, and I saw nothing to invite me to engage on their Side; I saw a World of Confusion in all their Counsels, and I always expected that in a Chain of Distractions, as it generally fals out, the last Link would be Destruction; and though I pretended to no Prophecy, yet the Progress of Affairs have brought it to pass, and I have seen Providence, who suffered, for the Correction of this Nation, the Sword to govern and devour us, has at last brought Destruction *by the Sword*, upon the Head of most of the Party who first drew it.

If together with the brief Account of what Concern I had in the Active Part of the War, I leave behind me some of my own Remarks and Observations, it may be pertinent enough to my Design, and not unuseful to Posterity.

1. I observed by the Sequel of Things, that it may be some Excuse to the first Parliament, who began this War, to say that they manifested their Designs were not aimed at the Monarchy, nor their Quarrel at the Person of the King; because, when they had him in their Power, though against his Will, they would have restored both his Person and Dignity as a King, only loading it with such Clogs of the People's

Power,

Power as they at firſt pretended to, *(viz.)* the Militia, and Power of naming the great Officers at Court, and the like; which Powers, it was never denied, had been ſtretched too far in the Beginning of this King's Reign, and ſeveral things done illegally, which his Majeſty had been ſenſible of, and was willing to rectify; but they having obtained the Power by Victory, reſolved ſo to ſecure themſelves, as that whenever they laid down their Arms, the King ſhould not be able to do the like again: And thus far they were not to be ſo much blamed, and we did not, on our own Part, blame them, when they had obtained the Power, for parting with it on good Terms.

But when I have thus far advocated for the Enemies, I muſt be very free to ſtate the Crimes of this Bloody War, by the Events of it. 'Tis manifeſt there were among them, from the Beginning, a Party who aimed at the very Root of the Government, and at the very thing which they brought to paſs, *viz.* The depoſing and murthering of their Sovereign; and, as the Devil is always Maſter where Miſchief is the Work, this Party prevailed, turned the other out of Doors, and over-turned all that little Honeſty that might be in the firſt Beginning of this unhappy Strife.

The Conſequence of this was, the Presbyterians ſaw their Error when it was too late, and then would gladly have joined the Royal Party, to have ſuppreſſed this new Leaven, which had infected the Lump; and this is very remarkable, that moſt of the firſt Champions of this War, who bore the Brunt of it, when the King was powerful and proſperous, and when there was nothing to be got by it but

Blows,

Blows, firſt or laſt, were ſo ill uſed by this Independant powerful Party, who tripped up
the Heels of all their Honeſty, that they were
either forced, by ill Treatment, to take up
Arms on our Side, or ſuppreſſed and reduced by
them. In this the Juſtice of Providence ſeemed
very conſpicuous, that theſe having puſhed all
things by Violence againſt the King, and by
Arms and Force brought him to their Will,
were at once both robbed of the End, their
Church-Government, and puniſhed for drawing their Swords againſt *their Maſters*, by *their*
own Servants drawing the Sword againſt them;
and God, in his due Time, puniſhed the others
too: And, what was yet farther ſtrange, the
Puniſhment of this Crime of making War againſt
their King, ſingled out thoſe very Men, both
in the Army and in the Parliament, who were
the greateſt Champions of the Presbyterian Cauſe
in the Council, and in the Field. Some Minutes too of Circumſtances I cannot forbear obſer-
ing, though they are not very material, as to
the Fatality and Revolutions of Days and
Times.

A *Roman* Catholick Gentleman of *Lancaſhire*, a
very religious Man in his way, who had kept a
Calculate of Times, and had obſerved mightily
the Fatality of Times, Places and Actions, being at my Father's Houſe, was diſcourſing once
upon the juſt Judgment of God in dating his
Providences, ſo as to ſignify to us his Diſpleaſure
at particular Circumſtances; and, among an infinite Number of Collections he had made, theſe
were ſome which I took particular Notice of,
and from whence I began to obſerve the like.

1. That

1. That King *Edward* the VIth died the very same Day of the same Month in which he caused the Altar to be taken down, and the Image of the Blessed Virgin in the Cathedral of St. *Paul's*.

2. That *Cranmer* was burnt at *Oxford* the same Day and Month that he gave King *Henry* the VIIIth Advice to Divorce his Queen *Catherine*.

3. That Queen *Elizabeth* died the same Day and Month that she resolved, in her Privy Council, to behead the Queen of *Scots*.

4. That King *James* died the same Day that he published his Book against *Bellarmine*.

5. That King *Charles's* long Parliament, which ruined him, began the very same Day and Month which that Parliament began, that at the Request of his Predecessor robbed the *Roman* Church of all her Revenues, and suppressed Abbies and Monasteries.

How just his Calculations were, or how true the Matter of Fact, I cannot tell, but it put me upon the same in several Actions and Successes of this War.

And I found a great many Circumstances, as to Time and Action, which befel both his Majesty and his Parties first.

Then others which befel the Parliament and Presbyterian Faction which raised the War.

Then the Independant Tyranny which succeeded and supplanted the first Party.

Then the *Scots*, who acted on both Sides.

Lastly, The Restoration and Re-establishment of the Loyalty and Religion of our Ancestors.

1. For King *Charles* the First; 'tis observable that the Charge against the Earl of *Strafford*, a
thing

thing which his Majesty blamed himself for all the Days of his Life, and at the Moment of his last Suffering, was first read in the Lords House on the 30th of *January*, the same Day of the Month six Year that the King himself was brought to the Block.

2. That the King was carried away Prisoner from *Newark*, by the *Scots*, *May* 10, the same Day six Year that, against his Conscience and Promise, he passed the Bill of Attainder against the loyal noble Earl of *Strafford*.

3. The same Day seven Year that the King entered the House of Commons for the five Members, which all his Friends blamed him for, the same Day the Rump voted bringing his Majesty to Tryal, after they had set by the Lords for not agreeing to it, which was the 3d of *January* 1648.

4. The 12th of *May* 1646, being the Surrender of *Newark*, the Parliament held a Day of Thanksgiving and Rejoicing, for the Reduction of the King and his Party, and finishing the War, which was the same Day five Year that the Earl of *Strafford* was beheaded.

5. The Battle at *Naseby*, which ruin'd the King's Affairs, and where his Secretary and his Office was taken, was the 14th of *June* the same Day and Month the first Commission was given out by his Majesty to raise Forces.

6. The Queen voted a Traytor by the Parliament the 3d of *May*, the same Day and Month she carried the Jewels into *France*.

7. The same Day the King defeated *Essex* in the West, his Son King *Charles* II. was defeated at *Worcester*.

8. Arch-bishop *Laud*'s House at *Lambeth* assaulted by the Mob, the same Day of the same Month that

he

he advised the King to make War upon the Scots.

9. Impeached the 15th of *December* 1640, the same Day Twelve-month that he ordered the Common-Prayer-Book of *Scotland* to be printed, in order to be imposed upon the *Scots*, from which all our Troubles began.

But many more, and more strange, are the critical Junctures of Affairs in the Case of the Enemy, or at least more observed by me.

1. Sir *John Hotham*, who repulsed his Majesty and refused him Admittance into *Hull* before the War, was siezed at *Hull* by the same Parliament for whom he had done it, the same 10th Day of *August* two Years that he drew the first Blood in that War.

2. *Hambden* of *Buckinghamshire* killed the same Day one Year that the Mob Petition from *Bucks* was presented to the King about him, as one of the five Members.

3. Young Captain *Hotham* executed the 1st of *January*, the same Day that he assisted Sir *Thomas Fairfax* in the first Skirmish with the King's Forces at *Bramham-Moor*.

4. The same Day and Month, being the 6th of *August* 1641, that the Parliament voted to to raise an Army against the King, the same Day and Month, *Anno* 1648, the Parliament were assaulted and turned out of Doors by that very Army, and none left to sit but who the Soldiers pleased, which were therefore called the *Rump*.

5. The Earl of *Holland* deserted the King, who had made him General of the Horse, and went over to the Parliament, and the 9th of *March* 1641,

1641, carried the Commons reproaching Declaration to the King; and afterwards taking up
Arms for the King againſt the Parliament, was
beheaded by them the 9th of *March* 1648, juſt
ſeven Years after.

6. The Earl of *Holland* was ſent to by the
King to come to his Aſſiſtance and refuſed,
the 11th of *July* 1641, and that very Day ſeven
Years after was taken by the Parliament at
St. Needs.

7. Collonel. *Maſſey* defended *Glouceſter* againſt
the King, and beat him off the 5th of *September* 1643, was after taken by *Cromwell*'s Men fighting for the King, on the 5th of *September* 1651,
two or three Days after the Fight at *Worceſter.*

8. *Richard Cromwell* reſigning becauſe he could
not help it, the Parliament voted a free Com-
monwealth, without a ſingle Perſon or Houſe
of Lords; this was the 25th of *May* 1658; the
25th of *May* 1660 the King landed at *Dover,*
and reſtored the Government of a ſingle Perſon
and Houſe of Lords.

9. *Lambert* was proclaimed a Traytor by the
Parliament, *April* the 20th, being the ſame Day
he propoſed to *Oliver Cromwell* to take upon him
the Title of King.

10. *Monk* being taken Priſoner at *Nantwich* by
Sir *Thomas Fairfax,* revolted to the Parliament,
the ſame Day nineteen Years he declared for
the King, and thereby reſtored the Royal Authority.

11. The Parliament voted to approve of Sir
John Hotham's repulſing the King at *Hull,* the
28th of *April* 1642; the 28th of *April* 1660, the
Parliament firſt debated in the Houſe the reſto-
ring the King to the Crown.

12. The

12. The Agitators of the Army formed themselves into a Cabal, and held their firſt Meeting to ſieze on the King's Perſon, and take him into their Cuſtody from *Holmby*, the 28th of *April* 1647; the ſame Day 1660, the Parliament voted the Agitators to be taken into Cuſtody, and committed as many of them as could be found.

13. The Parliament voted the Queen a Traytor for aſſiſting her Husband the King, *May* the 3d 1643, her Son King *Charles* II. was preſented with the Votes of Parliament to reſtore him, and the Preſent of 50000l. the 3d of *May* 1660.

14. The ſame Day the Parliament paſſed the Act for Recognition of *Oliver Cromwell, October* the 13th 1654. *Lambert* broke the Parliament and ſet up the Army 1659, *October* the 13th.

Some other Obſervations I have made, which as not ſo pertinent I forbear to publiſh, among which I have noted the Fatality of ſome Days to Parties, as,

The 2d of *September*, the Fight at *Dunbar*; the Fight at *Worceſter*; the Oath againſt a ſingle Perſon paſt; *Oliver's* firſt Parliament called: For the Enemy.

The 2d of *September*, *Eſſex* defeated in *Cornwall*; *Oliver* died; City Works demoliſhed: For the King.

The 29th of *May*, Prince *Charles* born; *Leiceſter* taken by Storm; King *Charles* II. reſtored: Ditto.

Fatality of Circumſtances in this unhappy War, as,

1. The

1. The *English* Parliament call in the *Scots*, to invade their King, and are invaded themselves by the same *Scots*, in Defence of the King whose Case, and the Design of the Parliament the *Scots* had mistaken.

2. The *Scots*, who unjustly assisted the Parliament to conquer their lawful Sovereign, contrary to their Oath of Allegiance, and without any Pretence on the King's Part, are afterwards absolutely conquered and subdued by the same Parliament they assisted.

3. The Parliament, who raised an Army to depose their King, deposed by the very Army they had raised.

4. The Army broke three Parliaments, and are at last broke by a free Parliament and all they had done by the Military Power, undone at once by the Civil.

5. Abundance of the Chief Men, who by their fiery Spirits involved the Nation in a Civil War, and took up Arms against their Prince, first or last met with Ruine or Disgrace from their own Party.

1. Sir *John Hotham* and his Son, who struck the first Stroke, both beheaded or hanged by the Parliament.

2. Major General *Massey* three times taken Prisoner by them, and once wounded at *Worcester*.

3. Major General *Langhorn*. 4. Collonel *Poyer* : And, 5. Collonel *Powell*, changed Sides, and at last taken, could obtain no other Favour than to draw Lots for their Lives; Collonel *Poyer* drew the Dead Lot, and was shot to Death.

6. Earl of *Holland*, who, when the House voted who should be reprieved, Lord *Goring*, who

had

had been their worſt Enemy, or the Earl of
Holland, who, excepting one Offence, had been
their conſtant Servant, voted *Goring* to be
ſpared, and the Earl to die.

   7. The Earl of *Eſſex*, their firſt General. ı
   8. Sir *William Waller*.
   9. Lieutenant General *Ludlow*.
  10. The Earl of *Mancheſter*.

All diſguſted and voted out of the Army,
though they had ſtood the firſt Shock of the War,
to make way for the new Model of the Army,
and introduce a Party.

In all theſe Confuſions I have obſerved two
great Errors, one of the King, and one of his
Friends.

Of the King, that when he was in their Cuſtody, and at their Mercy, he did not comply
with their Propoſitions of Peace before their
Army, for want of Employment, fell into Heats
and Mutinies; that he did not at firſt grant
the *Scots* their own Conditions, which, if he
had done, he had gone into *Scotland*; and then,
if the *Engliſh* would have fought the *Scots* for
him, he had a Reſerve of his loyal Friends,
who would have had Room to have fallen in
with the *Scots* to his Aſſiſtance, who were after diſperſed and deſtroyed in ſmall Parties attempting to ſerve him.

While his Majeſty remained at *Newcaſtle*, the
Queen wrote to him, perſwading him to make
Peace upon any Terms ; and in Politicks her
Majeſty's Advice was certainly the beſt : For,
however low he was brought by a Peace, it
muſt have been better than the Condition he
was then in.

The

The Error I mention of the King's Friends
was this, that after they faw all was loft, they
could not be content to fit ftill, and referve
themfelves for better Fortunes, and wait the
happy Time when the Divifions of the Enemy would bring them to certain Ruin ; but
muft haften their own Miferies by frequent
fruitlefs Rifings, in the Face of a victorious Enemy, in fmall Parties, and I always found thefe
Effects from it.

1. The Enemy, who were always together
by the Ears, when they were let alone, were
united and reconciled when we gave them any
Interruption ; as particularly, in the Cafe of
the firft Affault the Army made upon them,
when Collonel *Pride*, with his Regiment garbled
the Houfe, as they called it, at that Time,
a fair Opportunity offered ; but it was omit-
ted till it was too late : That Infult upon the
Houfe had been attempted the Year before,
but was hindered by the little Infurrections of
the Royal Party, and the fooner they had fallen out, the better.

2. Thefe Rifings being defperate, with vaft
Difadvantages, and always fuppreffed, ruined
all our Friends ; the Remnants of the Cavaliers
were leffened, the ftouteft and moft daring
were cut off, and the King's Intereft exceedingly weakened, there not being lefs than Thirty Thoufand of his beft Friends cut off in the
feveral Attempts made at *Maidftone*, *Colchefter*,
Lancafhire, *Pembrook*, *Pontfract*, *Kingfton*, *Prefton*,
Warrington, *Worcefter*, and other Places. Had
thefe Men all referved their Fortunes to a Conjunction with the *Scots*, at either of the Inva-
fions they made into this Kingdom, and acted
with the Conduct and Courage they were known

Z   Mafters

Mafters of, perhaps neither of thofe *Scots* Armies had been defeated.

But the Impatience of our Friends ruin'd all; for my Part, I had as good a Mind to put my Hand to the Ruine of the Enemy as any of them, but I never faw any tolerable Appearance of a Force able to match the Enemy, and I had no Mind to be beaten, and then hanged. Had we let them alone, they would have fallen into fo many Parties and Factions, and fo effectually have torn one another to Pieces, that which foever Party had come to us, we fhould, with them, have been too hard for all the reft.

This was plain by the Courfe of Things afterwards, when the Independant Army had ruffled the Presbyterian Parliament, the Soldiery of that Party made no Scruple to join us, and would have reftored the King with all their Hearts, and many of them did join us at laft.

And the Confequence, though late, ended fo; for they fell out fo many times, *Army* and *Parliament*, *Parliament* and *Army*, and alternately pulled one another down fo often, till at laft the Presbyterians, who began the War, ended it; and, to be rid of their Enemies, rather than for any Love to the Monarchy, reftored King *Charles* the Second, and brought him in on the very Day that they themfelves had formerly refolved the Ruine of his Father's Government, being the 29th of *May*, the fame Day 20 Year that the private Cabal in *London* concluded their Secret League with the *Scots*, to embroil his Father King *Charles* the Firft.

F I N I S.